Also by Cheryl Mendelson

Home Comforts
Morningside Heights
Love, Work, Children

Anything for Jane

Anything for Jane

A NOVEL

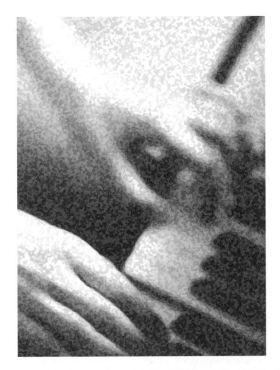

CHERYL MENDELSON

Random House
New York

Published in the United States by Random House, an imprint of The Random House
Publishing Group, a division of Random House, Inc., New York.

RANDOM HOUSE and colophon are registered trademarks of Random House, Inc.

Grateful acknowledgment is made to Random House, Inc., and the estate of W. H. Auden
for permission to reprint excerpts from "Vespers" and "Letter to Lord Byron," both from
Collected Poems by W. H. Auden. "Vespers" copyright © 1955 by W. H. Auden; "Letter to Lord Byron"
copyright © 1937 and copyright renewed 1965 by W. H. Auden. Reprinted by permission
of Random House, Inc., and the Estate of W. H. Auden.

ISBN 978-0-375-50838-7

Library of Congress Cataloging-in-Publication Data

Mendelson, Cheryl.
Anything for Jane: a novel / by Cheryl Mendelson.
p.   cm
ISBN 978-0-375-50838-7
I. Teenage girls—Fiction.   2. High school students—Fiction.   3. Children of the rich—
Fiction.   4. Middle-class families—Fiction.   5. Homeless families—Fiction.   6. Parent
and child—Fiction.   7. Conflict of generations—Fiction.   8. Social classes—Fiction.
9. Morningside Heights (New York, NY)—Fiction.   10. Domestic fiction.
I. Title

PS3613.E48A8   2007
813'6—dc22   2006050434

Printed in the United States of America on acid-free paper

www.atrandom.com

2 4 6 8 9 7 5 3 1

First Edition

Book design by Carol Malcolm Russo

For without a cement of blood (it must be human, it must
be innocent) no secular wall will safely stand.
— W. H. Auden, "Vespers"

I hate the modern trick, to tell the truth,
 Of straightening out the kinks in the young mind,
Our passion for the tender plant of youth,
 Our hatred for all weeds of any kind.
 Slogans are bad: the best that I can find
Is this: "Let each child have that's in our care
As much neurosis as the child can bear."
—W. H. Auden, "Letter to Lord Byron"

PART ONE

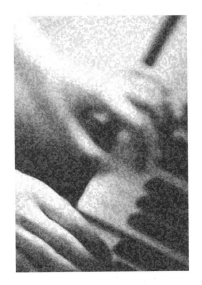

CHAPTER 1

G ood parents made bad citizens. That was Charles Braithwaite's opinion, a common one in Morningside Heights. The neighborhood was populated with conscientious liberals, people who admitted their own flaws—unashamedly, as Anne Braithwaite liked to point out. Anne could see how she and Charles were a little bit that way themselves. These socially concerned men and women tended to undergo a moral shock when they first held their newborns in arms. They would look down into the grumpy little faces and strabismic little eyes, and suddenly their hatred of cruelty and injustice would morph into a bloated sense of parental obligation. From then on, they orphaned all other causes and devoted themselves to cosseting their own children. Sometimes they comforted themselves with the thought that the children would go on to change the world—maybe just by existing, so obvious was it that their intense parental investment would pay off.

The youth of Morningside Heights took no drugs. After earning high SAT scores, they attended desirable colleges and entered the professions, the arts, or the academy, where they made substantial contributions. Eventually they formed stable relationships and went on to become parents in the mold of their own mothers and fathers. There may have been one or two who once or somewhere got into serious trouble, but offhand, no one can think of an example.

Which is not to say there weren't difficulties. Their reliable academic and professional successes aside, the children of these doting, hyperinvolved, and better-than-optimal families included *quirky* kids and *problem* kids in addition to the usual all-around *super* ones. Parents all too often experienced a moral aftershock when life confronted them with the unwelcome facts: that *great kids* can also be odd or troublesome and surprisingly hard to live with, that their fathers and mothers may someday see them off to college with guilty joy, and that sometimes a happy family produces a spectacularly unhappy child.

The Braithwaites were a case in point. They enjoyed the worldly blessings of health, money, and honor in a sustaining environment of mutual love and respect. Their quarrels and differences, free from the infection of malice, did not fester. But the eldest Braithwaite child was miserable, and her misery threatened the peace of the others both because they loved her and because she wanted to make them suffer.

Charles and Anne were musicians in their mid-forties. He was an operatic baritone who sang at the Met, mostly in secondary roles, and she was a fine pianist who had given up a performing career to teach and raise their four children: eighteen-year-old Jane, their unhappy daughter, who already showed promise as a soprano; Ellen, a precocious, caustic schoolgirl of thirteen; and two boys, aged nine and five. Both boys were musical and multiply talented, but the older one, Stuart, had a troubling tendency toward suspiciousness and eccentricity—due, in his parents' opinion, to the fact that he was quite small for his age while Gilbert, a genial, trusting boy, was unusually tall. This unequal endowment, with its profound consequences for the brothers' psyches, felt unjust to Stuart and also to his mother and father. But that was one of the dangers of marriage between the short, like Anne, and the tall, like Charles. "If we'd *both* been short," Anne said, "there'd have been no problem. Isn't it strange?" "Or if we'd both been tall," Charles pointed out.

The family's history paralleled that of their neighborhood. Anne had grown up in Morningside Heights, raised according to its long-standing tenets to invest her energies as deeply in liberal causes as in music. Indeed, she was an outstanding exemplar of what local parents yearned to produce—as good a progressive as a pianist (and as a pianist she had actually had a Carnegie Hall debut) but ultimately more interested in motherhood than either social progress or music. When she and Charles settled in Morningside Heights in the 1980s, they were typical residents of the shabby enclave of academics, writers, musicians, librarians, theologians, theater people, social workers, and film technicians who had always lived around Columbia University, to the north of Manhattan's West Side. Through a series of oddments and accidents, they evolved into equally typical residents of the richer Morningside Heights of 2004. The transformation was unusual. Most of the moneyed people in Morningside Heights had moved in, and the hard up had been pushed out. The Braithwaites were uneasy living the same luxurious lives as the rich invaders who, by bidding up the neighborhood, had cost so many friends their homes and worlds and left the Braithwaites themselves, along with others who had weathered the calamity, to stand as false proof that it had not happened. Newcomers spoke fondly of this likeable but somewhat peculiar family of musicians, along with other remnants of the old neighborhood—the people who managed to hang on and the institutions of learning, music, and religion they clung to—as part of the appealing local color that they had moved here for.

Despite the brutal economies that had emptied the neighborhood of so many poor, elderly, and old-style middle-class people, the twentieth-century culture of Morningside Heights was not entirely obliterated; Morningside Heights propagated ideas as successfully as it did children. Old-fashioned progressive views on child rearing survived the rent rises and exorbitant co-op prices and wove a subtle retro pattern into the post-millennium social fabric. Child worship and the dream of transforming society through the rearing of virtuous children were inspirited, not destroyed, by money and competition. So central did child rearing become to upper-middle-class ambition—both moral and worldly—that childlessness came to be considered one of life's major tragedies, and parental feelings grew so tender that one of the first rules of social intercourse prohibited public gloating over a child's successes.

"I told Rebecca's mother all about Jane's troubles," said Anne at the breakfast table, when the four Braithwaite children had gone off to school. "But she could smell the *nachas* anyway. I felt terrible, spreading gossip about my own daughter."

Rebecca's parents were a banker and a lawyer who had moved into the Braithwaites' building in 1996, when Rebecca and Ellen were both five. Rebecca's mother had taken in Anne's mothering of the Braithwaite children with the same emulous hunger with which poor girls absorb the fashion sense of rich ones. She had imitated Anne so closely that she had been forced to quit her job after a couple of years. Otherwise it would have been impossible to match the standards of the Braithwaite household.

"What gossip?" Charles asked, bristling.

"About Stephen, the suspension—among other things. I had to because when she found out that Ellen made all the honors classes, she went snarky. Poor Rebecca tried so hard, and she didn't get in any. So I sacrificed Jane."

Charles relaxed. "I guarantee she already knew all about Jane."

"Yes, but now she knows just exactly what we said in the fights, and about how they recommended the shrink and the Ritalin and all, and . . ."

Charles grimaced but had no remonstrances for his wife. To sacrifice some degree of family privacy to mollify Rebecca's mother, whose virulent envy had led her to cause difficulties between Ellen and Rebecca in the past, was reasonable. "How that woman raised Rebecca," he said. "How can it be that the child is so good and sensitive when the mother is such a lunatic?"

They considered the mystery. It was the kind of frustrating subject that tended to come up at this unpleasant, in-between time of day, after the children had left for school but before they managed to put thoughts of them aside and turn to work. They brooded over bowls of cereal-flecked milk and bite-scalloped crusts of toast.

"She may be pathological, but somehow she's raised a super kid. And if we're such great parents, why are all our kids so quirky?" Anne asked. "All right, I could see maybe one or two. It happens. But all four—that's no accident."

"Absurd," said Charles, offended. "Ellen isn't a bit quirky. Neither is Gilbert. Stuart's a bit of a problem, but—"

"Well, I guess there's my answer," said Anne, "if you can't even see it. You wait till Ellen has a boyfriend. You'll think Jane was a conformist."

"And there's nothing wrong with Jane except your mother." Helen preferred Jane, her first grandchild, over the others and in Charles's opinion spoiled her; that's why Jane had become impervious to criticism and correction. He would have been surprised to know that many people thought Charles and Anne themselves were at fault. They were too invested in this girl's unusual musical talents to see her for what she was. Or so people told each other, in the firm, didactic tones they used to condemn obvious parenting errors—but only when the parents were not around to benefit from the lesson.

Charles's reference to Anne's mother was an invitation to quarrel; they had been arguing about Helen and Jane for more than ten years. But Anne only gave him a look that accused him of breaching their truce on the subject. "I'm just hoping this obsession with Stephen will subside," she said, "now that she's a senior and college is on her mind."

The previous spring, Jane, then seventeen, had fallen for Stephen Delacort, a bright, troubled boy who lived on the East Side and attended a prestigious school that often shared activities with Jane's prestigious school. They met in the course of a joint production of *West Side Story* in which Jane played Maria.

"That's what I've been thinking," Charles said, more hopefully than confidently. "At a certain point, the romance of his problems is going to wear off, and they're just going to be problems."

"Yes, but until she gets to Juilliard and meets boys with interests more like hers, he really may be the best out there. I have to admit that sometimes I can see the attraction to Stephen, especially when she brings home anyone else."

Jane had had only three involvements with boys that her parents knew of, none satisfactory. Her first boyfriend was the profoundly depressed son of a Queens dry cleaner whose freakish math talent had earned him a scholarship to an elite private school. There, relegated to the sad society of the marginal, he stewed daily in a broth of social disregard and contempt until he fell to pieces. Jane comforted him in his torments for at least six months, until he had his breakdown, dropped out of school, crawled back to Queens, and disappeared. The second boy, like Jane herself, had great musical talent, but he was so peculiar that Anne and Charles regarded him as disturbed, perhaps slightly autistic. Jane, intolerant of her own family's smallest failure of understanding and empathy, accepted a complete lack of these qualities in this boy and exercised her own capacities for them on his behalf so earnestly that after three months she fell out of love owing to exhaustion. Jane's relations with girls were even worse than her relations with boys.

Charles knew that his own judgment, where the children were concerned, was often skewed by a lifelong sense of grievance that grew out of his own unhappy childhood and frustrated ambition. He had married Anne for her blithe hopefulness and good-natured insight, her tender, understanding heart, and he still loved her for these virtues. But he disliked her habit of sharing them outside their own family, especially with troubled people like Stephen. In Charles's opinion, Anne made a specialty of empathizing with the demented. Obviously, Jane imitated her. If the kids were quirky, Anne's accepting attitude toward offbeat and misshapen minds probably had as much to do with it as anything. Charles refused to see anything good or attractive in Stephen Delacort and despised him wholeheartedly.

When they were juniors, Jane and Stephen had been suspended from their respective schools after disappearing together in the course of Jane's class trip to Boston. Stephen had shown up at the Museum of Fine Arts in the middle of the tour, and Jane had sneaked off with him, whispering to classmates to tell Ms. Liu and Mr. Fein that she'd see them later. The outrage of Jane's teachers, who felt obliged to inform the police, as well as that of her classmates, the school officials, and her parents, was boundless—no matter that she showed up on time at the hotel for dinner, or that she had thought she was reachable by a cell phone that had in fact gone dead. Their behavior was grossly inconsiderate, selfish, and immature.

For several weeks after Jane's three-day suspension, Charles had re-

fused to let her see or call Stephen. He neglected to forbid computer contact, however, and the two of them had spent the entire period messaging
and e-mailing. Even so, Jane had been unable to eat during the separation
and, having been fashionably slender to begin with, grew so extremely thin
that her parents were alarmed. In defeat, they went to her room for the last
in a series of tense showdowns and agreed that for the next two months
she could go out with Stephen once a week, if she was home by ten, and
could have him over once a week. After that, they'd see.

Jane, at least, had had sense enough to be sheepish about her misbe-
havior, if not genuinely remorseful. But Stephen seemed indifferent to the
disapproval heaped on the two of them. When Charles tried to talk seriously with him, he didn't apologize, didn't even say he was sorry that people had worried. Charles detected something jeering in his eyes, something
snide in the angle of his hip as he stood there in front of him. More or
less, he was laughing in Charles's face. This was all the more frustrating because the boy had no parents whom Charles felt comfortable calling and
complaining to, for both of them were workaholic lawyers who had effectively abandoned their son except to appear at school to defend him
fiercely in his frequent jams. Yes, the kid had problems, but his solutions
were shallow, Charles told Anne.

Though Jane was often uncooperative and rude, she had never before
been guilty of this sort of mischief. It was obviously a case of bad influence, but why was Jane susceptible? Her school psychologist first explored
the possibility that she was not getting enough love and attention. After
all, she had Ellen, Stuart, and Gilbert to compete with. But this hypothe-
sis proved implausible, as did the alternative theory that Jane was rebelling
against excessive restriction. No, you would think these parents blameless
if you didn't know that in a case like this they couldn't be. The girl herself
would neither explain nor justify her behavior and insisted that she didn't
see why the incident was such a big deal. The only useful remark the psychologist could get out of her was her protest, "I wish everyone would
leave me alone. I feel like I'm suffocating. I feel like jumping out of my
skin," which sounded just a little like attention deficit disorder. That an
eleventh-grader should suddenly present with attention deficit disorder
was unlikely but, of course, not impossible. Maybe it had even been there

all along, undiagnosed. After all, Jane had a history of maladjustment at school; she had always hated it. On the psychologist's recommendation, the school suggested to her parents a complete psychological workup, perhaps a trial of Ritalin, but the very idea drove Charles and Anne into an irrational fury.

"Attention deficit?" Charles echoed in disbelief. "She reads all night long and memorizes entire operas. Her concentration is amazing. What are you talking about?"

The school had tried to explain that ADD occasionally affected some areas of personality and study and not others, but the Braithwaites stalked out of the psychologist's office, outraged. They knew, nonetheless, that there was something crazy going on with their daughter Jane.

"What is it you like about Stephen?" Charles asked her now and then.

After a sarcastic mime of reflection, Jane might reply, "His inner self—you know, his DNA," or something along those lines.

"What is it she sees in him?" Charles and Anne took turns asking each other, over and over. This morning it was Charles who began, with a manner so sincere that it suggested he thought Anne might actually have an answer. "Is it just that he's a good-looking rebel? Or that he doesn't fall all over her? That's so . . . clichéd. Anyway, I don't believe that's her psychology. She has too much self-respect."

"I don't know," said Anne. "She's attracted by his problems. I have no idea why—none at all."

There they let the subject drop, as they had done many times before, and rose from the table, Charles to go read through a new song cycle, Anne to prepare to receive her first piano student of the day. The trouble with Stephen was only the latest in a series of family upsets caused by Jane's almost constant distress. For invisible reasons, Jane was always either morose and withdrawn or spiteful and sneering. She had a maddening habit of calling home in tears in the dead of night from alarming or inconvenient places—Gray's Papaya down in the Village, the Hans Christian Andersen statue in Central Park, a friend's house in Sag Harbor—begging, demanding, to be rescued immediately. In a certain kind of mood, she would tell her world-famous voice teacher, in frank terms, about Charles's private opinion of the teacher's approach to certain aspects of vocal technique. When things got too tense at home, Jane would spend a few days at her grandmother's apartment and return, carrying a shopping bag full of presents, in a whistling, sassy good humor that never lasted long.

This particular morning, while Charles and Anne were talking about her, Jane, near the end of her bus ride to school, was on her cell phone talking to Stephen Delacort.

"I can't. I have a lesson. Anyway, they'd find out," she told him, ignoring scornful looks from Ellen, who sat at her side with a book open in her lap.

"Totally humiliating, yes, but it's just a matter of months until . . . No, I can't. It's not worth it—my lunch period is really short. . . . No, don't skip, don't . . . Sweetheart, you really won't graduate if you keep this up."

Ellen closed her book and stared at Jane contemptuously.

"But that's what I'm like, Stephen. I told you. Don't ask me to . . . I'm the good-girl type."

Ellen emitted a derisive snort, but Jane only glared back.

"You know what?" said Ellen, when they were on the sidewalk in front of the school gate. "You're a total hypocrite. I hate you. I've always hated you. My whole life, you've made our family miserable. I can't wait until you're gone." And quenching her rage by drinking in Jane's shocked and wounded expression, Ellen turned to enter the gate without giving her sister a chance to respond.

In some families, words like these between sisters might not count for much. They might express the passions of the moment, carelessly voiced, easily forgotten, soon replaced with their opposites. But not in the Braithwaite family. Ellen's may even have been the first sincere words of hatred that any one of them had ever expressed to another. They were often angry, but cold, long-standing hatred was not part of the family's emotional repertoire. Jane reeled from the blow. She was unable to parry Ellen's words because she had no counter-hatred to protect and inspire her. She had only a lifelong habit of believing in her own side of things and her own rights, and Ellen's ferocity had broken through that.

Jane entered the school gate and saw Ellen standing with a group of friends near the entranceway. Jane had few friends. Ellen had many. Those surrounding her at the moment were all short; Ellen, too, was short, and Jane was tall. Looking at the group of laughing, petite girls, Jane felt, for the first time, self-conscious about her height, as though it mocked the smallness of what was inside her. She had an odd new sensation, like feeling little, to which she could not put a name, so unfamiliar was she with a sense of humility.

There in the school yard under the feeble October sun, Jane plunged into crisis. The vague disgruntlement that was her normal mood gave way to angry despair, then molten remorse, and, finally, self-loathing. She bludgeoned herself so violently with dislike that she felt unsteady, as though she'd been actually knocked off balance and might fall. She questioned even the all-forgiving, all-embracing parental love that had always inflated her self-regard and insulated her from guilt. Nothing about her was good or genuine, and there was no way she could become so—at least no time soon. She anguished over lost opportunities—if only she had studied hard, like Ellen—and for a moment considered running away to devote herself to helping the migrant workers in Florida who were her grandmother's latest cause. She had to do something—something major—to save herself, but she couldn't think of what.

These reflections took only two or three minutes. Then habit prevailed, and Jane bobbed up out of her funk with the buoyancy of all adored, protected children. Her reaction to Ellen, so unlikely and out of proportion, was just one of those mental fits that young people on the brink of adulthood are prone to. If Charles and Anne had known about it, they would have understood perfectly. They would have said exactly the right thing.

CHAPTER 2

Gabriela Leon, a thirty-six-year-old woman from the Dominican Republic, had lived for many years in Manhattan Valley, a marginal neighborhood that separated the eastern edge of Morningside Heights from Harlem. She had two young daughters, Alita and Isabel. An older daughter named Cristina had followed a boyfriend back to the Dominican Republic last year. Gabriela and her family faced no unusual problems. The catastrophes that constantly threatened them were ordinary and typical, yet just as hard to bear as though they were full of fascinating novelty.

The Leons shared a small apartment in a tumbledown building that was intermittently without heat and water. For more than a decade, the landlord had refused to make repairs. Manhattan Valley was quickly going the way of Morningside Heights, and he wanted the tenants out so he could gut the building and put in upscale condos. But for the time being, the rent was low enough for Gabriela to afford on the wages she earned cleaning richer people's apartments. Her boyfriend, Juan Santiago, who worked off and on as a short-order cook, was often there, though he had his own place up in the Bronx somewhere, and her teenaged nephew, Andrés Valiente, the son of an unstable younger sister who drank and took drugs and often ended up homeless, was almost always there. For years, when Rosa had once again lost an apartment or moved in with a new rough man, Andrés had gone to his aunt and slept on her sofa. He had spent more time with Gabriela than with his own mother in his eighteen years, especially in the last four. Now when he had problems at school, they called Gabriela first, not Rosa, who for nearly a year had been unreachable by mail or telephone. Gabriela wished she could provide Andrés with a bed, but there was not enough space in her three small rooms.

Long ago, Andrés had set up his computer in a corner at Gabriela's, a powerful sign that he considered himself a permanent resident, for his computer was his lifeline, the one physical possession that linked him to the time when he lived with his mother. He periodically took it apart and upgraded it with great skill. It was a stock car of a computer, cobbled together from spare parts and amazingly speedy. It held all the pictures Andrés had of his mother, his father, whom he did not remember, and others now equally lost to him; his journal and other writings; years of his schoolwork; his e-mail correspondence dating back to the first he had ever sent or received; and his precious games. Insofar as his history existed, other than in memory, it did so on the friendly little machine. He switched it on as soon as he got up in the morning, to be greeted with its soft beeps, whirs, and clicks, and again as soon as he returned home in the evening.

Despite her kindnesses and good intentions toward Andrés, Gabriela was not pleased to have him on her hands. But what was she going to do? Throw her own nephew out on the street? Let him go live in whatever druggy hellhole in Brooklyn Rosa was sharing with crazy, dangerous strangers? When Rosa began her decline, Andrés had been a bright, outgoing, somewhat nervous little boy. By his teen years all the horrors he witnessed had transformed him into a withdrawn, bookish, and frightened adolescent who read and studied compulsively, avoided everyone outside Gabriela's family except for an occasional teacher, and had attracted notice for outstanding schoolwork. Andrés regarded himself as cynical and knowing, but an authentically childlike innocence led him to take for granted that his aunt would feed and shelter him when his mother collapsed. Gabriela wished him well but privately complained that she just couldn't feed one more—not a teenaged boy who ate more than she and her daughters together—even though he worked summers and gave her half his wages.

Juan scolded her about this attitude. "Andrés is going to give everything back to you someday," he said. "You'll see. You won't be sorry." But then, Juan himself had many a meal at Gabriela's. He chipped in when he could. When the TV died, he showed up within three days lugging a new one, and they never knew where it came from. He fixed anything that broke. When Gabriela got worried about the sparks that flew when the kids plugged something in, he fiddled with the wiring. He unclogged the kitchen drain and fixed the toilet. He drove off the drunk who started sleeping in the hallway outside their door, scaring the girls. When he got money, he'd hand her a twenty, sometimes much more, to pay for food or even their clothes. When Con-Ed turned off the electricity and gas, Juan had poked around and done things with cables and wires. Soon the power and gas had come back on, along with cable for the TV—and no bills ever came again for any of it. He figured that this more than made up for what Gabriela gave him.

Juan liked Gabriela's girls, aged ten and twelve, but mostly ignored them. He was very fond of Andrés and full of attention for him and his quiet exploits. He loved Gabriela because she was stalwart, maternal, and reliable. Most people he knew were crazy or crooked, and they dragged him down after a while. But Gabriela was a good woman like his mother had been, and she made a warm center for his life, just the way his mother had.

Gabriela was very much in love with Juan. He was a superior sort of man—better-looking and smarter than most. She liked hearing him talk. She relied on his practical help and advice. The problem was that he was feckless, and she was much older than he. She knew one day he would leave her for someone younger and prettier, but in the meantime she intended to hold on to him. She would suffer torments of loss again, as she had when her husband deserted her, but it was worth it.

Life had held its current tentative shape in the Leon apartment for nearly two years, so long that they had begun to take it for granted. They had given up worrying about the building being condemned or eviction or Juan disappearing or the dealers moving in on the hallway or the refrigerator going warm and dark again. Naturally, as soon as they were off their guard, unpleasant things began to creep up on them, small at first but growing. Gabriela always expected trouble to start with Juan, or Andrés, or Rosa, but this time it was Gabriela herself who was the problem.

One day, she woke up feeling tired and achy. She went to work but was scarcely able to complete her chores. When she was not better after a week, she saw a doctor, who recommended rest, vitamins, and aspirin and asked if she was having problems at home. She didn't get better; next she developed headaches and felt weak. She began working on Saturdays and Sundays so that she could bring Alita along to help her with things she could no longer manage, but most clients objected to having her around on weekends, and they were positively horrified at the sight of a twelve-year-old girl, who looked considerably younger than that, scrubbing their kitchens.

"I may be compromised in life. I've done bad things," one lady told Gabriela, "but I draw the line at child labor."

Gradually, Gabriela had to give up clients, and when she got to be months behind on the rent, she tried to get on welfare. Social Services sent her to a clinic, which diagnosed her illness as psychological, stress-related, and promised her a housing subsidy. But when the social worker came and saw their apartment, she said it was simply unsafe for the children. It was dangerous to use the gas kitchen stove for heat and to be carrying big pots of hot water from the stove to the tub for baths. Gabriela had to get them out of there. They dithered about this for weeks. Then, one day, the social worker mentioned foster care—just until they could locate a decent apartment, she said reassuringly—as though it wasn't obvious that Gabriela would never be able to afford a better apartment with the pittance of a subsidy they were offering.

Gabriela concealed from the social worker how badly this suggestion frightened her and, as a result, scarcely realized it herself until after the woman left. Then terror overwhelmed her. When Juan showed up an hour later, Gabriela was hysterical and shrieking, and all three children, even nearly grown-up Andrés, were white-faced with fear.

"I'll quit school and get a job," Andrés said.

"No way!" said Juan. "You graduate this year. You're going to college. No, you let me handle this."

This calmed them all down. Juan often had good ideas even if he didn't help pay the rent.

"You're not going to like this, Gabriela," said Juan, "but you gotta send the girls to your mother for a while. They stay here and the city takes them. That's it. That's the only way."

"My mother don't want them."

"I'll talk to your mother. Cristina will look out for them, and they can help your mother. They're big girls now, not babies."

The big girls were weeping hopelessly, but all five of them knew that what Juan proposed was the right answer. They had to get money for two tickets to the Dominican Republic, and the girls had to leave right away. You never knew—that social worker might show up with a court order tomorrow afternoon. The calm of inevitability gradually descended over them all.

"Okay, who do you know with a little cash? Who can you borrow from? You need three, four hundred."

Gabriela thought it over. "Maybe the lady on 117th," she said, "Braithwaite. She might do it. She knows I'm sick. She's telling me every week to see another doctor."

"Her—yeah," Juan said. "You call her. I'll call your mother. I'll say you're too sick to take care of them. It's not really a lie."

Within the hour, Anne Braithwaite had agreed to give Gabriela four hundred dollars for plane tickets, which would leave nearly sixty dollars to give to Gabriela's mother for expenses, and Juan had convinced her to take the girls in. He sweet-talked her, and told her how sick Gabriela was. "Look," he said in a low voice, in Spanish, "Gabriela wants to come too so you can take care of her, but I know—"

Here he was evidently interrupted by lengthy protest. "No . . . no, listen . . . no," he interjected, while Gabriela watched him, her arms clutching her middle protectively.

"I talked her out of it," Juan told her mother. "I told her that would be too much for you. But the girls have to come. We'll send some money—don't worry about money."

After his cousins went away, Andrés stayed on with his aunt in the Manhattan Valley apartment. They told the social worker that he lived with his mother but came over often to look after his aunt because she was unwell. Somehow, however, the promised housing subsidy disappeared with the girls. The social worker got suspicious and grew less helpful. Juan continued to show up as he always had, sometimes with good things to eat if he had had work anywhere, but his jobs never seemed to last. Gabriela missed her daughters painfully and couldn't stop worrying about them, but her health began to improve a little after they left. Maybe that psychologist was right. Maybe the stress of things had been too much for her. They grew hopeful that with a little more rest, she would get well and go back to work and retrieve her girls.

Then one afternoon Gabriela came back from a visit to the clinic to find strange men carrying their belongings down to the street and stacking them on the sidewalk—dishes, clothes, beds—in preparation for being carried off in a van. She had gotten all the eviction notices, but had done nothing about them, relying on the promised housing subsidy. Gabriela stood in the street screaming insanely, and ladies from the neighborhood came to take care of her. One of them gave her a Valium and made her lie down on her sofa. Then they called Juan, who arrived within half an hour and almost smilingly took charge. Nothing seemed to faze Juan.

"All her stuff is down there in the street. I gave the guys ten bucks to wait, but I gotta do something quick or they're gonna drive off with everything," he told the lady who had taken in Gabriela. Gabriela was still on the sofa, sobbing quietly now.

In the meantime Andrés had shown up, and he recognized the family belongings in the heap on the sidewalk. Indeed, this was by no means the first eviction he had lived through. It was after a similar event that his own mother had suffered her first serious breakdown. Andrés got agitated and teary at the sight of all their things, especially his computer, stacked on the curb ready for loading, and started shouting at the van man. Fortunately, Juan happened to come down from the neighbor's apartment then, for Andrés tried to take the computer, and he and the van men were threatening one another.

"Okay, here's what we're gonna do," Juan announced. He stared fiercely at the van driver and his assistant, then turned to look at the small crowd that had gathered, as though calling on them for support. "We just gonna take clothes, medicine, school stuff . . ."

"My computer. We have to take that."

"Okay, your computer. We gonna stack 'em in my room until your aunt gets a new place, okay? So, look, mister, you give me that paper where the rest goes, right? I sign for the lady."

They packed these belongings and themselves into a gypsy cab, for which they spent Juan's last twenty dollars, and headed for the Bronx. There, for the first time, Gabriela and Andrés saw Juan's place. It was the size of a large closet, and it smelled fusty. There was a small bed, a sink, and a bathroom at the end of a forbidding hallway. They stuffed in Gabriela's and Andrés's things, but it was so crowded that Andrés had to sleep on Juan's floor with their clothes as a mattress. In the midst of these problems, what Andrés obsessed about long into the night, lying on the floor, was his homework, how he wouldn't be able to turn in the English essay that he'd been working on for days, due tomorrow second period, because he had nowhere to set up his computer.

Early the next day, Gabriela showed up at the Braithwaites' apartment smiling and insisting that she was ready to go to work. Anne stared at her, shocked at how she looked.

"You're not," Anne said. "Gabriela, you're going home and right to bed."

"No, no! I just saw the doctor yesterday, and he said I'm improving. No kidding. It's just I didn't sleep well last night."

"Why not?" Anne demanded aggressively. It was obvious to her that Gabriela was hiding something.

Gabriela laughingly brushed her questions aside, but Anne was aware of several telephone calls in frantic Spanish during the course of the morning. That afternoon, Gabriela approached her, blushing.

"You know, I have an idea. I'm changing apartments. I'm moving to a bigger place, you know? I wonder, would you mind if I slept in that little back room for a few days? Just until I move—because my lease is up on the old place and the new place isn't ready yet. I was staying with my friend, but it was so noisy and crowded there I couldn't sleep at all. That's why I'm so tired."

Anne wanted to refuse but could think of no good reason to do so, and was embarrassed at the length of her hesitation before she replied. "Well . . . sure. I guess. Why not? You mean tonight, or . . ." Anne's discomfort, however, was at least mitigated by the idea that she might now have more of an opportunity to make sure that Gabriela got some rest. "They still say it's just stress?"

Gabriela made a sour face to show her opinion of the doctors. That night she slept in Anne's little office off the kitchen, which had been a maid's room when the building went up a century ago. Anne thought that Gabriela was probably the first maid to sleep there since 1929, when the Miller family, the prior tenants of 9E, suffered losses in the stock market crash. Anne refused to let her leave to get her things in the Bronx. She made her take a nap, and that night she supplied her with a nightgown, a toothbrush, and a change of clothes, and insisted she call for another appointment with the doctor at her clinic. Anne considered calling her own internist and setting up a consultation for Gabriela but decided against it. Charles was already annoyed with her for giving Gabriela the four hundred dollars for plane tickets—when they themselves were living on credit cards until the end of the month. He would be even more annoyed to learn that Gabriela was sleeping in the little office. If Anne also paid for her medical treatment, he would be angry—and he would be right. Gabriela deserved help, but the Braithwaites, obviously, had already contributed far more than their fair share of what she needed. She was only their employee for one day a week, and they paid her very well.

Charles was always accusing Anne of extravagance, and just today she had spent nearly $300 on groceries and okayed $2,700 worth of repairs on Stuart's three-quarter-sized violin. She would of course point out to Charles that it was a good instrument and the repairs would only increase its value. Anne never wasted money on clothes or jewelry or vacations and had no interest in the show-off kind of luxuries. But she believed in her family's right to eat well, and how could you expect kids to eat fruits and vegetables if all you offered them was the tasteless stuff they sold in chain markets? How could you offer them supermarket beef when mad cow was out there and the food industry bought off the regulators? And she believed in the right of her children to the best of educations and the best musical training.

Even so, she had to admit that the world was a strange place when she and Charles could spend many tens of thousands each year just on tuitions and camps, while Gabriela, so hardworking and honest, had to beg for a bed and accept obviously substandard treatment at a free clinic because she didn't earn enough to pay a doctor. Anne was honest enough to face these painful facts and generous enough to be uncomfortable, even genuinely unhappy, about them.

In the morning, when Anne went to the kitchen to make breakfast while the children got ready for school, she found the table set, sliced fruits set out, coffee brewed, and cooked eggs keeping hot on the stove. Anne had nothing to do but sit down and read the paper.

"These eggs taste like a restaurant," said Stuart, his eyes narrowed in judgment.

"I think they're delicious," said Anne reprovingly. She could not imagine what Gabriela had found in her kitchen to make them taste like this.

"That's what I mean," said Stuart. "I like eggs better than cereal."

"I like eggs better than cereal," said Gilbert, who had been doubtful about the eggs until he heard his older brother's verdict.

"When is she leaving?" asked Charles. As Anne had foreseen, he resented having this awkward visitor imposed on them.

"A day or two," Anne whispered, pointing at the closed door of the maid's room and putting her forefinger to her lips. But she knew that "a few days" was what Gabriela had actually said.

"You shouldn't complain, Daddy," said Jane. "If Gabriela asked to stay, she must really need to stay. She never asks for anything."

"I didn't complain."

Both Charles and Anne grew parentally attentive at Jane's remark. It heralded something. Jane wasn't one to notice whether people, at least adult people, were undemanding or needy. In fact, they could see how someone who didn't know her well would think that Jane had no moral ideas at all. After all, this was the girl who had simply failed to show up for her master class last week, a master class taught by the distinguished English tenor Henry Moss—this after days of pestering and pleading with Anne to arrange for her to be invited. Anne had given in against her own better judgment, for the class was supposed to be restricted to college students. But Jane was so desperate to be included that Anne made at least twenty telephone calls, groveled, called in every favor she was owed, and fought with Charles to get him to use his own influence with Moss, whom he knew slightly. Though the request obviously put Moss in a difficult position, he graciously agreed to admit Jane. But when the evening of the master class arrived, Jane never came, and Charles and Anne, who were seated among the auditors, had to stand up and make pitifully inadequate public excuses for her.

Argument about this calamity flared for days, Jane sometimes insisting that she had just forgotten and other times maintaining that since *they*, by their own account, had done wrong to wangle her a place in the master class, *she* had been right to stay away. That really brought them to a boil. They talked about sending her to a psychotherapist. Last night, Anne went so far as to call her friend Lily Freund about it. Lily, a psychoanalyst who knew Jane and the whole family well, counseled against suggesting anything like that to Jane.

"Of course, it would be different if Jane herself wanted to," Lily pointed out.

To Anne and Charles's surprise, Lily didn't seem to be particularly shocked by Jane's truancy, and they were happy to think that Jane, though selfish, impulsive, maddening, perhaps even a little cruel, was normal. Still, given her history of self-centered indifference, they were understandably skeptical when Jane preached patience and altruism on Gabriela's behalf. Besides, even before the night of the master class, Jane had withdrawn from her family in an exaggerated way. She shut herself up in her room, coming out only to sit at the dinner table and pretend to eat, not speaking at all. This morning, however, she consumed Gabriela's eggs with a good appetite and left the table biting on a piece of apple.

"I think maybe Jane broke up with Stephen," Ellen said when Jane was gone. "Rebecca's sister said she heard that at school."

"No," Anne said, "he's coming over tomorrow night. She told me herself."

CHAPTER 3

As the cab pulled up to his building on Riverside Drive, Michael Garrard could see, by craning his neck, that the lights were on in his twelfth-floor apartment. It was past midnight, and he had hoped Adriana would be asleep. While he considered what to say to her, he paid the driver and got his mail, and the doorman retrieved his suitcase from the trunk. It was odd how Adriana never fetched the mail. She lacks curiosity, he thought. There was at least three days' worth stuffed into the little box, and the doorman, with an apologetic air, handed him a couple of packages as well.

"Dr. Garrard, these came Thursday. Your wife didn't want to—"

"Oh, I know," Michael said, laughing a little. The doormen were so respectful of him, so nearly fearful of him in fact, that he had to go out of his way to make clear that he was not offended or critical. Their excessive deference was owing to their knowledge, gained heaven knew how, of his high standing in the medical profession.

Adriana was waiting for him, wan and intense in her robe, when he walked into the living room. He was sunburned and fresh after a week on the slopes.

"Why didn't you call when you landed?" she asked.

"I thought it might wake you. It was almost midnight."

"Well, it wasn't like you, and I got worried."

"So sorry, dear. Next time I'll be sure to call. Now, fill me in. What's new?"

He smiled at her in a kind way, which made her feel sad and even more worried.

"What could be new since I talked to you this morning? How was your flight?" She had nothing else to ask, having already heard a full description of the skiing in phone calls.

"Simply dreadful. Delays. Compulsive talkers sitting next to me. What did you do today? Tell me things."

Adriana looked at him anxiously. He sat beside her, put his arm around her comfortingly, stroked her hair, and nuzzled against her cheek. He often did this rather than talk.

"Took a walk. Ran into Barbara. We went for coffee, and she had a few interesting ideas."

"Tell me," he said again, with an encouraging little smile, both arms around her now.

"Oh, you wouldn't . . . It's nothing we should go into at this hour, when you've just gotten home. Want something, honey? Are you hungry? Want a glass of wine?"

"No, nothing. I'd like to shower and go straight to bed. Come on." He stood, pulling her up after him, and walked her to their room, his arm around her shoulder.

She got into bed and sat pretending to read but in fact silently watching him unpack. Then she listened to the showering noises. He climbed into bed, still slightly damp and smelling of soap and shaving cream.

By this time, they both were tensely conscious of the subject she was avoiding. The Garrards' marriage was being injured by its childlessness. After years of fertility treatments with the best doctors in the field, they had never gotten so much as a tentative diagnosis of the problem. All they knew was that it was likely that she, not he, was its source. They were both unhappy about it. He was wistful for the babies that never came—he wanted to adopt one or two, but Adriana, so far, had refused—and was sadly thoughtful about what sort of man he might have been, what sort of life he might have had, if he had become a father. Her unhappiness was keener and more ominous. While Michael became increasingly hopeless, Adriana grew more and more determined to get pregnant and her feelings more and more deformed by her childlessness, until the slightest allusion to babies or pregnancies or even the possibility of adopting could bring on hysterical tears. Five years ago, at the age of thirty-three, she had given up her work as a hospital publicist to devote herself full-time to the pursuit of conception.

She knew that any allusion to fertility issues now would be a mistake, and she had to suppress a second urge to tell him what Barbara had said about a clinic in California.

"So all in all," she said, still casting about for a subject, "the trip was a success? Enough good days?"

"Yes, barely," he said, leafing through a magazine. He glanced over at her, sitting up beside him on the bed, and saw that she was frowning and staring into her lap. "What's wrong? Something's bothering you."

"I think *you're* the one who acts like something's wrong."

"What are you talking about?" His mild exasperation was far more comforting than explicit reassurances would have been, but Adriana's perception tonight had an almost paranoid keenness.

"Michael, don't do this. I'd rather you just left than do this."

Examining her face curiously, Michael thought about this seriously for a moment but decided that she was mistaken. No matter what she said, she wouldn't prefer that he leave. Not at all.

"Adriana, these are vapors," he replied. His voice, deep and authoritative, was as reassuring as his words, and this time Adriana opted to believe him. She sighed, and he leaned toward her and kissed her. He would have made love to her, but she turned away—a rare refusal; she disliked passing up any chance to make a baby. Michael himself had been surprised at the erotism available in this new relation with Adriana, in which, he thought, she was becoming more of a patient than a wife. She was his patient, he was her nurse, and making love wasn't quite real anymore. It felt like acting, except it was himself, his own body, that he acted, to comfort and reassure her. The pleasure he took in this love-on-stilts was oddly vicarious but nonetheless intense.

Michael, who had married his wife for love, watched her deterioration over the years with some agony; then gradually he began to withdraw into his work, his friends, his various charities and causes. Though he had no wish to abandon her, things had reached the point that now they saw mostly different people, and his entertainments and friends came from the boards and organizations he volunteered for. He stepped back to avoid the undertow of her obsession. People began to say that he was seeing some-one on the side. He was not, but the circumstances made rumors inevitable.

For several years Adriana was unaware of her husband's growing alien-ation. Her immersion in her quest, together with his tact and considera-tion and even his genuine affection, blinded her to his withdrawal from their shared life. A few weeks ago, when he had suddenly announced his intention to take this solo skiing vacation, the truth hit her, and she got scared.

In the morning, Adriana came to the breakfast table determined to try harder to make him content: she must no longer burden him with her con-stant talk about fertility issues. But within five minutes her resolve wa-vered.

"Do you know what Barbara thinks?" she said, with a forced liveliness intended to disguise her urgency.

"What?" he said, quite as though he had no idea what she was going to talk about.

And when she did talk about it, Adriana knew, he would no longer show the slightest impatience. The realization gave her strength.

"Oh . . . she thinks . . . I need a vacation—as hard as that is to believe."

"I don't think it's hard to believe," he said. "Not at all. Of course you do. But can you survive a month or two until I can come with you? Let's not have *all* separate trips."

On hearing this, she looked at him crestfallen, as though he had said the opposite. "Oh, that's just Barbara," she said. "If her husband had gone off for a week, she'd insist on doing the same—just to be even, you know. I have no impulse at all to vacation without you."

Michael had opened his appointment book on the table and was reading. "Damn," he said. "I've got that roundtable on religious charities tonight—and it's a dinner meeting. It might be ten or eleven before I get back. Why don't you make plans to meet someone for dinner?"

"Oh. Oh dear," Adriana said. "Do you have to go?"

"I do. They've put it off until tonight just so I could attend. Remember, I told you about it week before last. Well, I'll try to leave early, but I can't promise. If you're out, don't worry about getting home. Just call and let me know your plans. All right?" Michael rose from his chair as he talked and pulled on his coat, arcing his long body over her for a brisk kiss.

Then he was gone, and Adriana felt a misery so potent that for more than half an hour it immobilized her. When she had partially mastered it, she rose unsteadily from the table, went to her computer, and found enough energy to open the day's research into comparative in vitro success rates in leading U.K., European, and U.S. programs. Galvanized by her initial findings, she spent hours on more research, e-mails, chat-room exchanges, and online orders of pamphlets and articles. She did not leave her desk to shower and dress until nearly four o'clock.

By late afternoon, Michael, a doctor of internal medicine and a professor at Columbia Presbyterian Hospital, had completed his rounds, hurriedly swallowed a sandwich at his desk while reading charts and reviewing test results, and examined fifteen patients. His private practice consisted mostly of moneyed New Yorkers with a sprinkling of wealthy people from elsewhere—Londoners, Californians, the occasional Arab, Italian, or Japanese. He liked to treat people who could pay out-of-pocket because that let him avoid the frustrations of dealing with insurance companies while earning enough to take on plenty of charity cases and, at the same time, practice medicine the way it should be practiced, spending enough time and prescribing exactly what was best for each individual. He gave his poor patients the same skill, devotion, and tenderness he gave the rich ones.

That he stood at the top of his profession was the opinion of medical experts as well as doormen and society matrons. His diagnostic skills were uncanny; his knowledge was vast. Moreover, he was a kindly man with gentle, warm hands who, when faced with suffering, became almost womanly in his need and ability to comfort, and he listened to his patients' stories with endless patience, a slight, faintly puzzled, encouraging frown on his face until he got it, whatever it was—diagnosis, cure, or palliative. He was effectual, decisive, impatient of dithering and bureaucracy, a striking character in every sense—even in his looks. He was tall and thin; his wiry hair, mostly still dark, sprang up in an energetic, boyish cowlick; and he had a narrow face with a profile that showed a perfect shallow arc from his forehead down the thin, strong nose to the slight recession of his chin. His mouth, thin-lipped and small, had a hint of an overbite. He was not glamorous; nor was he a glad-hander. He smiled rarely and spoke sparingly, expressing himself, though, with clarity, simplicity, logical orderliness, and sensitivity when he did, and the beauty of his voice was startling, unusually deep and calm, with pronounced head resonance and an obvious English accent despite his twenty years in the States. His colleagues joked that even Dr. Garrard's death sentences were a pleasure to listen to. It was easy to understand why so many moneyed people found their way to his matter-of-fact Fifth Avenue offices.

Michael was born in Manhattan, the child of a nineteen-year-old American girl and a middle-aged English businessman who was rich, handsome, seductive, and twice divorced. Tormented by her husband's infidelities, his mother committed suicide when Michael was still a baby, and the elder Garrard took his little son home to London despite the pleas and protests of his wife's family. In England the child was reared, with stoic reluctance, by his grandparents and aunt, with early and extensive reliance on the dying English custom of boarding schools for young children. His father had plenty of affection but no time for his son, abandoning him for long periods and offering by way of parental guidance mostly bon mots and witty rules of conduct that he imagined the boy would admire when he grew older. "In a restaurant, never take the first table you're offered," he would tell him, or "No woman is ugly in the dark." Michael grew into a lonely, awkward young man with unusual gifts in rhetoric and the sciences.

Although he had no family left in New York, he returned to study at Columbia because of a painful sense of weightlessness and directionlessness that he suffered in England. He took those feelings to mean that he didn't belong in England, that he belonged in his mother's world, and life in Morningside Heights quickly convinced him that this was correct. Even as a student, he saw how the neighborhood's dedication to family framed and formed an intense life of the mind. It was a startling and powerfully attractive combination to the intellectual young man, who had known so little of family and, to ward off loneliness, had immersed himself in politics and philosophy during his two years at Oxford, accepting the remnants of monkishness in that university's culture as natural to the enterprise.

When Michael married Adriana and plunged wholeheartedly into domesticity, he soared, feeling as though he had made up all his losses and would finally taste the sweet parts of life that for so long he had hungrily watched others enjoy. Now he had to make a deliberate effort not to become bitter. To his own surprise, he mostly succeeded.

CHAPTER 4

At five, Michael left his office and cabbed back to Morningside Heights, where he was to attend a meeting of the Ecumenical Council of Religious Charities at the Cathedral of Saint John the Divine, the huge Gothic monument to Manhattan Episcopalianism that loomed over the neighborhood. Michael was a founding member of this group, which consisted of about thirty people: businesspeople, lawyers, academics, but, of course, mostly clergy. Michael had become quite fond of one of the latter, an Episcopalian priest named Greg Merriweather from Saint Ursula's in Morningside Heights. Father Merriweather was a gentle, soft-spoken fellow who impressed Michael with his thoughtful fair-mindedness; he was accommodating and generous but also perceptive, hard to fool. If he had a flaw, it was a sometimes infuriating lack of self-assertion, though Michael thought he was not weak but self-doubting— as a result of some peculiar convictions along with excessive sympathy for the other's point of view.

After the meeting, a small group of council members, including Michael and Greg Merriweather, were going for dinner. Michael thought there was no point in injuring his wife with the knowledge that this dinner was not mandatory. He had made up his mind to spend as much time away from her as he could, trying to enjoy himself while causing her as little pain as possible. Sometimes truth had to be compromised to accommodate this program.

Hunger and food-distribution programs were the major topic of the meeting—soup kitchens, food pantries, home-delivery meal programs, food donations from restaurants, and more. Someone wanted to convince restaurants to adopt certain poor and elderly people and keep them fed from their leftovers, of which there were prodigal amounts. The discussion bogged down on administrative issues. A church volunteer program would be unwieldy, subject to breakdown. Father Merriweather, along with two others, was assigned to look into the possibilities and try to inspire various churches to work out arrangements with local restaurants.

Then there was a presentation on legal services for the poor in housing, criminal defense, and divorce and custody cases by a former legal aid lawyer turned poverty activist named Carla Winter—quite a depressing presentation from Michael's point of view. At least you had some hope of feeding poor people, even of providing them with medical care, but the wretched families and societies of the poor, he believed, were beyond anyone's help. Sometimes people saved themselves or their intimates, but the sort of devotion required for anyone else to help them—this was not available. It had never existed anywhere. How could it? You would have to provide each maimed soul with what he provided his own declining wife. This was not possible.

Michael was glad when the chair tapped the table with his glass and announced that they would adjourn. With the others, he followed Greg across the cathedral lawns to Amsterdam Avenue, which, despite its new eateries, was relatively deserted, crime-prone, and scruffy compared with thoroughly gentrified Broadway, and its air of flimsy makeshift continued to resist the grave, heavy purpose of the century-old institutions that lined its blocks—the cathedral at 112th Street; Saint Luke's Hospital at 113th; Columbia University with its great wrought-iron gates and School of Law at 116th, and the Renaissance palazzo, Casa Italiana, that housed its Italian Academy at 117th. Deserted by students, Amsterdam got darker and lonelier as they walked north, heading for Pisticci, a restaurant on La Salle

Street at the northern edge of Morningside Heights, where it meets Harlem.

"It's like walking back twenty years, isn't it?" Michael asked Greg. "Up here, things feel like Morningside Heights in the eighties."

"So I've heard," Greg said, and Michael only then reflected that Father Merriweather was not only relatively new to the neighborhood but considerably younger than himself. Twenty years ago he had probably been in high school. Michael had judged his age by his sober air rather than his looks.

After the empty streets and the meeting's gloomy discussions, they welcomed the noisy warmth of the unexpectedly crowded restaurant. Their group included Peter Frankl, the mild but sharp-witted president of a small local foundation, Carla Winter, and two or three others. Michael thought Peter an exceptionally decent man—"a *really* nice guy" was how his friends always described him—and enjoyed his company. Carla was difficult, but over a period of months he had learned to respect her quick mind and energy, and he wasn't someone who could withhold liking where he gave respect. He still felt an outsized resentment when Carla disagreed with his views, though, and he was perhaps over-ready to disagree with her. He'd noticed that social acceptances that contained an element of forbearance often played out this way, grudgingly. Just now Carla had quarreled with Michael's skepticism about programs that aimed at anything beyond food, shelter, and health care.

"Eighty percent of this social pathology you're going on about would disappear if you put a little money in these people's pockets," Peter was saying to Greg, in support of Carla.

Greg nodded affirmatively and shrugged skeptically.

Father Merriweather was certainly an exasperating man to argue with, Michael thought; it was almost comical.

"Sometimes," Greg replied, "but there are lots of people you can't help with money."

"I know that," said Peter. "But most you can. And eighty percent of the people the doctor says you can't help wouldn't be that way in the first place if someone had stepped in with cash back when—to pay a doctor or the rent or whatever."

"Well, I have to agree," Greg said, "that money could prevent a lot of human damage. Yes, really a lot."

"Father Merriweather, you also think that money wouldn't do much for a lot of them," put in Michael. "It'd be a lot more interesting if you'd say so instead of just seconding Peter."

"But Peter's making the most important point. I'm just talking about original sin. We don't really disagree."

Peter nodded agreeably. "That's right."

"I could swear the two of you are totally at odds," Michael said. "Peter, you don't even believe in original sin."

"I didn't say I did."

"I think wealth is much more damaging to people's moral health than poverty is," said Greg, as mild as ever. "There are lots of really good poor people, but very few good rich people. You wouldn't agree, would you, Peter?"

"I don't know," said Peter. "I really don't think in those terms. What about middle-class people, Greg? Do they count as rich or poor in this theory of yours?"

"Rich," Father Merriweather replied apologetically.

"Of course," Peter said to the others, laughing. "We're all sinners. Of course, that's what he thinks."

Michael, like Peter, was surprised to hear a colleague on the council talking in terms of moral health and original sin. He was beginning to think of Father Merriweather as Greg and to look forward to seeing him. Most of the time, he forgot that he was a priest at all. But every now and then he came out with these odd ideas and then he would seem foreign and peculiar again, the way he had when they first met. Of course, this was a council on *religious* charities, but Michael had been invited to join not through any religious affiliation but because of his reputation for work on behalf of various secular charities. In London, he reflected, you could have safely accepted such a position without running into any actual religion. Father Merriweather's very clerical collar made Michael feel queasy—the same way he felt when he saw those head-to-toe black burkhas, with only slits for eyes, worn by Muslim women on the Edgware Road in London. Both costumes announced someone's mad withdrawal from general humane rationality into something primitive and tribal, and Michael feared and disliked anything akin to madness. He could never have been a psychiatrist. His attraction to science was largely a response to his sense of the dangerous plasticity of reason in politics and philosophy—though he was aware that his attitude was dated and unpopular. No one but a few scientists any longer regarded science as a reservoir of truth, sanity, and respect for objectivity.

"But you don't think it's okay to let people go hungry or homeless because that's a faster ticket to heaven," said Peter, turning back to Greg.

Greg certainly didn't.

"But that's not consistent, is it, Father Merriweather?" asked Michael. "If poverty creates virtue, then why work to rid the world of it?" Michael had been a great debater at Oxford and he excelled in political argument, but he was also genuinely curious about Greg's views. What sort of human being became a priest, even an Episcopalian priest, in this day and age? What sort of person thought poverty encouraged virtue? Greg was surely no ascetic.

"Yeah. What garbage you're talking," Carla said, looking at the priest with benign contempt.

Michael took no comfort in Carla's support. Despite his own attitudes, he was always distressed by her open disrespect for religious views—and at a gathering of people working in religious charities. She was especially contemptuous of personal charity, the kind that pulled one child or one family out of the great mass of the poor, threw a rent deposit or a bowl of chili at its problems, and then smugly approved of its own virtue.

"On average, in my experience, rich people are much, much nicer people than poor ones," she said now. "It's one of the saddest things about poverty. It corrupts people."

Carla was tough and sour, and Michael liked listening to her as a kind of antipode of his own wife's supine sweetness. Adriana's mind never moved out of the circle of its own intimate concerns—at least it hadn't for years. Yet he wondered, listening to Carla, how any man could ever approach her sexually. He himself found her steely sharpness simultaneously appealing and repellent. He guessed she was somewhere in her mid-thirties—and not bad-looking at all, with her shaggy haircut, low-cut tight top, and short, close-fitting skirt. It dawned on him, having had such a thought, that poor Father Merriweather had too.

"What you're saying, of course, is profoundly anti-Christian," Greg was telling Carla, pouring more wine into her glass.

"What do you think, Peter?" Michael asked. "Should we chastise the Antichrist here or what?"

"Greg knows she just likes to pull people's chains," Peter said to Michael, seeing that he was on the verge of being offended on the priest's behalf.

Michael put his feelings aside, as the general opinion seemed to be that Carla was to be tolerated. When it came to Carla, everyone seemed to act as though they'd made a pet of some wild thing, some incontinent and unpredictably aggressive creature you couldn't blame for messing on the carpet or drawing blood with her claws.

"You're mixed up, Carla," said Peter in a voice so confidently yet respectfully disapproving that Michael half expected Carla to retract her views on the spot.

"Look, I despise religious charity," said Carla. "It fattens on the poor. It rationalizes poverty to give itself some reason to exist. I hate religion period."

"Then why did you want to be on the council?" asked Peter. The question was curious, not accusatory.

"Are you kidding? I'd bet that half the members have no religion. That includes the priests. As for me, I'll use anyone and anything I can—nothing personal, by the way. I love you all. Here's to friendship!" The others were perfectly willing to raise their glasses to this, and no one seemed to feel anything less than admiring warmth for Carla.

"Carla," said Greg, who had heard Carla argue this line before, "let's have lunch tomorrow somewhere quiet. I'd like to talk some more about this, someplace where we can hear each other."

"A Christian working lunch? I really can't."

"Later in the week maybe?"

"I don't do lunch," said Carla.

"Greg," said Peter, "she also doesn't do religious discussion."

Carla laughed.

Michael felt sorry for Father Merriweather, who seemed a little hurt. When the party broke up, he walked out with him, and taking advantage of Peter's precedent, he called him Greg. "Going home, Greg?" he asked. "Have time to stop for a drink? It's only nine-thirty." Michael intended to stay out as long as possible.

"Uh, sure," said Greg, brightening a little. "Except I have to stop at my friends' place and pick up some opera tickets. They're just on 117th. Do you mind?"

Michael, who was an opera fan himself, didn't mind, especially when he learned that the friends were Charles and Anne Braithwaite. He had seen Braithwaite at the Met often enough to learn to look for him.

The Braithwaites wouldn't let them leave once they were in the door. They'd assumed Greg would stay for a while and have a glass of wine with them. They insisted that Michael, whose unusual qualities they detected almost immediately, stay too, and Michael could not refuse. He found the domestic chaos inside entrancing. The apartment was untidy, noisy, and crowded with children, pianos, music stands, and books—so unlike the muted order of his own home. He eventually counted four Braithwaite children, the oldest a striking tall, slender beauty—a fine singer herself, they said—who was not interested in the guests. She was engrossed in un-smiling conversation with a boy her own age in the relative privacy of a deep window seat. Michael did not know why, but he felt a sympathetic ache watching this girl and boy in their difficulty, whatever it was.

When he left, at midnight, he was Michael to all of them, they had made plans to get together again, and he was to be given the ticket that he accused Greg of having wanted to offer to Carla.

"I doubt she'd care any more for opera than religion," he told Greg, who somewhat sheepishly agreed. "My wife doesn't go to the opera either."

CHAPTER 5

Carla's Saturday nights were reserved for big dates, even though this policy meant that many of them were spent at home alone. Friday nights were for minor dates and check-him-out dates. Sunday evenings were unplanned, but typically she had dinner in the neighborhood with some friend or other.

Carla had two regular Monday-evening meetings. The Ecumenical Council of Religious Charities met on the first Monday of each month, and the Legal Reading Group on the third Monday.

On Tuesday nights, Carla stayed home and read.

Most Wednesday nights, she went to dinner and then a film with some old friends.

The Thursday Night Club was a shifting group of about fifteen women, of whom eight or nine reliably collected each week at one of their homes for potluck dinner and a predetermined entertainment. They had gone through a forties/fifties film noir period, during which they watched every example of the genre offered by the Movie Place video rentals on 105th Street. That enthusiasm had led to a fascination with New York

City films from the thirties through the sixties. Lately, for several weeks running, the group had been learning to knit, taught by a member who was skilled in the art.

This evening, gathered in Carla's one-room-with-kitchen on 111th off Amsterdam, they had brought their scarves for binding off and fringing.

"We should all do a sweater now," Lisa, the talented knitter, said.

"Like hell," said Brett. "I've had it with knitting."

"What about knitting while we take turns reading aloud," someone suggested, "like in *Little Women*?" But this was rejected as too sleepy.

Soon poetry enthusiasts among them had shamed the reluctant into agreeing to spend several weeks reading modern verse. In the meantime, they all diligently bound off their scarves and snipped and traded yarn for fringe, heeding Lisa's suggestions about contrasting colors.

"Christ, Carla, do you ever vacuum? My scarf is coated with cat hairs. I'll have to have it dry-cleaned before I can give it to Barry. He's so allergic," Lisa said.

"I'm keeping mine for myself," said Brett.

"I guess I'll put mine away for the next birthday present I need," said Carla, oblivious of the general opinion that hers was the ugliest of the scarves. "People appreciate it when you give them something you *made*, you know?"

A long shriek from the kitchen, where three of the group had gone to begin laying out dinner, halted talk of knitting.

"What on earth," Carla said, rushing in.

"Roaches!" screamed Beth, pointing dramatically. "Honest to God, Carla, an army of them—all over that . . . that . . ."

"For heaven's sake. On that bowl covered with aluminum foil? So what?" asked Carla coolly. "They can't hurt you, Beth."

"You always have roaches, Carla," Lisa said. "Why don't you call an exterminator?"

"I give every spare penny I have to environmental groups working to clean up the air and soil and water. What sense would it make to spend money to have my apartment, my own kitchen, where my food is prepared, sprayed with long-lasting carcinogenic pesticides?" The others, looking around the cramped kitchen, saw that roach traps littered the floor and countertops—like garlic to ward off vampires, someone said.

"You know, it's not so healthy to have roaches either," Lisa pointed out. But Carla seemed firm in her opinion, and no one liked to take on Carla when it came to anything remotely political.

"They're really everywhere, aren't they?" Brett said. "Look—there're two crawling up that cabinet."

"Maybe they won't hurt you, but they can really kill a girl's appetite," said Lisa. "Who's going to lift up that aluminum foil and see what's under there?"

"Oh, come on," said Carla. "Grow up, everybody."

"Throw up is more like it," said Brett, gingerly lifting the corner of the aluminum foil to a chorus of horrified howls, as three insects were huddling in perfect stillness on its underside, apparently hypothesizing that they would be overlooked if they didn't move.

"I wonder why they like chili so much," said Lisa, who had begun giggling. "Look, they don't like fruit salad at all."

Carla, too, was working to stifle laughing.

"We probably can't even see the ones that drowned in that chili," Lisa said. "I'm not eating that. In fact, I'm not eating any of this food that's been sitting here. Someone call for pizza or Chinese."

"Hold on, Lisa," said Carla. "There's plenty of stuff in the fridge, totally safe."

"Oh, Brett, what a tragedy. All that chili you made!"

Lisa was willing to eat food from the refrigerator, but when they opened a cabinet to pull out plates, a roach scuttled out and up the door. Everyone waited tensely to see if she would refuse to eat from the plates, most intending to follow her lead. As she said nothing, soon they all had plates on their laps in the living room, but their appetites, except for Carla's, were generally feeble.

"Who made this eggplant?" Carla asked. "Truly delicious."

The roach night, all agreed, would be a memorable chapter in the history of the Thursday Night Club.

Carla told the story to Father Greg Merriweather the following evening when she went with him to Dynasty for Chinese food. After his fourth invitation, she had run out of excuses, and he had promised not to allude in any way to any religious subject.

"I can't remember the last time I actually sat and ate in a Chinese restaurant," she told him as they took their seats in the dark little room. "It's become a strictly take-out option for my friends."

"Really?" asked Greg innocently. "I come here all the time."

"They're tearing it down, you know," Carla said, looking around suspiciously at the many tired and dusty attempts at Chinese décor involving beads, bamboo, pleated paper, and crockery painted in oriental motifs. "Putting in an apartment building."

"Oh, too bad," Greg said forlornly. It was one of the few places left in the neighborhood he could afford.

"If you say so," said Carla.

"So you don't eat out much?" Greg asked. "Do you like to cook?"

"I eat at home a lot, but I'm not really much of a cook." Frustrated at being positively misconstrued when she had intended to come across as difficult, she mischievously began telling him all about the fiasco with last night's potluck dinner. She assumed it would put him off, but to her surprise he laughed. In fact, he tried not to laugh as much as he wanted to. She had thought he was humorless. As he was not, she made up her mind to call him Greg, the way Peter Frankl did. Carla had never set foot in a house of religion and found it embarrassing to call someone Father, especially someone her own age.

"Greg," she said, with an excessive firmness that somewhat startled him, "do you smell that?"

"What?"

"Sort of a sickening flowery smell?"

"I'm not sure, maybe . . . sort of."

"Someone's perfume."

"Yes, uh, I think I do," Greg said, sniffing conscientiously. "It's hard to make it out with all the food odors in here."

"Can you stand it?"

Greg thought hard. "You mean the perfume smell bothers you?"

"It really does. I have kind of serious chemical sensitivities."

"My goodness," said Greg. "Well, let's change tables."

"Would you mind?" she said. She sounded apologetic, but she was already standing and gathering her things as she spoke.

They moved to the far side of the restaurant; Carla looked scathingly at the perfumed woman as they passed her. The woman, however, didn't notice and continued to ply her chopsticks dexterously.

"Carla, you know, it doesn't make any difference to me that you're not religious," Greg said when they had sat down again.

"That's very sweet of you, but 'not religious' is sort of an understatement," Carla replied.

"Whatever you call what you're doing with your life," Greg persisted, "it's the same thing I'm doing with my life."

"Well, this *is* getting serious," Carla said, resolving not to respond in emotional kind. "You mean poverty work?"

"Of course. Being devoted to a cause, and being willing to be poor and . . . insignificant."

"There is that, yes, but as for doing the same thing with our lives— the resemblance is absurdly superficial. You're only trying to 'minister to suffering' as one of the jackasses at the last council meeting said. I'm trying to get rid of it. I'm only interested in attacking the systemic social conditions that produce it. No offense, Greg, but I think your soup kitchen work is contemptible and degrading to the poor."

"Did you grow up poor, Carla?"

"Sort of lower-middle-class strapped. My parents were divorced, and my mother was a dentist's receptionist—in Brooklyn."

"Aren't you going to ask me if I was poor?" Greg asked, smiling.

"No, because I don't think it matters at all. Hey, you promised no religion in this discussion, and I think you're on the verge of reneging."

"I thought we were just trading bios. Anyway, I grew up in foster care."

"What!"

"Yeah."

"Foster care! Were your parents druggies or something?"

"My father was killed in Vietnam when my mother was pregnant, and she was in and out of mental institutions from about the time I was five. No other relatives."

"Oh Jesus."

"Yeah," he said, nodding affirmation.

"Was this sort of middle-class foster care? I mean, out in the suburbs, split-level foster care?"

The waiter set platters on the table. Greg filled Carla's plate, then watched her take a hearty first bite. "More rural, poor working-class foster care," he said, helping himself.

"That's impossible! You couldn't have been raised like that."

"My grandparents were from a different sort of background, which I knew, and that seems to have been very influential in how I turned out. Or maybe Freud was right: it's all over by the time you're five. You're formed. That's what my friend Anne says."

"Greg, just how horrible was the foster care? How many placements?"

"About eight. Some were really horrible, some were okay. Mostly they were just depressing. But I got away at sixteen—went to college very young, got a scholarship."

"You can't imagine how this changes my image of you."

"Yes I can. That's why I told you."

"Why?"

"You know, Carla."

Greg couldn't meet her eye after this unhedged confession, and Carla had a chance to look at him appraisingly. It wasn't that he was bad-looking. Actually, he was fairly nice-looking—the glasses were okay. His mildness was soothing, too, and his refinement, and the subtle coloration that his anachronistic outlook gave his whole demeanor appealed to her. There it is, she thought. He senses that I'm half attracted to him, but he won't see that it's only half. Now that she knew why he had become a priest, she disliked it more than ever.

"I'll be honest with you, Greg," said Carla. "To me, your becoming a priest and getting religious as a way of responding to this wretched childhood you had is just doubling your misery. Not only did you go through all that, you end up stuck with this rigmarole that doesn't really help you—culturally dead rigmarole that keeps you marginal and down and in-effective. You don't do yourself or anyone else any good. But I feel sorry for what you went through. I really do."

"When someone told William Blake she felt sorry for him, he said, 'Dost thou pity me? Then I will love thee.' "

"That's horrible! That's absolutely horrible! He wanted to be pitied? That's a basis for a relationship, for chrissakes?"

Greg thought it over. "Why not? What's wrong with that?"

He poured tea into Carla's cup and spooned more spicy chicken with cashews onto her plate. He's certainly polite, she thought. In fact, as he was dimly aware, he liked feeding her. When she cleaned her plate, it gave him a good, satisfied feeling.

"Pathetic. I can't stand it."

They made aimless small talk for the rest of the meal, but Greg in-sisted on walking Carla home—as though, she thought, the prospect of anything between them had not just tanked.

"Do you like movies? Want to go see *Collateral* this weekend?" he asked.

"Greg, give it up. This is a no-brainer. Let's just agree to be vaguely ac-quainted. In a year, neither of us has to remember this conversation."

Greg was despondent when he left Carla at the door of her building, and Carla was remorseful even though, she told herself as she walked the three flights of stairs to her studio, she had done nothing wrong. In the long run, it was kinder to be blunt. In the night, she woke up and thought about what Greg might be like in bed—probably sweet and calm. But there would be no way to have a relatively uninvolved sexual relationship with someone like him. Oh, no, it would have to be all total and commit-ted or he would be terribly hurt, and Carla was too fond of him to allow that to happen—not that she wouldn't like a committed relationship with someone more on her wavelength. Wasn't there some failure of self-regard in his persistent interest in her, she wondered, some masochistic tendency? The idea quickly destroyed the sexual stirring she had just felt.

CHAPTER 6

Three weeks after the eviction, in mid-November, Andrés still had no place to set up his computer; there was no electrical outlet in Juan's room, let alone a tabletop to work on. He began staying at school late to finish his homework, and every night he slept on Juan's floor. Juan got him a weekend job helping a contractor, and that gave him cash for food. Despite Juan's help, Andrés was terrified. Before, he could usually drive fear out of his mind with books and schoolwork. But now his terror was so intense that his thoughts circled endlessly in his brain, day and night, and he couldn't read or think. His heart beat maniacally. If he fell asleep, he dreamed of falling and sat up gasping so audibly that a couple of times he woke Juan. Every day, he called his aunt, hoping she would have found a new apartment. One night, Juan called Andrés and said he wouldn't be home. Although Andrés was glad to have a chance to sleep on the bed, he got worried that Juan had found another girlfriend—so worried that he had a harder time than usual concentrating on his classes, and his teachers at City High, one of New York's elite public schools, had already begun to notice that he was slipping. Andrés called Gabriela as soon as his last class was over.

"Aunt Gabriela, how is everything?"

"Same. I went back to the clinic, and the doctor still says it's in my head or maybe it's mono or chronic fatigue syndrome. Maybe it'll take a long time to get better. And he didn't give me nothing for it."

"Look, I'll go try to find a place for you."

"No, I got no money yet, Andrés. I'm calling every day for welfare, but the problem is they keep saying nothing's wrong with me and I have to go here or there. They say I have to appeal."

"Aunt Gabriela, is Juan helping you?"

"He's trying."

"You heard from him at all?"

"I've seen him a couple of times." Gabriela sounded vague.

"He didn't come home last night."

"I know." She sounded so unconcerned that Andrés was relieved.

"So you get your homework done last night?" she asked. "School okay? You have to find Rosa. Did you try calling her friend Maria again?"

"School's okay, and I still can't find her. I keep calling everyone."

Gabriela heard trouble in Andrés's voice, and she could hear him breathing too hard into the phone. True, he was grown up now—he was eighteen, older than she had been when she had Cristina—but she could hear that he was fraying. Boys were not as tough as girls. "I have an idea," she said. "You come here and have dinner with me tonight. These people going out and not coming home till late. Come about seven-thirty, and I'll cook for you, okay? I don't have no one to eat with."

Andrés felt a little odd about visiting his aunt in some strangers' home, but he hadn't seen her since the eviction and he was almost ill with loneliness and fear. That night, calming himself with the knowledge that he was going to see her soon, he managed to do homework in the school library until it was time to ride the subway uptown to Morningside Heights. There was a doorman in the building, which intimidated Andrés, but the man seemed to expect him.

"You Andrés?" he asked. "Gabriela's nephew?" Then he continued in Spanish. "Go on up. But don't go in the first 9E door. Keep going to the next door. That's the service entrance, and she'll let you in there. I'll call her and say you're coming up." The man was surprisingly friendly.

Andrés found it comforting to be known and expected, and the band of anxiety that had been constricting his chest for weeks loosened. He smiled gratefully at the doorman and waved as the elevator door closed. On the ninth floor, Gabriela was leaning out the second doorway on the left, pulling an unfamiliar wrap around her. Although she seemed tired, she smiled and kissed him several times.

"I didn't know how much I missed you!" she exclaimed, and drew him into a neat room barely large enough to hold the bed and the desk that were its only furniture. On the desk sat a laptop, a fancy Mac.

"Whose is that?" Andrés asked, pointing at the sleek white computer.

"The lady who lives here. This is her office—except she never uses it."

"It's one of those new PowerBooks. Can I use it for a while?"

"Better not. Well, I don't know. You can't hurt it, can you?"

"Nah—I just want to play around."

"Not now though. Come talk to me while I cook."

Gabriela led Andrés into a large kitchen that held a professional-sized stove of stainless steel at one end and a huge industrial-looking refrigerator at the other. Granite and tile gleamed; copper-bottomed and shiny steel pots and utensils lined one wall; tomatoes and avocadoes ripened on a counter-top. On a large oak table sat a diminutive vase that held half a dozen daisies.

"Jeez," said Andrés, turning to eye all these wonders. "They're rich, huh?"

Gabriela lifted her hands, palms up, as though to say, "You see for yourself." But she had known the Braithwaites for many years and remembered the way they lived before they inherited this co-op and a pile of money; her relations with them had been forged when they were hard up. Despite her weariness, she proceeded to set out pans, slice cold chicken, cheese, and vegetables, and prepare rice, every now and then giving out a little moan or sigh. Andrés ate heartily sitting at the oak table. Gabriela had no appetite herself but took satisfaction in watching him eagerly consume what she had made for him.

When Andrés had finished and she had cleaned up so thoroughly that the kitchen showed no trace of her cookery, she walked him around the apartment. He exclaimed repeatedly over its size, was dazzled by the living room with its huge, gleaming, black grand piano, the amazing number of bedrooms—a large one for the parents and small, snug ones for each of the four children. The children's rooms gave him a bad feeling. They were all astonishingly outfitted, with computers, puffy comforters, book-shelves, photos, toys, and trophies, and everything was so, so cool. Andrés felt an overpowering impulse to surrender, just to deliver himself from ex-cruciating envy. But surrender to whom? To what? These people didn't even care if he surrendered; they weren't trying to hurt or defeat him.

Andrés followed his aunt back to the little room she was staying in, and she let him turn on the laptop on the desk. He found a manual in the desk drawer and soon was avidly exploring the potential of the machine.

"She could do a lot with this," he said. "Did she just get it or some-thing? There's nothing on here at all."

"I think she never used it," said Gabriela. She lay on the little bed, propped up with pillows, looking drained and wan. "They got it for her birthday a couple weeks ago, but she don' really need it."

"Want me to set up a few things for her?" Andrés asked hopefully.

"No, no, no!" said Gabriela. "Just leave everything like it was. Don't change nothing."

"Don't change anything," said Andrés.

"Don't ack like that with me. Who feeds you?" she snapped. Gabriela accepted no disrespect from the children.

Andrés thought to himself that no one fed him, usually, but he loved his aunt and he said nothing. She was just old-fashioned.

"You have to go now," she told him when he had been fiddling with the machine for twenty minutes, her voice hard because she knew he would find it difficult to leave and she had to make him.

Andrés nodded and immediately stood and pulled on his jacket.

"Aunt Gabriela, what about the mail?" he asked rather shamefacedly, for he knew that she had many more serious problems to worry about. "Some of the colleges are gonna start sending out acceptances soon."

"College!" she snorted. "You pay rent for your family before you spend on stuff like that. That school wants you to go to college, they can find us someplace to live."

Within minutes, Andrés was walking down Broadway, shivering in his light jacket, and, as his heartbeat quickened, the shivering became trembling. The subway ride through dark tunnels to the Bronx was long and dreary, and the nighttime walk from the station to Juan's place, down some deserted, dilapidated blocks, was always frightening. But tonight, after his visit, the fear grew worse with his heightened sense that he belonged nowhere and to no one, for that meant that he deserved whatever might happen to him. People expected kids like him to get knifed or shot or robbed, put down, shut out, whatever. He was the type of kid those things were supposed to happen to—unlike the kids who lived in the apartment where Gabriela was staying. This indifference of the world, its acquiescence to his terror and harm, he felt as a great weight pressing down on him, making it harder and harder to keep going.

He was relieved when he finally closed Juan's door behind him. Juan was not there, which was also a relief, for Andrés feared that Juan would soon tell him to find someplace else to crash. He couldn't blame him. There wasn't room here for two, and he didn't want to get Juan mad. His aunt needed Juan, and Andrés wanted to help her keep him. Maybe Juan was no saint, but he was a pretty good guy.

If Andrés could find his mother in Brooklyn, he would have to join her, a thought that filled him with dread. Her rage, the drugs, the strange people, guns, arrests—these were things he could not brave again. Once, when Andrés was twelve, he had called the police for help, and they had come and arrested his mother and put him into foster care with some stupid, weird lady somewhere in the Bronx where he was so frightened that he couldn't speak. They said he had to take drugs because he was so upset, which confused and further upset him. After all, they had thrown his mother in jail for doing that. One night, he used his school MetroCard to run off to Gabriela, and the social workers never showed up again. He knew, even then, that Gabriela didn't really want him the way she wanted her own girls, but she always took care of him.

Andrés wanted to take care of his aunt. He had to get money and rent a place for her—one with three bedrooms—and send for the girls and get everyone back together. Gabriela would get well if she had a home and someone to take care of her.

CHAPTER 7

The news about Stephen Delacort went through the school faster than the virus that hit its computers first period. Even without e-mail, everyone in the upper school had heard before lunch that Jane Braithwaite's boyfriend had been arrested for shoplifting and punching a security guard at Barneys. Jane became as notorious as Stephen himself, and after two teasing incidents, the headmistress called her in for a private talk. Jane had nothing to say to her and was observed stalking haughtily out of her office. The other students stared at Jane and let her see them whispering about her.

Charles and Anne heard the news from Ellen, who got home from school first. "She acts so superior, everyone hates her. It's totally miserable being her sister," Ellen told them bitterly, "and at the same school and everyone knows who you are just because your sister is horrible Jane Braithwaite. Katie and her friends are making fun of me all the time."

"Your sister is not . . . horrible," said Charles, with such coldness that Ellen was crushed. Ellen's problems were always overlooked. Jane was always favored, no matter what she did, no matter how much trouble she caused.

"Why is she responsible for what Stephen Delacort does?" Anne added. "Stick up for your sister, Ellen. We don't care what the girls at your school think."

The injustice of this choked Ellen into sullen silence, and she slipped off to her room and locked the door.

"We'll have to tell Jane she can't see him anymore," Charles said to Anne.

"She's eighteen now. She may feel within her rights to defy us. She'll think she shouldn't abandon him when he's in trouble."

"As long as she lives here, she's not going to see him," Charles said.

They heard murmurs from Gabriela's room, as Anne's office was coming to be known.

"Someone's in there with her again," Anne said in a low voice.

"A woman," Charles said, listening. "Not her sister, I hope." They had heard stories about Gabriela's crazy sister.

The door to Gabriela's room opened, and Jane came into the kitchen, her backpack slung on one shoulder and her coat on the other. "Hi," she said. She went to the refrigerator and peered in. "Do we have anything cold to drink?"

"Jane," said Charles, "Ellen tells us that Stephen was arrested last night."

"So I hear."

"We want you to stop seeing him. We have to insist on it."

"Whatever you say, Dad," said Jane, with a jeering compliance. She poured a glass of orange juice to the brim and walked out slowly, sipping as she went.

"So, if that's sarcasm, which it must be, do I or don't I insist on a promise from her?" Charles said. He was ashamed of feeling a great urge to hurt his daughter. He would have liked to say something that would crush her or . . . He would not explore the impulse further.

"I don't know," Anne replied. "I really don't know what she meant by that."

"I have a feeling Gabriela would."

"But I don't know how Gabriela's rules of confidentiality operate," Anne said. "I need to think about this for a while."

Charles went to his studio, and Anne heard awkward piano notes at intervals; he was working something out and then writing. He had only so much strength for these struggles with the children. Anne, left alone in the kitchen, stared at Gabriela's door and thought.

An hour passed before Anne knocked. After several moments, she heard the lock turn—Gabriela was actually locking the door now—and in a little while Gabriela said, "Come in." She was lying listlessly on the little bed. Apparently this was one of her bad days. Looking at her drawn face, Anne was convinced that mono or chronic fatigue syndrome or whatever this was had a large psychological component. So she had read somewhere. Gabriela was so depressed with the loss of her daughters, no doubt, that she couldn't get well enough to earn her living again. What she needed to escape the vicious circle was cash, enough to pay a deposit and rent for a few months. Anne had finally offered her another five hundred dollars, but she knew very well that five hundred dollars didn't touch the cost of a new place, what with the rents lately and hefty deposit requirements and all the little extra expenses of moving. She would have offered more, even though Gabriela already owed her four hundred for the plane tickets, but Anne would have had to borrow the money herself and Charles would have been furious. She decided that they were doing enough by housing and feeding her; they wouldn't go into debt for her as well. For all their apparent wealth, the Braithwaites were, in fact, always broke. Four sets of private-school tuitions, lessons, camps, clothes, doctors, dentists, and their household and professional expenses consumed their entire ample income.

As Anne stood in the doorway, she became aware of a figure on the floor at the opposite end of the little room, a dark, frail, and anxious-looking boy, with long black hair, one tiny silver earring, and books and papers scattered around him in a semicircle.

"My nephew, Andrés," said Gabriela, "visiting me—doing his homework." There was something weaselly in the way she spoke.

Anne remembered hearing once or twice about this boy, child of the wild sister, who had moved in with Gabriela a few years ago. She hadn't thought about him when Gabriela's troubles began. "Andrés," said Anne, gathering all this in mind and nodding in greeting. "But where are you staying now?"

"The Bronx," Gabriela put in quickly, "with my boyfriend's mother."

Anne, standing beside the desk, rested her hand on the laptop and felt that it was warm. She looked from Gabriela to Andrés, who appeared shyly uncomfortable. He had been using her laptop to do his homework. She should probably be annoyed, but she wasn't. Instead she said, "Andrés, don't do your homework on the floor. Sit at the desk. How can you write down there?"

"Kids always like to sit on the floor," said Gabriela unconvincingly.

"What year are you?" Anne asked.

"Senior," he said.

"My daughter is a senior," Anne said. "And what school do you go to?" He had no social grace at all, but he was so sweetly shy, Anne thought, that he was appealing.

"City," he mumbled, as though anticipating an unpleasant reaction.

"City!" she replied, and immediately was embarrassed at having reacted precisely as, obviously, he had dreaded. City was an elite public high school that was probably more rigorous academically than her own daughters' respected private school. That a boy with so many problems, with such a torn-up life, should be able to work at the City level—this was something unusual. "Great school. You must be a really good student. Look, if you need a computer, use this one," she said, blandly offering this permission as though it were not ex post facto. "And the printer too. There's paper here, see?" She opened a drawer and pointed to its contents.

Gabriela nodded at him, to prod him into speech.

"Uh, thanks," he said. "Thanks a lot."

His voice was shaking. What on earth was he so frightened of? He was terribly sheepish, too, looking at the book in his lap while he answered. Reading upside down, Anne decided that it was some work of political philosophy. Unlike his aunt, Andrés had no accent at all. He was raised here, no doubt born here—a citizen. Gabriela was illegal and her sister, Andrés's mother, probably was too.

"Don't tell him he's such a good student," Gabriela said sourly. "He's a lazy kid. He don't want to get a job. He only wants to read books all the time because he thinks he's so smart."

Andrés flushed at this, and Anne winced for him. For the first time she felt a moral gap between her and Gabriela, a difference beyond those of money and learning. Gabriela's open indifference, her actual hostility to her nephew's aspirations to do well in school, appalled Anne, for it was a first tenet of morality in Morningside Heights that you sacrificed every- thing to educate your children so that they could fulfill their potential and rise higher than their parents—in talent, knowledge, success, satisfaction, even in virtue. Especially in virtue, for everyone believed in the kids' good- ness. That was what made everything worth it. It was why the parents did what they did. Of course, when immigrants' children were the first gener- ation to pursue learning, they always had a hard journey, one that in- evitably orphaned them by teaching them to leave their parents' world and join another, where the parents weren't welcome. This was lonely, painful, and difficult even when the parents insisted on it and worked to pay for it, as Anne's own grandparents had pushed her father, toiling at menial jobs so that he could study at Columbia and eventually marry a girl like Helen Stein—pretty, well educated, and a talented musician! How did a kid do it when the adults in his life stood in his way?

"Gabriela, I'll be going," Anne said. "I didn't realize you had company. I just wanted to see how you were doing. You look—"

"Much better than yesterday," said Gabriela with a forced smile. She always maintained that she was improving. She always refused to see an- other doctor. On the windowsill stood a dozen or more bottles of vita- mins and various strange nutritional supplements. "Juan says he's looking at another place tonight—in the Bronx."

Anne saw that Andrés was embarrassed. He knew that his aunt was trying to con Anne and that Anne knew it, and he was ashamed. Poor boy, poor decent little chap. But just then Andrés stood, and Anne was sur- prised to see that he was not little but fairly tall; his apparent frailty was owing to his exceptional thinness—and his fearfulness.

Later that evening, at dinner, she described this encounter with Gabriela and her nephew. Charles frowned, but all the children except Jane were fascinated and full of questions. Ellen was outspoken against

Gabriela. How could she be that way—even if she was just his aunt and not his mother? Jane, who had come to the table looking irritable, ate very little and said nothing. She and Ellen energetically ignored each other.

The next day, while Juan took Gabriela out to some doctor who, Anne suspected, was a quack, a healer of some sort, Anne went into her room and opened the computer. She found a cache of files that obviously were Andrés's. There were several essays for English and history classes, and they were remarkably good. One file was filled with poems. He writes poems, she thought, melting toward him. They were vivid but chaotic and lonely, hard to understand. A couple about a girl were sweetly haunting. She wondered if he was writing them for a class. She found a file that looked like a journal or a diary, with dated entries, but resisted the temptation to read it. Undeniably, the boy had been spending quite a bit of time here in Anne's office with his sick aunt, and Anne had been completely unaware of it. Of course, he came in by the service entrance.

The following morning at breakfast, Jane and Ellen continued their silent warfare while their brothers, sensing the tension, noisily teased and tormented the rest of the family.

Ellen is right: it all comes from Jane, thought Charles. We're always sacrificing the rest of them to her. While Charles was ready enough to accuse his mother-in-law of this sin, he usually exonerated himself. This morning, though, he looked remorsefully at Ellen when she kissed him good-bye. But the more guilt he showed, the more reproachful Ellen was. And why not? he thought. His repentance removed any doubt she might have had about whether she was being treated unfairly. Charles could not imagine that either of his sons would ever cause a fraction of the heartache that Jane, or even Ellen, caused their parents.

Ellen and Jane rode different buses to school that day. At lunch, Mabe Alinsky, an eccentric girl with poor grades and plain looks, sat down beside Jane, who was alone at a table in the cafeteria.

"Your sister is really upset," Mabe said, squeezing ketchup out of foil squares onto French fries.

"What are you talking about?"

"Isn't your sister that little eighth-grader, Ellen? She's in the office crying. Some girls locked her in a janitor's closet. They were teasing her about you and your boyfriend. They said she had to go to jail or something."

"What?"

"That's what I heard."

Jane ran out of the cafeteria to the head's office, leaving her tray of food untouched. "Is my sister here?" she asked the receptionist.

"She's with the nurse now."

"What happened?"

"I'm not sure. You'd have to ask . . ."

But Jane was off to Nurse McCaughey, who allowed her to visit with Ellen as she lay on a little cot, her chest still heaving with an occasional sob and her eyes still red.

"What happened?" Jane asked, her voice full of awkward consideration for her sister's sufferings. They were not used to offering comfort to each other—or to accepting it.

"Go away," Ellen said, turning her back to Jane.

"I don't expect you not to hate me," Jane said. "But just tell me who did what, and I swear I'll make them sorry, Ellen. Trust me. I swear. Please."

"I just want you to go away and leave me alone. If it wasn't for you, nothing like this would ever have happened."

"Ellen, I broke up with Stephen weeks ago. I haven't seen him except when he came to our house that once. He tried to talk me into getting back, but I wouldn't. I swear, Ellen. What do you want me to do? Wear a sign on my back—NOT GOING WITH STEPHEN DELACORT?"

"I want you to disappear—from my life or at least out of this room."

"I'm going, but you don't need to tell anyone what I just said."

Ellen turned around and half sat up. "Why? So you can keep pretending you're going with an accused felon and get a lot of attention?"

"You don't understand, Ellen." Jane struggled for words. "For me, everything is like . . . like a cotton prison. I can't move, and everything's soft and suffocating. I know I haven't . . ." Jane's voice petered out, silenced by the hate in Ellen's face. It was the first appeal for understanding Jane had ever addressed to Ellen. In making it, particularly in so helplessly inarticulate a fashion to this much younger sister, who was a verbal adept, Jane was intentionally humbling herself. But the gesture was unprecedented, and Ellen could not read it.

"Oh, poor Janie!" Ellen said with vigorous sarcasm. "That's too bad. You're so nutty no one can understand you. But look on the bright side— you're extra good at mad scenes. Just don't use me as an excuse to do one at school. Don't do it, Janie."

Depressed and wounded, Jane left her sister with Nurse McCaughey, who had heard every word of the quarrel and looked pityingly and curiously at Jane as she walked out.

"They're already suspended," she told Jane. "They sent them home an hour ago."

Hearing this, Ellen thought bitterly that no matter who got hurt and no matter how much at fault Jane was, everyone always ended up feeling sorry for her, never for Ellen.

CHAPTER 8

Andrés's performance at school had slipped so radically that his case was discussed at a faculty meeting that week.

"Maybe it's just senioritis," one teacher said.

"It's worse than that. He looks seedy and beaten up. Seems to me a little like the problems when he was a freshman," said the counselor, Ms. Goldberg.

Mr. Ling, Andrés's history teacher, thought Ms. Goldberg, a psychologist, had an amazing ability to detect hidden things. That was her job, he supposed, but it bothered him.

A new teacher had to be filled in. Andrés, they told him, had been arrested on drug and assault charges during a bust at his mother's apartment when he was fourteen. He had heatedly insisted the drugs were planted, but no one believed him. His mother, beyond any doubt, not only used drugs heavily but had been dealing in a minor way. When a policeman handcuffed her during the bust, Andrés attacked him with his fists. But for the strenuous efforts of a court-appointed lawyer and a kindly judge, he would have been sent to a juvenile facility. Instead he got a short suspended sentence and probation until he was nineteen. His mother had also narrowly avoided prison time, but Andrés, furious with her and frightened of her deterioration, had begun sleeping mostly at his aunt's place and for the past two years had seen little, and lately nothing, of his mother. His father had disappeared many years before that—no one knew where to. Some said California or maybe someplace in South America.

Those at his school who knew anything about Andrés's background thought of him as something of a miracle. That a boy as bright as he, as seemingly good-hearted, should have come out of that sort of chaos was not easily explained. Many of his teachers, like him, had been poor. They had been immigrants or immigrants' children; they, too, had seen hard things and lived in tough places. But they had all had life jackets of some sort—good families or good neighborhoods or something. That Andrés should have been formed in the hellish world he grew up in, that his fine mind should have developed there, defied understanding.

Andrés was aware that they thought this, that they studied him looking for weaknesses and damage. Whenever he slipped, he knew, they decided right away that he was beyond help or that he was on a slide to the bottom; to them, his slips were social pathology, not ordinary ups and downs. They were wrong, of course, that he was so inexplicable. Although he did not remember his father, his father had been very smart. Everyone told him that. His mother was not so dumb either, although you couldn't tell anymore, she was such a crackhead. And when he was little, Gabriela said, Rosa sang to him and read to him and taught him his letters and numbers. Gabriela did the same for her girls.

"He's not using, is he?" one of the teachers asked.

"He's pretty strung out lately. Big circles under his eyes. Looks very skinny," said Ms. Goldberg, "and I hate to say it, but not so clean."

None of them wanted to believe it, but drugs were the obvious explanation. No one would have blamed him much. If ever a kid deserved to feel something other than despair, if ever a kid had cause to want to get numb, it was this kid. Mr. Ling, though, thought to himself that Ms. Goldberg had a remarkable ability to get little things right and big things wrong. It was not her place to speculate to the kid's detriment. He felt uneasy.

"Okay, who's gonna talk with him?" asked the new teacher, who, with no warm feelings toward Andrés to blind him, thought the case fairly clear.

"Forget it. He doesn't talk. Andrés doesn't talk to anybody," said Ms. Murdoch, who taught English and creative writing. "He writes. He listens."

"Actually," said Mr. Ling, "he said something to me a couple days ago. He asked me how you give college admissions a change of address."

"Well, that's a good sign," said Ms. Goldberg. "He's still thinking in terms of college. He almost didn't apply, you know. Tom, you want to talk to him?"

"No, he's not really comfortable with me," said Mr. Ling, adding as an afterthought, "Get Matt Redding to talk to him."

The others were doubtful about this suggestion. True, Andrés was a computer jock, and Matt, a computer science teacher, *should* have known him well. But Matt was as silent and asocial as Andrés—not someone who would know how to talk to a boy using drugs. Mr. Ling insisted nonetheless. Many times he had watched Andrés stay comfortably silent with Matt Redding for hours at a stretch in the computer lab. Besides, Mr. Ling, himself a reserved man, felt more at ease with Matt Redding than with all these nosy, talkative social science, psychologist types. He guessed that Andrés would feel the same way.

And that was how it happened that on the last afternoon of school before Christmas vacation, as Andrés was leaving the computer lab with other students, Mr. Redding called him back. He studied Andrés's face and concluded, to his own satisfaction, that there were no drugs in the case. Andrés was not the druggie type. Although his colleagues didn't know it, Mr. Redding was an excellent judge of such things, having done drugs more or less nonstop in his own recent youth. Andrés's soul was visible in every part of his face, if you knew how to look—and so was his agony. No numbing going on there. "So, Andrés," he said, "how come you look so bad lately? You got trouble?"

Andrés thought it over, then nodded.

"What kinda trouble?" Mr. Redding was also used to trouble. He had grown up with nothing but.

Andrés shook his head. He didn't want to tell, Mr. Redding concluded. In fact, Andrés would have told him everything if he had just
asked once more, with different words. Mr. Redding weighed doing that,
then called it the other way. He didn't want to feel like a tool for that idiot
Goldberg. He changed the subject.

"I hear you've been doing a lousy job in some of your classes."

"Yeah."

"I want you in here tomorrow. You spend the day, and you start catching up."

"Can't. Gotta work."

"Work!" Mr. Redding thought this over. "Okay, then right now. Get
out your books. Pizza on me in two hours. Then I'm gonna show you
something about setting up a mail server."

Andrés smiled a little and lowered his backpack to the floor. An
evening playing around on the computers, and pizza with Mr. Redding,
who never talked except about computers, was a prospect filled with pleasure when he had been anticipating fear and loneliness. Warm relief
flooded his body like a drug.

"Hey, can I turn my cell phone on in case my aunt needs me?"

"Sure, school's out."

Mr. Redding didn't send Andrés off alone into the darkness until past
ten. And then he worried. The boy's escalating anxiety was obvious as he
pulled on his coat, hoisted his heavy pack to his back, and inwardly prepared to face whatever it was that he had to go face out there.

"Merry Christmas," Andrés said, with no smile, and he waved good-
bye to Mr. Redding.

He was on his way to Juan's, but he feared that Juan was getting tired
of him. What would happen now, with school out, when he had nowhere
to go all day long? Would Juan let him stay in his room? He would go
crazy. There was always the library. And Andrés was looking for another
job; the construction was only two days, and they needed money badly.
Usually you could get something on Christmas vacation when the stores
hired extra help, but this year, so far, Andrés could find nothing.

"It's because you look so bad," Gabriela told him the next day when
he called her from the construction site on his break. "You come sleep

here in my room tonight. I'll wash your clothes and you can take a shower. And you have to get a haircut, or tie it back. I'll show you. Then you go looking for something first thing in the morning. Christmas only three days off."

Andrés knocked softly on Gabriela's door at about eight that night, a bag of his clothes slung over his shoulder. Inside, Gabriela was ready for him. A sleeping bag was rolled up at the foot of her bed. An ironing board leaned against the wall, and an iron sat on the windowsill, next to the bottles of pills. Gabriela held up a black elastic. "For your hair," she said, "so you don't have to spend for a haircut."

"How'd you get all this stuff?" he asked, worried. "Do they know?"

"I asked Jane. She's nice. She don't tell nobody."

Andrés was ashamed to have his need exposed to Jane, and Gabriela knew it. Jane was always buying little things for her with her allowance—aspirin, toothpaste, delicious fruits from some fancy grocery on the East Side.

"It don't matter what she thinks. Anyway, she's nice. She don't think nothing bad."

"Does she know I'm going to sleep here?"

"I didn't tell her. I just asked if I could borrow her sleeping bag."

They washed clothes in the bathtub and laid them on the radiator to dry. Andrés slept deeply on Gabriela's floor, wrapped in Jane's sleeping bag. The next morning, he ironed his clothes smooth. When he was ready to go, he looked almost sharp, with a fresh shirt and jeans, his still-damp hair combed by Gabriela into a neat ponytail at the nape of his neck.

"Just like that actor," she said, looking at him with satisfaction. "How you say it—Liam?" She pronounced it Lee-*ahm*.

"*Lee*-um. Liam Neeson," said Andrés, smiling at her.

He hoped Gabriela would say something about Christmas, but she didn't. She probably wanted Juan to stay over on Christmas Eve, so she wouldn't want Andrés too. He whispered good-bye to her and slipped out.

The day was cold and overcast. He was hungry, but he didn't stop for breakfast. He wanted to save his money to buy Gabriela something for Christmas even though she had said, "No presents this year. I'm not getting you nothing, so I'm telling you no presents, Andrés. I mean it." At the corner of Broadway and 116th, Andrés stood and tried to decide on his first stop of the day, shivering and suddenly feeling like the debris that swirled on the sidewalk in the gusts of icy wind.

CHAPTER 9

M ichael Garrard left his office at midday to go Christmas shopping. He had told Adriana that he would not be home for dinner that night, and she had not objected, knowing that he would be out buying presents for her. But she did not know that he finished his shopping by early evening and then headed back uptown to have dinner with the Braithwaites, Greg Merriweather, and Carla Winter.

Jane answered the door when he rang.

"Bergdorf's, Tiffany's," she said, dispensing with a greeting and examining his bundles with uninhibited, greedy curiosity. "What's this CD—music for your wife? Jazz. Does she like opera too? A fur? Really a fur! Sable. Mom, look."

Anne came to welcome their guest just as Michael unzipped a garment bag and displayed a fur jacket of ingenious design, eliciting admiring "ahs" from Anne and Jane both. Anne and Charles had qualms about furs. But Anne so admired the jacket's beauty that—she argued with herself—after all, she couldn't consistently object, as her whole family wore leather shoes and belts. Besides, she couldn't be judgmental about a friend's Christmas present for his wife. Of course she had to fuss over the coat.

"Can I try it on?" Jane asked.

"No!" Anne said. She was surprised that Jane, too, really seemed to like the jacket and wanted to put it on; just six months ago she had been flirting with vegetarianism. Anne knew that this was not mere politeness on Jane's part. She had made some sort of hero of Michael. It would not occur to her to be critical of his judgment or taste. Jane seemed as eager to resolve doubts in his favor as she was to do the opposite where her parents were concerned. For a moment, Anne resented her daughter's injustice.

"Of course you can try it," Michael said, with a slight smile that for him, Anne thought, was like other people grinning ear to ear.

Jane slipped on the jacket and ran to look at herself in the hall mirror. "Oh, it feels so, so good," she said, running her hands over it and rubbing her cheek on its collar. "It looks really great with jeans, don't you think?"

"It looks good with Jane, I think," Michael said to Anne.

Anne responded with proper parental modesty. "What doesn't look good on eighteen?" she said. With great care, she helped Jane rehang the jacket and replace it in the elegant bag.

"I should be ashamed to drag you into the kitchen," Anne said, "but Charles is cooking and he wants company. Do you mind?"

"Not at all," Michael replied, sounding stiff, almost indifferent, though in fact he was pleased to be invited into the kitchen, and Anne knew it. He had begun to feel more at home with the Braithwaites than he did in his own apartment. After only three or four visits, they had adopted him in the way that families so often adopt singletons. They acted as though he wasn't married, but they knew he was. How that had happened, none of them quite knew. Of course they had made the ordinary friendly inquiries about his wife. He supposed they took their cue from his reluctance to talk about her and his ignoring opportunities to suggest a get-together.

In the kitchen, Charles was holding a pasta maker in place on the table and shouting instructions at Stuart, who was cranking its handle and crowing at the sight of ribbons of noodle emerging from its teeth, while Gilbert stood by insisting tearfully that it was his turn. Pots steamed on the stove. The countertops and floor were strewn with bits of vegetable matter, flour, and crumbs.

Within ten minutes, Anne had restored order and quiet. Michael had a drink in his hand, and Gilbert sat on his lap playing a game on his cell phone. He gave the child an occasional parenthetic instruction, in a low voice, while pursuing the adult conversation about last month's election. Anne saw that he liked Gilbert and easily split his attention between the child and the adults; Gilbert listened to what Michael told him in that deep, resonant, respectful voice, and obeyed, which impressed and touched Anne. So few men had that skill, of knowing how to make things clear to very young children. How sad that Michael had no children. Greg had told them about the Garrards' long struggle with infertility and how his wife refused to adopt. Just as Anne thought of this, the doorbell rang, and soon Jane led Greg and Carla into the kitchen.

The Braithwaites had not yet met Carla, but they were aware that Greg was unusually interested in her. Michael observed their meeting, fascinated. Greg would never come closer than this, he thought, to introducing a girlfriend to his parents, and if I were Greg's parents, I doubt I would be terribly happy about this choice. Carla was wearing her usual short, tight skirt—sexy, he thought—and her hair was ragged in the currently popular style. As she shook hands, she gave a noncommittal grimace to the Braithwaites, which announced unmistakably that she did not care whether they liked her and that Greg might be serious about her but she was not serious about him.

Michael told Greg, when Greg first showed an interest in Carla, that she was not likely to respond to his attentions—or perhaps anyone's. And observing Carla's coolness to these warm people of whom he had become so fond, he was mystified by Greg. Perhaps it was just that Greg found her sexy. That he could understand, but lots of women were sexy. He refused to believe that Greg was one of those clergymen who were so repressed that only a woman as brazen in every way as Carla could overcome his inhibitions. No, watching Greg with her, it was more as if he filtered all that out of his image of her. God knew what Greg's private version of Carla might be.

"Carla," Michael said, rising to greet her with his usual near-smile.

"Dr. Garrard," she said, with a grin that was more aggressive than friendly. Now he perceived that she was a bit tense, out of her element, he supposed.

Jane had gotten a brotherly squeeze from Greg and the same indifferent response from Carla that her parents had received. "By the way, Dr. Garrard," she said, turning to go out again, "if your wife doesn't care for the coat, it will always have a home with us."

"That's good to know," Michael replied. How extremely charming a girl she was.

Anne explained to the newcomers. "He's bought his wife a beautiful sable jacket for Christmas. Jane and I are all envy."

Carla looked disbelievingly at Michael. "I suppose it's not exactly news to you that a lot of people think slaughtering mammals for their pelts is disgusting," she said with stoic distaste. This speech, a shocking breach of decorum in the well-meaning Braithwaite household, silenced all of them for several awkward seconds.

"One more case where we'll have to agree to differ, won't we, Carla," Michael replied. "Don't you think we should let it go for the sake of our hosts?" He managed to imply a delicate disdain with the polite words.

Anne thought that Carla would be squelched, but she immediately came back at him. "No," Carla said defiantly, and continued in an exaggeratedly rote style. "People who encourage killing little creatures so they can buy status symbols should expect criticism wherever they are. Their hosts should be glad."

"What are you *talking* about?" Jane demanded, staring at Carla. It was not much of an argument, but her tone of contempt was exquisitely persuasive. "Greg, why don't you tell her to cut it out?"

This outburst left Michael once more speechless and Greg blushing, but Carla actually seemed to be more comfortable. She was swelling with a retort when Charles broke in. "Enough," he said, addressing Jane but intending to cut off Carla. He sympathized with his daughter's reaction, but she shouldn't be rude to a guest—even an impolite one.

"Carla," Greg began hesitantly, evidently feeling duty-bound to second Charles, "when in Rome, you know . . ."

"That covers when and where you can belch, not moral matters, Greg. You're never entitled to be silent about moral matters."

Greg, Michael thought, seemed like a man trying to get his unruly dog back on a leash.

Taking Jane by the arm, Anne drew her out of the room. She approved of the strain of respect, or even reverence, in Jane's affection for Michael Garrard. The adults felt much the same about him, and Jane hadn't said anything the rest of them weren't thinking. Anne didn't know what to say to her. "Of course you're right, sweetie," she began, "but she's our guest too, and maybe—"

"How could Greg be with someone so awful!" Jane exclaimed, earning a sarcastic frown from her mother, who had asked the same question about Jane herself on so many occasions.

"Maybe she's one of those people you have to get to know," Anne suggested, to Jane's scorn. "Look, sweetie—"

"I'm going to eat with Gabriela," Jane announced. "We'll order out."

"Fine," Anne said. This was probably the best solution. She didn't want to force Jane to apologize, Jane wasn't volunteering to, and Anne doubted very much that Carla would. She and Charles would have to apologize. And, in fact, when she reentered the kitchen, Charles was already telling everyone how sorry he was.

"Yes," Anne added, to Michael's amusement, "we're really so, so sorry, but teenagers are volatile, and she's been through some tough times lately." Maybe Jane had done them all a favor, she thought; now we can ignore the real offenses and sit down together in peace.

"She's just loyal to her friends," said Michael, who had enjoyed novel sensations on having a beautiful young girl publicly defend him so warmly against Carla Winter. Now, watching the only two completely innocent people in the room ingenuously apologizing to the others for those others' own bad conduct brought him as close as he ever came to laughing out loud.

Anne's eyes met his just then, and she sniggered. With this, the crisis was over—but not the argument. As soon as they were seated at the table, Michael, always a willing debater, reengaged Carla.

"This theory of yours," he said, "that you're not morally free to leave others to their own mistakes—it's quite popular on the right, I notice."

"What do you mean?" she said.

"So many of them think they're morally required to prevent others from acting in ways their own consciences permit—on abortion, say, or gay marriage. They want laws to force people to conform to *their* moral choices."

"To their *religion*," interjected Anne. "They want to make everyone obey their religion."

"There is the biggest difference in the world between people like them and me," Carla said.

"Which is?"

"That they're wrong about abortion and gay marriage, and I'm right about furs. Besides, I don't *make* them have abortions. Look, that tolerance argument doesn't go anywhere. Greg, you don't *tolerate* people inflicting the death penalty. You vote for laws to abolish it."

"I think there's an in-between position," said Charles, "when we decide that the law shouldn't take sides in a particular moral debate. The question is, should wearing furs be left to individual conscience or should the law impose a morality on us?"

"Very well said, Charles," said Michael, the former debater. "It's easy to pile up reasons why abortion should be left to the individual conscience. So a fortiori—"

"Exactly," said Anne. "Furs clearly—"

"—which is not necessarily to say that whatever people decide is fine," Greg said, "or that we shouldn't try to persuade them to change their minds."

The four moderates, their speeches interrupting one another in a genial fugue, basked in their harmony, nodding agreeably at one another, muttering "of course" and "certainly," but Carla found all the peace and unity distasteful. "Personally," said Carla, "I would definitely vote for a law to forbid selling fur coats. But even if we agreed that we shouldn't have a law like that, it would still be wrong to kill animals for their fur and you'd still be obligated to tell people that. And the fur really is a grotesque present for your wife, Michael."

"Fortunately, she won't think so at all," Michael said, thinking, however, not about his wife but about Jane trying on the coat. He noticed now that Jane's place at the table was empty, but he stopped himself just in time from asking where she was. Of course, she was staying away because of the argument. He hoped she wouldn't have to miss her dinner on account of him.

"Besides," Carla went on, "people are so mixed up about morals nowadays, you have to be outspoken."

"Again, that's just what the right thinks," Michael put in agreeably.

"So what, Michael? The point is, people are mixed up. They don't get upset about terrible, terrible things. They don't care—unless it's about kids. The only thing anyone is sure of is you should be nice to kids. What is the worst crime anyone could ever possibly commit? Child abuse. Why is nuclear war wrong? Because it's terrible to fry children. Forget about a few billion adults who might also get incinerated. And a lot of people aren't even sure about other people's kids."

"You're exaggerating," said Anne, "kind of aggressively. Were you ever tempted to be a prosecutor?"

"Never!" Carla replied, aghast.

"Also," Michael said, "when you choose to be so outspoken about fur coats you contribute to the muddle you're describing. It's hard to be outraged about the right things when so many people are outraged about so many absurd and misguided things. But take away the exaggeration," Michael went on, turning from Carla to address the others, "and she's got an interesting point. It's true that children provide today's moral archetypes, and it's strange—as though people can't understand why you shouldn't mistreat adults."

"Yes, that's generally true with Carla," said Greg, with a sidelong look at her. "You have to use corrective lenses and hearing aids to cut out the distortions in her ideas, but then you're left with something to think about."

While this debate occupied those in the dining room, Gabriela rose from her bed in the little room behind the kitchen to open the service-entrance door to a deliveryman from Nacho's Kitchen. Savory odors blew in as she paid, and Jane and Andrés, inhaling them, smiled.

"I'm starving," Jane said.

Gabriela served their portions with the same maternal pride she would have felt if she had cooked the food, but in fact, she hadn't even paid for it. Anne had tucked two twenties into Jane's pocket for the dinner. They ate burritos, Gabriela on the bed, Andrés on the floor, and Jane at the desk. The room was more crowded than ever. There was a radio now on a little stand in the corner. It played Latin music softly while they ate and grew happy. They talked aimlessly, and Jane told them about losing her temper just now with Carla Winter.

"What?" Gabriela asked, full of scorn. "She don't like killing animals?"

"*Doesn't*," said Andrés.

"But she eats meat, right? I mean, Christ ate meat."

The young people paused in their eating to think. They weren't sure about that. They looked at each other.

"Fish, I know," said Jane.

"Yeah . . . fish for sure," said Andrés, considering. He started to snicker for no particular reason, and that made Jane laugh. They all laughed.

"Anyway, he's so nice, Dr. Garrard. Oh, Gabriela! You should see *him*. He'd figure out what's the matter right away. He's brilliant, and so, so sweet. I'll ask him—"

"No!" said Gabriela. "I seen enough doctors. I don't want—"

"*Have* seen," said Andrés.

". . . no more—"

"*Any* more."

". . . doctors. Andrés, you making me mad. You don't like the way I talk, you can get outta here."

Jane saw him shrink slightly at this, even though of course Gabriela didn't mean it. "How do you like City?" she asked him. She had noticed the school insignia on his backpack.

"All right."

"Lots of homework."

"Always."

"Are you . . . where are you applying to college?"

He didn't answer immediately, then said, "I'll never get in."

"Think positive. Where'd you apply?"

"Chicago, Stanford, Wesleyan. A couple other places."

"Those are good schools. Don't tell me, you're some kind of math genius or something."

"Nah. Where do you want to go?"

"I'm going to Juilliard. I already know—I'm already studying with someone there," she said, and seeing the question coming she added, "I sing—opera-type singing—and play piano. Voice major, piano minor."

"She's really something too," said Gabriela, who had often heard Jane practicing.

Andrés laughed. "Major in voice?" he said. "I never heard of anything like that. Sing for me. Come on."

Jane thought, swallowed, then cleared her throat and sang, *"Mon coeur s'ouvre à ta voix. . . . Ah! réponds à ma tendresse! . . ."* She gave them one full verse.

"What is that—French? You believe she can sing like that in French?" Gabriela said proudly to Andrés. *"He* knows French," she told Jane, who was flushed, for she had sung with great intensity—as though she were on a stage.

Jane looked at Andrés with sly curiosity.

"That was beautiful, but I don't really know much French," he said, as flushed as Jane.

"He always says things like that," said Gabriela. "He gets all A's in French." Now that Jane had shown off, Gabriela was not averse to touting her nephew's accomplishments.

Andrés shook his head in such a convincing denial that Jane would have believed him if his red face hadn't proved how well he understood French.

"What was that?" he asked.

"Delilah singing to Samson," Jane said.

"Ah," said Gabriela, nodding.

The Braithwaite dinner had just ended, and Michael and Greg were carrying plates into the kitchen—while the Braithwaites searched for their copy of *Against All Enemies* to lend to Carla—when Jane's voice floated in, high and sweet.

"That's Janie," Greg told Michael, smiling at the expression on his face. Michael listened intently until she stopped.

"Good God," he said. "How extraordinary. She's just a child." A young, innocent, and passionate Dalila—it was unsettling.

"The child of two professional musicians. And don't let her fool you," Greg said in a lower voice, after glancing around to be sure they were alone. "She sings beautifully and I love the kid, but she's kind of a brat— very difficult and spoiled, egotistical. Have they told you about this last boyfriend of hers?"

Michael found it all hard to believe. What explained the sweet, open look—the look she'd greeted him with—on the face of a girl going through so much, feeling so much? He contrasted all that upheaval with the calm, dry misery of his own life with Adriana, compared the feelings of their lovemaking to those described in the aria, and was overcome with chaotic, sad longings of a kind he'd forgotten years ago.

Charles came in with more plates. He had heard Jane from the next room. "I didn't know she knew that," he said, with an uneasy undertone in his voice. "Interesting how it changes when it's so high and girlish, eh?" Michael guessed that Charles, too, was slightly unnerved.

Andrés fell asleep on the floor of Gabriela's room and woke up in the morning wondering if Jane was going with anyone. She didn't seem like a girl who was going with anyone. He sneaked out early to begin job hunting again, though he had begun to think it was hopeless—especially on Christmas Eve. At least it gave him places to go besides the library or Juan's room, and it filled the time. On Gabriela's suggestion, he tried department stores: Macy's, Bloomingdale's, and Lord & Taylor. Then he tried three Gap stores with no luck. He spent the day traveling from store to store on the subway, filling out futile applications, and sitting in hallways waiting for supervisors to return from their lunches and breaks. He had plenty of time for more reverie and for recalling the aria Jane had sung.

Gabriela had told him to sleep at Juan's tonight, and Andrés gave up his job search at about four to ride up to the Bronx. He bought a present for Gabriela though she had told him not to—a pair of fuzzy slippers, bright red. They cost fifteen dollars, but she would really like them and she wouldn't scold. Tomorrow he would take her the present, nicely gift-wrapped by a lady in the store who asked him if they were for his mother. On the subway, he opened his bag to peer in at the package. That was a mistake, he realized immediately, as it drew the attention of a blank-faced boy who began to eye the bag. Andrés guessed that the boy was not very old, sixteen or so, but he was big—maybe two hundred pounds and over six feet tall. When the train doors opened at his stop, Andrés dashed out. Despite the cold, he sweated as he ran up the station stairs, aware that the boy was behind him, increasing his speed, and he broke into a run when he reached the dark of the street. He made it to the barbershop on the corner, with the boy close behind. Inside, the spicy sweet smells of gels, shampoos, and shaving cream made the danger seem unreal. It was not possible that a world of threat existed outside the doors of this serene room, with its evergreen wreaths, tinsel, red ribbons, and candy canes, crowded with tranquil men getting their holiday haircuts.

Andrés stood gasping and sweating inside the door. One of the barbers, a plump man with a highly sculpted close cut, eyed his ponytail with interest. "You wanna get rid of that?" he asked curiously.

"No. Okay if I just sit here for a few minutes? Someone following me."

Several of the men turned to listen and now noticed Andrés's terror.

"Whatsa trouble here?" said one, looking up sternly from his magazine. "Who followin' you?"

"There he is—that's him," said Andrés, pointing through the glass of the door to the big boy, who was leaning nonchalantly against a streetlight post at the corner. Andrés tried to sound calm, but he was still breathing hard from his sprint and his face was tense. A couple of the men stood and craned their necks to see, and they got a look on their faces that Andrés recognized, a look that meant they were ready for fighting. It surprised him that they would have such a reaction on his account, and oddly, it made him feel warm and good. For why would anyone help him if he didn't deserve it? This was how his feelings reasoned, even though he recognized that it was irrational.

"You stay here a minute," one of the men told Andrés soberly. He and his friend went out and said things to the boy that made him take off—going east, Andrés noted, with relief. He himself would be heading west.

"He gone" was all the man said when he came back in.

"Next time," said his friend, "you don' be so scared. You be tough, people leave you alone."

Andrés was ashamed. He knew this was true, but he would be just as scared the next time. He was cowardly. Still, he was grateful, but the men waved off his attempts to thank them.

"Well . . . Merry Christmas," Andrés said awkwardly as he turned to go.

"You take care now," said the man without a smile.

"Take care," the man's friend said, settling down with a newspaper.

When Andrés lay in Juan's bed that night, he felt so good that it made him nervous. He began sifting through the events of the past twenty-four hours, looking for dangerous angles, threats that he might have missed. He often did this, trying to feel safe enough to sleep, though it often made him feel more, not less, anxious. Tonight, for once, he liked the reminders of the day, especially the memories of Jane singing and the men in the barbershop who chased off the boy. These incidents seemed to him to be connected, although he knew they couldn't be. He fell asleep thinking about them.

CHAPTER 10

On Christmas Eve, presiding over his own table of guests, Michael made a private vow that would be difficult to keep: never again would he give a dinner party with Adriana. He was not sure how he would break this to her, for they were used to having three or four a year. Slowly and stealthily—just being unavailable or unreliable until she gave up? There was cruelty in that. Abruptly? "Adriana, dear, I just despise the whole routine. From now on, we'll go *out* with our friends." After all, not everyone had dinner parties. Somehow, he would have to convince her, he thought, because he had passed his tolerance threshold.

Michael tended to form inalterable resolves—always out of the blue. He never saw himself coming. This new one arrived with the same fixed and out-of-nowhere determination that led him to refuse to go back to Oxford after two years there reading politics, philosophy, and economics; to confine his relationship with his father to brief letters every year or two; and to engage in a private life separate from his marriage to Adriana. Overall, he was a highly deliberative man, but swiftly decisive nonetheless.

Adriana had invited a small group for this Christmas Eve dinner. There was an older couple, the Westons, whose middle-aged children lived in

California. The husband had held ambassadorships in the Ford, Reagan, and Bush I administrations, and had once served on some charity board or other with Michael—by this time, neither of them was really sure which. The Kaplans, a happily childless fortyish couple, were extremely rich friends from their tennis club. There were two single women Adriana's age, one a friend from college, the other a former colleague from the hospital. The lone single man, an unfriendly fellow, was a journalist of some sort. It was obvious to Michael that the only commonality among the guests was childlessness; those present either had no children or were old enough to be Adriana's parents, with children her own age.

The Garrards were gracefully and coolly hospitable, and the guests all smiled and behaved themselves. There was a hired cook, and their own maid served. Everyone ate, laughed, told anecdotes, and talked with their right-hand and left-hand neighbors, except for the single man, who would not speak to Adriana's college friend, suspecting her of having designs on him. He thought the Garrards had invited him only out of desperation for a single man, and he accepted only to avoid being miserably alone on Christmas Eve. But, though the conversation jogged briskly along—about the election, the war, the city—it was extremely boring to Michael. Was that because no one cared enough about anything or because no one dared to speak frankly in this group where convictions and loyalties were hard to read? For whatever reason, the people all failed to be in love with one another. As far as Michael could see, none of them ever had been in love with anyone or anything, unless it was long, long ago.

After dinner, they returned to the living room, where there was a brilliant Christmas tree, all in silver and gold and crystal—quite a contrast to the haphazard one the Braithwaite children had decorated. Nearly everyone accepted brandy, but only the journalist drank any. Then, one by one, they all set down the snifters, paid their compliments, and escaped.

"Well, it was fine, wasn't it?" Adriana said, scanning her husband's face when the last guest, the college friend, had departed.

"Everything was perfect," he said, and he kissed her and even managed a smile. "I'm so exhausted. Let's go right to bed."

"Don't you want to open presents?" she asked, her face clouding childishly. She sensed that he had disliked the dinner, that something had

changed in him. But, frightened to admit this to herself, she sought reassurances. As always, he knew that he had frightened her, and he moved
quickly to repair the damage.

"Well, we could, couldn't we? Isn't it odd how we can't get straight
what our tradition is? One year we insist on Christmas morning, and the
next Christmas Eve. But we always start with different ideas—like the
O. Henry story, isn't it. We each say what we think the other wants. Truthfully, I prefer Christmas Eve, but since your family always waited . . ."

"We'll compromise," said Adriana, smiling, thoroughly taken in and
warmed by the comparison with the loving young couple in the story.
"We'll each open one tonight and the rest tomorrow."

"Excellent," he said. As tired and moody as he was, it would have been
hard to manufacture convincing enthusiasm about many Christmas gifts.
One, he could manage. Besides, Adriana had not mentioned any subject
connected with fertility for at least seven hours, which softened him toward
her. "And do we pick for ourselves or let the other person pick for us?"

"The other picks."

Michael hoped she would approve of the fur jacket—a Bergdorf
shopping aide who understood her taste had helped him select it. But
being unsure, and not yet ready to erase the pretty memory of Jane wearing it, he decided to choose something more certain to please. He handed
Adriana the smallest package under the tree, and her delight so gratified
him that he almost believed he loved her. He had commissioned a friend,
an artist who worked in metals, to design a bracelet of platinum and dia-
monds. It was delicate and sparkling, so lovely that Adriana gasped when
she saw it. She was susceptible to that kind of thing. And his little smile,
which sprang from compassion, doubled her joy, entirely duping her into
trusting that after all he still loved her.

Then she selected a small, flat, rectangular package for him. In it, he
found a framed photograph of a young woman holding in her arms a tod-
dler who looked happily into her eyes; she looked back at the child dot-
ingly, sweetly. He'd never before seen this picture, but Adriana assured him
that it was he himself with his mother in 1958, when he was about two.
She explained excitedly how she'd gotten the photograph from a friend of
the family. Michael stared at the picture uncomprehendingly. He had

never seen his mother's love before or, for that matter, heard about it. He'd grown up encouraged to think that he'd lost her before he knew her, that he was fortunately too young to miss her or grieve for her, that she was a crazy thing, insane.

"I knew you'd be surprised," Adriana said eagerly. "I was too."

Michael thanked her rather gravely, staring at the soft-eyed girl in the picture. Then he went into the bathroom, locked the door, and let tears run down his face.

CHAPTER 11

On the twelfth day of Christmas, the Braithwaites took down their tree, and the children prepared to return to school. Ellen and the boys felt the gray hopelessness that schoolchildren always feel at the end of the holidays, when the days are short and cold and the next vacations unimaginably far off. Jane so disliked school that she had always suffered more than other children at such times. But this year she felt her spirits rise—even though the winter term stretched infinitely before her and even though her classmates, stricken with senioritis, succumbed to dreary inertia. Jane was energized. She had an overpowering feeling of wanting to get on with things, of there being a show that had to get on the road.

On the morning that school resumed, she was out the door a full twenty minutes before Ellen. School itself, however, provided nothing that answered to her sense of portent and possibility. By the end of the school day, she had begun to feel low. By the time she got home, she was sinking into disappointment and despair although she did not really know it, any more than at the day's start she had known she was waiting for something. She simply came home, went to her room, and surrendered belatedly but wholly to the gloom the others had felt anticipating this day.

Charles and Anne, who noticed how eagerly she had run out that morning, surmised that something had happened at school to produce this letdown. Anne went to Jane's room twice but found out nothing. At dinner, Jane refused to come to the table. Only when the other children were sleeping and Anne and Charles were reading in bed did Jane leave her room. Charles and Anne heard her door open and her quiet steps in the hallway.

"She's going to get something to eat," said Anne, her voice hushed so that Jane wouldn't hear.

"I'm sick of this," Charles said, at normal volume. "I'm tired of worrying about Jane. I'm sorry if that offends you."

"Well, actually, it doesn't," Anne said.

"And I don't want to talk about it," Charles said.

"Me either," she said, after a moment's thought.

They switched off their lights. In half an hour, Anne was sleeping, but Charles was still awake. He had not heard Jane come back to bed. He lay there, restless and listening, for another thirty minutes, then, with a sigh, got out of bed. The door to Jane's room was closed, but there was a faint light at the end of the hallway; maybe she was still in the kitchen. Or maybe she had left a light on.

Barefooted, he walked quietly past the boys' rooms and turned the corner into the kitchen, where, to his shock, he saw a man leaning into the refrigerator, illuminated by its light. The man jumped when he saw Charles.

"Oh, hi," he said. "Just getting something for Gabriela. Sorry. Hope I di'n't wake you."

"Who are you?" Charles demanded. "What are you doing here?"

"I'm Gabriela's friend. She call me and say she was sick, so I come over to help her out. She feeling too bad to get something to eat herself, so I'm getting her something."

Charles stood there, confused and trembling, staring at the man.

"Juan Santiago," said the man, ingratiatingly. He was beginning to take control of the situation. "Okay, I just give her this," he said, holding up a plate. "Don't worry. I'll take care of her." And he opened the door to Gabriela's room, which was dark, and went in.

Charles heard Gabriela's low voice, and Juan's "Shh" before the door closed behind him.

Back in bed, Charles shook Anne. "Gabriela's got a man in there," he told her in a whisper. "He was in our refrigerator."

Still asleep, Anne understood this literally at first; her mind struggled to make sense of it with a series of unlikely dream images.

"He said he was taking her something to eat," Charles continued. "Scared the hell out of me."

Anne woke up. "Her nephew maybe. Was it—?"

"No, this guy was older—maybe thirty. Hispanic guy."

"Oh my God, Charles." Anne sat up in bed. "What did he say?"

"He said she called him because she was sick and he was getting her something to eat."

"This is impossible. We can't have this."

"I guess I have to go tell him to leave. What time is it?"

"It's nearly midnight. Wait," Anne said, "let's think. Surely he'll just leave now. I mean, really, what's so awful about her friend visiting her? And I did tell her she should take anything she wanted in the refrigerator."

"Her lights were off."

They thought about that. They decided that it would be better to talk to Gabriela about this in the morning.

When morning came, they had had very little sleep. Jane, too, looked taut and tired when she appeared at the breakfast table. She nibbled on some toast and stood to go.

"What's wrong?" Anne asked. She wished the question had not come out sounding impatient. "Please don't say 'Nothing.' "

Jane gave her a reproachful look. "Do you know—is Gabriela up?"

"No," Anne said, too firmly. "She had a bad night. Don't bother her now. Why do you have to talk to Gabriela anyway?"

But Jane could not bear any conversation with her parents. "I want to get to school a little early this morning," she said. "See you later."

Charles bent toward her for a good-bye kiss, but she ignored him.

"Who's going to talk to Gabriela?" Anne asked Charles, when the other children had also left for school. "Me or you?"

"I will," he said. Until now, he had left the matter of Gabriela entirely in Anne's hands. Obviously that had been a mistake.

"What are you going to tell her?"

"I'm going to give her a deadline for moving out and tell her that until then no more strangers wandering around our house—daytime, night-time, anytime."

Anne nodded. She was not sure she herself could say such things to Gabriela, but Charles was right. It was time to reclaim their home.

Charles tapped on Gabriela's door at about ten o'clock. It took her some time to answer it, and she was obviously surprised to see Charles rather than Anne. Sitting on the edge of the bed in Anne's nightgown and robe, she looked very ill, he thought.

Anne, who was near tears at the prospect of Gabriela's being forced out when she was so sick and poor, didn't stay in the kitchen to listen. She went to wait for Charles in his studio.

"Well?" she said, when he appeared in what seemed only a few min-utes.

"They've got a place lined up for February," he said.

"We knew that already. What if it falls through, like the other places?"

"We'll cross that bridge when we come to it."

"What did she say about the man?"

Charles walked to the piano and opened a book of music. He was al-ready leaving this conversation behind. "Oh, I forgot to mention it," he said.

"You for—" But Anne stopped herself. This man Juan was, effectively, Gabriela's husband. She had been with him for years. How could they tell her that her husband had to stay away? Of course he wanted to look after her and make sure that she ate something. What was so awful about his midnight visit to their refrigerator? Anne understood that Charles, too, had realized these things.

"It'll work out," she said. "I'm not really worried about it. I'm more worried about Jane."

"Think how easy life would be without Jane," he said.

"I try not to," Anne replied.

PART TWO

On a wet January afternoon, Juan greeted the doorman, Wilfredo—everyone called him Willie—like a brother, and Willie responded in the same spirit.

"How's she doin'?" asked Willie.

"Tired alla time. It's mono," said Juan. "Or maybe this chronic fatigue syndrome—like mono. Takes a long time to kick it."

"Huh," said Willie, shaking his head sympathetically. "That's rough. Tell her I said feel better."

Juan arrived on the ninth floor just as Charles Braithwaite closed the door to 9E and turned toward the elevator, his eyes fixed on the newspaper he had just picked up. Juan pirouetted and ducked down the stairwell until the elevator doors closed on Charles. Then he went to the Braithwaites' service-entrance door and opened it with a key.

"Hey, baby," he whispered to Gabriela. She lay on the little bed, her arm over her eyes.

"Were you careful?" she said, lifting her arm and looking at him. Her eyes were sunken and her skin sallow.

"Very. Her husband was going to the elevator when I got off, so I hid down the stairs."

Gabriela nodded. "You're soaking," she said.

"It's pouring," he said, "and then gonna turn to snow. It's bad out there."

He stripped off his coat and hung it on the back of a chair, pulled off his shoes, and lay down on the bed next to Gabriela. "You too tired?" he said, stroking her hair and kissing her.

"I'm not too tired, but Andrés will be here any minute."

Juan swore, but he didn't sound angry. Gabriela caressed his face and curled against him. In fact, she was much too tired, but she wanted to keep Juan wanting her and satisfied with her. She already caused him so much trouble that it was a miracle he still came back—and always tucked a bill or two under her pillow when he left.

Juan didn't really expect her to be interested in lovemaking. Asking was a sort of polite gesture on his part, to make her feel good—because she looked like hell and she was scared he'd take off. Juan had no intention of doing that. The sicker Gabriela got, the less capable he felt of wronging her. Juan seemed no less breezy and smiling than he'd ever been, but in fact he was terrified by Gabriela's illness and, despite his room in the Bronx, he felt homeless because Gabriela had no home. Until all this happened, he'd had no idea that she'd become the fixed point upon which he leveraged his freedom and courage, the way his mother used to be. Juan thought about this as he lay beside Gabriela and also about how he was learning some of life's big lessons, things people told you someday you'd learn, and now he really had: you never appreciate anything the way you should until you're afraid of losing it. That was so true. Juan took great comfort in the fact that this was something people had told him to expect.

Andrés showed up in half an hour. "Why's the subway always so slow when it pours like this?" He put his sopping coat over Juan's and sat in the only chair. "Let's get something to eat," he said. "I'm starving."

"I'm broke," said Gabriela.

"I got fifteen bucks," said Andrés. "Not enough for Thai. Pizza?"

"Wait," said Juan, "I got . . ." He pulled a wallet out of his pocket. "I

got more than twenty, and I found out I know this guy at the West End—
he'll give us a break. I temped with him once someplace. Let's get some
burgers."

"Yeah," said Andrés.

He handed his cash to Juan, who took five and handed the rest back.
Then Juan called someone at the West End. Before long, a boy with mes-
tizo features showed up carrying a large, warm, fragrant brown bag. Juan
tipped him generously.

"Remember, be quiet," Gabriela whispered, pointing at the door to
the kitchen. "They're in there cooking right now."

Juan and Andrés nodded, and Juan turned the radio on low. His
friends at the West End had loaded the bag with free extras, and the three
of them enjoyed a silent feast. Andrés, who had had no dinner the night
before, ate ravenously.

"Look how he eats, and he's still so skinny," said Gabriela, who had
little appetite herself. She spoke softly but Andrés heard. "He never . . ."

Juan looked at Gabriela, and that was enough to stop her. He rarely
corrected her, but he knew when she was wrong, and it put him off when
she talked, as she often did, about Andrés eating so much. Gabriela resented Andrés being here instead of her girls—as though what happened
was *his* fault—and she refused to admit that he was supporting himself,
working construction weekends, and wasn't always getting his meals. The
kid was so exhausted and thin, you'd think she'd feel bad. Instead, it was
almost as though she were starting to believe what she told these people
here, that he was living with Juan's mother—who had been dead seven
years now. Gabriela thought Andrés should quit school and go to work to
help support her and bring back her girls. She had gone to work herself
when she was sixteen. If Juan didn't fight her, she would have insisted, and
Andrés would have obeyed; he knew he owed her. But Juan wanted Andrés
to go to college, and he understood that he himself, not Andrés, was the
one who should get an apartment for all of them. He knew perfectly well
that Gabriela thought so too, but she found it easier to be mad at Andrés
than at him. That didn't make her a bad person. She was just a human
being in a lot of bad trouble. So when Gabriela went too far, he only

straightened her out. He never got too mad. He looked soberly at Andrés, who avoided his eye.

On the other side of Gabriela's door, Anne was pulling things out of the refrigerator and cabinets, preparing to make dinner. "I smell food," she said to Jane, who had just come home from school and was scouting for snacks. "French fries or something."

"I don't smell anything," Jane said blandly.

"You can't smell that? Maybe Gabriela got takeout," Anne said, "although she should just help herself in the kitchen. I keep telling her that. I mean, if she's going to be here, she may as well eat decently and save her money. All that takeout can't be good for her."

Jane knew that Gabriela always ordered out when she had company, which seemed to be more and more often, but she said nothing. Gabriela had been sleeping in the little room for more than three months now, and to Jane, she seemed sicker this week than before. She had ups and downs. Periodically, she felt well enough to do a little housework or cook breakfast for the family or entertain the little boys in her room. The children always saw far more of Gabriela than Anne did. They all liked Gabriela and ran little errands for her, and no matter that she spent half her time resting in bed, they were getting used to having her there and had begun relying on her to do up French braids for Ellen and Jane, speak Spanish with Stuart, and play Mouse Trap with Gilbert. For nearly a week, she had been too sick even for that sort of thing, yet the children continued to wander in and out of her room until about five o'clock, when she always told them that she needed a little privacy—as though until then she considered herself to be on call.

Anne was worried about Gabriela's health, but yesterday when she urged her again to go back to the doctor, Gabriela claimed that she'd seen him last week and had another appointment for next week, and she denied she was any worse than before. Anne didn't ask about the new apartment, but Gabriela volunteered that it would be ready in time—February. She sounded confident. It would be none too soon, Anne thought, for she and Charles had begun to ask themselves whether they were just going to accept the fact that Gabriela lived with them now, as an invalid, or whether they would have the courage to throw her out if she didn't leave in February.

It was a relief to think that she would get on her feet and bring the girls home—and it was fortunate that Juan, who Gabriela said was staying with his mother in a one-room apartment, was willing to carry them all this time while Gabriela was too sick to work. Anne doubted she and Charles would be able to ask Gabriela to move out. Where to? Certainly not to a shelter—not as sick as she was. Anne sometimes thought she herself should get in touch with the city welfare agencies and insist they do something, but when she suggested anything like that, Gabriela protested vehemently and Anne backed off.

After dinner, Jane slipped off to her room and called Gabriela on her cell phone.

"Is Andrés there?" she asked, shyly, because she was aware that this question would cause upheaval on the other side of the kitchen door. Gabriela's face showed her displeasure when she passed the phone to Andrés, notwithstanding the innocent puzzlement on his, and she was stern-faced when he announced, without emotion, that Jane wanted help with her math homework and that he was going out to meet her in a café on Broadway.

"I'll be back," Andrés told Gabriela and Juan. "I won't be long."

Jane got there first and watched Andrés come in and look around for her. The place was filled with Columbia students working on laptops. She had never before encountered him outside Gabriela's room, and seeing him here, on this neutral turf, she formed radically new impressions. Before this, he had been someone belonging to Gabriela, but now he was his own person, with something forceful about him. He was tired-looking, but not self-conscious and shrinking the way he sometimes seemed in Gabriela's room. He was about her own height, and his face was narrow, olive-toned, sensitive—or sharp, maybe, keen, as though he were on high alert for something—with a strong, thin nose. His long, straight black hair was tucked behind his ears. He didn't smile when he saw her at one of the little tables in the back, papers, pencils, and a math book already spread out.

They got coffee in enormous paper cups and, to Andrés's surprise, ac-

tually did math problems for nearly an hour. He had thought she probably wanted to talk about his aunt, maybe to tell him that her family was
really getting mad about the whole thing. Instead he explained polynomial
functions to her.

He was terribly serious about it all, and organized and clear too, with
the manner of a peer, not her housemaid's nephew. He matter-of-factly
took himself to be smarter than she, and he was very smart, she realized.
He grasped quickly not only the problems but the terms of her confusion,
for she hadn't invented her need for help.

"What a good teacher you are," she said, all grateful sincerity, when
they had closed the books and she was zipping her freshly solved problems
into a case. "I really get it now, and I'm terrible in math."

"No, you're okay. You just needed to have it explained," he said. He
wanted to be encouraging, but coming from him to her this sounded—at
least it felt—like trying to butter her up. He tried again. "I mean, that's
advanced, what you're doing. I'm surprised they give you that."

"Why, because it's a girls' school? I can't believe you said that. Listen,
I'm dumb at it, but you should see my sister and some of the other girls."

Andrés couldn't help letting his frown relax and one corner of his
mouth pull back, his first smile of the evening, but it lasted only a second.
Jane seemed to him foreign, more foreign than Asian kids at City who
hardly spoke English. Yet he was absolutely certain now that she was trying to be friends with him, although he didn't know why she would want
to. It was all the more embarrassing that later he intended to sneak back
into her home and maybe even sleep on the floor in Gabriela's room, as he
had three nights this past week. Juan was probably going to stay over too.
A couple of times, both of them had stayed, Juan in the bed and Andrés
on the floor. They were all secretly going to sleep in Jane's home, uninvited. The bizarrerie of it hit him with renewed, painful force. The only
thing that could have made it worse was to have her realize how much time
he had spent thinking about her.

"Andrés," Jane said. "I have to confess." She was suddenly full of
something serious, and Andrés, shaken by her change of tone, tried to pull
himself together.

"To who? What?"

"You."

"Come on," said Andrés nervously.

"I read your poems on my mother's computer."

"Oh." His face was full of dread. "She said she didn't mind if I used it."

"I really like them."

"No," he said.

She didn't know what he meant. "I *do* like them," she said, thinking that perhaps he doubted her sincerity.

There was a hard-breathing silence.

"Did you read other stuff?" Andrés asked, finally.

"The journal . . . yes, I did. I was going to say that next." Jane's voice quivered, and she could feel her heart rev.

Andrés breathed an expletive. "But it's my own fault."

"Kind of, it is, because it's our laptop—anyway, my mother's. It just so happened that I borrowed it for school Monday. Still, once I saw what it was, I should have stopped reading, and I didn't. I read all of it. So I'm sorry, really sorry."

"It's okay. It's more my fault." Tears of shame burned in his eyes; it took a great effort to hold them back. Everything was in the journal—absolutely everything. If she told her parents, they'd throw Gabriela out. But that wasn't the worst.

"Here's a CD with some of your files," Jane said, handing him an envelope. "I got worried and I deleted them so no one else would read them."

His lips formed "Thanks," but she heard nothing.

"And I just want to tell you one more thing," Jane said in a slightly hoarse voice, looking at him urgently.

"Okay."

"I think about you all the time too."

It was nearly ten when they returned to 635 West 117th in the freezing rain, now turning to snow. Jane walked in first, alone. Andrés waited around the corner for several minutes before brushing himself off, going in, and getting on the elevator, with a wave to Willie, the doorman, who thought this a good occasion on which to look completely unconscious.

In the morning, Andrés slipped out at seven, leaving Juan and Gabriela asleep. As he got out of the elevator in the lobby, Charles Braithwaite, unshaven, in T-shirt and jeans, got in; he had been down to pick up a newspaper left at the wrong doorway. Charles registered Andrés as a new young face in the building—evidently going to school with the backpack and the City insignia. Whose kid is that? he wondered, and he felt uneasy, remembering Anne's story of the nephew on the floor in Gabriela's room who also went to City. Charles resolved to ask the doorman who the kid was, for he hadn't known there were any new families in the building.

That evening, Jane announced again that she intended to meet a friend in the neighborhood—Andrea somebody or other—and do homework. Charles and Anne were pleased that she had a new friend. Maybe with all the Stephen Delacort problems behind her, Jane was beginning to find more acceptance among her peers.

All that week, Jane's mood continued to sweeten. One afternoon, she clung affectionately to Anne and regaled her with school news. She curled up next to Charles on the sofa in the evening and asked him thoughtful questions about vocal technique. She even asked them to listen to her sing a new piece she was working on.

"She hasn't been like this since Ellen was born," Anne told Charles, "so pleasant and funny and reasonable. It's like she had a chip on her shoulder for fourteen years, and suddenly it's gone."

One day after school, Jane found Greg Merriweather drinking tea with her father in the kitchen, and she surprised them by sitting down to chat. Anne soon joined them, followed by Ellen. Greg, who had been on intimate terms with the family for years, was astonished at this friendly new edition of Jane, which seemed to be the one her parents had always believed in but no one else could see at all. Ellen, who had not yet taken in her sister's transformation, listened suspiciously to Jane's talk. Jane never said anything at family gatherings. She muttered privately to her father or mother, or she made faces, ironic rejoinders, angry denials, and unavoidable factual admissions.

"Daddy, I was playing some of your old stuff," Jane said, with the melting warmth of reconciliation. "Led Zeppelin, Boston, Dire Straits, Kansas, and all that stuff. I think maybe I'm going to put together some CDs of oldies."

Ellen rolled her eyes and sighed loudly.

"Someone pay attention to Ellen," Jane said, "before she blinds herself or chokes or something. Don't worry, Ellen. Everyone notices you."

"Jane gets along so well with the older generation," Ellen said, clasping her hands in mock admiration. "She likes all the same stuff—the same operas, the same rock groups. Some people think she's a suck-up, but I—"

"Ellen, for heaven's sake!" Anne said.

"The generation gap is over," said Greg, in a too-obvious effort to neutralize the quarrel. He was surprised by Ellen's hostility.

"They do like our music," Anne said.

"And clothes and movies and books and politics," said Greg.

"Not really," Jane said, sipping a cup of coffee—instead of her usual cold drink—with a grown-up air that startled them all. "I wouldn't mind being like Mom and Dad, but I don't think I am. Actually, I kind of wish I related to people the way you do, Mom."

Ellen groaned her disgust. "Echh. What is *this*? New Age Janie?" she said. "First it was opera diva Janie and then teenage brat Janie. You should have costumes for your roles—like Barbie. Cowboy Barbie, Comrade Barbie, Alcoholics Anonymous Barbie."

"Ellen, I think you'd better take your juice and leave the room," said Charles.

"Go," Anne added calmly, to make it clear that she supported Charles.

"My feelings aren't hurt," Jane said, to their surprise, although she gave Ellen a scathing look. "She doesn't have to go for me."

"How forgiving. Saint Barbie," Ellen said with a pious expression, and began to giggle uncontrollably.

"Ellen, if your sister is willing to tolerate this, you may stay," said Charles.

"Great," said Ellen, still giggling, "because I would hate to miss this conversation." She tried to drink and sputtered in her glass from giggling.

"Janie, what *did* you mean—about relating to people the way I do?" asked Anne. "I almost thought you were offering me a compliment."

"Oh, funny, Mom. You're almost as funny as Ellen. What I mean is, it doesn't matter to you how rich or important people are. You treat everyone the same because to you everyone really is equal. Other people aren't like that."

"Your father is," Greg said.

"Yeah," Jane said, "but not as much as Mom."

"Egalitarian Barbie," muttered Ellen, and she suppressed renewed tittering.

"It's not funny, Ellen. It's just stupid," said Jane. "Why don't you save this routine for your puerile friends—because it's not going over very big here."

"Actually, you're very much that way yourself," Anne said to Jane. "It can get people mad at you."

"Oh, Janie would hate that," said Ellen, shaking her head in mock sympathy. She was surprised but not mollified when Jane smiled a little at this.

"In fact," said Greg, "Christ was crucified for getting people mad about things like that."

"Messiah Barbie," Ellen said.

Everyone else ignored Greg's comment, which came uncomfortably close to crossing the line that divided acceptable allusion to facts about religion from unacceptable outright religious talk.

"You really think I am?" Jane asked her mother. "Because it's important."

"Of course it's important, and, yes, you are like that."

"You and Ellen both," Charles said. He stroked Ellen's hair, which was curly like Anne's. Jane's was straight like his. Both girls had preferred curls when they were younger, and Jane had been bitterly envious of her sister's. Now things were reversed. "All of you, I hope. In your case, Jane, it's certainly part of why you've had so much trouble at school. When other girls think they're a big deal, you let them know you don't necessarily agree, which makes them resent the attention you get all the more. And they decide you're a phony because you also don't act the way they would if they were in the spotlight as much as you are. Socially speaking, you go around tilting at windmills a lot."

Everyone thought this over. Charles had never said or thought such things before. It had come to him just this moment how life as his and Anne's child might possibly be confusing and difficult.

"Aren't you going to go for it, Ellen?" asked Jane, with a snide look at her sister.

"I don't think Quixote Barbie is particularly funny," said Ellen.

———————

CHAPTER 13

A t the doorway of a Juilliard studio, Jane said good-bye to her voice teacher. Then she ran down the escalator steps beside Avery Fisher Hall and hurried to Tower Records across the street at Broadway and Sixty-sixth. She went upstairs and looked at a new recording of *Don Giovanni*. The room was nearly empty, and a lush performance of Mahler's First was playing at high volume. Besides Jane, the customers looking at classical CDs included two elderly men and a middle-aged woman who, judging from her forlorn expression as she compared discs, was flummoxed by the prices. Jane put down the *Don Giovanni* and went to the Bach recordings, which she flipped through with one hand, clutching her cell phone in the other. When it rang, she answered it breathlessly, and the two aged men glared at her.

"Where are you?" she asked, hastening to a corner where she could hear over the Mahler. "I'm here already—upstairs. Be right down."

Andrés, unsmiling and apparently indifferent, was waiting for her at the foot of the escalator. "This one," he said, holding up a CD.

"Okay, let's pay," she said.

"Don't you want to look around for a little while?"

"Let's go someplace and talk," she said, pulling him by the hand toward the checkout counter. He gave in. They each contributed seven dollars to the purchase. Andrés knew he should not spend the money, but he said nothing.

They walked to a nearby café and ordered espressos at the counter.

"You take it," Andrés said, handing the CD to her. "I don't have anyplace to play it."

"I'll download it, and you can borrow my iPod tomorrow," Jane said.

He hesitated, then agreed. "I hope you like it," he said, and abandoning his indifference for a moment, he looked at her with an appeal in his eyes. "It's not like . . . innovative or anything."

They had met several times since the night when Andrés helped her with math homework, but with each meeting things grew cooler between them despite how hard Jane tried to be entertaining and understanding and, today, to look good in tight new jeans.

"I don't care," she replied. "I'm not cool. I'm not trying to be cool. I don't fit in."

Andrés all at once turned scarily cool. He looked at her with his chin lowered, his expression neutral, and his lips pressed tight against any weak-minded disclosures. Compared with Andrés in this new mood, Jane thought, Stephen Delacort was the warm teddy-bear type. She knew how she must sound to him, and loathed herself.

"Why not?" he asked, adding in a needling voice, "You're rich like them."

"Not like them. When I was thirteen, we got an inheritance, but until then we were sort of hard up. My mother always got my coat ten sizes too big so I wouldn't outgrow it fast. For years, I had to wear this enormous quilted down-stuffed thing she got on sale. I looked like a mattress."

"You *are* rich," he said. "Even before you were thirteen you were." It felt rude to refuse to smile, but satisfying too.

"I know," she said.

This was capitulating too strategically, and the falseness in her voice disgusted both of them. Avoiding her eye, Andrés picked up the check and studied it. Jane felt almost panicky at the thought that he might leave.

"My little sister is really embarrassed by me," she offered. Again it was the wrong thing to say, but some demon in her seemed determined to make her act like the girl his face showed such contempt for.

"She's cool, huh?" said Andrés, digging in his pocket for money.

"Not really, but so far she can kind of fake it. Actually she hates me. Everyone does—except my grandmother."

Andrés chafed at her easy humility, which made him want to make her feel the real thing.

"Why?"

"Because I get more attention at home, and I'm a loser at school. I don't have friends. I got a bad reputation because my last boyfriend was always in trouble. Once I got suspended because of him. The other girls say I'm phony and think I'm better than everyone else just because I've been onstage a couple of times." She was coming across badly—false, full of herself despite her self-deprecatory offerings. It was maddening.

"Why do you say things like that all the time?" he asked her. "You think it's gonna convince me you're not too good for me? You know what? That makes me sick."

Jane, wounded though she was by a tone not far from hatred in his voice, looked at him thoughtfully, her face deeply flushed. "Mm," she said, nodding, her thin dark brows forming S curves of concentration and enlightenment. She got it now—it was so obvious.

She looked like her father, but she acted like her mother, Andrés thought, when she did that. His heart began to beat fast with what he had done—speaking so roughly to a girl like Jane. She'd probably never heard such mean talk before. He was ashamed of the words, and of the pleasure he took in wounding her.

"I'm sorry," she said, sounding more authentically herself, if not particularly apologetic—nor all that hurt either.

"That's stupid. You're not sorry," he shot back at her, again with malice in his voice.

"Yes I am," she replied self-righteously. "It's not stupid to be sorry. Maybe I was stupid about you, but let me tell you something, Andrés. You're just as stupid about me. I mean—'why-aren't-you-like-them-you're-rich-too?' How dumb is that, huh?"

"Hey, you bought it, didn't you?"

"I was just trying to be nice."

"To a retard."

"I *was* willing to believe you were dumb—about that stuff. I thought I just liked someone who maybe was . . . inexperienced in some ways. I didn't *know* you were feeding me fishhooks."

"Yes you did. But I'm sorry," said Andrés sheepishly. He smiled a little and glanced sideways at her. "Fishhooks?" he repeated, with a small amused laugh.

Jane showed her relief in a deep sigh, and Andrés leaned over, gave her a quick kiss on the cheek, and grinned at her. He was relieved too, and just like that, things were all right again.

Mutual confidence and ease mysteriously restored, they exploded in pent-up talk. They gripped each other's hands and pulled unconsciously as they chattered, so that they semicircled and swayed in an unconscious dance on the counter stools.

Andrés confessed how desperate he was to get to college in the fall, Jane how she hated the thought of going to Juilliard. With the help of her teacher, and without her parents' knowledge, she was trying to arrange an audition for a part at the City Opera. Her plan was to leapfrog school, jumping immediately into the real world of music. What need would there be to go to conservatory if she was already a successful performing musician? Andrés was surprised to hear that she wanted to quit school; he talked gloomily of how Gabriela wanted him to drop out of school, go to work, and support her family. She would have insisted, only her boyfriend wouldn't let her. Gabriela wouldn't do anything that got Juan really mad. Yet Andrés knew that he should quit and go get a job. He owed that much to Gabriela, but, he told Jane, he was selfish and also cowardly in a lot of ways. He had run out on his mother too. Andrés's self-deprecation, unlike Jane's, came from the heart, and horrified her. She pressed him urgently to stick it out at school. She knew her parents were broke, but maybe she could get money for Gabriela from her grandmother.

"No, no," Andrés protested. "This is between you and me. Whatever we say is just for us. Don't make it so I can't tell you things, Janie."

Jane agreed to this reluctantly. She saw that he was coming apart, close to tears, and she let him change the subject without comment.

"You should go to Juilliard if you really want to be a singer that much," he said as they probed their pockets for money to pay the check. He watched, amused, as Jane struggled to pull bills out of her extremely snug jeans. His own jeans were baggy; he retrieved his dwindling roll of dollars and extracted two. He considered trying to pay for her espresso but decided against it. She would protest, and, besides, he was really broke. "Jane, you think maybe you just like to give your parents trouble?"

"I used to, but lately I stopped," Jane replied. "I don't blame them now."

"That's nice. You're a really nice girl."

"I don't think—"

"I do," he said. He sounded so sure that she almost believed him.

CHAPTER 14

―――――――

"I should never have let myself get talked into this," Carla said, with a baleful look at her companions.

With Greg Merriweather, Michael Garrard, and a woman wearing the in-the-know look of the real estate agent she was, Carla was riding a creaky old elevator operated by a man who, she thought, was equally old and creaky. He sat on a small, leather-covered seat at the right of the elevator door and pulled levers to stop and start his vessel. The elevator crept upward slowly, emitting alarming groans, as though burdened beyond its strength. They were on their way to see Morningside Heights's only billionaire—at least he was rumored to be a billionaire—a man named Wyatt Jesse Younger.

Younger's offices were all located here, in the building in which he had been raised and where he still lived. It was a nondescript, run-down place on 112th Street, just catty-corner from the U.S. Post Office; it smelled of a hundred years of cabbage soup, haphazard trash collection, and neglected kitty-litter boxes, but it remained marginally middle-class. Only recently had the building attracted a few of the sort of moneyed sophisticates who had already transformed the rest of the neighborhood. Four years ago, an intrepid young couple who had not heard the rumors about Younger's wealth bought two one-bedroom apartments directly under his and proceeded to gut and combine them, making a great deal of noise and dust, while complaining endlessly at board meetings about the roar of Younger's enormous stereo speakers. Younger had responded vigorously, and the quarrel ended with the young couple's exit a year and a half ago. Bought out by Younger, according to the real estate agent. Sort of forced out, she added, with a vague air, and the result was that no one wanted to buy into the building anymore.

"Now if anyone wants to sell," she said, "they go see Younger, and a lot of them do because he pays top dollar. I handle all the deals, so I'm over here all the time."

The real estate agent, who was the civic-minded friend of an Ecumenical Council member, had put this expedition in motion. She had urged her friend to contact Younger and ask for a contribution. Younger's willingness to buy all the apartments in the building that went up for sale was apparently part of his own personal anti-gentrification campaign—or so the real estate agent guessed. Maybe he would take an interest in helping local poor people.

"In twenty years, he'll own the whole building," she said. "There'll just be him and some old folks who lived there when he was a kid." She leaned forward confidingly and whispered, "He's kind of eccentric."

The old elevator operator shook his head scornfully and spoke for the first time. "Not eccentric—rich!"

Michael smiled at this, for he himself had observed how often the freedom that money bought was mistaken for eccentricity. Most of the rich people he'd met were conventional and conforming, and their apparent nonconformisms were merely self-indulgences that their wealth permitted. This was proved by the fact that the wealthy were all very much like one another—sought the same status symbols, wore the same clothes, congregated at the same places, had the same air. Meet one billionaire, you've met them all, Michael thought. But it was a small thought, unbecoming. He pushed it away.

In any event, Younger promised to be something other than your run-of-the-mill billionaire. He was Morningside Heights's own version of the thing: the offspring of a supervisor at the local post office and a house-wife; educated at public schools; a dropout from City College after only a semester. Though he had his own jet (or so it was rumored), he never got invited to fund-raising dinners with heads of state, and was not the sort of billionaire who was himself head of a type of state without borders. Certainly he was not to be classed with a Soros or Buffett. They said he made his money on Wall Street off regulatory loopholes. Before they closed the holes, he had accumulated enough capital to play the market in more ordinary ways, supposedly very cleverly, but no one was very curious about how Younger made money. The most interesting fact about him seemed simply to be that he had done so before he was twenty-five. He was still short of thirty.

"Very few people in the building have laid eyes on Younger," explained the real estate agent, "since he made his own little private entrance. Some-times you see his car pull up and he jumps out and hustles in there with a baseball cap pulled down over his face. Otherwise, he's invisible."

A year ago Younger had bought the doctor's office on one side of the lobby, along with exclusive rights to the old-fashioned little elevator. Then he knocked down a wall so that the elevator could be reached from the doctor's office, and summoned the ancient operator out of retirement to run it, so that he no longer shared public spaces with his neighbors. They could no longer gossip about remarks he made or clothes he wore riding on the elevator or collecting his mail from the lobby, or pass on such tid-bits to the curious.

"See? Most people would envy you your chance to get a look at this fellow close up," Michael chided Carla.

Greg had noticed that Michael could not speak to Carla except to offer sly jibes, reproaches, and corrections. When the three of them were together, Greg found himself continually putting out little conversational fires that might otherwise have blazed into quarrels.

"But I've never heard anything really interesting about him," Greg said, "unless you think buying and selling gazillions of legal fictions on tiny margins is interesting."

The old man at the elevator controls snorted, as though offended, and pulled the lever to open the door on the tenth floor, where the real estate agent exited.

"My seller's here," she said. "Good luck. Just remember—he can be a little . . ." But the old man closed the door on her final speech, and they continued upward without her advice. On the eleventh floor, the elevator stopped again, and they peered into a dim hallway with flaking paint in the mustardy color favored for lower-middle-class housing in the seventies. Boxes, apparently stuffed with papers, were stacked along one side. They stepped out warily.

"Are you sure this is the right floor?" Michael asked the elevator man.

"Eleven. Younger offices," he replied. He pulled the door closed and was gone.

The hallway was dark and the bare floor gritty under their feet. The twelve doors on the floor all had plates with letters but no names; no one answered the first half dozen at which they rang.

"I think Younger's bought up the whole floor," said Michael. "No one seems to live here anymore."

The door to apartment K, they discovered, stood open, displaying a disorderly collection of old furniture, trash bins, and battered file cases, but no one answered their calls. At last, at the far end of the hall, they found a corridor that showed signs of renovation. It, too, was lined with closed, locked rooms, and was dark except at its very end, where a light shone out from door frames on both sides. They stopped before one of these that seemed to be the source of music, and Greg put his ear to the door and listened intently.

"Purcell," he said decisively, as though that clarified matters.

Michael shrugged and rapped on the door. Despite what he had said to Carla, he was skeptical of the value of this begging expedition. They had written to Younger only in a what-have-we-got-to-lose spirit and never expected to hear back from him, let alone be invited to meet him.

"Come in," called an exaggeratedly affable baritone, and the Purcell suddenly ceased.

They stepped into a large book-lined room furnished in a luxurious version of professorial style—oriental carpets, Rauschenberg prints, hand-rubbed cherrywood cabinets and desk, a glamorous cutting-edge computer, and high-design lamps. A microfiche reader, a great gray sixties antique, hulked in a corner. And behind the desk, which sat in a windowed bay, was the obvious master of these money-infused scholarly facilities— a handsome man in his fifties who appeared to glow with good-natured self-delight. He had one of those permanently youthful faces, and his hair, although it was silvery gray, fell boyishly on his forehead. He swept it back in a habitual, refined gesture. Behind him, down a narrow hallway, they saw a maze of smaller rooms from which emerged the sounds of typing and, occasionally, a soft, businesslike conversation. They had not known what to expect, but all this was nonetheless surprising.

The man at the desk looked at them with benignant condescension. "Well?" he asked with a laugh—a rather superior laugh, Michael thought with distaste.

"Mr. Younger?" Michael said hesitantly.

"Oh, no, no," said the man, laughing more heartily. "I'm flattered to be taken for a man of such extraordinary talent, but I'm a mere scholar."

"Sorry to trouble you, but we seem to be lost. Can you tell us where Mr. Younger's office is?" Michael was austerely polite, for he particularly disliked the style of bragging that disguises itself in outright reversals of a person's real convictions—especially when it simulates modesty.

"Not so fast," said the man, holding up his hands warningly, and his tone shifted. "You are?"

"My name is Michael Garrard, and these are my colleagues from the Ecumenical Council of Religious Charities, Carla Winter and Father Gregory Merriweather."

The man observed Carla and Greg with cheerful stoicism. "We invited only you, Dr. Garrard," he said reprovingly.

"The letter to Mr. Younger was from all three of us," Michael replied, thinking how easy it was to dislike this man, knowing nothing at all about him. "And I'm not authorized to act without my colleagues."

The man behind the desk was oddly distant for a moment while, apparently, he thought things through; then he reverted to his original buoyant good humor. "Well, all right then," he said. "So, let's hear your pitch."

"Hear what? Who *are* you?" Carla asked irritably.

Greg made discreet pacifying gestures in Carla's direction, but Michael, for once, was not troubled by Carla's rudeness.

"We came to see Mr. Younger," Michael said. "We have no idea who you are, and I'm afraid we've nothing to say to you."

The icy edge in his voice cut through the stranger's condescension. "Oh, I apologize," he said. "So sorry. What was I thinking of? Selvnick is my name. Around here, they call me *Professor* Selvnick because I used to be a professor of philosophy—just up the street." Selvnick pointed with his thumb over his shoulder. "Now, Mr. Younger supports my philosophical work. Sorry I have no chair to offer you."

The absence of chairs for visitors was odd—and on purpose, Michael decided, for the fellow smirked as he apologized. The name Selvnick was familiar, but he could not recall where he'd heard it. He was certain that he hadn't seen it on any correspondence with Mr. Younger.

"So you're a sort of . . . house scholar?" Greg asked. He was trying to come to grips with the idea of a philosopher tooling away here in a lair of capital.

"In a way. Mr. Younger is my patron."

The visitors waited for some explanation of this somewhat overly sentimental description of Professor Selvnick's relationship with Younger.

"You know—like Machiavelli and Giuliani de' Medici, or Hobbes and the Cavendishes," added Selvnick, seeing their puzzlement. "In return for Mr. Younger's generous support, I dedicate my scholarly work to him and offer him my personal guidance on the moral, social, and political implications of his business—and on whom and what to support with the rest of his money." Professor Selvnick looked modestly sideways at his astonished visitors with this last disclosure and chuckled. He seemed to laugh a great deal.

"So . . . literally, you mean?" said Greg. "He's literally your patron?"

"He is, yes. Why is that so strange? The arrangement helps both of us. He had absolutely no idea what to do with all his money, but now he's used it to buy himself some moral and political expertise. And I can do far more good in this role than I ever could as a scholar and teacher."

A genuine fool, Michael thought, dismayed. He glanced at Greg, but Greg wouldn't meet his eye. Well, it would be a fruitless expedition and a waste of the afternoon, but here they were. They might as well go through the motions of making their request. Besides, Michael's curiosity was aroused by the social atavism of medieval-style patronage flourishing right here in postmillennium Morningside Heights.

"I wonder," said Michael, "how Mr. Younger decided that he should support *you* and that it was *your* advice he wanted rather than anyone else's. Did he . . . advertise? Research philosophical treatises?"

"Actually, I contacted him—told him I was looking for a patron and explained my ideas, gave him a few books and articles. He was absolutely fascinated." Selvnick interrupted himself to grin and laugh. "But let's get down to business here. Mr. Younger asked me to scout you out. So I've looked at the work your organization does—very well meaning but terribly misinformed. It's just giveaways—housing, food, clothes. Not something we really have any interest in. You don't seem to realize that we're libertarians here. We don't believe in welfare."

"But our organization—" Greg protested.

"—encourages dependency and irresponsibility and rewards slackers. You know, private charities can be as bad as the welfare state at breeding the something-for-nothing mentality. The poor need to work. That's their salvation. We believe in personal independence, freedom, and responsibility—that means private charity to aid the deserving poor, not freeloaders. And minimal government."

The trio from Morningside Heights—eyes fixed on the floor, wall, and ceiling respectively—shared their reactions to this speech by some telepathic means. Only now did it dawn on Michael that this man was surely *Richard* Selvnick, the libertarian guru—the professor who years ago had written a defense of libertarianism that eventually succeeded in converting thousands to its congenial tenets about the primacy of property rights and the market as the foundation, in fact the very core, of personal freedom. Such ideas, which had had enormous influence across the political spectrum, had been fiercely debated in Michael's undergraduate days.

"Minimal government that ensures market stability and controls foreign governments in the interests of multinational corporations?" said Carla. "What an original opinion for a billionaire. How did he ever think of it?"

The remark was childish, but in Michael's present state of mind it had a certain witty charm. Now it was Greg who wanted to rein Carla in. She had an unfortunate knack for making the most commonsense, defensible ideas sound like subversive quackery. She damaged her own causes, mostly for the pleasure of creating offense. But why offend prospective donors? It was some comfort that these peculiar people on 112th Street were probably not really prospective donors. Greg gently nudged Carla's foot and frowned ambiguously.

She glared at him. "What, Greg? Is that root canal still bothering you?" she asked loudly.

"What sort of charities *are* you interested in?" Michael asked Selvnick.

"Education! We give out a load of fellowships and internships and support dozens of scholars at universities. We operate two think tanks and several weblogs. And we're doing educational radio and TV shows about small government, the tyranny of unions, the benefits of deregulation." Professor Selvnick gave Carla a look of cheerful defiance.

"But what do you do for the poor?" Greg asked. "This sounds like a political movement, not charitable work."

Selvnick looked at them with an expression that annoyed even Greg. He'd seen it a hundred times on PBS interviews: the amused, neutral look of the superlatively confident academic who has been set up to give a crushing response to some Neanderthal politician or businessman.

"Libertarianism," said Professor Selvnick, "is the *only* way to help the poor. There are poor people because taxes destroy jobs, and there are taxes because there are bloated governments. Making people pay taxes for social security or public television or educating ghetto children sounds noble, but in reality it's taking people's money against their will, which means they're forced to work for nothing. And what's that but slavery? Slavery for some and dependency for others—bad stuff for everyone." With an air of triumph, he looked at Carla.

"What about forcing a man to pay just half of one of many billions that he acquired without doing a goddam thing?" Carla asked. "What if the game in which he acquired his billions was stacked?"

"We're wasting each other's time," said Michael, feeling warm toward

Carla, "and, I must say, I can't see why you invited us here if you'd already made up your minds."

"Well, A, we invited *you*, not them," said Professor Selvnick, waving his finger at Greg and Carla. "And, B, I didn't say we'd made up our minds. Let me hear your arguments. Maybe you can talk us into something. But I warn you, I'm a tough logician. I respond only to reason—reason and fact." He smiled and sat waiting with an eager expression.

"Let's get out of here," said Carla.

"We'll just be going," said Michael.

"Oh, *don't* be so defeatist. You might as well take a stab at it. What have you got to lose? Besides, you can't get out."

"What do you mean?" asked Michael.

"I mean, you can only leave this floor by our private elevator. The operator has to come for you."

"You may as well call for the operator then. We're formally withdrawing our request for a donation," said Michael, turning to go.

"Not so fast," said Professor Selvnick, holding up a finger. His face briefly assumed the same faraway look they had seen earlier in the interview. "There's another matter Mr. Younger wants to discuss with you."

"We have to be going, and we'd appreciate your . . . freeing us."

"You're making a mistake, Dr. Garrard. This is a medical matter— something he wants to talk with you about privately."

"Oh, so that's it," Michael said.

"A house call," Carla said. "I can't believe it. No, actually I can believe it."

Michael sighed and thought for a moment, head bent, before answering. "I'll be happy to see Mr. Younger in my office. Just have him call for an appointment. If it's anything serious, he should be sure to make that clear to—"

"That's not how Mr. Younger operates, Dr. Garrard."

"You'll call the elevator, please," Michael replied.

"I am not authorized to do that," said Professor Selvnick with an apologetic but amused smile. "I am so sorry. Please just be patient. Mr. Younger wants—"

"So we'll take the stairs," said Carla.

"The stairwell is locked off," said Selvnick, smiling with a combination of embarrassment and amusement. "You have to understand that a man like Mr. Younger can't be too careful."

Carla pulled out her cell phone. "No service," she said, snapping it closed.

"Mr. Younger wants to make a deal with you, Dr. Garrard," said Professor Selvnick, "in private. Why are you making such a big thing out of that? Oh come. Allow for an eccentric."

"I'm not interested. I've been drawn here under false pretenses. Call the operator, Professor Selvnick, or—"

Michael was distracted by the appearance of a slight young man leaning against the doorway of Selvnick's office. He had thin, sandy hair and undistinguished features on which was displayed a mix of self-importance, self-doubt, and—somewhat unnervingly, thought Michael, studying his face closely—fear.

"Dr. Garrard," said the man. "I'm Wyatt Younger. I want to talk to you in my office." He had a slightly nasal tenor voice, and despite his peremptory words, he sounded ordinary. His alleged eccentricity could be detected only in his air of troubled distraction and the fact that he wore something like a carpenter's apron of coarse unbleached muslin with pens, pencils, a handheld computer, eyeglasses, and several other unidentifiable lumpy objects arranged in its many pockets.

"I'm sorry, but I have to be going," said Michael.

"I told you, you can't leave until the operator comes," said Professor Selvnick, who had reacted to Younger's appearance as though it were the unexpected punch line of a good joke.

"Did either of you ever hear of something called false arrest?" Carla asked. "Let me explain wha—"

"Please," said Professor Selvnick, elongating his vowel to indicate refined condescension and deprecation. "How about a little common sense?"

"*Someone* around here could use some," Carla responded.

"Don't bother," Greg said to her under his breath. "He feeds on opposition. Leave him alone."

"Yeah, okay," she said indifferently, as though Greg had misunderstood her.

"We'll just wait in the hallway," said Michael, in a firm, frigid voice. "I'm sure the operator will be here soon." And he led the way, past Wyatt Jesse Younger, who looked reproachfully at Selvnick as the three visitors made their way to the door.

"It's good you don't have any chairs," Carla said to Selvnick over her shoulder as they filed out, "or we'd be tempted to stay and talk." The self-satisfaction on Selvnick's face, she noticed, had given way to nervous disgruntlement.

"If I'm not mistaken," she said, as Michael rapped against the door of the elevator in the hallway, "Younger is none too pleased with Selvnick. Selvnick looked like a kid with a bad report card at the end there. Well, how long are they going to make us . . ."

The elevator appeared before she could give voice to their shared anxiety about being trapped in the dismal hallway—too soon to have been summoned by Michael's knocking. Younger must have told Selvnick to call. The three were silent in the elevator, while the old operator observed them with a mixture of curiosity and satisfaction. They walked silently through Younger's miniature lobby, with its worn doctor's-waiting-room furniture and ample stock of year-old copies of *Time, Newsweek, Business-Week,* and *People,* out onto the street, where they expressed their relief only by breathing deeply of the fresh, cold air.

Michael spoke first, when they had walked nearly a block. "An earpiece!" he exclaimed, his eyes wide with discovery. "That insufferable man's office was wired for a mike, and he was listening to instructions from Younger on an earpiece."

Greg smacked his forehead and groaned. "Of course."

"Why are political nuts always into these weird technological things?" Carla asked, beginning to grin.

"I don't believe I've ever uttered these words before," Michael said, "but I need a drink. *What* an unpleasant experience."

They made their way to a pub on Broadway and drank, seated at a sticky table in a dark, shabby room that reeked of beer and rancid food.

At 4 P.M. the place was empty but for two or three aged and impoverished hard drinkers who indulged in malicious staring at the amateurish new-comers with their relative youth, respectability, and ample funds.

"But think about it," Carla said, when they started on their third round, "That guy Selvnick calls himself a libertarian, but he was more or less holding us there against our will," said Carla. "He *imprisoned* us."

"That's a bit paranoid, Carla," said Greg. "He just likes throwing his weight around."

"Likes money too," said Michael. "There's a man who likes lots and lots of money and power. Naturally he writes a philosophy that makes virtues out of his flaws. Small ideas and big money—a very, very bad combination."

"I wonder how much *Younger* likes money and power," said Greg, a slightly boozy slur in his words. "Too bad we didn't get a chance to talk to him. I've heard that he never went to college but he's an autodidact—reads everything and gets cranky ideas. Never talks to anyone. Someone like that might be easily influenced by a slick guy who has all the credentials."

"That suggests another paranoid theory to me, Greg," said Carla, "although not to you. And that's my problem with you." Carla, evidently, had lost her train of thought. "You can dance all around a paranoid conclusion and never even notice it's there, never be tempted to draw it. I mean, Michael, Greg is the kind of guy who would notice he'd been stabbed and say, 'Gosh—what is this knife doing between my ribs? Maybe someone misplaced it! I'll take it right over to the lost-and-found.' So innocent! You know what Greg is? He's the opposite of para-noid. There ought be a word for it, like . . . 'trustoid'—someone who thinks no one is out to get him, someone who's always sure that every-thing's going to be all right—and there's no convincing him otherwise, despite the evidence."

A slight convulsive movement of Michael's chest and shoulders sug-gested that he thought Carla funny. "But what paranoid theory, Carla? You mean that Selvnick has undue influence over Younger and is using Younger's wealth for his own self-interested purposes?" he asked. "That's not paranoid."

Greg snickered unduly, to his companions' surprise. Greg had drunk too much. Carla looked at him with real affection.

"You see," said Michael, "when I was young, I gave up studying politics and philosophy because I realized . . ." Here Michael stopped and sat staring with all the appearance of thoughtfulness though he, too, had actually lost his train of thought.

"Younger's okay, I bet," said Greg after a long interval, having forgotten that he was waiting for Michael to continue.

"What, Michael?" Carla demanded impatiently. "What did you realize that made you give up studying politics—which I never knew you ever studied, by the way."

"I realized," said Michael soberly, though he was not, "that political debate became futile once people started forming personal commitments to theories like libertarianism and neoconservatism and Rawlsian liberalism and socialism and all the others. Because from that point on, they'd no more interest in reality—only in being on the winning team, or, among academics, in gaining professional status. Self-interest disguised as political virtue took over. It was very ugly back in the late seventies, and it's only got worse. To me, it's a sure sign of bad character when someone signs on to some political ism in that committed, club-member, religious way. There is no such thing as an honest ism-ite. That's why I fled into science."

"Down with ism-itism!" cried Carla. "Or should it be ism-ism?"

"But I wonder if Younger is an ism-ite," said Greg. "Ism-ist."

"My guess, based entirely on gossip," said Michael, "is that he's a limited man with too much money for his own good but not a particularly bad man. Perhaps he's even well intentioned, which would be fortunate, considering that anyone with his kind of money and power is effectively beyond the control of law and government—I mean, if he wanted to, he could probably have us all murdered without consequence."

"Michael, your paranoia is very simpatico," said Carla, squeezing his hand on the tabletop.

"So much for money from the libertarians," Greg said, and he circled with his finger overhead to signal the waiter for a fourth round.

They drank on. At one point Greg again giggled uncontrollably—just because Carla accused Michael of being patronizing when he (A) insisted on paying for all the drinks, and (B) refused to join them in a final round—and at another point, Carla, in a speech whose eloquence at its emotional peak was hardly marred by a brief alcohol-induced grammatical lockup, conveyed to Michael how she had never appreciated him the way he deserved and that she would always, always be there for him. In the end, the three of them were the best of friends.

CHAPTER 15

———————

Some days later, at breakfast, Michael and his wife discussed adoption. The subject had dominated their conversation for at least two weeks, and something went askew each time it came up. As they spoke, he looked at his newspaper and she at her laptop, which sat on the table next to her cup.

"Adriana, we've said all this before. My feelings are what they are, and these arguments you make don't change them. Why not adopt a baby since you want so much to be a mother? The older we get, the harder adoption will be."

"But I want to *have* a baby. I want to be pregnant."

He looked her full in the face for the first time in the conversation. Her sadness moved him. "Dear, I'm sorry you haven't had that chance. But isn't it time to adopt? Of course, we can still do everything in our power to try to get pregnant. But having a child to raise in the meantime might help. It might help you to . . . to relax and enjoy yourself more, get some perspective. Think how lovely and cheerful it would be to have a little baby to take care of and play with and get to schools and lessons and all that."

"You don't understand at all."

There was silence for several minutes, broken only by the muted click of Adriana's keyboard. Up on one of her fertility chat rooms, Michael thought. Last night, in their lovemaking, he had almost been unable to function, and he had had to make excuses about being particularly tired. He was getting out of his own control, and he had counted on being able to carry on the way he had been; it was his only plan in life.

"Let's think about egg donation again," said Adriana.

"Adriana," Michael said, pausing to collect his thoughts. "You know that egg donation is not a good option for us. Until we understand why you always miscarry, no ethical doctor will put a donor through it. The chances for success are too poor. Besides, you know you have no intention of proceeding with it." He stood and went to the window, where he leaned on the sill and looked out at the gray morning sky.

"*What* are you talking about? You've done nothing but create obstacles. You're more concerned about some perfect stranger of an egg donor than me. And you've—"

"—made three appointments to go for initial counseling, all of which you've broken."

"And I'll tell you why—because you think it would be your baby, not mine."

Still staring out the window, Michael plotted the forward trajectory of his married life into a future that seemed as dreary, as devoid of color and warmth, as the wintry sky. Adriana sounded paranoid to him lately, irrational. He recalled the soggy conversation with Greg and Carla, which reminded him that after a meeting at the hospital that evening he was expected for drinks at the Braithwaites'. The thought was a reprieve from despair.

"And you made the appointments with people you knew would say no," Adriana went on.

"I made the appointments with leaders in the field, who also happen to be very responsible people," he replied. "Really, I'm still willing to look into it. But no matter what else we do, let's try right away to adopt. Egg donation is too iffy for us to rely on."

"I'll think it over," she said, with a strained reasonableness.

This, he knew, was a refusal. She had been thinking it over for years. He had to face it: she would never agree to adopt a child. Now she would begin to search for help from fertility doctors at the questionable fringes of medicine. In fact, some of the people she was already talking to counted as quacks in his opinion. "I've got to go," he said. "I'm late. Remember, I'm not coming home for dinner tonight. I'm going to—"

"I don't care where you're going. You don't want to see me, that's all." She ran out of the room, and he heard their bedroom door slam shut.

That evening, when the Braithwaite boys were in bed and the girls were finishing homework in their rooms, Charles and Anne set out glasses of wine, sighed, and collapsed side by side onto the sofa. At dinner, Jane had confronted them with the disturbing news that she and her voice teacher had arranged for her to sing a major audition at City Opera.

"It's too soon. You're too young," Charles told her. "You'll destroy your voice."

"Not if I handle things right. I'll have an agent or a manager or something. I'll get good advice."

"What manager are you going to find who's going to protect you from directors and rehearsal schedules?" Anne said, a mix of protest and defeat in her voice. Jane was making a bad mistake, but there would be no talking her out of it. This moment had been coming for years. "You're not ready, physically or musically. You need so much background that Juilliard will give you. But it doesn't have to be Juilliard. We understand if you'd prefer to get away from us and New York. There's Curtis, Eastman, Yale—"

"I don't want to go to school," Jane replied, all cool patience, as though she had planned her argument ahead of time. "I know I'll probably understand more and sing better in five years, but that's no reason not to start now if people want to hear me. Lots of sopranos started when they were my age—Maria Callas, Renata Scotto, Geraldine Farrar. Joan Hammond was only seventeen. They didn't all ruin their voices like Maria Callas either."

"Those days are gone, Jane," said Charles. "When most of those women came up, singing still happened by accident. Training was hit-and-miss. Things are more scientific and professional now. Education counts so much more, and women's lives are different."

"But I don't like the way things are now," Jane said. "I don't like schools. I don't belong in school, and I can't do things that way."

Charles and Anne, too, objected to the corporate model that now governed professional music, but they thought that Jane would be able to ascend its ladder more easily than most. Rebellion was for those with no options. Fortunately, the likelihood was that she would fail the audition and be sent away with some kindly encouragement: Very good, little girl, but grow up and continue your studies and come back to us later. Even if they offered her a part, it was unlikely to tempt her. Jane would not be interested in singing three lines from left stage while someone else sang the great arias. Moreover, she was not well suited for those insignificant parts; she brought them too much attention. Jane might not want to continue her studies, but she would find it unavoidable—the same as everyone else.

They came to this conclusion just as Michael called to apologize. He would be at least another half hour.

"If that would keep you up too late, just say so, Anne," Michael said. "I know you get up at dawn."

She insisted he come.

"Well, maybe for just an hour then."

"He thinks he's the only grown-up in the world," said Anne to Charles. "He's always taking care of everyone, but he won't let anyone take care of him. Michael is a very paternal sort of man."

Charles smiled. Anne herself was so motherly that her parental valence almost always exceeded that of her friends. There was satisfaction in seeing her demoted to childhood, to taking advice and receiving explanations rather than giving them. "To me," Charles said, "it's just a doctorish mentality."

"But the way he doctors is parental. I know that his mother died when he was a baby and he was sent so young to boarding schools and all that, but after Lily met him she said he seems like someone who's been mothered."

"Whatever that seems like."

"And he's so intuitive with young children," Anne said. "What a tragedy his wife is infertile. He's going to miss this experience from both sides—he never had a real parent and he'll never be one either."

"It's not necessarily so tragic. Why shouldn't Michael and his wife just relax and enjoy their freedom?" Though Charles was a doting father and an affectionate husband, he had at times found it hard not to resent the burdens of rearing four children and supporting a wife whose earnings were insignificant. He could easily see an enviable side to Michael's predicament.

"They should if that's what they want. But Michael really wants kids badly, and according to Greg, his wife won't adopt because she's obsessed with getting pregnant. That sounds ominous to me. Being pregnant and raising children are two very different things. Some women want one and not the other. There are women who love being a mother and hate being pregnant—and vice versa."

"You liked both. You sound unsympathetic, and you don't know the woman. It's not like you. When Merrit wanted a baby so much she was half-crazy and depressed, you were all sympathy."

"No, I am sympathetic. I wouldn't have given up easily if it had happened to me. I just have a feeling that this is all a lot more complicated than it sounds. Look, the fact that we've gotten so close with him and never laid eyes on her says something very dire about that couple, and thinking as highly of him as I do—"

The doorbell rang, and they heard Jane shout, "I'll get it."

"Hello," Jane said to Michael in a voice heavy with meaning, as though she, personally, had been waiting for him.

"Is something wrong?" he asked curiously, taking off his overcoat and laying it in her outstretched arms.

"Sort of. Not really. I mean, no, nothing's wrong. I just wanted to ask you something."

"Ask away."

"Well, it's a favor, and I don't want my parents to know. Can I call you?" She spoke in a near-whisper, glancing anxiously behind her; her eyes were big with daring.

"You don't want your parents . . ." This was worrisome. He had to think for a moment before he could consent to receive a private call from the Braithwaites' eighteen-year-old daughter. "Well, I suppose . . . of course you can call. Wait," he said, patting his pockets. "Here." He extracted a card from his wallet and handed it to her. He told himself that it would be some girlish nonsense, nothing to worry about, but he continued to feel uneasy. Jane looked and saw that it was a business card, with his office address and number, and she nodded with satisfaction. Yes, that was what she wanted.

She was hanging up Michael's coat when Charles and Anne appeared at the other end of the hallway.

"Michael!" Charles called in welcome.

"Here again." Michael gave his barely there smile.

"Greg told us about your adventure," said Anne, smiling and handing Michael his brandy.

His smile broadened slightly. "You must have seen him yesterday then, because he was still feeling unwell the day before."

"Unprecedentedly hungover. And Carla too, right?"

"So I hear. But I've not been able to reach him or Carla this evening, and I've had extraordinary news on that front this afternoon. Here, have a look at this. Do you mind if I just try Greg again?" Michael handed an envelope to Charles and pulled a cell phone out of his pocket.

Charles pulled a letter out of the envelope and read aloud to Anne, while Michael tried first Greg, then Carla.

"It's from Wyatt Jesse Younger," said Charles, with a snort at the name. " 'Dear Dr. Garrard, Enclosed please find a check made out to the Ecumenical Council in the amount of'—I don't believe it—'2.5 million dollars'! Good God, Michael. But there's a string—'. . . yours to cash on condition that you join me and a group of friends in a conference on libertarian ethics, January 28, 2005'—someplace in Maine. If you can't attend, return check . . . Will fly you there in jet, put you up, et cetera."

"I don't know about this. These are strange people," said Anne, and she called across the room, "Michael, don't go."

"Don't go where?" asked Jane, who had run off to hide Dr. Garrard's card in her backpack.

"Are you joking?" Michael asked, looking quizzically at Anne with the phone to his ear. "Of course, I'd certainly rather not, but with this much money at stake, I couldn't possibly refuse to . . . Carla—at last!" The Braithwaites could hear Carla's shriek from across the room when she heard about the check.

"Carla thinks I should write back counterinviting Younger and Selvnick to attend a meeting of our council. That way I wouldn't have to see them alone, on their turf," Michael said, sitting next to Jane on the sofa.

"What a good idea," said Anne.

"Amazing how rational and practical Carla can be in her advisor role when she's such a madwoman personally," said Charles. "It's a very good idea. This Maine thing is going to be a collection of ideologues and fanatics, and I don't care how big the bribe is, you'd be out of your mind to put yourself at the mercy of this man's plane or hospitality."

"Why?" asked Michael. "I don't mind trying to get Younger to one of our own meetings, but I'll certainly attend this Maine conference to get the money if he says no. How could I not?"

Michael's manner made it clear that he was not persuadable on this question—and that he disapproved of Charles's and Anne's caution. Charles contemplated the moral rift just exposed and reconsidered for a moment. But he himself would not attend a conference of wackos no matter how much money it cost his favorite charity—especially in light of that story about the odd professor refusing to call the elevator. Emotionally, it would be beyond him to tolerate the irrational talk and behavior for more than an hour. Charles saw Jane looking from Michael's face to Anne's and knew before she spoke that she would side with Michael.

"Yeah, how could he not?" Jane asked Anne. "It would be incredibly selfish to pass up all that money for poor people just to avoid listening to some political garbage. There's not really any danger."

Jane's tone was even more accusatory than her words, and Charles could see that Anne was hurt. It wasn't fair either, because Anne was the least selfish human being he had ever met, the most willing to take other people's point of view, no matter how foreign or unsympathetic, the freest with her time, labor, and sympathy, and even the most capable of giving away what she had—at least once she was sure she'd taken care of her own. How could Jane be so unfair to such a giving mother!

"You're right, sweetie," said Anne, with a frank air. "I'm putting minor detriment to a friend above major help to strangers."

Michael said nothing, for this was just the truth—and Anne had put it very well. How generous of her, to admit her error so openly, candidly.

"But don't go, Michael," Anne pleaded. "It just doesn't feel right to me that you should go."

Now Michael was mystified. How could Anne recognize so clearly that her position was false yet stick with it? Jane exhaled loudly, through her teeth, in the way teenagers do to express forbidden contempt. Her whole life, her parents had driven her crazy doing what Anne had just done.

Charles felt sorry for Anne. She wasn't selfish—just protective. He felt as she did about Michael's flying off to Maine in Younger's jet to convene with lunatics.

"Here's another idea," said Charles. "Make it just ten or so people from the council and invite them here. Anne and I can subdue eccentric libertarians—especially Anne. She's poison to fanaticism. She personally destroyed the young socialist group at her high school just by attending meetings faithfully."

Anne reacted to this suggestion with the same relief that she had when Charles made one of his calming paternal interventions in the children's quarrels. "That's a good idea. Of course, we can handle them," she said. "Make it for dinner, Michael. It's the least we can do."

"You're joking," Michael said, but they insisted that they weren't.

"Make sure you invite Peter," she said. "And we can ask Morris and Merrit, Charles. They love to argue politics."

"So it's settled. Done," said Charles. "Invite Younger, Selvnick, and ten or so of your colleagues on the council to dinner here, and don't return the check yet. Just offer to return it and tell him your invitation stands with or without it." Charles was authoritative, in charge, even though he saw that this made Michael feel awkward. Just as Anne said, Michael wasn't used to being protected and directed; Charles took plea-

sure in having made him accept such treatment. It avenged Anne, and re-
deemed her too. He was pleased with himself.

"He'll accept too," said Anne. "You watch."

Michael could not resent their interference, though it made him feel
shy and embarrassed. The Braithwaites might have been deficient in their
sense of charitable obligation, but they got things right when friendship
and loyalty were concerned. He hovered at the edge of judgment about
these new friends, then decided to continue to be fond of them despite
their blind spot. In fact, he loved them all the more.

At one o'clock that morning, when Michael was long gone and the rest of
the Braithwaite family were sleeping, Andrés and Jane lay on her bed,
watching the end of *The Matrix* on her tiny DVD player. Jane had met him
at the door at half past eleven, while her parents were still laughing and
talking with Dr. Garrard, and Andrés had slipped in, carrying the red bag
with the DVD from the video rental store. The two slipped past Ellen's
room, into Jane's, and locked the door. They began watching lying on their
stomachs, six inches apart. But by this time, Jane was nestled comfortably
against his chest, his hands were in her hair, then on her shoulders and,
tentatively, on her back and belly, and he occasionally pressed a kiss on the
top of her head. When the movie was over, she turned her face up to his
expectantly, but with obvious effort, he held back.

"We better not get started," he said. "Too risky."

"We already got started," she said.

"No more," he said. "Don't do that, Janie." She was stretching herself
out against him, kissing his neck and shoulders when he withheld his
mouth. He sat up and, with gentle skill, wrestled to get a grip on her
hands and pressed them up against her own mouth. "Hey, you like to
dance?" he asked, turning his restraining grip into a caress.

She saw with surprise that he really intended to resist her, and sitting
up to look at him, she fell in love. His thin face showed such a struggle of
wistfulness and determination, and his eyes were so tender, that she
couldn't help it.

"I love . . . to dance," she said, awed by what she felt for him. The pressure of her feelings opened cracks and faults in her thinking; whole continents of her mind slid unpredictably here and there.

"I'll take you dancing Saturday night, okay? I know a great place. But you have to tell your parents a story where you're going, and now I gotta go. Look—it's past one. I have a test first period."

Jane was entranced by the prospect of going dancing with Andrés. They gathered his things and, in their stocking feet, Andrés carrying his shoes, padded down the hallway to the door. When he said good night, he smiled and kissed her on the mouth—just enough of a kiss to leave his taste with her. To keep it as long as possible, Jane did not brush her teeth that night.

CHAPTER 16

On Saturday night, Carla made dinner for Greg at her place. Overall, he thought, sitting on her sofa afterward, the evening was turning out to be dreadful, an experience to be recollected in irritability—far from what he had expected. The roaches were appalling, not nearly as funny as they had sounded—not funny at all—and his appetite deserted him. After about an hour, the ubiquitous cat hair had him tearing, sneezing, and constantly dripping at the nose. His allergy had never been so severe. But, then, Carla's apartment probably posed an Olympian challenge to the immune system. Its ambience was inhospitable to any weak-minded yearning for comfort or beauty or pleasure, for indulgences spiritual or physical.

Carla was a classic example of a Morningside Heights political ascetic. Greg's priestly work brought him in touch with many of these. Such people would tell you they loved good food and good times, and they aspired to bonhomie. But in fact, when it came to the aesthetics of daily life, they were blind and deaf. Greg detected these deficiencies in Carla, but still he pursued her because she was an extraordinary woman. He had never met anyone else with her passionate dedication, her strength of will and energy, her genuine indifference to what anyone thought, her radical egalitarianism. Next to Carla, other women seemed colorless, conformist, conventional, and passive. Greg liked looking at her too. He liked her thin lips and shaggy hair, her tight little figure.

"Coffee? Tea?" she asked him, falling into a chair next to the sofa, where he sat with his arm stretched invitingly across the back.

"No thanks," he said in a stuffed-up voice, and his arm fell to his side as he gave up hope of getting it around Carla.

"Good," she replied, with a sigh of scornful relief.

"You look tired," he said.

"I'm dead," she said. "It's hard to come home and cook all night after working all day."

"Oh, er . . . sorry. Sorry you went to all the trouble."

"Yeah, especially when you didn't want anything to eat anyway. What, did you stop off for pizza on the way or something?"

By now, Greg had repeatedly discovered that Carla was an unreasonable human being, but he kept forgetting it in his admiration for her good qualities, and over and over again he was forced to rediscover it. This made for a dizzying cycle in his mind of alternating and conflicting opinions and emotions about Carla. Though the cycle had begun soon after he met her, Greg became fully conscious of it only now.

"Don't look at me that way," said Carla irritably.

"Hm?"

"Like you're about to ask me whether I get chest pains after meals or exercise."

"Sorry. I just couldn't help wondering about that."

Carla wouldn't smile, and there was another long, burdened silence.

"Carla," Greg said. "I'm just not afraid of you. No matter what you do, I'm not going to be afraid of you."

"What an icky thing to say." In fact, that sort of talk made Carla shudder with distaste. Still, there was something to what he said. She was rough, and Greg was soft. Intimacy with her could only injure such a gentle person, and until now she had attributed Greg's unwarranted trust in her, his emotional unguardedness, to pure naïveté, lack of experience and insight. Evidently, he understood more than she had realized.

"And you don't need to be afraid to be nice to me—"

"Shut up, Greg."

". . . like you think that's going to mislead me into—"

"I've had it with this. I don't want to have this talk with you, and I'll ask you to leave if you keep it up. Actually, yes, just go, okay?" She stood up and headed to the closet to get his coat.

"I'll stop," said Greg.

Carla hesitated, but she still didn't like the way he looked at her, as though he was thinking that mucky stuff even if he wasn't saying it.

In fact, what Greg was thinking was that he had to try to reform her. Of course, he knew you weren't supposed to do that. You were supposed to accept people the way they are; they could only change themselves. But Greg had never really been persuaded by that kind of thinking. You couldn't—shouldn't—think that way about someone you loved. Greg was startled to find that he was arguing with himself about how to love Carla. Neighborly, brotherly love, he tried to tell himself, but he knew better, and besides, he had noticed that brotherly love often turned enthusiastic about the other kind. He pushed the theological rationalizations aside. You're just plain in love with her, he told himself. You're in love with someone you think is impossibly obnoxious and the worst dinner companion and cook you've ever met.

"So, the counteroffer worked, and Charles and Anne are going to host the libertarian duo," Carla was saying. "That's a relief. Garrard going off to Maine with that pair—they would have locked him up in a lobster trap or a woodshed or something until he converted to libertarianism. You know, when he said those guys could have us murdered and the law wouldn't interfere, he was right. If they decided to hold him, no one would ever be able to prove a thing."

"You're being paranoid again."

"Even Michael said it's not paranoid."

"Carla, why don't you practice law anymore?"

"I can't take it. It was all crooked plea bargains forced on people because they were just too scared of the long sentences to insist on a trial. Then I lost a case. One of my clients—just a young kid, twenty years old—got twenty-five to life, and I was the one who convinced him to turn down a plea bargain because he was innocent. I saw where they sent him, and what they did to him. I was so upset, I had to take a two-month medical leave for emotional problems. That's why I just work for groups and organizations now, never individuals. If I make a mistake, no one goes into a living hell or anything. Jesus Christ, are you crying?"

"Well, what you're saying is worth crying about," he said, "but no. Allergies." He wiped his eyes and blew his nose.

"Absurd to cry," Carla said. She still suspected him of crying. She swung her legs over one arm of her chair and reclined against the other. "I used to cry a lot. Now I'm happier. Strange, but right now I have such an urge for a cigarette, and I haven't smoked one for more than ten years. Hey, let's go get ice cream, all right?"

"If you want, but it's kind of cold for ice cream. You want to come to my place and have a glass of wine? Someone gave me a really nice bottle." Greg wanted Carla, but Carla's apartment was unendurable. "It's just a few blocks. Don't you want to see where I live?" he asked hopefully. He stood and held out his hand to pull her up.

"Wait a minute. You live in a goddam church, right? Oh, no. No, no, no. Forget that. Besides, you'll insist on walking me home, and we'll spend half the night running back and forth."

"I swear I won't offer to walk you back, and I don't live in the church. I have a couple of rooms in the ... uh ... in the parish house." He was momentarily embarrassed to be living in a parish house. "It's my home. I have visitors just like anyone else. Come on, Carla."

This time she took his hand and let him pull her out of the armchair. He was stronger than she expected, and somehow the warmth and firmness of his hand was surprising. *Maybe I imagined he was immaterial,* she thought. *The holy spirit or something.*

As they walked down a hallway in the parish house at Saint Ursula's, they encountered the rector, a bristly old man with a long thicket eyebrow. He eyed Carla skeptically, then nodded and moved off too quickly for introductions. He seemed to be heading somewhere with great purpose.

"His bedtime," Greg remarked, then regretted having let himself appear so knowledgeable about the rector's intimate habits. Carla, he saw, was thoroughly uncomfortable. He had never seen her without the buffer of her cool. Her novel vulnerability made him feel remorseful for insisting she come over.

Carla looked curiously around Greg's miniature apartment. It was, in fact, to her taste, a very nice room, warm, boyishly neat and organized except for a scattering of CDs and books, prints of Renaissance paintings of saints on the wall along with some framed French posters, and a desk with a computer and stacks of papers. There was a kitchenette at one end. She peered into a small bedroom off a short hallway.

"It's very Greg," she said. She walked to his desk and studied the papers lying there. "Oh, God, you write the *Saint Ursula's Biweekly Newsletter*? Greg, we have to do something about you." She had pulled herself back together, a little anyway. She was still nervous, and Greg felt protective toward her.

He uncorked his bottle and poured a large glass for both of them. It would help her relax. They sat on his sofa and sipped. Greg sat close to her with an arm stretched out behind her on the sofa back. She seemed unaware of this for a time, but after he poured her a second glass, when his arm sank gently to her shoulder, she pulled away and stared at him coolly.

"Greg, we're both over thirty. Don't act like a high school boy trying to trick me into kissing you."

"Then don't act like a high school girl who doesn't want to," he replied, somewhat belatedly. It had taken him a good twenty seconds to figure out what high-schoolish thing he might have done.

"How about a thirty-five-year-old who doesn't want to? When was your last girlfriend?"

"About eight years ago. When was your last boyfriend?"

"That depends on how you define 'boyfriend.' "

"I mean someone serious."

"Maybe never. Let me tell you something, Greg. I can't stand your wishy-washiness. I can't stand the way you never push back. You're soft and weak, and that brings out the worst in me and you make me hate myself. But you're smart and available and not bad-looking, and I'm really lonely, so we keep falling in together. We've got to stop it or bad things are going to happen."

"I think you're wrong about me and everything—everything," said Greg, without hesitating this time, "especially about what you want."

"Did you hear what I just said to you? I can't stand the fact that you're not even insulted. That's sick." Carla stood and went to get her coat off a hook near the door.

"You just don't understand yet, Carla," said Greg, hearing in his own voice the patience with which Anne Braithwaite spoke to Jane.

Carla looked at him bitterly. "Oh, the hell with it," she said. She threw the coat on the floor and went back to the sofa, curled up in Greg's lap, and kissed him. At first, he was astonished at how sweetly she did this— not at all the way anyone would have imagined. But his second thought was: No, of course. This is what I knew.

Hours later, Carla crept out into the chilly dawn, before anyone else in the parish house stirred, and Greg waved to her from his second-floor window. Then he stood alone in his room in a state of something like ecstasy.

Earlier on that same Saturday evening, Jane had run into Greg as she hurried south on Broadway. A guilty conscience caused her to greet him with an excessively bright friendliness, for she was on her way to meet Andrés at Broadway and 116th. Andrés was already standing there when she arrived, leaning against the railing of the subway stairs. He watched her approach with his hands in his pockets, his face unreadable. She thought he looked very cool, with his hair slicked back and a red and gold braided bracelet fastened festively around his bony wrist. He turned and fell into stride with her as soon as she came up, and they skipped down the subway steps side by side. But they didn't look each other in the eye and smile a little until they reached the bottom.

The club Andrés knew was in Queens; they rode two different subway lines to get there. By the time they arrived, it was already packed with a young, mostly Latino crowd. The music, audible at the door as they paid the cover, was some kind of salsa. Jane recognized the rhythm but didn't know the dance; she didn't know any Latin dancing, in fact, except the old-fashioned kind that they still taught in ballroom-dance classes. The two of them followed a long, shabby hallway to a room that was smaller than Jane had expected, and dark, crowded, and loud. A deejay sat on a raised platform on the far side, leaning over to talk to three men with po-maded hair, dark blazers, shirts, and ties. The floor was worn wood, smooth from use. Good for dancing, Jane thought, but she detected some roughness in the atmosphere, some threatening current that seemed as though it could suddenly gather strength and flow in any direction. You couldn't know what was going to happen here. Jane moved closer to An-drés in the dimness and noise, somewhat timidly surveying this scene, and they automatically reached for each other's hands. Then Jane's fear gave way to a surge of exhilaration.

"How do you know about this place?" she asked Andrés, gripping his hand excitedly now.

"My oldest cousin, Cristina, she loves this place. I came here with her a couple times."

"With your cousin?"

"Why not? We both like to dance. There's a lot of people to dance with here."

"I would have thought you were too shy to do that."

"I'm not shy," he said, but he smiled shyly. "Come on." He pulled her by the hand. "Let's dance."

"You have to teach me this. I don't know how."

Andrés was pleased to oblige, and Jane caught on quickly. "You do like dancing, don't you," he said happily, his hands on her waist. And watching her concentrate on her steps and hips, excited and intent, he had a moment of such joy that he couldn't risk looking in her eyes.

They danced for nearly two hours. Then they were tired but even more elated; now they had a common secret history in this expedition and an immense sense of shared possibility. Anything could happen—and anything that happened would belong to both of them.

"We better go," Andrés half shouted into Jane's ear, over the din.

"It's only ten-thirty," she said. "I told them I wouldn't be home till midnight."

"Subway is slow on Saturday night," he said, and he pulled her by the hand toward the exit. But they had luck catching trains and got back to Morningside Heights quickly. "Let's go down to Riverside and walk," he said, looking at his watch.

"My parents would die," she said, and happily followed his lead down 116th Street, "but it's perfectly safe. I go down after dark all the time."

"You had lots of dance lessons, didn't you," he asked, as they strolled along the promenade, hand in hand.

"All my life. If you want to be in opera, you have to know how to move nowadays. And you can't be fat."

"Jeez. Like what kind—ballet or modern or what?"

"Both, and also ballroom and minuets and you name it. And acting, improvisation. You want to have every advantage because it's so competitive. It all gave me a stomachache, but if I do well at this audition—" Jane said, stopping in the middle of her thought.

"What?"

"I don't know," she said, shrugging. "I guess it would still be good."

Andrés thought he understood her. She was implying that things were so different now, she wasn't sure what she wanted anymore, and *he* was what made them different. That shook him. He didn't know if he wanted her to take him that seriously. Nonetheless, his mood plummeted as midnight approached. In a few minutes, he would no longer be Jane's partner in some shared world of limitless possibility. Jane would return to her safe, affectionate home and her attentive, competent parents. He would go up to the Bronx and sleep on Juan's floor, or if he couldn't stand that idea tonight, maybe he would try to sneak back into Jane's building and sleep on the floor in Gabriela's room, even though Gabriela would be mad. It would hurt Jane, he knew, even to be confronted with the facts of his life. She would have been destroyed if she had to live them.

"Jane, I'm on probation," he said.

"So is my ex-boyfriend," she said. "What did you do?"

"Nothing. But they said I was dealing drugs. Actually, it was my mother's boyfriend's stuff. There was a bust and he stuck it in my pack so he wouldn't get caught with it. I was only fourteen, but they didn't believe me. I got a suspended sentence and probation until I graduate. They told me I had to admit it or they'd send me away to some juvenile facility, so I said I did it but I didn't. It made me crazy because I never touched any drugs, never sold any drugs. I hate drugs. I hate dealers. You couldn't ever hate them the way I do."

"Andrés, this is really bad," Jane said. The street lamp exaggerated the shadows of anger and pity on her face.

Andrés regretted telling her. He shouldn't have anything to do with a girl who was so soft and easily hurt, but that, though it was true, made him angry. After all, she started the whole thing.

"You ought to . . . hire a lawyer and sue them," she said.

He gave a short, dry laugh. "That wouldn't be too smart. Jane, you know what? You shouldn't hang around with me. It was fun tonight, but now I'm starting to think we better cool it. With me around, things could get too scary for you."

"You're really wrong," Jane said, hurt in her voice.

She suddenly climbed up onto the stone wall that ran along the promenade at the edge of a bluff, with a drop of nearly thirty feet on its opposite side. Jane stood on the wall, with the lamplight on her face, and looked down at Andrés. He glanced up at her, then continued walking, ignoring her as she kept pace with him up on the wall.

"Hey, Andrés," she said, "watch this." She picked up her pace to a run and executed a series of balletic leaps in the near-dark, all on the wall. She terrified Andrés.

"Stop it. Get down!" he yelled, and he began running to catch up. "Jane, stop it. You're crazy."

He sounded so panicked, so grief-stricken, that she did stop.

"What, do you think that impresses me or something?" he said. "If you break your neck for no reason? Fake danger. That's what people like you think scary is. Like bungee jumping or mountain climbing." He laughed contemptuously.

"People like me? That's not very friendly," Jane said, sitting down on the wall. "Why are you so down on me all of a sudden?"

"But I already see, Janie. You can't do this. I can see you won't be able to handle it. It's not a matter of giving you a chance or being unfriendly. It's just too hard. And you've got everything to lose and nothing to gain. Unlike me. I can't do that to you."

"You're always weighing who gets more and who gets less. You're underestimating both of us. I wish you would understand. My life is messed up. I'm in trouble, and I'm all alone. But you could help me. Please, Andrés."

———————

CHAPTER 17

On Monday morning, standing outside the school gate, Jane pulled a battered business card out of her jeans pocket, studied it, then made a call on her cell phone.

"Is Dr. Garrard in? This is Jane Braithwaite calling."

Michael took Jane's call immediately and asked her to come to his office after school. At a little past four, she sat in his East Side waiting room with several wealthy thyroid and kidney patients until a white-clad nurse led her through a maze of tiny rooms to an office that, though simple, seemed elegant to Jane, who still received the care of a pediatrician in a shabby, child-pocked medical suite.

Michael rose to shake Jane's hand—as though she were adult, an equal, she thought—and invited her to sit on a sofa. He sat next to her in an armchair. Feeling suddenly shy, she delayed having to look at him or talk by pretending to study the objects on the table before her—a modern statuette, a book about ancient medicine, and what Jane thought was a rock used as a paperweight but was unexpectedly light. It was inscribed to "Milli."

"Milli?" she asked.

"When I was a medical student," he said, "they called me Milligram—because my initials are m.g."

"Milligram," Jane repeated, with a little laugh, looking at him finally. "Milli for short."

Michael looked at her with the expression that, with his friends, passed for a smile.

"So, tell me what it's all about," he said, with an encouraging, if puzzled, frown. Michael found Jane disarmingly attractive. Her attempts to be adult and serious were, if anything, even more charming than the playfulness he had seen in her at home.

"It's about my . . . it's about someone who I think is really sick who won't go see a doctor. She tells my mother that she goes to the doctor and it's mono or chronic fatigue syndrome or something like that, but I found out she was lying. She hasn't seen a doctor for a long time. I'm really scared for her."

"And you want me to . . . ?"

"Or if you can't, maybe try to help me get her to someone else? But you see she's really poor." When the moment arrived, Jane was too embarrassed to ask him to examine Gabriela. It occurred to her only now that she was asking him for a lot.

Jane's genuine anxiety for her unnamed acquaintance moved Michael, which was not surprising, for he was also moved by her childishly bony elbows and the way her collar was tucked half under and half out of her sweater. He sighed and frowned a little more deeply. "All right," he said. "Now. It would help, in this sort of situation, if I knew who we were talking about and what the circumstances are. Why is this your problem? Why not go to your parents?"

"I can't."

"But I think you have to. Jane, this doesn't sound like something they'd have any reason to be angry about."

"Dr. Garrard, did my parents ever mention to you anything about someone staying in Mom's office?"

"Someone was staying there before Christmas—your maid, wasn't it? I heard you singing to her in there. Is this who you're talking about? But why on earth can't you tell Anne?"

"I'm afraid they'll make her leave if they know she's lying. They talk about it all the time. She said she wanted to stay for just a couple of days, and she's been there for months now. She told them she has an apartment lined up for February, but she doesn't. My parents are so annoyed. They'd never ask you for help, and they'd never let me ask you either."

"Well . . . hmm. And how do you know she's lying about seeing a doctor?"

"Her nephew."

Jane blushed unexpectedly—needlessly, it seemed to Michael. He grew thoughtful, and his expression changed. He looked at her benignly, a breaking understanding detectable only in a tilt of his head. Jane nonetheless detected it.

"Things are really complicated," she said, grimacing and avoiding his eye.

Michael stretched his upper lip down to his lower and pondered for a time. "Even if she would agree to see someone—me or someone else," he said at last, "I couldn't agree to keep secrets with you from your parents. Let's go back a minute. Just what is wrong with her?"

"Gabriela Leon is her name. She's weak and gets all these headaches and sweats, and she says it hurts here"—Jane pointed to her side—"and sometimes everywhere. This week she hardly ever got out of bed. She has a hard time just walking to the bathroom. But my parents don't know how much worse she is because she fakes it when she sees them. She sits up and stands, like she's okay. She's afraid they'll call the city and get her sent off to some awful hospital for poor people."

"How old is she?"

"About forty, I guess. I'm not too sure."

Now Michael turned slightly away from Jane and thought again, staring into space for what seemed to Jane a very long time, so long that she started slightly when he spoke again.

"Jane, I agree with you that this sounds serious," he said, decisiveness in his voice now. "She must see a doctor. So I'll agree to see her but on condition that you tell your parents that you spoke to me about it."

"They'll be mad."

His narrow lips made another feint at smiling. "You can handle it."

She bent her head to consider this. "I suppose," she said.

"And that would be the right thing. I believe you've done the right thing to come to me. Now do the right thing and tell your parents. Agreed?" he asked, holding out his hand.

She shook it and nodded. "But what if I can't talk her into coming?"

"Then I'll make a house call."

"Would you really? Thank you very, very much, Dr. Garrard. Andrés is going to be so relieved."

"Her nephew?" he asked, indifferently, his eyebrows lifting a little.

"Yes. He lived with her until she started staying at our place. But he's only eighteen. He's a senior in high school. He tries to help her. He has a weekend job, but he has to buy his own food and he can't pay for—"

"Of course not," said Michael, in a way that deprecated the possibility most comfortingly to Jane.

He walked Jane to the door, and the white-clad nurse, who wore a plastic badge that said MARIE COLLIER, returned to lead her back to the waiting room.

"So I'll expect to hear from you soon," he said as Jane put on her coat. "You know, we mustn't delay." His voice was both serious and tender.

Jane smiled so gratefully at him that Ms. Collier looked from her to Michael and back, curiously. "Cohen waiting for you in three," she told him.

Michael picked up the patient's file from his desk and, on his way to the examining room, tried to imagine what it must be like to be the parent of a vivid, volatile young woman like Jane. He wished he hadn't promised Adriana to come home for dinner.

CHAPTER 18

T he storm over Jane's visit to Michael's office was violent but brief, erupting as soon as she got home and subsiding before dinner. She should have gone to her parents. She should not have imposed on their friend. Charles and Anne were angry and mortified. They phoned Michael to apologize, but he insisted that he was pleased that Jane had called on him. She had felt obligated to keep secret from her parents what Gabriela had kept secret, he said, and while that was probably a mistake, it was a good-hearted, well-intentioned one. Michael only wanted to talk about when he could see Gabriela. Anne went to Gabriela and, now that Jane's concern had sharpened her perception, she saw with horror how she had deteriorated in just a few days.

"I'll bring her in right away—whenever you tell me to," Anne told Michael. He could hear the alarm in her voice. "She's very bad. I'm not even sure she can walk. I had no idea—"

"Then have her taken to the hospital—tonight," he said. "Call an ambulance. I'll call ahead for you so they'll be expecting her. And I'll come right away."

"This is very, very good of you, Michael, and—"

"Anne, can you get hold of someone in her family? She should have her own people there with her."

Anne promised to try to find someone, but this request sounded ominous to her. In a few minutes, she went to Gabriela's room carrying an overnight bag.

"The doctor says you have to go to the hospital tonight. I'm calling an ambulance. He'll come to you there. And we need someone to go with you. Who should I call?"

"I'm not going," said Gabriela.

"Yes, you're going," Anne said. "You're going if we have to tie you up. Charles is calling an ambulance right now. I'll pack a bag for you." Anne opened a dresser drawer and was surprised to find jockey shorts and T-shirts among Gabriela's things. She looked at Gabriela, who looked back but said nothing. "Phone numbers, Gabriela. You want to be there all alone? Who are we going to call?"

Gabriela began to cry. "If I go in there, I'll never get out again. I know it," she said. Her voice was hoarse and broken by sobs.

Anne sat on the bed and patted her shoulder. "Lots of people are afraid of hospitals," she said. "Gabriela, such a good doctor, our friend Dr. Garrard, is coming to see you there. He helps all kinds of people. Last year when the archbishop was sick, who did he see? Dr. Garrard—same as you. So don't be afraid. He'll help you, I know it. Give me phone numbers. Come on. You want to leave the doctor standing there waiting for you? And he's at Columbia Presbyterian—the best."

"I never been there."

"The best. Everyone's so nice at that place. I had all four babies there. Where are your phone numbers?"

They heard a gentle tapping at the door.

"My nephew," Gabriela said.

Anne opened the door to Andrés, who looked startled to see her.

"Your aunt is very sick, Andrés," said Anne. "We're taking her to Columbia Presbyterian Hospital, and a friend of ours, a very good doctor, is going to look at her. Can you go up there with her?"

"Sure, yes," he said breathlessly, lowering his backpack to the floor. He looked at Anne with frightened eyes. Poor boy, she thought. He's too young for this.

"Call Juan," said Gabriela. "Juan will come."

"Yeah," said Andrés. He pulled a cell phone out of his pocket and soon was speaking rapid Spanish. "He's in Queens now on a job," he told them. "He'll meet us at the hospital as soon as he can."

"That's fine. Andrés, I'll wait with you there until he comes."

"No," said Gabriela and Andrés together.

"I'm sorry, but I will. He's too young, Gabriela. Be sensible. Andrés, you hold on to this bag for your aunt, and see if she needs anything else. I'll go get ready too."

Anne walked out, leaving the door between the kitchen and Gabriela's room standing wide open for the first time in months. It seemed strange. Jane, who was in the kitchen, stared through the doorway into Andrés's teary eyes. The wall had come down now, and she had done it. If Gabriela died, would Jane have killed her? If she had just stayed out of it, wouldn't things have gone on in a magical, mischievous way forever? Jane broke into silent sobs, and Andrés, looking furtively around, came out of Gabriela's room and kissed her.

"Don't worry," he whispered.

"Maybe I shouldn't have called the doctor," said Jane.

"No, it's good," he said. Anne's voice approached, and he quickly stepped back into Gabriela's room.

Juan stayed in the examining room with Gabriela while Anne and Andrés sat in the waiting room. It was more than an hour until Michael came out to them. He pulled Anne aside.

"Tell me," she said.

"This is probably very serious, whatever it is. We can't be sure until the test results come in, but leukemia is the main thing we're worrying about. And if it is leukemia, it's a disgrace that they didn't manage to diagnose it at that clinic she went to. In fact, my main hope is that it's so unlikely that they would have missed it that it's going to turn out to be something else."

"But if it is leukemia?"

"They would treat her here. The problem is, treatment is usually useful at an earlier point in the disease. Everything would depend on how she responds. There's a good drug, but it's less effective in advanced cases. And she's too sick now for a bone-marrow transplant. The delay will have been very damaging. But let's not talk about all this until we know more."

"Will you talk to Andrés?"

"Of course."

Michael and Andrés paced the waiting room, in grave conversation, for a long time. Twice Andrés almost gave in to tears. Finally Michael put his hand on his shoulder and beckoned Anne to come to them.

"Andrés, where do you live?" he asked. He now looked at Andrés and saw that he was not well. Too thin—his color, his posture. Something wrong here, he thought—something more than his being upset about his aunt. Earlier, Michael had been too distracted by Gabriela's situation to pay attention to him. This boy was seriously run-down.

Andrés blushed. "Um, really with my aunt but lately with . . . with Juan's mother up in the Bronx."

"Well, that's a bit of a trip for you, so you'd better say good night to your aunt and go home now. She's resting, and Mr. Santiago is with her. You should get some rest too—and eat something. There's nothing anybody can do until we get the test results. You can come back tomorrow during visiting hours, and there's a number you can call anytime to find out how she's doing."

"I'll give it to him," said Anne. "But, Andrés, stay at our place tonight. It's closer. You can have Gabriela's bed."

"No, I better not—"

"I insist," said Anne. "We can go back together." And she held his hand.

Michael looked down at Anne tenderly. How good she was. She would not send the troubled boy off alone into the night any more than she would send Gabriela out of her home. But would she make this offer if she knew what Michael guessed about Jane and Andrés? Actually, he thought, she might, and that was a comforting thought because he suspected the boy was lying about living with Juan's mother. He wondered where he did live. This was a good boy, if he was any judge, and he would keep his guesses to himself.

Anne and Andrés took a cab from the hospital back to Morningside Heights, and Anne asked questions. She was very skilled at asking children questions, and this boy was hardly more than a child. How long had he lived with his aunt? Did he ever see his mother? Did he like school? Had he heard from any colleges? Did he stay in touch with his cousins who were now with his grandmother (whom they would call as soon as they heard something definite)? This is an unusual boy, Anne thought as she listened to his responses, and the perception increased her horror at his situation in life, the outlines of which emerged through her questions. This boy, unsupported and unprotected, was trying to do for himself what she and Charles together, with all their resources, found hard to do for their privileged, secure children—and he was on the verge of succeeding. She remembered that Andrés had had no dinner and had refused to have anything at the hospital.

"You have to have a sandwich when we get home," she told him. "I insist. Look how thin you are."

Jane came into the kitchen when they returned and looked questioningly at Andrés behind her mother's back. He shrugged helplessly.

"Jane, Andrés is going to stay over tonight," said Anne. "He can have Gabriela's bed. Would you please get some fresh sheets? We're having sandwiches. Want me to make you one too, sweetie?"

Charles joined the three of them at the kitchen table, and they discussed Gabriela over the late supper.

"Dr. Garrard is one of the finest doctors in the city," Charles told Andrés reassuringly, "and also a very good man."

"I could tell," Andrés said. He would have expected to be shy and ill at ease with these rich, accomplished people, but in fact he was comfortable, maybe more at ease than at Gabriela's, where they didn't really want him and thought he was stuck-up and a smartass. As long as he didn't look at Jane, he felt at home. She avoided looking at him too, and spoke to him only once.

"Are you going to school tomorrow?" she asked him.

"Yes," said Charles and Anne together. Their parental instincts were awakened on this boy's behalf; *they* would be responsible for Gabriela, and he must continue a child's life.

"You'll feel better if you keep busy," Anne told him. "Call your aunt before you go in the morning, and if you want, call me on your lunch hour and I'll give you news. Don't worry. If there's any emergency, we'll get to you—but from what Dr. Garrard said, there's not going to be. And you can go up to the hospital after school."

He nodded obediently. He didn't mind letting them decide these things for him. His brain was too tired.

In a few minutes, he was fast asleep in a real bed with sheets and blankets and a pillow—a rare luxury—and feeling it safe at last to let down, he slept so deeply that Anne had to shake him awake in the morning, and he looked up bewildered into her face.

"That is a very nice boy," Charles said at the breakfast table after Andrés had left for school. "Obviously quite bright too. Stuart, eat your cereal."

"I want eggs," said Stuart miserably, "like Gabriela makes." His disappointment was odd, for Gabriela's eggs had appeared on the breakfast table only twice.

"Dr. Garrard is taking care of Gabriela," Anne said to Stuart. "Isn't that good?"

"Of course Andrés is bright," said Jane, whose heart had beaten quickly at her father's words. "He goes to City, you know."

"Against all the odds. He's one of those kids who beat the odds," said Charles.

"Not us," said Ellen. "We're ordinary kids with undeserved advantages and privileges. It's all because you got us educational toys."

"Never!" said Anne. "I gave you what fit your emotional lives. I figured the rest would take care of itself." Of course, wise parenting had given her children big advantages in life, but surely they were not advantages stolen from other people, she told herself. To be a good parent, you needn't exploit or underpay or exclude or commit any of those other social crimes that keep other people down unfairly. We're obligated to be good parents, no matter if it does improve our children's chances for Harvard or Carnegie Hall.

"I *want* toys," said Gilbert resentfully.

Charles would have been surprised at his wife's musings on their children's advantages, for he himself sat wondering whether the understanding, care, and affection they had lavished on their children had disadvantaged them, made them less strong and good, even less sensitive, than a boy like Andrés who had never been given anything.

"*That* must be what's wrong with us," said Jane. "Our development was stunted because we didn't have educational toys."

CHAPTER 19

Gabriela was diagnosed with a chronic type of leukemia that, untreated, had entered a crisis. They would begin treating it now, but they were not optimistic. Michael told Anne that the mishandling of Gabriela's case had probably cost her years of life. He was distressed by the case—by the medical incompetence, Gabriela's self-neglect, her ignorance and terror, and Juan's and Andrés's grief.

"You'll take medicine," Michael told Gabriela, "and we'll see how you do. We may try other things later."

"But I have to stay here?" she asked him.

"For a while. As soon as you're stronger, you can go home and come in for treatments. Right now, we want to watch you."

Her eyes moved back and forth as she considered this, and Michael suspected that she had nowhere to go but to the Braithwaites. He would have to speak with them.

Juan and Andrés, too, realized that Gabriela had to have a home.

"If she had a place," said Andrés, "maybe she wouldn't ever have gotten so sick."

That made sense to Juan. Not having a place to live broke you down.

Juan himself had felt kind of that way ever since Gabriela lost her apartment. People always died when they didn't have a place—like the lady who lived on the sidewalk on 110th Street by Central Park all those months, then one morning she's dead on a park bench, sitting upright—only in her forties.

"I'm gonna quit school and get a job," said Andrés.

"No way," said Juan. "With—what?—four, five months until you graduate?"

"It doesn't matter. I'm not going to college. Even with a scholarship, I couldn't afford it."

"It'll work out. They're gonna want you bad. Look, *I'm* gonna get a place for Gabriela. We'll bring her home, and everything will be fine. Take my word. Hey, I know a guy who has leukemia for fifteen years. We'll take care of her. She'll be fine."

"Juan, I have to stay at your place for a while. I can't stay in Gabriela's room anymore."

"That's okay. Pretty soon I'll find a place for all of us, and we'll get the girls back. That'll cheer her up."

"Where?"

"Just leave everything to me. You don't realize how much money this is gonna take—say eight hundred, nine hundred a month, plus big deposits, plus some beds and a lot of stuff. We need a couple thousand at least—maybe more. It's not easy to pick up that kind of bread."

When Michael heard that Andrés was talking about dropping out of school to get a job, he called on his charitable connections, pulled strings, and smoothed things at the hospital so that Gabriela could stay despite her Medicaid problems. Gabriela would be taken care of, he told Andrés. His job was to try to graduate even though it would be hard to concentrate.

Andrés didn't talk to Juan about getting an apartment for nearly two weeks, but he could see that Juan had begun making efforts. He made many calls from the hospital waiting room, took unexplained trips, and once disappeared altogether for three days. Andrés got worried, and Gabriela told him sternly that he was not to call the police—as though he would make that mistake twice.

Just as living in Anne's office had come to feel routine and normal, so now did a life that revolved around Gabriela's hospital room. With treatment, Gabriela began to feel a little better, which calmed everyone. Andrés did his homework in the room, showered in its shower, and even slept there when the other bed was empty—as, unaccountably, it often seemed to be—and one of the friendly nurses was on duty. Otherwise he slept on the floor in Juan's room. He met Jane when he could—on the way to the hospital or afterward, in the park if it wasn't too cold. Soon Jane began to visit Gabriela with him, and it quickly became an open secret among the four of them—Gabriela, Andrés, Jane, and Dr. Garrard—that the young people were a couple. Michael had a bad conscience about keeping Charles and Anne in the dark, but he had grown very fond of Jane and Andrés, and after all, it wasn't really any of his business. He often slipped a couple of twenties into Andrés's shirt pocket and was irritably insistent if Andrés protested, and he told the cashiers in the hospital cafeteria not to charge Andrés for meals but to save the slips for him to pay. Andrés quickly began to put on weight, and his color and posture improved— changes that Michael observed with satisfaction.

Jane, too, tried to take care of Andrés. She lent him a laptop for doing homework, sat with him in the laundromat on 109th Street, and brought him little bags of cookies and apples along with videos for watching in Gabriela's room. He accepted her gifts and was greedy for her company. But in five years, he thought, he'd probably be selling jeans at the Gap or waiting tables in one of Juan's restaurants, writing poems on napkins during his breaks, and she'd be an opera star or something. He clung to her, full of guilt for intruding his darkness into her bright world. He thought of his life as a war and Jane as something delicate and lovely that had wandered innocently into his battles—like a kitten or a butterfly. He was so busy fighting and so worried that she'd get hit by crossfire that every day he found less and less pleasure in her presence.

Andrés felt guilty toward Charles and Anne, too, especially now that they were doing more than ever for Gabriela. But he would never agree to tell them.

"They'll understand," said Jane, unwrapping a sandwich one afternoon in the cafeteria and placing half in front of Andrés. "They like you."

"That doesn't mean they'd like you to be with me. You'd be better off without me, and they'll know that. They'll be mad because you never even would've known me except they were nice to my aunt. Their own kid gets hurt because they tried to be nice to someone."

"You just don't understand people like them."

"People like them? Maybe so. Remember one day I said something like that and you said it wasn't friendly?"

"I only meant you don't expect people to see things your way and have sympathy, but there are people who do. My parents would."

Jane picked up her sandwich, put it down again, and absently stirred a cup of tea. The odors of neutered cafeteria foods took her appetite.

Andrés studied her face curiously. She looked so serious and sad now. That was because she loved him. She was always telling him that she loved him. He never told her that, he thought, first with remorse and then with a satisfaction that surprised him. Until this moment, he hadn't noticed his growing hard-heartedness toward Jane, and now that he did, it seemed natural and justified. She was so childish; she had a childish delusion that everything would always turn out all right. Mom and Dad could fix anything. It infuriated him, and he wondered if he loved her at all.

"What really gets to me," he said, "is that your parents actually raised you to think like that, so you wouldn't be worried and afraid. But I was raised to be afraid and worry. That was my main protection in life. If I went around like you, I woulda been dead or locked up or in a straitjacket a long time ago. It gets me mad, the way you think—like it's one more way you're spoiled. It's not fair."

"You're making things up about me," she said. "I promise you my parents *will* understand. They always do." Her voice shook delivering these confident words, too loudly, in the cafeteria, where now the only sound was the dull clatter of plastic trays, dinnerware, and chairs.

"Not this time," Andrés said.

"Why not tell them and see?"

Andrés shook his head. He would not say so to Jane, but there was no point in telling her parents and causing a lot of heartache when it was only a matter of time until one of these arguments between him and Jane was fatal. He'd seen how it happened with his mother and her boyfriends; he'd watched Gabriela calibrating how far she could safely push Juan, steeling herself against his inevitable loss. Andrés thought that he was taking advantage of Jane, but he couldn't help it—not yet anyway. She gave, and he took—just like Juan and his mother's boyfriends, and, from what he'd been told, his own father. He promised himself, though, that when the time came to part from Jane, he'd be different from men like that. He wouldn't just disappear without saying anything and get a new phone number. He'd tell her first.

One night, when Jane's parents were away and her grandmother, who was babysitting, had dozed off on the sofa with a book spread open on her chest, Andrés sneaked into Jane's room for the second time. She begged him to come, and on that particular night he was not heroic enough to insist on a lonely subway ride to the hospital to take his chances on finding a bed there. But he was different with her, stiff and cool, not at all like he had been before. He lay on her bed with an arm flung over his eyes.

She sat beside him cross-legged and bit her nails. She wanted to say important things without putting him off, and Andrés was always a critical listener. "Andrés, I want to be your lover," she said. It came out awkwardly, whiny.

Andrés rolled over impatiently. She stretched out alongside him, put her hand on his back, and kissed his neck. "Please, Andrés, please, please. If I don't take this chance, maybe there'll never be anyone else."

"What are you talking about?"

"What if you're the only person I'll ever love?"

"What a baby you are," he said bitterly.

"Realistic. I just know what I'm like," she replied, feeling offended but also silly. She could not help seeing everything from his point of view as well as her own, but she knew that sometimes people loved this way only once—like her own mother and her mother's friend, Merrit. Merrit had spent ten lonely years trying not to love someone and ended up marrying him anyway. I'm like my mother, she thought. She could hear her mother in the words she had just uttered.

Andrés thought it over. Despite his impatient reaction, he was inclined to believe what Jane said. Women—his mother, Gabriela, lots of women—did sometimes seem to love men forever. So although he didn't know why Jane loved him, he believed that she did and that, therefore, it was possible, even probable, that she would never be in love with anyone but him. In that case, he'd committed a bad crime by getting mixed up with her, but since he had, didn't he now owe her his love? Following this twisted mental route, Andrés took nearly five silent minutes to work his way to the conclusion, long obvious to Jane herself, that he was in love with her, and having reached it at a moment when he was lying beside her, looking into her eyes, breathing in her scent, suddenly grateful and astonished that such an odd, generous, beautiful girl actually existed, he naturally wrapped his arms around her and began kissing her frantically, completely disarmed against the terrors that had muted and numbed all his feelings for weeks.

Now it was Jane who grew frightened. She stopped kissing him back and pulled away with her arms crossed protectively over her chest, her hands balled under her chin. Andrés raised up and looked at her, confused. "Janie, I never did this before," he said. "Can you . . . like, help me? How come you're making your fists like that?"

"I don't know. I never did this before either. What do you want me to do?" She sounded, for Jane, timid.

"Just—guess," he said desperately. He bent back down to kiss her. She unclenched her fists and put her arms around him, and he felt her chest shake with a silent laugh.

"See? No penalty for guessing," he whispered after a little while. "Janie, Janie, I love you too."

Late that night, Juan showed up at his room, exhausted and tense, after several days' absence. Andrés was already there, beguiled into a blissful, fearless sleep by extraordinary memories, with Jane's smell still on him and his inner alarms still disengaged. By the time he had stolen out of the Braithwaites' apartment, it had been too late to go to the hospital.

"Andrés," Juan said, shaking him awake, "I want you out of here for a couple days. Can you stay somewhere?"

"I don't know. I guess."

"So go now."

"Now? It's two in the morning. I have school tomorrow."

"I don't care, just . . . *mierda!*"

Someone was banging on the door.

"Pretend you're asleep," Juan whispered. He waited until Andrés closed his eyes and then opened the door a crack.

"You got it?" said a voice.

"I got it, but you were supposed to call me first," Juan said.

"Hand it over."

"Show me the bread," said Juan.

Andrés, his eyes closed, heard shufflings and rustlings.

"All right," someone said. "You're under arrest. You have the right to remain silent and all that . . ."

Andrés sat up, terrified. Three rough men stood in Juan's doorway pointing guns at Juan and, when they saw him, at Andrés too.

"Who's this? Your partner? You're under arrest, too, kid. Don't talk or you'll get yourself in trouble."

"Why you arresting him?" Juan cried. "He don't know nothing about it. That's my girlfriend's kid, and she's in the hospital, I swear. He don't know nothing."

"You have such an honest face. Why don't I believe you?" said a rough-looking man who was unshaven with a knit hat pulled down over his ears. He grabbed Andrés by the hair and pulled him out of Juan's bed. "Get dressed," he said. "Who are you? What's your name?"

The blood pounded so hard in Andrés's ears that it was hard to hear what they were asking him. He couldn't answer. His hands trembled, and he couldn't tie his shoes. Of course, now he would be charged and certainly he would lose Jane and a chance for college and instead he would go to prison, but he didn't worry about those calamities. What tormented him was missing his physics test, second period tomorrow morning. For hours, all the way to the precinct and in the holding pen and before the judge, he worried about the test so much that he hardly knew what was going on around him.

After a while, a man from legal aid showed up and announced that he would get Andrés released on bail. He went with Andrés to a courtroom where a sour-faced judge presided at a big desk. Andrés was still having trouble collecting his thoughts and concentrating on what was going on. He heard them talking about sending him to some home or maybe foster care pending trial because his aunt was too sick to supervise him and no one could find his mother.

"I won't go," he said to the lawyer. "I'm eighteen. Can they make me?"

They decided they couldn't, or at least wouldn't. They would assign him a social worker, and the social worker would be responsible for finding housing for him. Then someone asked Andrés something—he couldn't understand what.

"I have to get back to school," Andrés replied, his voice faltering, to the room of strange faces spinning round him, "or I won't graduate." This speech sounded absurd and false in his own ears and actually seemed to make the judge angry.

"That's the least of your troubles," he snarled. "Do you know how much cocaine you had in there?"

"None—I had nothing, Judge," said Andrés. "I was just crashing there. I didn't know—"

"Enough," said the judge, shaking his head in disgust.

Late that afternoon the social worker, a wryly sympathetic black man, drove Andrés to a shelter in the Bronx.

"It's an SRO, really," he said, "single-resident occupancy, for the homeless. You'll get a little room to yourself." They went into a lobby that smelled of urine and disinfectant. People with drugged, barren faces moved around aimlessly or sat on plastic chairs watching a television mounted high on the wall, set to CNN. Screams and shouts periodically sounded at a distance, but no one paid any attention. Two armed security guards leaned on a counter and stared curiously at Andrés, who seemed too young and scared to be abandoned in such a place.

"There's supposedly no one dangerous here," the social worker told Andrés, "but I wouldn't go making a lot of friends."

"I'm not staying," said Andrés, looking around. "Everyone's crazy here."

"Don't tell me that," said the man. "That cell phone still working? Give me your number." Andrés complied.

They had dealings with a frowning man at a desk who sighed and got up to take Andrés's picture. In a few minutes, he handed him a photo ID.

"You need that to get in here," said the social worker as he left. "Don't miss your court dates. That's the worst thing you can do. There's your lawyer's number. When he calls you, you answer. You stay in touch with him, all right?" He handed Andrés a MetroCard and left.

A little while later, Andrés stood alone on the sidewalk near the shelter, considering whether to call Jane. When the police had returned his cell phone, he found more than fifty messages on it—all from her, he felt sure. Gabriela would have told her what happened. Of course, Jane would be devastated by his arrest. He would have to break up with her despite the things they had said that last night. He felt as though he had damaged her, contaminated her life with the bitterness of his. But it also seemed to him that it was her fault. He had let down his guard so that he could love Jane—and look what happened.

Andrés rode the subway to Juan's neighborhood, hoping to shower and collect his things, but his key no longer opened Juan's door. They'd changed the lock. They'd probably thrown his things out, all his clothes and schoolbooks and papers—and his computer.

Andrés was frantic at the loss of his school things, and even more upset about the computer. He ran up and down the stairs, to the roof and the basement, trying to find the building super to ask what had been done with everything, but as usual, the super was gone, no one knew where. Anyway, Andrés knew he would have thrown it all out. The computer was gone forever. Everything was lost—his only pictures of his parents, the journals and games and other remnants of his childhood and school life. Now he really was no one at all. For several moments he felt dizzy as he fell into the void of nonbeing where prisoners and the homeless live. Before, he had always managed to find something to grasp on to, but now he fell and fell, on his way to annihilation—until he remembered his aunt.

He rode the subway to the hospital. Gabriela just looked at him, and told him to use her shower quick, before they put someone in the other bed who might object. Then Andrés sat at her bedside and looked at her, seeing how sick she was. She was worse. She would die, he realized, and tears ran down his face. He loved her even though she could not really love him. She resented the demands he made on her strengths and resources. Still, she was good, and she had always come through for him. She kind of liked him. He could tell she was glad to see him and felt sorry for him.

"You feel bad?" he asked her. He himself now felt strangely numb.

She nodded feebly.

"I won't talk about it," he told her, "but I want you to know I didn't do anything."

"I know," she said. She sounded weak and resigned. "Juan called. He told me how it was."

"But they're going to send me to prison."

"Juan says no. He says they can't prove nothing against you."

"Doesn't matter. They'll lie, like before."

"Juan knows about stuff like this."

"They changed the lock on his door. I couldn't get in. Is he out yet?"

"No. And stay away from him. Don't call him. You hear me?"

"Aunt Gabriela, can I sleep here tonight? They sent me to a shelter. It's really bad."

"No. Someone's getting the bed soon." She thought for a moment. "Give me your phone. You go out for a while. Come back in ten minutes."

Andrés went to the waiting room and paced, full of love for his aunt, who, sick as she was, still tried to help. No matter what happened, even on her deathbed, somehow she managed to take care of him, like he was her kid—and she didn't even love him that way. As long as she lived, he had a place in the world, some right to be in it, but when she was gone he would be like a scrap of paper in the wind.

Returning to Gabriela's room, he heard her saying on the phone, ". . . about an hour. On the bus, yeah. Okay, thank you."

"They say come on the bus. Subway's not too good at night. You can sleep in their room."

"Braithwaites? They don't know?"

"About you and Jane, no. They know you got arrested. Now I'll tell you. It was a big mistake to get mixed up with her. Now you see." That was all Gabriela said by way of reproach.

"Wait," she said as he put on his coat. "Anne brought this. A letter come for you at their place." She took a stained, beaten-up envelope from a drawer and handed it to him.

Andrés looked at the return address—the University of Chicago— and carefully opened it. They accepted him with a full scholarship. He didn't tell Gabriela. She would sneer. Anyway, he wouldn't be going anywhere now.

CHAPTER 20

"He could well be innocent, Carla," said Anne. "That's what you're not getting."

After Andrés had left for school that morning, Anne and Charles had called Michael, along with every lawyer they knew, and it did seem as though everyone they knew was a lawyer—Carla, Peter Frankl, even Greg had been a lawyer before he went to seminary. The calls had produced an impromptu meeting in the Braithwaites' living room this evening. Anne was sitting on the sofa with her arm around Jane, who had been crying and now was curled up against her mother, a sob shaking her shoulders every few minutes. Anne had been taken aback by how personally Jane took Andrés's troubles. Apparently she had become quite friendly with him through visiting Gabriela. Jane had come to Anne for comfort for the first time in years. Anne was astonished to feel needed by this daughter—and for such reasons.

"He's lying, Anne," said Carla. "They never admit it. I know these people. You don't."

Jane lifted her head and stared at Carla with bitter fury.

"On the contrary," said Anne, pulling Jane back and putting a finger on her lips. "You've never even met them, while I've known his aunt for ten years and talked to the boy over and over, about intimate things too. He's staying in my home now. You don't know him, and I do. Besides, whatever he did or didn't do, he doesn't deserve prison."

Peter Frankl listened thoughtfully. Anne's moral position was impeccable, Carla's disgraceful. But he thought that Carla was more likely right about the facts. You came to have a feel for these kinds of things when you had Carla's experience with them.

"What do you think, Charles?" he asked. Charles looked depressed, and he had said little.

"I'm not at all convinced he did it," he said.

Peter suspected that Charles thought Andrés had probably done it but, like Anne, could not bear to think he would go to prison for it. No doubt everyone but their daughter thought that way. It was just too sad to think he might not even have done it, because if he *was* innocent, there seemed to be little anyone could do for him. It was easier to believe Carla.

"Of course, guilty or innocent," said Carla, "what they'll do to him is evil. I know that better than you do, Anne. You realize, he's facing many years—eight to twenty and they're likely to ask for more than the minimum. The sentences are mandatory—even if the judge wants to give him less than eight, he can't. And he violated his probation on a prior drug conviction."

"He may have been innocent the first time, too," said Anne. But this sounded unlikely even to her own ears, and she sighed in frustration.

Peter thought it most improbable that at fourteen Andrés would have been charged unless it was absolutely certain that he had been mixed up in the dealing. So many children were—even at younger ages. On the other hand, what was a fourteen-year-old boy whose mother turned his home into a drug dealership supposed to have done? March to the local precinct office, turn in his mother and her boyfriend, and beg to be taken off to foster care?

"Anyway, I can't take the case. This is not what I do," Carla said. "I'll fight laws. I'll back organizations. I don't take criminal clients."

"But Carla, you—"

"Don't press her, Peter," said Greg gently. "She can't do it. You and I are lawyers too."

"You're not criminal lawyers," said Carla, "and the case is unwinnable in any event. Charles and Anne, it may seem strange that here we have three lawyers and none of us can do anything for him, but criminal law in this city is not something you jump into without experience."

"What you should do," said Peter, "is get him an experienced criminal lawyer. They've appointed a free lawyer for him, but you can't count on a good defense from a court-appointed attorney. Too risky. But Carla may be right: the case may not be winnable no matter who the lawyer is."

"Lies or not, looks to me like they've got him," Carla said. "So, what we need is someone who can get him a good plea bargain."

"Then he'll go up for a few years," said Peter. "That's bad, but you can stay in touch and help him when he gets out. You'll be there for him. We all will."

Anne was touched by the way Peter gradually took on his friends' concern for a boy he didn't know. He was such a good man. She winced when Jane burst out at him.

"You say that like it's nothing. A few years in prison! He can't," cried Jane, tears once more spilling onto her cheeks. "He'll be destroyed. You don't understand, Mr. Frankl. Andrés isn't tough. He's gentle and sweet. He just got into Chicago with a full scholarship. Besides, he almost went crazy when they made him plead guilty the last time. He just couldn't stand that again, and he wouldn't last a day in prison. You know what happens in prisons, Mr. Frankl. How can we just say, well, too bad—that's the law."

Peter knew all too well what prisons were like. All of them knew about prisons. And if it were his kid—he shuddered.

"Chicago will withdraw its acceptance as soon as it hears he's being tried for dealing cocaine," said Carla. "Peter, I know the lawyer we want. We have to get Mark Berman—he's the plea-bargain man in cases like this."

"If Andrés is acquitted, he'll have no trouble with Chicago," said Anne.

Michael listened to all of them carefully, with an eye on Jane's face. He felt himself in an intolerable position, keeping secrets from Anne and Charles, but his concern about Andrés was nearly as strong as Jane's. "I myself need to think more about this," he said. "I'll help any way I can. I'll give money for a lawyer. Carla, why don't you call Berman, then, and see if he'll take the case. But I have a feeling there're things that can be done here that we're not considering. Don't any of us know someone with influence in the D.A.'s office?"

"That occasionally works if the kid is *someone's* kid," said Peter. "Otherwise it can backfire. Here again, the right lawyer could give you a realistic answer on what could be accomplished by the back door."

"Stephen Delacort," Jane said, bitterly, "who is totally . . ." She broke off, reconsidering the disclosure she had been about to make to her suddenly overattentive parents, and began again. "Someone like him gets off because his father donates money to politicians, but no one can help a wonderful boy like Andrés."

The adults did not respond to this plaint. That sort of thing was too common for them to feel the rage Jane did, and it all was more complicated than she allowed for.

"My instinct," Anne said, looking at Jane, "is that we have to change their take on Andrés. We need to get the police and the prosecutor and the judges to look at him as a kid, like a middle-class kid—as one of us. We have to show up on his behalf, be there in the courtroom—whatever."

"And my instinct," said Carla, "is that approach is a good way to send this kid away until he's got gray hair. That is just laughable, Anne. Listen to me. You want the toughest drug defense lawyer in the city. You want the guy the big dealers hire, because they're the ones who get good deals and know how it all works."

"I just don't see that," Anne said to Charles in an aside. "She may know about drug cases, but I know about kids."

"Of course let's get him a good lawyer who can do what you want, Carla," said Michael, "but, in the meantime, I'm with Anne. I don't think a plea bargain is good enough."

Jane's soul, which had been about to explode out of her skull, shrank back to its ordinary size. She despised and mistrusted Carla. She had faith in her parents and Dr. Garrard.

"Who's going to talk to Andrés?" Greg asked, as he, Carla, and Peter stood to go.

"I will," said Michael. Michael thought that Andrés was innocent, and he could see that though Anne argued only for the *possibility* of Andrés's innocence, in her heart she was convinced of it, almost against her own better judgment.

"He'll be back from the hospital any minute now," Anne said, looking at her watch, "if you want to wait."

They were all in the kitchen, keeping Charles company while he cooked, when the doorbell rang.

"I'll get it," Jane said emotionlessly. She ran to open the door and leaned forward to kiss Andrés, but he turned his face.

Jane had waited for Andrés at the subway station that morning. He'd told her then that they had to break up, and she had cried. He knew he owed her another conversation about it.

"Please, don't do that," she begged. "You make everything worse."

"I can't do this, Janie."

"What do you mean?" she said. "You're being stupid. Why don't you ever call me back?"

"I can't talk about it now."

"I'll sneak into your room when they're asleep," she whispered.

"No," he said. "I mean it, Jane—don't come. Just call me later. I'll answer."

When the two of them appeared in the kitchen, Anne thought that Andrés looked better than he had in the morning when he left. Then he had seemed stunned and disoriented, but now he just looked like a miserable boy. Jane didn't dare talk to Andrés in front of her parents, who were alert now to an excess of feeling on her part toward him. They didn't understand it yet, but Jane knew they would, sooner or later. Michael guessed how things stood between Andrés and Jane when he saw Andrés slip off into Gabriela's room while Jane's back was turned; she looked surprised and anxious when she turned and discovered that he was gone.

Excusing himself, Michael rapped on Andrés's door and spent nearly an hour talking with him. Afterward, Andrés still expected the worst, but he responded to Michael with a touching rise in courage. Not only were people offering to help, but some, at least—the ones who mattered most—seemed to believe every word he said. Back when he was fourteen and let himself be pressured into a false guilty plea, no one had believed him. He had been cowardly—too afraid of jail to stand up for himself. All he'd had back then was the brittle courage that came from ambition, obligation, and necessity, and it wasn't enough.

"Charles," Anne said as they lay reading in bed that night. "Someone should adopt Andrés. I don't mean legally. I mean—"

"I know what you mean. But we have too many young children. We can't do it. Maybe an uncle, something like that. That's the best I can do."

Anne nodded. "I just hope not an in-law."

"What?"

"Did you hear Jane comparing Andrés with Stephen Delacort? I think she has a crush on Andrés."

On the one hand, Charles had detected this already himself, but on the other, he preferred not to think about it because he didn't know what to do about it. "We shouldn't say anything to her," he said.

"I had thought about asking Mother if Andrés could stay with her. Then I decided that he might run off or something if we asked him to go. He feels connected to our home, and he's too shaky to uproot. Besides, he'd know why."

Charles had nothing to add. He did not particularly like the idea of asking ask the boy to leave because they suspected their daughter of having a crush on him, especially when they had no evidence that he returned her feelings. On the other hand, why didn't he have every right to protect the safety and peace of his family against threats caused, however innocently, by a boy who was, morally speaking, a stranger to them? They wanted to be generous to Andrés, but they owed him nothing.

"The only possible objection to this boy is that he's extremely unlucky," Anne said.

"Maybe so. But I'd still do everything in my power to separate him and Jane, if it came to that, because I don't want her to have to deal with his problems," said Charles. "Anyway, it's just a crush. If we leave them alone, it won't last more than a few months. They don't really have anything in common. Worst case, it lasts through her first semester at Juilliard. If we try to keep them apart, it'll just make her more interested in him. The best thing for now is to act as though we don't see anything."

"For now, yes," said Anne. Despite her belief in Andrés's innocence, she, too, would have done whatever she could to separate him from Jane.

And although this partial resolution was unsatisfactory, it let them fall into a restless sleep.

Jane and Andrés, meanwhile, were discussing the same subject on their cell phones. He was adamant about breaking things off, and her pleading only made him angry. After all, Jane had demanded his emotional disarmament and, when he complied, things went disastrously wrong. In his muddled feelings at least, Jane was the ultimate cause of his calamity. She was also a soft, overtrusting girl who would be fatally infected by exposure to his life's miseries. He would not disarm again, nor would he let her make him into a destroyer, a murderer of her innocence and safety. If you tried to put together two people as different as Andrés and Jane, naturally chaos and disaster would be the result.

"I can't," he told her. "I don't want it anymore, Jane."

The coldness with which he refused her was as foreign to her experience as being trusted was to his. It broke every rule, defied every expectation, of Jane's upbringing that he should not respond to her deep grief with mercy and compassion. At the same time, the sense that he unjustly held something against her was terrifyingly familiar.

CHAPTER 21

J ane's audition was scheduled for ten-thirty on a Thursday morning. She had been duly excused from school, and after several family councils, it had been determined that her grandmother, Helen, would accompany her, not her parents, who feared that their presence might inspire a repetition of the master-class fiasco. Although Charles and Anne opposed Jane's having this audition, they knew that memories in New York were long. Jane might develop a reputation for unreliability and unprofessional behavior if she pulled such a stunt twice. Now that she had asked to audition, she had to show up and sing well.

Jane announced that she would sleep at her grandmother's the night before. Helen was more open than Anne or Charles to the idea that Jane might not go to Juilliard. Besides, she could tell Helen more than her parents about Andrés. Not that she could tell even Helen that Andrés was— at least had been—her lover. Helen would tell Anne. Helen might spoil Jane, but she constantly defended Charles and Anne against Jane's attacks; she would never conspire with Jane against them.

Late on Wednesday afternoon, Jane sat in Helen's crowded sixties-era kitchen at a folding-leaf table that would seat four when fully opened and just fit under a small window on an air shaft that supplied ventilation but almost no light. It was the table at which Anne, her brother Paul, and their parents had eaten all their meals. The room would have looked shabby to strangers, but Helen still took great satisfaction in having an eat-in kitchen with a window. She and Gil had been proud and happy when they got the place—so good for the children, so sound-impervious for lessons and practicing. On a Formica countertop pocked with random burns and cuts and stained pink here and there, an electric teakettle began to whistle, and Helen made two cups of hot sweet tea with condensed milk—their shared taste, Anne and Ellen couldn't bear it—while she listened to her granddaughter. Helen could tell that Jane was in love from the way her voice went satiny and singy when she talked about Andrés. A musician herself, Helen noticed such things immediately. It was really quite wonderful, the responsive wiring that bypassed consciousness yet seemed to shape Jane's voice to her emotions far more intimately than in the ordinary person. That's what made her so good, of course. Jane did not know how obvious she was to her grandmother, for she had never talked about Andrés with anyone before; nor had she ever really been in love before, though she had thought she was.

"Nana, he's such a wonderful boy. No one really knows it. He's kind and fun, and he understands everything. He writes poetry. He . . ." But Jane remembered that she had no business knowing what a good dancer Andrés was.

"Yes, darling," said Helen, restraining considerable sadness and dismay. "I'm sure he is." She had heard all about Andrés from Charles and Anne, and she could only be miserable upon detecting how intense Jane's feelings were for him.

"But it's so hard to explain what it is about him. He's the best friend I ever had," Jane said, tears beginning to flow, "except for you."

This was getting dangerously close to telling all, and Helen didn't press her. Jane was so in love with this boy who was in such terrible trouble. Helen was one of those rare grown-ups who were brave enough to recognize the awful agony of young love when it went wrong. She had known suffering like Jane's only once in her own life, when her husband died just before Jane was born. Jane, her first grandchild, had been her consolation then. Helen began to cry too.

"He's like no one else," Jane said. "He wants to understand everything and do good things. He's all on his own. He thinks for himself. He's the first kid I ever knew who was really a mensch, Nana. People don't know that about him, but it's true."

"You've always been looking for someone like that," said Helen, wiping her eyes with a tissue. "Those are rare qualities. Of course you value them." Helen would not cause Jane more pain by reminding her of what was undesirable about Andrés. From what Anne had told her, it sounded as though the boy probably *was* some kind of passive participant in a drug sale, and the police probably had good reason to think so. That didn't make what they were doing to him right, of course. The drug laws were a disgrace to a civilized country. And the boy didn't ask to be brought up by malefactors. On the other hand, the injustice of the drug laws and Andrés's unfortunate family life didn't make him proper company for her granddaughter, either.

Taking the long view of Jane's tragedy, she feared that she herself was to some extent its ultimate source. She had raised Anne, and Anne and Helen together had raised Jane, to be a person of broad sympathies. She had taken both girls among the poor and beaten, to shelters and soup lines, tenements and greasy spoons, so that they would know the mucky depths of the city. She had exposed them to books and plays that opened their eyes and quickened their perceptions with love. She had given them rational, objective explanations of how it happened that they had so much and others so little.

This moral education, kindly and eloquently offered, would have sunk deep into any sensitive child's soul. Helen was aware that in Jane's case it was all the more successful because every lesson from Helen was reinforced at home by Anne. Jane absorbed from her parents the same empathic techniques for gauging and mastering the world as Helen taught, and she exercised them on the realities she encountered.

"Nana, lots of kids at my school think I'm an alien," Jane said. "But Andrés understands. He really understands everything."

"You should've gone to public school," said Helen in despair. "La Guardia—even Hunter. I told Anne . . ."

Helen had not foreseen that progressive child rearing could pose danger to the children by giving them overly broad sympathies or excessive optimism and confidence, for she, and Charles and Anne too, had broad sympathies. They would all gladly welcome boyfriends and girlfriends for the children from different religions, races, and nationalities. But Jane had done something Helen had not thought psychologically possible for a well-raised, well-loved girl—something she should have avoided instinctively, as Anne did, just by following her heart. She had chosen out of her class. Some people might see special virtue in this, but Helen, thinking it over, was not inclined to—even though she believed that a good society would have no classes. Class barriers, when the classes were as far apart as Jane's and Andrés's, did not give way to romance without great sacrifice and damage. Helen thought it was a mess-up, mad—a choice that sooner or later had to lead to catastrophe along Romeo and Juliet lines. In a ghastly way, Andrés's calamity might be Jane's only salvation. This was all Helen's own fault. She indicted herself, while, simultaneously, she pleaded for acquittal on the grounds that the danger was not foreseeable. After all, Anne and her brother had never loved out of their own world.

"Janie, I'm sorry that someone you care about is in such terrible trouble," she said, "and I know he deserves better. But you're very young and this . . . friendship . . . would have ended anyway, probably sooner rather than later. High school bonds can be very intense, but they don't last. And Andrés is not from your world. Sooner or later, that would have been a big strain. That can't really help you with what you're feeling now. I understand that. But in one way or another, you were going to have to go through this unhappiness. You were going to have to give him up. I'm so sorry, darling." Helen spoke gently, her voice congested with tears.

Lonely in her troubles, Jane had yearned for comforting words from her grandmother. She had so confidently expected them, moreover, that only after several moments did the real gist of Helen's speech dawn on her and begin to anger her.

"No, I wasn't," she said then, giving her grandmother the resentful glare that heretofore she had reserved for her parents. "I wasn't going to have to go through this. And I'll always . . . I'll always . . . care about him as much as I do now. I don't know what world you think I'm from or he's from, but wherever he lives, that's where I live too."

Helen was wounded, but she knew better than to oppose Jane at a time like this. "All right, sweetheart," she said. "I was wrong to try to get you to look at things the way a sixty-seven-year old sees it."

"You mean all distorted and stereotyped?" Jane gave her grandmother another hard look.

Helen closed her eyes and sighed. She shouldn't have tried to say such a thing to an eighteen-year-old in love. "I just wanted to help you feel better," she said. "I know you like this boy a lot, but he's brought so much suffering into your life already—even though he certainly never wanted to. If you cling to him, there'll be infinitely more. You know that's so, sweetie. It's such an old story. You don't need me to tell it to you."

"You are *so* wrong," said Jane. "He's the one who saved me. I was misérable before. I was dying. And now I'm not." And she stood and swung her pack to her shoulder.

"Jane, don't leave this way," Helen pleaded. "Stay and let's talk some more. I'm on your side. Really I am. Let's be friends, and we'll go to the audition tomorrow."

Jane stalked out, refusing to look back at her grandmother. It made her feel queasy to be so hard on Helen. She never had been before. But she feared that if she softened or tried to make friends, Helen might tempt her to betray Andrés. It was easy to feel confident when opposing her parents, with Helen's affection at her back. But when she opposed Helen, she was orphaned entirely. As she walked the six blocks home, she turned over in her mind the truth that though people might try to help Andrés, no one would help her. No one would be in favor of her being with him—not even Andrés himself. Not even Dr. Garrard, who had so much sympathy for Andrés and, she believed, for her affection for Andrés. And if Helen herself opposed Jane's going with Andrés, then Andrés had probably been right: so would her parents. She could see that now. She had always complained about feeling alone, but this was a different, scarier kind of loneliness.

Anne was surprised when Jane showed up just as she was preparing to have dinner with the boys, for Charles had a concert and Ellen was having dinner at Rebecca's. "Jane, did you forget? You were supposed to go to Nana's."

"I was just there," Jane said coolly. "I felt like coming home."

Anne hesitated. Did this mean that Jane wanted Anne to go with her tomorrow?

"Mom, I might cancel that audition."

Anne filled Stuart's and Gilbert's plates and poured herself a glass of wine before answering.

"Why's that?" she asked. She let herself sound as tense as she felt.

Stuart and Gilbert watched their mother and sister warily. The fights between Jane and their parents frightened them.

"There's nothing to worry about, boys," said Anne, bending to kiss Gilbert's cheek.

"I'm so upset that I don't think I could do it," said Jane.

"Let me point out that if you can't do it when you're upset, then you could never be in opera anyway, because in opera you have to sing even when life's full of trouble, which it often is. That's the deal."

"Yeah, Jane," said Stuart, with a knowing nod.

"You don't know anything about it, Stuart," Jane said.

"He knows," said Anne. "He's had to play at hard times—like the day he didn't make the soccer team even though he should've."

"Yeah," said Stuart, looking at Jane resentfully.

"What are you singing anyway?" Anne asked. She sat down to eat with Gilbert and Stuart and set no place for Jane. Jane noticed. She left the room without answering her mother's question, and when she had gone, Anne, Gilbert, and Stuart cleaned their plates and then had seconds and dessert—berries from South America with cream.

The following morning, Jane went to her audition alone except for her teacher, who arrived at the last minute and sat outside the audition room straining to hear what she could. Jane performed creditably. The kindly auditioners paid her compliments and thought that the sad, willowy girl had extraordinary talent and unusual musical depth for one so young, but they did not know what to do with her. They thought she should probably go to school even if she was so accomplished. After all, nowadays a young singer in this business was in her late twenties, not her late teens. They thanked Jane graciously and said that they would "be in touch." But Jane had the feeling that the audition had turned into something else by the end. The auditioners began to behave as though Jane wanted not a part but their disinterested career-planning advice. It was maddening.

Jane's teacher had no idea what the result would be. She told Jane that her singing merited some sort of offer, but she had a bad feeling that Jane might never hear anything definite. She had seen this sort of dithering response to a good audition in the past. Alas, they were all bureaucrats. They found it hard to be excited by talent, though they knew they were supposed to be. What excited them was someone reliable, someone who showed up and didn't get sick and always was in voice—who could competently sing a variety of roles from a variety of periods in the accepted manner without cranky ideas, someone who would not make trouble or scandals and fit into a complex social hierarchy, a system. Jane's teacher groaned to herself when she kissed Jane good-bye and watched her walk, dejected, into the subway station at Sixty-sixth Street. She was an elderly woman who remembered when things had been different. Fifty years ago, Jane would have been a star and audiences would have become especially fond of a girl they had watched grow up as a performer. She would have matured through performing rather than schooling—in her opinion, a more natural and favorable way to develop. Today, no one knew what to do with a girl like Jane. They had a business to run.

Jane was not as discouraged as her teacher. She had sung well, and therefore there was hope. She was prepared to compromise a great deal to avoid school. And because hope tends to generalize in the mind, Jane soon found herself thinking that there was hope for Andrés too. When Jane wanted something badly and thought she deserved it, she expected to get it—no matter what Helen and her parents and teacher said. It was easy for her to believe, contrary to all evidence, that the audition would lead to a substantial role, charges against Andrés would be dropped, and she and he would then reconcile. Her elders would have been appalled if they had been privy to her thoughts, so infected with fantasy and wish, so unchastened by reality. For looking at all her prospects with as much cold neutrality as she could muster, Jane told herself that everything would probably end well—though not for months and months. She prepared herself for a long siege, all alone.

CHAPTER 22

Charles and Anne went all out for what they had begun calling the Libertarian Dinner. They conferred with Michael on wines, knowing that his expertise exceeded theirs. They cooked: Charles's fish soup, Anne's fritto misto, Ellen and Jane's cake of ground almond and beaten egg whites.

The children, however, even the older ones, were not to join the party. Jane, Ellen, and Andrés were in charge of getting the younger ones bathed and bedded down. Then the three of them were going to watch the second and third of the *Matrix* movies in Charles and Anne's room. Charles and Anne had debated the wisdom of allowing Andrés and Jane to spend the evening together in that cozy way, in a bedroom yet, but Jane and Andrés had been so convincingly distant with each other in the weeks since his arrest that they had begun to think the danger had passed. Besides, with a houseful of people walking by and Ellen there and Charles and Anne going in and out all evening, it would be all right. Anne propped the door open with a chair.

Carla, Greg, and Michael arrived for drinks at seven-thirty, Peter and several other members of the council showed up just before eight, and the

Braithwaites' old friends Merrit Roth and Morris Malcolm came a few minutes later. Wyatt Jesse Younger and Professor Selvnick were expected at eight. But by nine, the guests of honor had still not appeared and the other guests were already a little tipsy.

The time passed quickly for some. Michael Garrard and Morris Malcolm, a molecular biologist at Columbia, quickly discovered common interests and acquaintances. Michael thought Morris's wife, Merrit, very pretty in a worn-out sort of way—definitely a bit anemic—and fun to talk to, and he warmed to learn that Merrit and Anne were girlhood friends who had both grown up in Morningside Heights. Their conversation moved energetically from science to politics, libertarian politics in particular.

"I'm sort of conservative myself," Morris said, "but libertarianism is juvenile bunk."

"It's not *all* bunk," said Merrit, a liberal who taught and read widely in political and moral theory. "There're some progressive, sensible elements in libertarianism—on civil rights, on women—"

"No there aren't," said Morris, rudely interrupting Merrit's list. "There's no such thing as a sensible political theory. I don't care—Plato, Hobbes, Rawls—they're all schlock thought, duded-up prejudice."

"Exactly," said Michael. "No reality check in them."

"Exactly," said Morris, beaming at Michael in a comradely way.

Morris was a bit abrasive, thought Michael, but very likeable. "These grand theories make people stupid," Michael said. "They let them off the hook morally, and tempt them to accept naïve, single-note answers to the most complicated practical questions."

"Pure wish fulfillment—in one way or another it all comes down to ego and greed," said Morris emphatically.

"Exactly," said Michael. "Liberal education should do more to inoculate people against them."

"Scientists!" Merrit said with scorn.

"The thing is," Morris went on, "sooner or later reality intervenes, and the theories look irrelevant. This new outbreak of libertarianism would have been over years ago if a lot of university professors and think-tank fellows didn't make their living off it."

"Interesting you say so," said Michael, and he explained how Younger, under the apparent influence of Professor Selvnick, was financing the academic dissemination of libertarianism.

"Too bad they're not coming," Carla said. "I love to argue with libertarians. But we should have known. I'm famished."

Anne handed her a cracker with cheese and poured more wine all around.

"They'll be here," Greg said at twenty past nine.

"Yes, they're just establishing their dominance by being late," Charles said.

At nine-thirty, Willie called up to announce them. His voice over the intercom, to Charles's sensitive ear, was faintly sarcastic.

It was a cold night, and the newcomers were imposing in enormous topcoats. Watching Charles greet them, Michael thought again that Younger was not entirely well. He had some pain or discomfort; he was fatigued. Michael had no diagnosis, only misgivings about the man's health. Tonight he was pale and slouched and looked much older than he was. His youthfulness, in any case, was of a particularly bland and understated type—not so much callow as flavorless. It was very odd, that eccentricity should be colorless and characterless. No, he was not well, Michael thought again, watching Younger struggle to get out of his heavy coat, even with Charles's assistance. It concerned Michael, but it wasn't as though the man lacked resources or self-interest. Besides, he'd offered to see him at his office.

"There they are," said Michael under his breath to Merrit, "the *éminence terrible* and the *enfant gris.* I'd better go help Charles with the introductions."

Merrit knew Selvnick by reputation, and she laughed. But neither Michael nor Charles could induce Younger to pay attention to anyone's name. He wandered around the room, studying the piano, the violins, and the music stands arranged in the far corner. Finally he collapsed, as though weary, into a seat opposite Michael, next to Professor Selvnick.

Anne watched Younger attentively. He was a worried man.

"It looks like *Masterpiece Theatre* in here" were his first words of the evening, addressed to no one in particular.

"This is how the contracted, welfare-state bourgeois liberal lives—all my Ivy League colleagues have places pretty much like this," Professor Selvnick replied glowingly.

"Not the welfare-state bourgeoisie," said Carla with scorn. "You libertarians are so sixties in your thinking."

"Very true," said Peter with a smile that conveyed both mischief and approval of Carla. "This is the postliberal, protofascist-state, starved remnants of the bourgeoisie."

"But you grew up in this neighborhood, Mr. Younger," Anne said, pouring wine for him and offering a plate of hors d'oeuvres. "You've been in a dozen apartments just like ours."

"No, because he had no friends," Professor Selvnick replied. "His mother was a homemaker; his father had some administrative position at the local post office and eventually died of Lou Gehrig's disease after a long illness. Neither of them had much interest in books or ideas or the arts, and after his father got sick the family was hard up." Anne was annoyed, but Younger seemed not to object to Professor Selvnick's speaking on his behalf. Selvnick sounded practiced, as though he had given this talk before, or as though he thought it his job to offer the public a biographical sketch of his patron.

"Mr. Younger developed his interest in business from watching *Wall Street Week* on PBS," Selvnick continued, though no one had asked, "and started out investing his birthday checks from his grandmother—at the age of seven! He wrote a fan letter to Louis Rukeyser asking for advice."

"Other kids played with toys," Younger said with some satisfaction. "I played with my calculator, and stocks and bonds." These were the first words that he had addressed to anyone other than Selvnick.

"I see. Your parents' troubles scared you," said Anne. "Did they go along when you started playing with money, or did they try to get you interested in Legos?" She was leaning forward, with genuine parental interest in her voice. She had often wondered what she would have done had any of her children shown such atypical tastes.

Younger did not know the answer. Her intensity disarmed him, and he stared, blinking at her, as he fumbled for a grip on her questions.

It wouldn't have occurred to me, Michael thought, to take the psychogenic approach to a man like Wyatt Jesse Younger, whose wealth and power dominated Michael's own perceptions of him. Anne always ignored all the ordinary social clues, yet with her twisty little trains of thought, she got so many things right. You could even call her clear-sighted. He settled back to watch her pursue her game. After all, wasn't it a skill something like his own at diagnosis? You had to respect results. Michael knew he had a bit of a crush on Anne. It was innocent enough, but he was ashamed to feel a moment of antagonism toward Charles and Morris for having wives with agile minds and a certain physical appeal despite their middle age and, in Anne's case, rather ordinary looks.

"He has an extraordinary genius for his work," Professor Selvnick was saying with parental pride, ignoring Anne. "It's a total passion for him—his only real love in life. No interests or hobbies. Never had a job. And he's entirely self-educated—didn't go to college. That's why we're such a successful team. He's everything I'm not and vice versa."

"Mr. Younger, you like music, I'm sure," Anne said. She had watched him studying the musical paraphernalia.

"I like music," said Younger, looking reproachfully at Professor Selvnick, to whom this response seemed to come as a surprise.

Anne was detaching him from Selvnick, Michael thought, and to avoid a smile he stretched his upper lip down to meet his lower one. Even Wyatt Younger responded to Anne. In fact, now he looked at her expectantly.

"So you watched *Masterpiece Theatre* too?" Anne asked. "Did you see *Pride and Prejudice*? I was in that. I had a bit part playing the piano in the background. What were your favorite series? *I, Claudius*? *Jude the Obscure*?"

Again Younger didn't answer, though he looked benignly on Anne. Her energy made his failure to reply seem sluggish, and maybe, Michael thought, that's just what it was. Anne talking with Younger was like an antelope dancing with a sloth.

"I also . . . uh . . ." Younger hesitated for a moment.

"Cards?" Anne mused, looking into his face. "Chess? I know—philosophy! I'll bet you read Hegel or . . . Mr. Younger, did you ever read Spinoza?"

Younger did not answer, but he smiled. "I'm hungry," he said. He liked the game but would not let her know if she had scored. Here was a man, thought Michael, who liked power a great deal. Charles, on the other hand, who was also observing intently, thought that anyone who circled Anne as warily as this fellow did was a very frightened man.

"Well, let's eat," said Charles. "Give us ten minutes."

He and Anne briefly conferred in the kitchen, as they reheated the food and filled a basket with breads. "Very grandiose," she whispered.

"They'd say autistic nowadays," he replied.

"No," said Anne. "Not a bit. He's just bizarrely inexperienced, ill informed, and socially immature—but not really the worst guy in the world. I can't wait to talk to Lily about him. Selvnick wants to pretend that he's an idiot savant, but he's not. He's just a smart man who's not educated enough to be sure he's really wonderful, and he needs to prove to himself that he is or he'll doubt he deserves what he's got. But he's too egotistical even to admit he needs teachers. No, he thought he'd just read the works of a few historical geniuses and buy himself a Selvnick."

Wyatt Jesse Younger, at that moment, wandered listlessly into the kitchen, with Professor Selvnick hovering behind him—the one looking for a meal and the other looking out for his meal ticket, Charles thought.

Younger sniffed. "What is that?" he asked suspiciously.

"Fish soup," said Charles. He ladled broth into a cup and handed it to Younger, who tasted it cautiously, then unceremoniously helped himself to more.

"You're not supposed to—" Professor Selvnick began with a genial laugh.

"He knows," Anne said. "He doesn't care."

Younger sipped broth and looked at photographs of the Braithwaite children stuck to the refrigerator with magnets.

"Are your children here? Four children! Where are they?" he asked, as though the idea of their children had taken him by surprise.

"They had their dinner earlier. The little ones are asleep, and the big ones are watching movies in our room," Anne said.

"The *Matrix* movies," Charles said, watching Younger. "Seen those?"

"I don't go to movies," Younger said.

"You should meet the children, Wyatt," Anne said, on impulse using his first name.

Younger's curiosity energized him, and he followed Anne to Jane, Ellen, and Andrés, who were stretched out on the bed, Ellen in the middle, watching a young man in a long, flaring black coat perform a magic dance of flying jiujitsu moves against a multiplying horde of identical enemies in suits and ties. The young people looked away from the screen unwillingly and, after offering sullen, one-word responses to Anne's introductions of Younger, resumed their watching. Younger, transfixed by what was on the screen, moved to an armchair on the other side of the bed and sat to watch with them. Anne could not persuade him to leave. Finally she left him there to go help Charles.

He would not come when they called him to dinner, and he looked up with the same irritable expression as the three teens when Selvnick repeatedly interrupted the viewing to try to persuade him to join the adults. He refused to budge. He was comfortable and well entertained where he was.

"We'll have these movies waiting for you when you get home tonight," Professor Selvnick said gaily. But Younger told him to go away.

Anne thought this a favorable development. "We'll bring him a tray," she said when it was after ten and Younger still could not be persuaded to come to the table.

"But really," Professor Selvnick said, following Anne back to the dining room, "we have business to attend to. Mr. Younger is needed."

As though we could do anything about it, Charles thought. Surely an edge of worry was beginning to cut through Professor Selvnick's thick self-delight. Charles didn't care; Professor Selvnick got on his nerves. "What's the point?" he replied. "He's having a good time. Leave him alone." But it occurred to Charles to worry about whether the children could handle Younger. Suppose he began making demands or being difficult. He went back to the bedroom and found the movie paused and Andrés giving Younger a plot summary.

Younger waved brusquely. "Okay," he said. "Start it again."

Charles stayed long enough to feel sure that Younger didn't intend to interrupt the viewing repeatedly, and when he returned to the table, Peter was trying to draw Professor Selvnick out. There was something lawyerly in his approach, something leading or manipulative, thought Charles. He didn't mind.

"So you've been offering Mr. Younger guidance, I hear," Peter said.

"Extraordinary soup," said Professor Selvnick, his eyes rolling upward in appreciation. "Yes, that's my job—he pays me for my moral and political expertise. He said he wanted to avoid doing anything wrong, and I convinced him that the best way to do that was to hire the services of a good philosopher, someone qualified to point out ethical pitfalls. And he'd already read about Descartes and Hobbes and Spinoza and so many others having patrons—nice guess there, Anne!"

How on earth did she pick Spinoza out of the hat? Michael wondered, humbled with admiration.

"Why, before he met me," Selvnick continued, "with a fortune of billions, he'd never given away a cent. Now he's head of an empire of think tanks, lobbyists, university chairs. Every year, he distributes millions to academia."

"But only to libertarians?" inquired Peter. "I'm especially interested because I run a foundation myself, and we also have to decide who to give money to, like you do, even if we don't have nearly as much to hand out."

"Mostly," Professor Selvnick said, an unconvincing note of regret in his voice. "We don't believe in social engineering, you see, so why should we try to do any—or give money to people who want to? It just doesn't work." Selvnick looked around benignly and laughed in a friendly way. "Wish it did, to tell the truth." Selvnick prided himself on knowing how to talk to people, unlike the average academic. He knew that people were more receptive to new ideas that were offered with wit and good humor by someone who sounded like them.

"So you've advised him to set up an ideological empire in which your own ideas rule," said Michael, "backed by a fortune that gives whoever controls it more real power than many of the world's nation-states and makes you, potentially, the world's most influential and powerful thinker, quite apart from any merit to your ideas. For you can't believe *he* is any judge of that. So it's fortunate that you can be sure you're right about everything—and that you have no interest in holding power yourself."

Carla looked at Michael adoringly; Charles and Anne, too, turned worshipful eyes on him. It was so satisfying to have someone put one's own chaotic thoughts into effective, logical language.

"Scientists," Morris said in his wife's ear, nodding in self-congratulation, as though he himself had uttered these lucid words.

"I'm no relativist," Professor Selvnick retorted, shaking his finger at the doctor. "I believe in truth. What did you call this, Anne—fritto misto? Divine. Look, of course I'm human and fallible, but not nearly as fallible as the average Joe. After all, I'm paid to spend my time thinking about these things. Most people just don't have that luxury. Besides, I've got above-average brains, and I'm at ease with abstractions. Most people, by definition, are average in intelligence. So, there's a natural division of labor here. I help others decide what to think about moral and political issues just as physicists tell them what to think about string theory. That's my job."

"But doesn't democracy presuppose that when it comes to politics and morals, people think for themselves? At least enough to vote intelligently?" asked Greg. "I must say, your ideas are rather . . . surprising— especially coming from a libertarian. I always thought libertarians believed in the individual over all else."

"But libertarianism is all for any kind of *voluntary* submission—to reason or to superior people—whatever. As far as I'm concerned, you can sell yourself into slavery if you want. A lot of people would be better off, just as they'd be better off taking competent advice on politics and morals. The only question is whose advice is worth having. Would you rather have some fundamentalist quack or me—who has no prejudice against gays, blacks, or women and believes in evolution and stem cell research and the science behind the claim of global warming?"

There was a general, thoughtful silence at the table.

"That's a tough call," Carla said.

"I should think that more than IQ, education, and opportunity are necessary to qualify one to give valid moral advice," said Michael, "because a person could have all that and still be——"

"An asshole?" Carla said. "A total fool?"

"Or bad, even evil," said Greg.

"Oh, I knew this was coming. God!" Professor Selvnick chuckled.

"Just common sense," said Peter. "I'm an atheist like a lot of other people here, but I agree with Michael and Greg. So, tell me, what if it turned out that you, or others in your position, were deficient in . . . well, in virtue?"

Professor Selvnick suddenly looked inward, as though attending to his thoughts. In fact, he looked so deeply contemplative that for a moment Anne thought she had misjudged him, that he was intimately engaged with Peter's question. But then Selvnick stood up abruptly. "Excuse me, please," he said, and hurried out and down the hallway to Charles and Anne's bedroom. Charles hesitated for a moment, then excused himself and followed him.

"Good movie," Younger was saying as Professor Selvnick entered. "You lost *that* argument, Selvnick."

"No, no, Mr. Younger," Professor Selvnick said with a laugh. "I simply hadn't finished yet. Their point is old and decrepit. I have an unanswerable, brand-new response. You see——"

"Not now. I want some dessert."

"Us too," said Ellen, though the children had already had dessert.

Younger listened to the children's discussion of the movie with silent attention, enthusiastically eating almond cake. Andrés's reactions particularly captivated him. Andrés, like the boy he still was, for the moment could put his miseries aside and take films, cake, and safety for granted. Charles, Anne, and Michael watched him with the painful mix of satisfaction and sorrow that was becoming their shared characteristic reaction to him. Jane seemed never to look at him. Anne was certain now that there was a breach between them.

"Let's take off," said Younger to Professor Selvnick, swallowing the last crumb of his third piece of cake. He suddenly looked much more wan and drained than he had earlier.

Professor Selvnick thanked the Braithwaites effusively for their hospitality and told Michael gaily that he *still* hadn't heard the last of them.

"But you lost the argument," Younger repeated, pulling a pen and a scrap of paper out of his pocket. He scribbled and handed the paper to Michael. "There's my number. Give me yours." He paused, then added, "Okay?"

He had figured out, Charles thought, that Michael wouldn't accept orders.

Michael looked at the number, mystified. He had no wish to call Wyatt Younger at his unlisted number. He extracted his card from his wallet and gave it to Younger.

"No, your unlisted number. I know you have one. That's my private number I gave you," Younger said. "Er . . . you might as well keep that check," he added, looking askew at Michael.

Younger was determined to ensure that he had direct, certain, and privileged access to the reluctant doctor, and, Michael thought, there was still going to be some medical angle to all this. Unsure how to respond, he looked to Charles for a cue, surprising himself, for he never permitted himself to rely on another man's judgment in place of his own—hadn't since he was a fledgling doctor terrified of killing some patient in his ignorance.

"You mean you want the number that only his wife has?" Charles asked Younger. "That doesn't make sense. Michael, I suggest you open a personal line for Mr. Younger and pay for it out of that check. Mr. Younger, he'll call you and give you that number. No big deal."

"Good idea," said Michael, nearly smiling at this solution, "if Mr. Younger can accept that." Not without profit, he thought, had Charles Braithwaite spent eighteen years dealing with childish unreasonableness.

"Good idea," said Younger, with satisfied seriousness, and he ambled out wearily, trailed by Professor Selvnick, who called out effusive good-byes and thanks over his shoulder.

As soon as they were gone, the council members erupted in loud rejoicing and gloated over the unlibertarian programs to be made possible by the windfall from Younger. The Braithwaites congratulated themselves on promoting an atmosphere that softened up Younger. They were generous to each other on that score. Anne thought that Charles had been brilliant with him, and Charles thought that Anne had cracked his shell and gotten him away from Selvnick. Only Michael was not completely satisfied with the evening; walking back to his apartment on Riverside Drive, he contemplated the prospect of future dealings with Wyatt Younger in a less than celebratory mood.

CHAPTER 23

For several weeks, Andrés lived the life of a normal American boy in the Braithwaite household. It was new to him, but he quickly found it natural. He had seen it on television and read about it all his life. He slept in a bed, showered when he woke, put on fresh clothes that mysteriously and reliably appeared in his room. Then he rushed through breakfast, stuffed his backpack with books and papers, and ran out, calling responses to questions and injunctions—Will you be home for dinner? Are you visiting Gabriela tonight? Don't forget your appointment with the lawyer!

Despite his difficulties with Jane and his legal problems, Andrés flourished under this regimen. He slept well, put on weight, and made a dramatic start at pulling up his grades. The counseling service at school wondered whether getting busted was not the best thing that had ever happened to him. The improvement in this boy's functioning now that he was neither using nor dealing was remarkable. But when Ms. Goldberg said as much to him, he answered her with a four-letter word and a look of loathing and got suspended for a day. He used the time to study and aced a difficult physics exam when he returned to classes.

Jane, meanwhile, declined. She became increasingly irritable and silent and sat up half the night reading or listening to music or simply staring. Her grades plummeted, and she and Ellen resumed their bloodletting quarrels. She's right back to where she was last fall, Anne told Charles.

One morning, Jane left home before Andrés and waited for him in the rain outside the subway station. "We have to talk," she told him. He could see that she was strung out, with deep circles under her eyes, pale skin, wet hair streaming onto her shoulders. He agreed to meet her after school at her grandmother's apartment while Helen was away. Jane had her own key and a bed there—Anne's childhood bed, which now was kept made up, mostly for Jane, but also for Ellen or their little cousins when any of them stayed over. Jane and Andrés had hardly spoken in the time that he had lived with her family; they had never touched. But soon after Andrés rang her grandmother's bell, she begged him to get into the bed with her.

"Stop it, Janie. If you can't do this, I'll move out," he said. "I can see it's bad for you, having me around."

"It's not having you around that's hard. It's *not* having you. You know that," she told him.

"You have to forget about me. It would be easier if you didn't have to see me all the time."

"Why isn't it hard for you?" she demanded.

"I didn't say it wasn't . . . It's just . . . I never thought you were mine. But you thought you had me. So I'm just where I was before, but you . . . and . . ." But Andrés could not tell Jane that love between them meant mutual destruction, for he hardly knew he thought such a thing, and in any event, Jane would simply have argued with him.

He would not be tempted back to her, but her tears and distress cut loose feelings for her that had been safely bound and gagged all these weeks. She had the satisfaction of seeing him cry. She calmed down after that. The change in her, when he wept, was striking.

With some experience of his strength of will, Jane now believed him when he threatened to move out. The thought that he really would go off to some grim shelter in the Bronx if she persisted silenced her.

"But after your trial?" she asked, as he put on his coat and heaved his pack onto his back.

He could see that she felt better despite his refusals, despite his dangerous situation. "If I'm not in jail," he said. "If I'm going to Chicago . . . but it's probably going to be jail."

"Why do you say that? You've got a really good lawyer. Anyway, if you think you'll be convicted, why not take a plea bargain? Maybe you could get, like, community service and then . . ."

He shook his head impatiently. "On a plea bargain, I'd still get prison and then for the rest of my life I'm an ex-con. You think Chicago is gonna say, oh we'll just defer your admission until you're out of prison? And my record couldn't ever change after that because pleading means I swear under oath I really did it, even though I didn't do anything. Nothing. And what if they say I have to testify against Juan? I can't do that. Even if I knew something, which I don't, I wouldn't testify against Juan."

But Jane could not be persuaded into these fears any more than he could be persuaded out of them. They parted, Jane more peaceful and he more disturbed, especially when she grabbed his arm as he left and told him that if he went to prison, she would wait for him.

He walked out alone so that no observant neighbor would see them together. Jane followed in half an hour, but instead of going home to Morningside Heights she went crosstown to Dr. Garrard's office, where the receptionist was expecting her.

Michael's morning conversation with his wife had been particularly grim that day.

"Adriana," he had said, looking with dismay at her face. "You look unwell this morning. Didn't you sleep?"

She shook her head.

"Would you like to take something tonight? I could get you something very gentle and harmless—"

She cut him off. "No," she said firmly, as she had in the past. What if she became pregnant while taking some drug?

In silence, they ate soft-boiled eggs with toast.

"Then, I think—consider this seriously—I think you should see a psychotherapist."

"There's nothing wrong with me or my mind." She was offended.

"I know that. But I think you're so unhappy and anxious and tired that you're not making good decisions. You're not thinking straight. Why not allow yourself the luxury of a neutral sounding board? Someone who can help you sort things out."

"Psychotherapy has no cure for disappointments. It's normal to be sad about them."

"Yes, but—"

"You really have no sympathy at all. You don't understand that a woman might be profoundly miserable about not being able to have a baby."

"I think I do sympathize—deeply. I feel those things too, although probably not as much as a woman does. But, most important, I'm sure that I'd be happier if we adopted a child. I wish—"

"Stop, Michael. I'm only thirty-eight. Lots of women have babies even in their forties. It's too soon to give up."

"But I'm forty-eight. And it's not giving up, though you see it that way. Adriana, I'll tell you the truth. Sometimes I think you're not really interested in motherhood or child rearing. This obsession with becoming pregnant is—"

"I'm finished talking about it. I can't bear this."

Michael went silent. She would run out of the room if he persisted. He went to his office in a gloomy state that persisted until midmorning when the receptionist told him that Jane Braithwaite had called again. Then for the rest of the day he so looked forward to the girl's visit, scheduled for late afternoon, that he had to ask himself a terrifying question. Am I in love with her? he wondered. He could give himself no clear answer. He absolved himself of explicitly wrong motives, of seductiveness or, for that matter, seducibility. No, they were not flirting at the edge of anything like *that*—and, besides, it was clear to him that she was in love with Andrés. But being around her made him feel something like being in love. She made him aware of how different things might be. Life could be filled with delight, hope, cheer, beauty, fulfillments. It could be the opposite of what he had with Adriana. Michael even wished just that he had a daughter like Jane. That would have been enough. It wasn't, perhaps, so much that he was in love with her as with the idea of life that her existence tempted him to believe in. As these thoughts went wilding in his mind,

Jane herself appeared, conducted to him by Marie Collier, who was surprised by his manner in greeting the girl. Ms. Collier had never seen him so warm or human.

Jane's mood was strikingly different from what it had been the last time she had come. Now there was humility, or perhaps doubt, coloring her lightheartedness and self-approval. A complicated love affair would no doubt do that to a girl.

She avoided coming to the point—for it was obvious that she was burdened with some urgent communication. They laughed about Wyatt Jesse Younger, who, Jane told him, had questioned them closely about the plot of *The Matrix Reloaded*. She asked after Gabriela, whom she didn't visit so much lately, and told him, avoiding his eye, that Andrés kept talking about moving out. The boy was too straightforward, Michael saw immediately, to tolerate their situation. Like Jane, Michael found unbearable the thought of that stem-of-grass of a boy alone in the harrowing shelter the city provided for schizophrenics, alcoholics, and felons. He made a note to call the Braithwaites about it, even though the subject was so delicate.

"So what is it?" he asked, with courteous directness, after they had traded all possible items of news.

She looked at him with a poignant, resigned smile. "I took a home test—actually three of them—and it looks like I'm pregnant."

This missile exploded in Michael's brain with stunning effect. He was unable to respond for a full minute. Had he really just been wishing for a Jane in his own life? Was this catastrophe his own fault for not telling Charles and Anne what their daughter had been up to? And how could such a thing have happened in the first place? Charles and Anne's daughter would surely know how to avoid getting pregnant.

"How on earth did it happen?" he asked, irrelevantly from Jane's point of view, when he was again capable of speech. It was the only thought he had that he trusted himself to utter.

"It was just one time . . . we . . . we were not so careful. I mean we tried to be, but, you know, we just . . . messed up."

"What does Andrés say?"

"I haven't told him yet. Look, I know you're going to tell me to tell my parents, and I will. But not until I tell Andrés, and Andrés already has too much to worry about—his aunt, the drug charges. He doesn't need me to be a problem. I'll tell him after the court case is settled. That won't be too long. So I'm asking you not to press me to tell before that."

"Do you know how far along you are?"

"It happened about seven weeks ago, in early February."

"All right. We'll take a blood sample and confirm everything. Call me tomorrow. It's too late for results tonight. And Jane . . ." He paused to consider his words. "Have you thought about what you're going to do?"

"Oh, I'll have the baby. It's Andrés's baby."

"Jane, this is something to think hard about. You and Andrés have years and years ahead of you for having babies. You should both go to college and study and work. You don't want to miss out on all that."

"I hate school, Dr. Garrard. I'd rather learn on my own. I begged my parents for home schooling for years, but they'd never let me. I don't want to go to Juilliard. I just want to sing. I'll keep on the way I am, studying privately."

"And the baby?"

"Next to Andrés, the baby is the happiest thing that ever happened to me. I never knew. I had no idea it would be so wonderful to be pregnant."

She couldn't know, he thought, what she's in for, how her life will change, how it feels to be always responsible, and Andrés, for a dozen reasons, was even less able than other boys to do his part. Michael realized that one likely outcome of all this, indeed the probable outcome, was that Jane would soon be the mother of a baby whose father, though innocent, was imprisoned. The baby would be adolescent and Andrés's own youth would be over, perhaps, before he was released. In a civilized country, how could such things be allowed to happen? The possibility raised an oppressive sense of horror, followed by the dawning of the cruel and obvious ironies of the case—that he and Adriana, with all their maturity and resources, were being destroyed by their childlessness while the lives of this careless girl and boy and that of their child would be ruined by its untimely birth. How fiercely Mother Nature resisted all efforts to civilize these generative processes.

"Jane," he said, in a voice of affectionate persuasion, "wouldn't you rather enjoy just being young and in love with Andrés for a while, without diapers and night feedings? You'll miss so much." He couldn't yet bring himself to allude to the possibility of Andrés's conviction.

"I disagree. All that stuff people want me to do—I don't want any of it. I just want Andrés and my baby and my singing."

"And what if Andrés doesn't want to be a father so young?" he asked gently. "Most boys don't. What if—"

"He will. I know him. That's why I can't tell him yet. He'd start saying he has to quit school and work. But he should go to college. He's different from me. He loves his studies. And he won't go to prison, Dr. Garrard. If a jury sees him and hears his story, they'll believe him just the way we do."

Michael decided not to bring up any of the multitude of practical obstacles that loomed so obviously over Jane's childish plans for motherhood. He was dismayed that she should be in such a vulnerable position and should have so little common sense or realism about it. But no sooner had he registered this feeling in one part of his brain than another began to discard logic and denigrate difficulties and to see things much as Jane saw them. Of course the girl was entranced with the idea of having a baby. It just showed what a lovely girl she was. What sane human being could not understand that? Andrés, Jane, their baby, singing, and Chicago—how completely wonderful it sounded. But these sweetly sympathetic emotions were soon soured by envy, as he recalled how old he had grown, how unlikely to have any such joys in his own diminishing future.

Michael's envy was incurable; you could only cure envy by acquiring whatever it was you envied or by renouncing it. He would have to bandage it up and endure the hurt. By the time Jane stood to go, he felt committed to aiding her and Andrés however he could. He expected the Braithwaites to behave well when they heard the shocking news, but he knew Charles. Charles would be devastated. He would probably do everything in his power to convince Jane to terminate the pregnancy. Michael was miserable about deceiving Charles and Anne. For a few weeks he would keep Jane's secret. Then, when the trial was over, he would refer her to an obstetrician, and she would tell them. The question entered his mind whether his own wish for a baby was somehow operative here, but even if it was, Jane was not a minor and, as a matter of professional ethics, he had no right to breach her confidence. He had advised her to tell her parents; she herself would have to decide when to do so.

He instructed Marie to take Jane's blood and send it for the proper tests. Marie was too professional to show any surprise at this, but the girl was obviously very young and unmarried and the doctor was beside himself, as upset as Marie had ever seen him.

———

CHAPTER 24

The following afternoon, Adriana Simmons-Garrard had a phone
call from Marie Collier, who had just seen the results of Jane
Braithwaite's blood tests. The subject was awkward, but Marie was a
friend. For years, she had been a confidante in Adriana's fertility problems.
Until recently, she was neutral in the disputes between Adriana and her
husband, but as Adriana became more and more angry with Michael, so
did Ms. Collier, an unmarried woman with a vicarious interest in her em-
ployer's marriage as well as a great deal of intimate information about it.
She decided to risk Dr. Garrard's finding out, and she told Adriana her
suspicions.

Adriana was at first disbelieving and then stunned into silence.

"But don't tell him I told you," said Ms. Collier.

"I'll have to. How else could I know?"

"Then don't say I suspected him. Just say I happened to mention
something about how upset he was over a girl who was pregnant."

Adriana confronted him the moment he arrived home. "Who is this
pregnant girl Marie was telling me about?" she demanded, her face pale
and her eyes near to overflowing.

Michael stared at his wife. The unprecedented hardness in the way he looked at her reinforced her suspicions.

"What are you talking about?" he asked coolly.

"You know very well."

"She is someone who's entitled to seek my advice in confidence, Adriana, and you have no right to know or ask anything about any patient of mine. Marie is very wrong to have mentioned that girl. But since she did and you're so upset about it, I'll tell you that she's the daughter of . . . of friends of Greg Merriweather, who sits on the Ecumenical Council with me."

Adriana didn't know what to make of this. Puzzlement mixed with her anger. "I'm still waiting for you to explain this," she said.

"I never will. What right do you have to ask such a thing of me?"

"Am I supposed to take that as an admission?"

His face darkened, and something dangerous came into his expression. This visible fury undermined her own rage and made her doubt herself.

"You can see how I would think . . ." she said, faltering.

"No, I can't," he replied. "Not at all."

He went into their room, changed clothes, and left without speaking. He had never walked out like that before—without saying good-bye or telling her where he was going or when he would return. He frightened Adriana, which, again, reduced her anger and suspicion. All at once he seemed good and trustworthy. What had she done? She opened the door and called to him where he stood at the elevators. "I'm sorry, Michael," she said, tears beginning to stain her face. "Please come back."

But the elevator door opened, and he got in without answering. Was it possible, he wondered as he strode down Riverside Drive moments later, that all his tolerance and sympathy had actually helped make Adriana crazy? Should he have been harder on her all along, for her own good? For surely she was something very close to mad now, and she had not been ten years ago when they married. She had been fragile, though, he recollected. There had been something obviously shatterable about her. That eggshell quality had been part of the attraction. Perhaps he had wanted someone who needed him for more than his love.

The idea set a process of thought in motion, and as he walked aimlessly, he marshaled the evidences and consequences of this—his excessive patience, his tolerance of her narrowing life, his refusal to make demands on her, and, at the same time, his growing dislike for her and withdrawal from her. The insight was energizing. At the end of this mental review— which came when he found himself on the Columbia campus, standing at the entrance to Butler Library—he had also come to clear conclusions.

He would tell all this to Adriana, and they would try together to re-form the marriage. He would oppose her. He would make demands on her—insist on proceeding with an adoption, insist that she control her obsessions, broaden her horizons. He, in turn, would have to give up his separate life, the activities she couldn't share and the friends she didn't know. He would gradually begin to see less of them. She would demand that of him, and she would be right. He wiped tears from his face in the darkness, then entered the library and wandered the corridors.

In one hallway, he stopped at a bulletin board that posted notices for public lectures, a student Shakespeare production, something about cam-pus e-mail and downloading films, various items "For Sale" and "Wanted to Rent," and two that announced "Egg Donors Wanted." Adriana wanted to put up one of these. She had said that everybody advertised on cam-puses, especially at Ivy League schools where you'd find the best eggs. One of the notices specified that the donor should be Jewish and have fair complexion and average-to-above-average height, documentably excellent SAT or IQ scores, while the second also wanted someone of stellar intel-ligence, five feet seven or taller, blonde, good at sports, Christian, of Irish, Italian, English, or Ukrainian heritage. He was struck by the desire for genes of a certain national or religious origin—an idea that anyone with the slightest knowledge of either genetics or history would laugh at. These people, he thought, wanted to construct a version of themselves out of someone else's history and genetic material. It was very peculiar that those who posted these ads showed such complete indifference to the donor's moral and emotional life. They emphasized appearance, brains, health, and athleticism. You never saw anyone asking for donors who were good, generous, loyal, courageous, affectionate, kindly. Was it that they didn't be-lieve these things were inheritable even partially? Or was it more, as he sus-pected, that their motives were entirely derived from ambition—that their greatest concern was that they would be forced to raise a child who would not confirm their superiority? People who on some level knew how little they deserved their many privileges, he thought, were particularly prone to needing superior children.

Michael went to the reading room, where he sat pretending to study a scientific journal but actually watching the students with an irrational intensity, wondering what it must be like to have raised one of those vital, lovely young souls, with their silly haircuts and jeans, and their hopefulness and warmth, so obvious behind the conventional cynicism of their generation. What must it be like to have the right to adore and help one of these puppy-people, to visit on weekends, to admonish and comfort and plan gifts that would inspire smiles and embraces?

Surely, if Adriana and he adopted a child, she would mother it affectionately, he told himself. Surely, though she was now so concerned about getting a certain kind of baby, when she had one, like other women she would love her child just because she was its mother. She would end up one more happy victim of the parental delusion that one's own infant is irresistibly lovable, beautiful, and brilliant. But he couldn't stop arguing with himself about it.

CHAPTER 25

"Look, let me make this clear," said Mark Berman, slouched lazily behind his desk. "You take this deal, or you're probably going up for, I'd say, fifteen years. It's a class A-I drug felony, you violated probation on a prior drug offense, and you can't look remorseful if you keep insisting you're innocent. I negotiated a better deal than you had any right to expect—four years, maybe parole earlier. There's no choice."

"I can't testify against Juan. I don't even know anything about what he did, and I can't swear under oath I did something I didn't do. I didn't do anything."

"Okay, I'll make it even more clear. You take the deal or I walk. I'm not taking you to trial. This is friggin' stupid. They'll get Juan regardless. Your testimony isn't going to convict him. Just say what they tell you to say. They're trying to be nice to you. You can't go to trial. You can't go on the stand—they'll rip you to shreds. You got no witness except Juan, and he has zero credibility."

"I can't help it. My only chance is to go to trial. I can't go to prison. To me, four years, fourteen, twenty-four—it's the same. My life is over."

Berman was a man of about fifty with the opaque expression of all criminal-defense lawyers. He had represented dozens of clients charged with drug offenses, and there were no troubling ambiguities in this case, no anguishing probabilities. Everything tilted one way. He had already told Andrés's friends that in a trial consisting of Andrés's word against that of the undercover cops, he would be convicted.

"They're going to say they heard Juan and Andrés talking—'they got us' or something like that," Berman told Charles, Greg, Peter, Carla, and Michael on a conference call the following day to discuss the plea bargain. Peter was on the speakerphone in his office on 107th Street with Carla; Greg and Charles were on extensions at the Braithwaites'; and Michael was in his East Side office. "Or maybe 'I told you not to meet them here.' Or that Juan told them about his partner—anything that will show Andrés was in on it."

"But Juan and Andrés will both deny it," said Charles, sitting beside Anne at the kitchen table. Anne anxiously studied Charles's face; she could see that he was not happy. Greg, who was listening on the hall extension, looked very upset.

"Their word against the cops'," Berman said in the same indifferent style. "The jury will believe the cops—especially those cops. They're slick on the stand."

Peter sat behind his desk, leaning back, looking at Carla, who sat in front of it, leaning forward to hear the speakerphone. "Andrés could be very convincing too, if he were handled right," he said. Peter had talked with Andrés about his case several times. When he was talking with him, he tended to believe the boy was innocent, but later, when he stood back and considered matters coldly, he was swayed by Carla. "Juan . . . I don't know him. Regardless, okay, I guess you've convinced me on the odds, and we've tried to talk Andrés into taking the plea deal. He just won't. He's terrified of prison, and he says he's innocent."

Andrés's friends had all been as disturbed by the advice to accept a plea bargain as Andrés himself, and they had had even less success than Berman in persuading him to take it, perhaps because they, too, believed four years in prison was unconscionable—even if Andrés, desperate to help his aunt, really had tried to deal drugs. Peter had briefly argued to Andrés that the false swearing would perhaps be justified to prevent his being even more deeply wronged, but he'd given up. How could he be persuasive when he himself would have refused to swear to falsehoods under oath? Greg and the Braithwaites felt the same way.

"And the judge can't go easy on him?" Charles asked Berman.

"He can give him, at best, the mandatory minimum sentence, which is eight years, or he can approve the plea bargain. His hands are tied. And he can give him up to twenty years if he decides to stick it to him. Something in between eight and twenty would not be surprising because of the violation of probation."

"This is breathtakingly wrong," Charles said. "It's barbaric on every level."

"How perceptive of you," Carla responded to Charles's staticky voice. "Yeah, tens of thousands of the people in prison in this country are serving barbaric sentences for small offenses—and just about every one of them is poor. The laws are appalling. There's no more right to a trial— hardly anyone gets a trial. Everyone's forced into plea bargains because sentences are so extreme they can't risk a trial. And you wouldn't believe how often the wrong people are convicted because of cops who lie and crooked, brutal prosecutors who care nothing about justice and everything about their own careers. And on top of it all, the costs of defending yourself are ruinous unless you're really rich. But no one notices any of this until it happens to *their* pet poor person."

"Carla," said Peter, with the kind of patient anger that she so often inspired. "I think everyone understands all that. Why do you have to make a speech every time someone worries about Andrés?"

"People, I've got work to do," Berman said with sarcastic ennui.

"The prosecutor is a human being," Charles said. "Why is he going after this kid of all kids? He doesn't have to do it."

"Like this kid is so special," Carla scoffed, before Berman could answer. "Like all the other ones deserve what happens to them. The prosecutor thinks Andrés is just one more Dominican dealer. He thinks he's scum. He *believes* in putting people away in cages where they're treated like animals until they're weak and old and broken, all burned out and crazy and helpless. He thinks you're a liberal pansy. Frankly, it makes me a little sick, the way you make this kid into some special case while you ig—"

At this point, Peter figured out how to engage the mute button on his phone.

"Is there a chance Andrés would get sent to one of the nicer prisons?" Michael asked.

Berman snorted. "None of them are what I'd call nice. Anyway, the answer is—there's absolutely no guarantee—especially if the judge is mad at him for not taking the deal and insisting on a trial. Listen, there's nothing but bad news here—unless he pleads."

"Assuming he doesn't, how long until his trial?" asked Greg.

"Not long at all, I would guess," Berman said. "The case is open-and-shut. They're basically ready to go. I could try to delay, but what do we gain?"

"By all means, try to delay. At least let's get him graduated before all this happens," Peter said. Everyone heard annoyance in his voice. "I mean, if there's a legal miracle, this kid's going to the University of Chicago in the fall with a huge scholarship."

"It won't help legally," said Greg, "but, yes, let's try to hold them off until summer."

"I told him yesterday that if he didn't take the plea, I'd walk—I wouldn't take him to trial."

"Are you serious?" asked Charles.

"No, but I wanted him to think I was."

"Won't work," said Greg.

"And on appeal—" Charles began.

"Forget it. He's not getting out on bail pending appeal, and he'll lose his appeals."

Berman's threats convinced Andrés that prison was inevitable. He began to refuse meals and to come home late every night. There were signs that he had abandoned his efforts at school. After three weeks, he called Jane and said he wanted to talk. They met in Riverside Park, where crocuses and daffodils had begun blooming. Jane was tense, waiting to hear what he would say. Her ability to read Andrés had improved simply from being in the same household, despite his silence and his distance; he wanted to tell her something painful.

Now that she had heard the terms of the plea bargain, Jane passionately opposed Andrés's accepting it. She told him so even though she feared that this would send him into deeper retreat. But he had no response at all. He walked beside her, his hands in his pockets, black hair flying in the wind—so thin-looking from the side that he suggested some stylized, sculpted image of a boy. They sat on a park bench for what seemed a very long time before Andrés could tell her what he had come to say.

"All these guys," he said, gesturing broadly at the people drawn into the park by the fine spring weather, "I used to think they were nice. I wanted to be like them. But they're not really nice."

"*I* never thought they were nice," said Jane.

Andrés laughed because that was true.

"They're only nice to themselves—their own kids, their own kind," he said, looking around at the people strolling, walking dogs, and sitting on benches with their eyes closed and their faces upturned to the sun. "They're really kind of mean when you get to know them."

"Nice only to their own kids," said Jane. "Greedy and selfish and envious and mean to everyone else."

"Except a few of them," said Andrés.

"My parents, Dr. Garrard—just a few are really good," said Jane, and thought for a while. "Peter Frankl."

"Aunt Gabriela, Greg Merriweather," said Andrés.

"Be careful," said Jane. "If the list gets too long, we might have to start loving humanity."

"Oh, no. I can't see loving *everyone*," he said, and for the first time he looked her in the eye, which meant, she knew, that he loved *her*, and that made her brace for what was coming.

"I'm moving out this weekend," he told Jane. "What's coming down is really bad. I don't want you or your family mixed up in this. It's hard to explain."

"It's hard to explain because it's so nutty," she told him.

"See you later," he said, rising. "I just wanted to tell you that—so you wouldn't be surprised or anything." Jane knew he would cry if she pleaded and that he would hold that against her, so though her own tears flowed, she was mute.

He waited only a minute before walking off alone, leaving Jane on the bench, where she sat until nearly sundown hoping he would return. It had been difficult to resist calling him back to tell him she was pregnant. That might have held him, but it might also have been more than he could bear. When it began to grow dark, she cried a little more, and then she went home.

"Someone tell Andrés dinner," Anne said that night, draining linguine in a colander. Jane ignored this request, and Ellen called his cell phone.

"He says he's not hungry," she said.

"Tell him just to come anyway. No, wait—Janie, can you get this on the table? I'll talk to him."

Andrés was lying on Gabriela's bed with his arms over his eyes, and when he lowered them, Anne saw that he looked exhausted.

"You'll feel better if you just sit with us, even if you can't eat," she said. "Come on."

"No, thanks, really. I'm just . . . too tired. Besides, you all need some times when I'm not there." He would not look at her.

"No we don't. Listen, I won't insist tonight if you promise me you'll have dinner with us tomorrow. Will you promise?"

Andrés would not, and his eyes fixed on something outside the window.

"Did you see Gabriela today?" Anne asked.

"She's bad today."

"I talked to her this morning, and I could tell she was worse again," Anne said, and impulsively she took his hand. "Andrés," she began again, after waiting in vain for him to say something, "you're having trouble in school, aren't you?"

"It seems kind of pointless now," he said coolly.

"Believe me, it isn't. If Charles or I can help . . . I was wondering if you'd like us to hire a tutor for you, or more than one even. You missed a lot when you were so upset. Listen, we could arrange for you to—"

"No," he said, embarrassed. "No, I couldn't do that. Anyhow, I'm doing fine."

But the next day, when Anne got up her nerve to call and inquire about his grades, a counselor at the school, a Ms. Goldberg, said that if they judged by the past few weeks alone, he'd be failing every subject.

"You have to make allowances," Anne told her. "This is a traumatized boy. He has serious legal problems, his aunt is getting sicker every day. He has great difficulty concentrating. Please, Ms. Goldberg, don't let people lean on him too much. Help him out."

"I am very aware of all that, and I don't disagree with a word you've said. In fact, I talked to him about it a couple of days ago, and I told him he should drop out."

"You told him . . . Oh, I know you meant well, but please don't tell him that. School is his one hope. He needs to graduate so he can go to Chicago in the fall. It means everything to him. Please, just help him graduate. Trust me on this. I know this boy, and what's best for him is to graduate. Listen," said Anne, her voice suddenly bright and friendly. "Suppose I come down there and talk things over with you—maybe meet a couple of his teachers. After all, I'm sort of in loco parentis right now."

"That would not be appropriate. We talk to his social worker, his lawyer, and his aunt when we need to. Everyone responsible for this boy thinks he'd be better off if he just drops out. Otherwise there's a good chance he'll flunk out, which would be worse. He's under way too much stress. It's already led him to make some very big mistakes. Maybe he can avoid making more if he defers graduation until he gets himself straightened out."

"The social worker has only laid eyes on him twice, his aunt is too sick to pay any attention, and his lawyer . . . Look, Andrés is staying in our home. We're the ones who know what's going on with him."

"Mrs. Braithwaite, I'm sorry. I know *you* mean well. But it would not be appropriate for us to talk about our students with just anyone. There are legal issues, issues of confidentiality. I've already said more than I should have."

Anne was used to charming guidance counselors and school heads and teachers on behalf of her own children, but this one treated her with suspicion. Something in her voice bordered on disrespect.

"It's all prejudice," she told Charles as they read in bed that night. "Every doubt is decided against him—at school, even in criminal court where that's supposed to be illegal. I never really had to deal with it before. It enrages me. I can't get over my conversation with that horrible woman—or yours with the lawyer either. She seems to think there's no question but that he's guilty, by the way."

"She can tell him to drop out all she wants, but he won't do it," Charles said. "I think he'll graduate. I'll check in on him tomorrow and make sure he gets some work done. Maybe a little moral support..."

A meal, a bed, friendship—these things went for nothing in this situation, Charles thought, even though they were so hard to give. They were at the far limit of his and Anne's moral capacity, and even so, they were not enough.

Anne called Lily Freund, her psychoanalyst friend, to discuss Andrés's situation. They were on the telephone for more than an hour. Lily was concerned and begged Anne to send him to her. "A little supportive counseling," she said, "is all I'd be able to do, but that can make a big difference. It could really help his concentration, his confidence."

"I'll try to get him to call you," Anne promised. But the following morning, a Sunday, there was no answer when Anne knocked at the door of Gabriela's room, and when she looked in, she discovered that Andrés's things were gone. He had left a note on her desk saying that he would be staying at the shelter until the trial. It would be easier for everyone. He couldn't stand bringing so much trouble into their lives and getting the kids upset. Thank you for everything, he said, but he was starting to be too much trouble.

PART THREE

The Garrard family, with its patient, wise father, its gentle and lovely mother, and their longed-for delightful infant who, every month, failed them, was malignantly unhappy. Its misery had reached some dangerous stage in which it infected everything that was said and done in their gracious apartment. Michael diagnosed their deterioration as the product of a collision of personal and societal weaknesses. Their society, or at least the part of it that survived in Morningside Heights, was itself so debilitated that it could offer nothing to equal child rearing as the moral center of life, thus condemning legions of people, the single and infertile and the bereaved, to deadly moral deprivation. Surely, he thought, this was a historical novelty, a new form of cultural depravity even, for it created people whose selfish devotion to their children meant unfeeling indifference to anyone else's, yet convinced them of their own warm humanity. Andrés's case had brought this home to him. The paradoxical flip side of child worship was escalating cruelty and hardness.

"Oh, yes, that's psychologically unavoidable," Anne's friend Lily said one night at dinner, when Michael made the point. "Parenthood is a natural reservoir of narcissism. Where else could greed and ego disguise themselves as altruism? And when narcissistic personalities become parents, the whole phenomenon escalates. Those parents become the last people in the world who'll worry about other people's children, and they'll hate poor people's kids most of all. You'd expect them to be merciless and sadistic, and they are. And I agree, Michael, the juvenile justice system is where you find the most horrendous evidence of this."

"Oh, dear, Lily," said Anne. "Do you think Charles and I are like that?"

"Of course not," Lily said, taken aback at the suggestion.

But Jonathan, Lily's partner in a childless and, their friends surmised, sexless relationship, felt that Lily had come uncomfortably close to condemning the Braithwaites and all the other parents in the neighborhood. Not that any of them were innocent. Of course they weren't. It had all gotten so bad that now when people began to have children you almost said good-bye to them. Having kids meant withdrawal from friends, society, and social responsibility. It drove Jonathan crazy, but if he or Lily were to say anything like that, they'd sound like a pair of bitter old spinsters or cranky old bachelors—he wasn't sure which. Jonathan looked at Michael, another childless man, who might be expected to be thinking similar thoughts, but couldn't interpret the frown on his face.

In the weeks that followed this conversation, Michael thought of it often. Lily had put her finger on part of what troubled his own marriage. Didn't he and Adriana exemplify how those corrupted attitudes toward family life played out in the bosom of a childless family? Whatever the cause, his unfinished little family was dying, and he began to fight for it. He administered painful remedies, braving the patient's agonized screams. He sacrificed his own happiness, limiting his prospects to those his invalid wife could share. For over two weeks, he was stern and demanding with Adriana, and her attitudes began to shift.

"Michael, I know you've been right all along. We should have adopted a baby long ago," Adriana said at the breakfast table.

She waited for a response, but none came, and she continued. "Let's try now. Please, Michael, forgive me. I was wrong. You have to understand how fraught all this is for me. I make mistakes."

He thought for a few moments, and she watched the hardness on his face begin to break up—around the eyes first. His brows lifted slightly, and he shifted his glance downward.

"What are you thinking? Are you willing to go ahead with an Asian adoption?" he asked coolly, folding up the morning paper.

She hesitated. "If we're sure there's nothing possible in the States. But shouldn't we look here first?"

"If you like."

Adriana's tension increased at this tolerant indifference. "Well, don't we want a baby as much like ourselves as possible?"

"I have no idea."

"Michael, surely that much is obvious."

"Not to me."

Adriana grew teary, and he felt remorseful.

"I don't mean to be difficult, Adriana, but actually I do feel uncomfortable setting up criteria, trying to come up with an adopted baby who would resemble what we imagine our biological child would be. That seems not very fatherly or motherly to me."

She looked perplexed; his way of thinking mystified her. She, of course, would want to find a baby that she could feel sure would be tall and dark, as they were, and very bright—one that strangers would casually accept as theirs so that she would not constantly be reminded of her infertility. Adriana would think it obvious that they should do this. Many people would. He, Michael, was the peculiar one, fearing some sort of moral slippery slope in this ordinary wish for a child like oneself.

Adriana looked sadly across the breakfast table at Michael, and he felt sorry for her. She was trying hard to please him and did not know how. He weakened in his resolve to be more demanding of her, despite the fact that doing so, so far, had brought her nearer what seemed to him something like sanity.

"Anyway, I doubt we'll have choices," he said. "If we could find a healthy baby who needs a home, I'd consider us very lucky." These were the friendliest words he had uttered in days.

There was a pause during which Adriana stealthily observed Michael, slight motions of her eyes betraying that she was frantically weighing her options. Her plotting, to him, was transparent, with a furtive, animal wiliness and a shocking coldness toward him that made her seem like a predator, though an unintelligent one, for she seemed unaware that he was much stronger and more dangerous than she. From the heights of his superiority, Michael was even more sorry for her as he felt the futile grip of her tiny claws.

"Don't be angry, Michael," she began, smiling fearfully, "but I've been wondering about one thing."

He looked at her curiously. She was so evidently terrified yet convinced that she had to risk some enraged reaction from him.

"That girl . . ."

Ah, he thought. She scanned his face urgently.

"What will she do with the baby? She's not married, is she?"

"How do you know?" he asked.

"You know that Marie told me."

"And what else did she tell you?"

"Just her name. I found out the rest by myself. I looked in her file in your office one night when you were gone, and then I . . ."

"Good God, Adriana. You know that I'll have to fire Marie now. And I'll have to change the locks on the office doors and forbid you ever to go there again. Surely Marie made you promise not to tell. Why did you break your promise to her?"

"You're so strange, Michael. What do you care if I broke my promise to Marie?" Adriana cried. "That's not what's important here."

"I'd like you to understand how wrong it was and what damage you're doing to people around you."

"You have to help me or I'll die," Adriana said in a small voice, her breath catching oddly. "I'll die."

"What do you mean?" he asked, in the controlled, serious voice with which one demands that a child tell the truth.

"If you won't help me with this, I'll kill myself. I won't be able to stand it."

"*Kill* yourself? You're saying that because you know how my mother died. You think I won't risk it."

"I'll do it, Michael. I don't care what you think about my motives. I'll do it."

"This is real madness, Adriana."

"I *mean* it, Michael."

"And what help do you want that you think I'm withholding?"

"This girl's baby—did you ever think how perfect it would be for everybody if *we* adopted it? It would be physically like us, and bright. And she shouldn't be raising a baby at her age. She's got a future—she's major talent. Her parents have four kids already. They're not going to want to raise their cleaning lady's grandson. They'd probably be delighted if you offered to . . ." Adriana began smiling tentatively, as though she felt sure of her persuasiveness.

"Did you hire a detective, Adriana? You've obviously done more than read my office file. But you don't know this girl or these people or the situation. I do. You must believe me when I tell you that there is no possibility that the girl you're talking about would give up her baby for adoption. Not the slightest chance. You must stop this madness." He stood and went for his coat and briefcase.

"You could at least talk to her."

"No. You'll just have to accept this. It would not be ethical for me to approach her on the subject even if it weren't hopeless—which it is."

"I'm begging you, Michael. Please, help me. Please. This baby would fix everything. This baby would be special."

"I refuse to discuss my patient with you, Adriana. I think you had better see a psychiatrist."

As he left the building, stepping out onto Riverside Drive, a thought occurred to him that made him wheel around and hurry back. He reentered the apartment quietly and went to Adriana's office, where she was sitting at her computer, back to the door.

"Adriana," he said. She jumped and gasped, but closed the window that was open on her computer before she turned around.

"Ah! You scared me," she said.

He went to the computer and, leaning over her, reopened the window, on which was visible a directory entry showing the home address and telephone number of the Braithwaites.

Michael took Adriana's frightened face between his hands and stared at her for a moment with the icy expression that had become familiar to her in the past weeks, before this morning's brief relapse into kindness.

"If you do that," he said, "I will divorce you." And he left again.

He had not known until that moment that he wanted to divorce her. The realization immediately brought to life his love for her. He considered all the facts that argued against divorce. Adriana was obviously going through some sort of breakdown. She needed his help, although not the help she thought she needed. She might well attempt suicide. What difference did it make if her behavior was manipulative and wrong? If she weren't mentally disturbed, she would not do this. He had to get hold of himself and act in her interests.

Moreover, growing calmer, he had to admit that the idea of adopting Jane's baby had enormous appeal even to him. Why shouldn't Adriana have felt as she did? He wanted a baby perhaps as much as Adriana did, if less madly, and he could so easily love Jane and Andrés's baby. But was Adriana fit to mother a child? Perhaps if she had a baby in her arms, she would become so. Maybe it would cure her, even save her life. Yet, it would be an experiment, doubtful of outcome, and he had no right to expose an innocent child to Adriana's debilitated mental state. In any case, how could it be better for Jane's baby to lose the sweet young mother who wanted it so badly and loved its father so much—especially given Adriana's deteriorating condition? On the other hand, if Andrés was convicted, wouldn't the balance of everything tilt and wouldn't the child be better off with him and Adriana? Michael could not help wishing for the baby and thus feeling things he preferred not to feel about Andrés's fate. Nor could he help fearing and crediting Adriana's threat to kill herself. His anxiety on that score was suddenly so intense that for a moment nothing else mattered except saving Adriana.

Yet in the next moment he felt an even more powerful protectiveness toward Jane. Of course, he and Adriana would not adopt her baby—or any baby—not to save Adriana's life, not to save the baby from its own father, who was, after all, innocent and good. But neither would he divorce Adriana, any more than he would if she had AIDS or couldn't walk. He could not desert her when she was ill, not even if her illness seemed, at times, indistinguishable from wickedness.

As Michael walked slowly down Riverside Drive, all but stumbling in his distraction, with his eyes on the sidewalk, these preoccupations warred with the brilliance of the late-spring morning, its breezes carrying the smells of freshly turned earth and flowers from the riverside promenade. He struggled to banish a morbid sense of Adriana's deterioration as decay.

On reaching Broadway, though, Michael helplessly absorbed the energy of the crowds rushing to work with their briefcases and laptops; or to classes, their arms full of books with rousing titles; or to lessons, carrying fat black cases pregnant with unknown instruments—all of them, with the easy coordination of the practiced, talking on cell phones and sipping out of paper coffee cups while dodging pedestrian collisions. In the vital atmosphere of the street, Michael felt a teary relief.

He hailed a cab and arrived at his office with time before his first appointment to study a set of lab reports that arrived by messenger just as he did. He had been worried about what these reports would tell him, and they were so engrossing that he entirely forgot Adriana and all their difficulties. At nine, Marie Collier ushered in Wyatt Younger, who looked tired and ill. Marie could tell from the way the doctor looked at her that Adriana had betrayed her, and the knowledge brought with it, belatedly, an acute sense that she had done wrong, along with the realization that her job was over. Pale and dejected, she left the two men alone.

"Mr. Younger, I have good news," Michael told his patient. "I'm very sure you've been misdiagnosed. You've been wise to come to me, although I quite understand your loyalty to your family doctor—especially after all he did for your father. But whatever it is you've got, it's not Lou Gehrig's disease. I don't believe you're dying. I believe you might have Lyme disease, and I want to start you on—"

"Call me Wyatt," said Younger, with an open, childish smile.

CHAPTER 27

"Trial in May?" Carla said. "They couldn't wait until school is out? What scumbags. So there'll be a sentencing hearing maybe as soon as June. The case is so simple. He'll be locked up by summer—actually, as soon as he's convicted, May—for the rest of his youth, maybe the rest of his life because people die young in prison. It's over, Greg. Don't take it so hard. There are millions of Andréses in the world. Just because you happen to know this particular boy who . . ."

Greg had by now taken on Andrés's case with a degree of dedication that maddened Carla. He made many trips to the Bronx to visit him at the shelter, sometimes alone, twice with Charles, and he called his lawyer several times a week. Through the Ecumenical Council, he had found a Catholic organization to help Gabriela. It had paid to have her moved to a hospice on Staten Island. That was best for her but hard for Andrés to get to. It was all but impossible for him to visit her after school and make it back to the Bronx at a decent hour. Gabriela was lonely at the hospice and cried for her daughters and for Juan, who could not make bail. To Greg, it seemed as though she always gave Andrés a grudging welcome— kindly but stinted. She held something against him.

Greg remembered how bad it felt to be a teenage boy with no family, and his situation had never been as terrifying as Andrés's. He knew that shelters for the mad, bad, and broken were scary places and that it was hard to sleep through the howls and sobs that broke out all night long and only died off when the sun rose. The idea of Andrés alone in there or traveling back there from the hospice late at night frightened him. Andrés got more and more tired, hollow-eyed, and thin. Greg asked the rector for permission to let Andrés move into his apartment, but the rector, after thinking about it, refused. They had limited resources to help the poor, and Andrés's case was no more, and perhaps less, sympathetic than scores of others they knew of. Andrés was welcome to get in line for one of their twenty beds for homeless men, but, otherwise, felons and drug dealers were not going to be sleeping in the parish house. They weren't prepared to handle the problems that such people brought in with them. He was sorry.

The rector looked the other way, though, when Carla showed up, and she and Greg took care to keep her comings and goings discreet. At this moment, close to midnight, they were together in Greg's bed. Somehow pillow talk, once again, had degenerated into political debate.

"Carla," Greg said, "I wish you wouldn't talk about it that way. What is this statistical morality of yours? Why don't individuals count for you?" He wasn't wearing his glasses, but her face was so near that he could see her well without squinting.

"Christian charity!" she said. "You feel so virtuous, like you earned your way into heaven because you take on a boy here or an old lady there and you *give* people things that they have a right to. Then you decide you don't have to worry about millions of others in exactly the same boat who don't get any help. And it sounds so noble: helping real flesh-and-blood individuals, warts and all!"

"I don't think that if I help Andrés in a personal way I'm off the hook for the millions," Greg said patiently. "You know I don't, because I work for systematic causes too. Why would you think so ill of me?"

"I do people more good than you."

"No doubt you do. But I still think—"

"Stop. You know, Greg, this doesn't work."

"What?"

"You and me."

"Yes, it does. It works, Carla."

She heard grief in his voice. "It was so obvious right at the beginning. We are such different types," she said.

"You're always making up stories about what I'm like—like you don't even want to know me," Greg said.

"Greg, sweetie, you are a straight-arrow, gentle, prissy priest. I am a godless, atheist ruffian. We belong together like Christopher Robin and Emma Goldman." Carla swung her legs out of the bed and began reaching for her clothes. Greg was particularly partial to Carla's pretty legs—so much so that he surprised himself.

Still, he loved Carla not for her legs, nor for any of her other good points, but Carla didn't believe it. She didn't believe in love. She always thought the legs came first. You had a list of traits you wanted people to have—like good legs or money or love of hiking—and then you loved someone who had enough of the items on the list. Greg had learned that it didn't work that way, and he had to admit that he was not entirely clear on what it meant that he loved Carla "for herself" or why he loved Carla rather than any of the thirty-seven single Episcopalian women at Saint Ursula's who were quiet, smart, congenial, sweet, refined, compatible in their tastes, habits, and religious beliefs, and sometimes pretty too. Once Greg met Carla, he had stopped his desultory attempts to date such women, who were a lot like him. From then on, Greg wanted only Carla, a woman who provided almost none of the items on his own pre-Carla list of desirable traits—which definitely hadn't even included legs. He and Carla were like puzzle pieces that were shaped quite differently but fit perfectly together; neither alone made a picture but the two together did—if only she would see it. He told her that. He told her that he'd never even known who he was until he got together with her, that loving her had illuminated and energized his entire life. But she hadn't much liked that kind of talk.

"See, Carla, you treat me like a type, a statistic, like you don't know me personally or something. You just want to avoid . . . Don't go, Carla, please." He reached around her waist and pulled her back down. "How could you leave now?"

"You overvalue sex something terrible," she said, allowing herself one last pleasurable embrace. They lay curled together spoon-style, and he kissed the back of her neck and shoulders. But soon she struggled to free herself again and resumed dressing, and Greg changed the subject so that she would not leave.

"Carla, is Berman doing a good job for Andrés?"

"Let's put it this way: no one could do better."

"He's so unsympathetic. Andrés gets into a bad state every time he sees him. It concerns me. I'm not sure he's really thinking much about strategy for a trial, either. I mean, I know I'm not much of a lawyer my-self—"

"I'd say he earned his fee with the plea bargain Andrés turned down."

"He says he's not going to put Andrés on the stand, and so far it looks like there won't be any witnesses for the defense."

"So? It's a reasonable-doubt case. He's going to say the prosecution didn't carry its burden. That's not crazy. He'll do good cross-examination."

"Something feels wrong to me. He's not putting enough effort into this."

"What's wrong was turning down the plea bargain. Berman knows he's licked in a trial. The plea bargain was the only way."

"You don't really think Andrés should testify falsely against Juan, do you?"

"It wouldn't be all that false. Do you really believe that, coming from his background, Andrés never had the thought that Juan occasionally dealt a little?"

"As a matter of fact, I feel pretty sure of that. Juan has no record. Carla, I think it's important for everyone, especially Andrés, for you in particular to really understand—"

"Greg, you make me crazy. This case is already lost. I gave you my best advice, and you ignored it. You and your friends were too busy being saintly to listen to me or Berman, and now this kid is going down. You

have to understand, though—I don't care. I told you that from the beginning. My aim is to change the laws and the prisons. This boy or that man
are not my concern. You're not going to change me, Greg."

"Carla, please just let me try to explain something to you."

"Can't, Greg. I'd better go. I told you it would come to this." Greg was
still under the covers but sitting up now with his arms wrapped around his
knees, his face buried in them. He stayed like that while she dressed and
strode briskly around the room collecting belongings that were strewn
here and there.

"Come on. Kiss me good-bye," Carla said when she had pulled on her
coat.

Greg wouldn't raise his head. "Better just go," he said, his voice muf-
fled by the blanket.

She could hardly hear him, and mistook his sadness for anger. She
hesitated for a moment, then opened the door. "Bye," she said softly, looking back at him.

Now, how did that happen? she thought, walking home, shivering in
her short jacket and skirt. She hadn't intended to break up—not yet anyway. She had just wanted to put things on a different footing—make Greg
understand how it really was between them. But she had a feeling that he
wouldn't call anymore. By the time she reached her apartment, she was
thoroughly miserable, and when she switched on the light in the kitchen,
the sight of roaches scurrying everywhere sickened and depressed her.

CHAPTER 28

For the third morning in a row, Jane was sick in the bathroom she shared with Ellen.

"What's wrong with you?" Ellen demanded, looking on with disgust as Jane hovered expectantly over the toilet, gasping. "Why are you going to school when you're vomiting all the time?"

"Some flu bug. I feel fine as soon as I throw up."

"Yeah, but usually you try to stay home if you chip your fingernail."

"I can't miss rehearsals this week." Jane had a part in the school play.

"I should have known. Ego conquers all. And here I was wondering whether you were either pregnant or going bulimic on us."

Ellen was now alert to how much her sister had changed. Something in Jane's face made Ellen feel sorry for her. She regretted teasing her, but constant verbal battery on her sister was a lifelong habit.

On Saturday morning, Ellen awoke again to the sound of Jane retching in the bathroom. She went into the kitchen and came back with a glass of ginger ale. "This is supposed to be good for nausea," she said.

Jane was suspicious but drank the soda and got back in bed.

"You better tell Mom you're sick," said Ellen. She was beginning to find the whole business a little frightening. "If you don't tell her, I will."

"I can't," said Jane. "I'm begging you, Ellen, don't tell her." Jane's expression was so urgent that Ellen knew. She knew, and Jane saw that she knew. Ellen stared at her sister, her hands pressed over her mouth, as though she had to hold back her voice. It was frightening but exciting. There was something ecstatic about it. She got into Jane's bed beside her.

"Is it Andrés?" she whispered.

Jane nodded. "I'm begging you, Ellen."

"I won't tell," Ellen said, after thinking hard. She was so agitated by the news that she sounded breathless, as though she had been running.

Jane trusted Ellen's promise. Ellen was mean but honest and reliable.

"When did it happen? How far along are you?" Ellen asked.

"Going on four months. They're saying the baby's due October twenty-seventh."

"Jane—a baby this fall! What are you going to do?"

"We can get married when his trial's over. But he doesn't know yet. I didn't tell him because he's just got too many worries right now."

Ellen had been alert to both the affair between Andrés and Jane and the breach. She didn't question Jane's confidence. "But where will you live? What will you do? Are you sure he wants to get married?"

"We never talked about it, but he'll want to. We'll figure everything out. He's going to Chicago. Maybe I'll go out there with him. I don't really want to go to Juilliard. I want to take care of the baby. I'll study privately."

"Oh, yes," Ellen said fervently. Jane's having Andrés as a boyfriend was amazing, but the main thing, of course, was the baby. A baby was an extraordinary thing, so out of reach yet so easy to get. She would take Jane's word for it that Andrés would want to marry and raise their child.

Jane discovered the depth of her own passion for the baby when she saw it reflected in Ellen's eyes. We got this baby-crazy business from Mom, she thought. The new sense of being like her mother was comforting this time. She had always resented her mother's pregnancies, but now that she herself was pregnant, she understood. She understood not just her mother, but life. Babies were the secret. Babies were the answer.

"And maybe I could audition for parts. Or work part-time and we could take out loans," Jane continued. "I could teach at home like Mom. I think I could really teach. But I don't know yet."

"Mom and Dad will die. Especially Dad."

"Ellen, why aren't you mad at me for making trouble again?"

"I don't know," Ellen replied with a silly smile. "He's nice, Andrés. I really like him. I know he didn't do the drug stuff. Anyhow, I wouldn't care even if he did. He's the best boyfriend you ever had. I kind of had a crush on him too, but I knew he was too old for me and he liked you. Besides, this is just—I don't know, so . . . interesting. You're gonna be a mother, and I'm gonna be an aunt. No one can stop us." Ellen gripped Jane's shoulders and shook her excitedly.

Jane had not expected any sympathy, and she discovered how badly she wanted some when tears of relief filled her eyes. Ellen seemed to understand everything—at last. She seemed to feel what Jane did. The two of them whispered for another hour, until they were interrupted by the little boys, who came in shrieking and shouting and jumped on the bed, privileged to make this assault by their mother's order to go wake the sleepyheads.

Anne detected the new alliance between the sisters less than three minutes after they walked into the kitchen—the way one handed the juice pitcher to the other, the eye contact, their coordinated response to the boys' quarrel over a favorite mug. She also knew that Jane had been crying. This, she guessed, was about Andrés. She could well imagine that Ellen had been sympathetic on that subject. Anne, too, felt sorry for Jane, but mostly she felt glad that they had broken up.

Anne would have been surprised to learn that her thinking on this subject was exactly like Andrés's. There was no way that Jane, or her parents, could share their own safety with Andrés, and Andrés's dangers would inevitably bruise Jane and all of them. Merely knowing Andrés, just being intimate with someone so miserable, was dangerous. It destroyed their peace of mind to have to weigh constantly whether they owed anything to this stray boy who had insinuated himself into their home, to whom they had now committed great amounts of money and emotion—though not enough of either to satisfy their consciences or to save him.

Charles arrived last in the kitchen, unshaven, mussed, and innocently puffy-eyed, black hairs and a few gray ones curling over the neck of his T-shirt. Ellen and Jane seemed oddly embarrassed by his kiss, and Anne, all but in tears, embraced him needily. He patted her shoulder and looked at her in bleary mystification. Thankfully, at least his boys were normal, understandable human beings. They screamed joyfully when he scooped them up, one in each arm, rubbed his scratchy face against their silky skin, and gave each a loud, smacking kiss on the neck.

"Is Michael coming tonight or not?" Anne asked Charles when he was fortified with coffee and his usual Saturday omelet. "I called him three times, and he won't give me a straight answer. I think he's avoiding us."

"I get the same feeling," said Charles. "He's not coming—I forgot to tell you."

"Did we offend him?"

"No, he's got problems or something."

"His wife," Anne said. "It's strange how he never brings her over." She did not miss the swift look that passed between her daughters. But what secret understanding about Michael Garrard and his wife might the two of them share? They've been gossiping together and making things up—that he's getting divorced or something, Anne thought.

"Does he hear from Libertarianism Inc. anymore?" asked Jane.

Oh, very good, thought Anne. Very good change of subject disguised as the opposite.

"He calls him Wyatt now," said Charles. "He sees Wyatt fairly often. Michael debates Professor Selvnick, and Wyatt listens."

"Creepy," said Jane.

"I know they gave him all that money," said Anne. "But imagine spending your free time chatting up those two. Poor Michael. I don't think any amount of money would be worth it. Charles, maybe you should call up Michael and meet him for a drink or something."

"I tried. Can't pin him down."

"Well, that's really a mystery. *That's* not on account of his wife," said Anne. Again, she observed the girls telegraphing something across the breakfast table. Whatever the reason was, it was no secret to them.

Jane hadn't seen or spoken to Andrés for weeks. She called him several times a day, but his cell was never on. She e-mailed him at his school address, and he never answered. She asked Greg if he was all right. Fine— a little depressed, naturally, Greg said. Greg had been the first one to hear that he had a trial date. Jane had written it down on her calendar. She would be there pulling for him—she would skip classes. He would be acquitted, and then they would be together again. Jane was relieved that the trial would soon be over and told herself again and again that he would not be convicted. Such a catastrophe was too enormous to think about, even though Greg and Dr. Garrard both kept hinting that she should prepare herself for the worst. She hadn't any idea at all how to prepare herself to lose her lover, the father of her child, let alone see him shattered by the inhumanity and sadism of prison life. Her grandmother and mother had told her all about the horrors of such places, but they had also taught her that she would never suffer them. Her mind simply spat out the indigestible idea that Andrés would. When Andrés was first arrested, Jane had been so upset that she could not conceal it. Fortunately, everyone seemed to think it natural that she should take a friend's misfortune hard. But, as a resolution grew near, Jane grew more and more calm. She trusted Greg and Dr. Garrard to stand by Andrés and help him. They were the sweetest, kindest men in the world; they believed in Andrés's innocence. Jane leaned on them, but even more on Ellen.

Every night, in Jane's room, the sisters whispered their secrets. They grew closer and closer until, finally, they were rather in love with each other. Ellen listened faithfully to Jane's reports on her weight gain, her symptoms, what Dr. Garrard said or thought. She was sensible and strong. She hid crackers in her room for Jane to nibble on to fight nausea. She reminded Jane to take her folic acid and multivitamin. She used her allowance to buy books on pregnancy, childbirth, and babies at the bookstore, and the two of them read, lying side by side on the bed, and afterward tucked the books under the mattress. Jane thought that Ellen was the smartest, nicest, best sister anyone could ever have.

"Are you going to have an epidural or natural childbirth?" Ellen asked her.

"I think I'll have an epidural for the first one," said Jane, "like Mom did. And then when I have more babies, the labor should go easier, and I'll do without."

"Yeah," said Ellen, with a serious nod. "Can you believe this, Jane? You're really going to get a big belly and go through labor and all that. And who's going to be with you at the delivery? Mom?"

"Are you kidding? Andrés will be there!" said Jane, shocked at the question.

"Jane, Daddy and Greg think Andrés might be found guilty. Aren't you worried?"

Jane shook her head.

"You're sure he loves you?"

Jane nodded emphatically. She had seen his tears. She knew that he had gone up to the shelter only because he loved her so much, and that was also why he was angry.

"Maybe you should tell Nana."

"She'd tell Mom. Don't get cold feet on me. It's just two weeks now until the trial. Then I'll tell. Don't—"

Jane stopped, alert. "My cell. It's Andrés," she said, frantically digging for the phone among the books and pillows strewn on her bed. But it was a strange voice, a woman's. "Who?" Jane asked the caller. "I don't understand . . ."

Jane listened, her politely puzzled expression gradually giving way to suspicion.

"This has nothing to do with you. I don't want to talk to you anymore," Jane said, and snapped the phone shut.

"What was that all about?" Ellen asked.

"She said she was Adriana Garrard—Dr. Garrard's wife."

CHAPTER 29

"If you had my life," Andrés told Greg one Sunday afternoon, a week before his trial, "you wouldn't believe in God either." Greg had brought him a bagged lunch at the Staten Island hospice where Gabriela lay, half-stuporous, drugged and weak.

Greg considered telling Andrés a little about his own childhood, then decided against it. "Your aunt believes in God," he said.

"She's ignorant. She doesn't even know what evolution is, or global warming. She thinks you can make deals with God—you just promise to do something he wants, and then he'll do what you want." Andrés's snicker was scornful, but Greg also caught a note of boyish lightheartedness in it. That must be what Andrés would be like if the world let him lead an ordinary boy's life. His troubles made it hard to know him. All Greg ever saw of Andrés was a glimpse now and then, like the one he'd just had. Jane probably saw more, but as far as Greg knew, she hadn't been in touch with Andrés for weeks.

Greg himself visited Andrés often enough to have grown accustomed to the signs of homelessness in his looks. Even so, this afternoon he was dismayed by how underfed and sad the boy looked—and unwashed.

There were always creepy guys hanging around the bathroom, Andrés told him, and he wouldn't shower when they were there.

"Andrés," Greg said, "next weekend, before the trial, you have to come stay with me. We'll get you a haircut and some nice clothes for court, and you can rest and pull yourself together."

"Well, maybe I . . . Greg, I'm sorry I don't believe in God."

"It's okay," said Greg shyly. "So you come to my place Friday, right after school." Greg would brave the rector for a few days.

Andrés nodded, looking absently around the little lunchroom. Even though it was humiliating to need help so desperately, Greg's offer was very welcome.

"Andrés, you keep saying it's the end of your life if you're convicted. That worries me," Greg said. "I don't think it's true. It'd be very, very bad, but you're young and strong. You'd get through it. You'd have lots of friends—the whole time and when you get out. And we'd keep on fighting for you. You wouldn't be abandoned. So you've got to fight too. You're a good fighter."

"I don't want to anymore," Andrés said. "I been fighting a long time."

"Maybe you won't have to. But if you do," Greg said, "I'm with you every minute. A lot of people will be."

"That's just what a priest would say. Sorry man, but it's not true. When the door locks, you'll be outside, and I'll be in there all alone."

"Why don't you get in touch with Jane?" Greg asked abruptly, blushing. "She's always calling me about you."

Andrés ignored this. "I have to get back to Gabriela now," he said, standing.

"I have to go too," Greg said. "There's a thing I'm in charge of at Saint Ursula's this afternoon. So I'll see you Wednesday at the shelter, and, remember, Friday you come to my place."

Andrés returned to find Gabriela sleeping, her mouth gaping, her face swollen and yellow, and her scalp shining obscenely through wisps of salt-and-pepper hair. He sat in the visitor's chair and took her hand, but she slept on for nearly an hour.

"So what you gonna do?" she asked, when she awoke and saw him beside her. Her voice was the same as always—the only thing about her that was.

Andrés shrugged, indifferent, incurious.

"Run," she whispered.

He shook his head adamantly.

"Don't worry about the bail. They're rich. Run. They be glad, I bet."

"No, I want an acquittal. Anyway, I'm not going to prison."

"You're crazy," Gabriela said in a tired voice. But then she looked at him suspiciously. "Better go to prison than burn in hell, Andrés."

"There is no hell," he told her, picking up a magazine that lay on her bed table.

"See, you think you're so much better than us with ideas like that. Where did all that ever get you? I told you—if you just went out for a job two years ago, none of this would be happening, none of it, not my kids, not Juan, not—"

"Maybe so," he said, his voice shaking. "But I thought if I went to college, I could buy you a nice house. Juan said—"

"You and Juan make me sick." Gabriela swallowed tears and groaned a little as she turned on her side. "How could people be so bad, to lock up Juan in a cage? No bail for him—he *would* run. They're right he would."

"Time for me to go," Andrés said, and he hurried out. He kept his head down as he strode out, but the nurses saw anyway that his face was wet.

"Poor kid," said one.

While Andrés was riding the ferry back to Manhattan, Peter Frankl, Carla Winter, and Michael Garrard discussed his case with increasingly sodden despair in the same seedy Broadway pub where the postmortem of the first meeting with Younger and Selvnick had been conducted.

"It's the proverbial train wreck in slow motion," said Peter. "It's riding the plane plunging to the ground with its engines out or the car on a collapsing bridge. There are no human forces that can intervene to prevent the catastrophe you see coming. It's too late."

"What a way you have with metaphor, Peter," said Carla. "But there are actually plenty of human forces that could prevent it. The judge could prevent it. The prosecutor could prevent it. The newspapers might have been able to help—if there weren't so many kids up on absurd drug charges that one more isn't news. It's just that they won't, and we can't." She drained her mug of beer.

"Michael, this will sound hard," she went on, seeing that he was deeply depressed by the discussion, "but you can't take on this boy's problems. They existed long before we met him. It doesn't help him if we throw away our life jackets and drown with him. We are entitled to the peace in our own lives."

Peter and Michael looked thoughtfully at each other.

"I guess I can't see it that way," Michael replied, "which is not to say I don't act as though I did."

"Me neither," said Peter. "I can't see that we're entitled to peace."

"You say things like that because you've never tried it the other way," said Carla. "I have. Take it from me. Tormenting yourself about poor people's problems goes nowhere."

"Poor people?" asked Michael. "Seems irrelevant. That's where you get it wrong, Carla. Not for poor people. Just for this one young fellow who—"

"In the movies," Peter continued, uncharacteristically voluble and oblivious in his half-drunk state to whatever Michael's point was, "there would be a dramatic illegal rescue—violence, jailbreaking, shooting the hanging rope as they put it around his neck, whatever—and then the good guy would get to prove his innocence and in the end he'd come back a hero and be legally vindicated, right there in the courtroom, and the judge would pat him on the back. But somehow the point is always supposed to be that the law is good. Why is that supposed to prove that the law is good? Why doesn't that prove that the law doesn't work?"

The other two stared blearily out the pub window.

"Well, none of us stodgy middle-class types are about to ride up to the prison on our white horses and become outlaws in a rescue attempt, are we? You know, though, Anne doesn't think he'll go to prison," said Michael, containing a yeasty burp with the back of his hand. He was high but not yet drunk. He had been dragged off by Carla and Peter on a Sunday afternoon, following an Ecumenical Council special meeting. Although he had been avoiding everyone in that circle, the two of them were insistent—to the point of incivility—that he come with them to talk over Andrés's situation. He had not been able to put them off the way he did Anne, who was so sensitive.

"She's pathologically optimistic," Carla said. "Sometimes I just can't stand to listen to her—it's insane."

"But she called the election, you know," said Peter, tipsily indifferent to the irrelevance of this comment. "Called it for Bush all along. Of course, she thinks eventually it'll hurt the right."

"She has her own kind of realism," said Michael, "sort of psychological. She's intuitive that way. Wonder what she thinks of Berman. Greg doesn't trust him."

Peter was not too high to notice that Michael was still clearheaded. He could probably do heart surgery dead drunk, thought Peter, whereas I couldn't tie my shoes.

"Greg is wrong," Carla said angrily. "Berman's doing the only thing he can do."

"But how d'you know, Carla?" said Michael. "Have you gone through it all to see where you might poke holes and such?"

"I'm not going to do that, but I'll guarantee you Berman did."

"I'll tell you what," said Michael, staring at her with candid dislike. "What gets to me, Carla, is how you take such satisfaction in all this. You're so happy you're right. You're so pleased to be able to sneer at Anne, so delighted that Andrés is going to be hideously punished for insisting on his right to a trial. It's hard to take." He stood and, succumbing at last to his drinks, staggered slightly and stepped on Peter's foot. "Sorry, Peter. So sorry for everything . . . foot. Bad temper. I've got to go. You know, I'm not a very nice fellow. Don't worry about . . ." He continued talking as he walked away, his voice trailing off to an inaudible mutter.

Carla, for once, was hurt—so hurt that she sat staring at the table, unable to recover herself.

Peter felt for her, but he could understand Michael too. Carla's attitude toward Andrés's case had always grated, but Michael had behaved badly, as he would realize when he sobered up—as he seemed to realize already. Evidently, he was in some kind of trouble of his own—marital, Peter suspected.

"Come on, kiddo," he said to Carla. "Walk you home. You know he was drunk and upset. You have to ignore it. Hey, where's that thick skin of yours I've always envied?"

But Carla was not to be jollied out of her funk.

"Why don't you call up Greg?" Peter said. "He'll be free by now. He'll know the magic words."

Carla didn't want to explain what had happened between them. She wished Peter would leave her alone. It hurt to be reminded that she could not call Greg.

CHAPTER 30

On the Saturday afternoon before Andrés's trial, Adriana Simmons-Garrard sat in a café drinking mineral water and watching the door anxiously. She knew only that Jane Braithwaite was eighteen years old, five feet ten inches tall, and brunette. She had been waiting for fifteen minutes. The girl was late; perhaps she had gotten cold feet.

After another fifteen minutes, a tall girl in jeans with long dark hair knotted severely at the back of her head, who might have been pretty if she were not scowling, stopped in the doorway and looked around the room. Adriana stood and waved timidly. She hadn't expected a high school student to have such an intimidating air.

Jane walked to her table and gave Adriana an icy look. Adriana, too, was tall and dark-haired, but she wore sleek, expensive-casual clothes. Jane knew and disliked the style, which, with its sly allusions to cost and quality, was designed to express satisfaction not only with the wearer's privileged place in the world but also with the world itself—and to disguise its boastfulness as modesty. Jane grasped all this instinctively. She also detected a jarring contrast between Adriana's style and something frantic, out of control, in her eyes.

"Jane?" said Adriana. "Please, sit down. Can I get you something?"

"No. Just tell me what this is about."

"I was beginning to think you weren't coming."

"I almost didn't."

"Jane, I found out you were in trouble, and I think I can help you."

"Why do you think I'm in trouble?"

"Oh, Jane. Look, I know what's going on. I also know who the fa-ther is."

"But how? I don't believe Dr. Garrard would tell you."

"Husbands and wives tell each other lots of things."

"Did he tell you to call me?"

"I'm not going to talk about my husband—except to say that he's a very good man and he would be a good father. Jane, you have to decide what you're going to do about the mess you're in."

"This is none of your business," Jane said.

"You must need someone to talk to about it. I mean, Michael is won-derful—but he's a man. Of course you can't go to your parents."

"I don't know why you think that."

"You know, it's a bizarre coincidence that you end up seeing my hus-band about this because we've just decided that we want to adopt a baby. I've been trying to get pregnant for years."

Adriana stopped to give Jane a chance to respond, to ease gradually into the idea. But Jane only sat and stared at her.

"You're going to Juilliard in the fall. You have exceptional talent and a happy future ahead of you. This boy will probably go to prison. He's a troubled person, and he's too young to be a father anyway. You're too young too. But you can give your baby a happy home with everything—love, security, well-educated parents—and you can get on with your life."

"I would never give away my baby," Jane said. "If I had known that's what you wanted, I would never have come here. You said you wanted to talk about Andrés."

She stood to go, her eyes burning with a sure anger, an arrogance, that nonplussed Adriana. She could not imagine how an eighteen-year-old came to have so much self-righteous certainty about these difficult mat-ters—in which she had no experience. It irked Adriana, who, in her own

mildly mad way, had a sense of her own deserts that rivaled Jane's. I have
to make her see reason, she thought. It was so obvious that her plan was
best for all concerned that Jane's resistance angered her.

"Don't go yet, please. There are things you probably haven't thought
about. Listen to me," said Adriana. "If your boyfriend is convicted, they'll
start gathering all kinds of information about him for sentencing. What
if it comes out—about you and him? That he got you pregnant? Do you
think that's going to do him any good?" Adriana looked down awkwardly.
"The judge might hold it against him. It could cost him extra years in
prison."

"What are you talking about? Why would anyone find out?"

"Well, if *I* know, others might. The prosecutor will probably find out,
right?" Adriana avoided Jane's eyes as she said this.

"Are you threatening me? You must be crazy. Listen, if you were the
last woman on earth, I would never give you our baby."

"Wait, Jane," said Adriana. "Look, I can help you make sure they don't
find out. Because, you know, they go poking around, and they're sure to
find out you're his girlfriend, and you might start to show by then. But I
could find you a place to stay somewhere. Also, I could make sure no one
else tells them. That's what I'm trying to tell you. I only want to help. But
the right thing is for you to let us raise the baby. You can talk to Michael,
my husband. Don't tell him you saw me. Just tell him you want to put the
baby up for adoption. He'll . . ."

Jane gave Adriana a lethal look and strode off while she was still talking.

Adriana had expected nothing like this. She had assumed she would
have the upper hand. Jane, she thought, would be worried, frightened,
guilt-ridden, weepy, intimidated—grateful to have strong, competent
adults take over for her, terrified of causing harm to the boy who got her
pregnant. Instead, walking home from the café, Adriana felt all those
things herself. She shouldn't have said what she did about the prosecutor
finding out. Jane might tell Michael. Why had that thought not deterred
her to begin with? She had simply overlooked the possibility. Indeed, the
shock of the real-life Jane, with her expertly murderous disdain, brought
Adriana once more to near-sanity, just as her husband's anger had done.

For several hours, she had an excruciatingly realistic consciousness of the strangeness of what she had done. The girl had said she must be crazy. Michael, too, thought she was crazy. Adriana began to have an idea of what they meant. But the bracing, cold shock of an oppositional reality began to fade before the evening, spent alone at home, was over.

I must not give up, Adriana had begun to think, looking out over the river at twilight. This girl is doing the wrong thing, and I have nothing to lose. Her heart pounded when she heard Michael open the door, but she quickly saw in his face that he knew nothing.

Jane herself, meanwhile, was not nearly so coolly calm as Adriana thought. She shook as she walked away from the café. Would the judge really hold their affair against Andrés? She could well imagine that he would consider it irresponsible, antisocial behavior and that no one would believe her if she insisted that she was the more guilty party, that she had pushed Andrés and he had been reluctant. But would the judge find out? Had Dr. Garrard actually discussed her pregnancy with his wife or asked his wife to call Jane? With natural savvy that had heretofore functioned only in sororal or schoolgirl warfare, Jane saw that this was unlikely, particularly given Adriana's insistence that Jane not tell him about their meeting.

That night she and Ellen talked it through and decided that she would have to speak to Dr. Garrard. There was no other way.

"This time I'll come with you," Ellen said.

"No, he'd freak," said Jane. "He already feels terrible about keeping secrets from Mom and Dad."

Jane called his office the next day, the Sunday before Andrés's trial was to begin. She told his service that it was an emergency; he called back within minutes and heard enough on the telephone to agree to meet her in his office within the hour. He was agitated and distressed by what she told him, and by having to explain the disgraceful history involving his wife and Marie Collier.

"I'm sorry. I am so sorry," he told her, over and over, agonized. "And she nearly threatened, you say. Dear God. Tell me again exactly what she said."

"She said that if Andrés was convicted, they'd investigate him for the sentencing and dig up dirt on him, and that if *she* knew, then others might too, and someone might tell. But I thought she meant that *she* would. And then she said she could find me a place to stay and she'd try to stop anyone from telling—if I'd go along with her. I'm sorry, but I thought maybe she was . . . a little . . . maybe a little . . ."

"I think so too. She's a bit unbalanced, but not enough that you could lock her up—at least until now. What is in her head that she thinks you'd actually give her your child after she'd . . . Jane, you mustn't let this upset you any longer. First of all, no one knows about your pregnancy but her and Marie Collier, and Marie is very angry with Adriana and in any case would never be a party to this. So that part of it is utter nonsense. The only person to fear here is Adriana herself, and I'll control her. So, as awful as this experience has been, you mustn't worry. I won't let anyone harm Andrés this way."

"Anyway, I don't believe he'll be convicted."

"I don't know," Michael said, hesitantly. "We should probably prepare ourselves for anything."

"Dr. Garrard, do you think I'm too young to raise this baby?"

The question took him by surprise. Until now, Jane had been all confidence and determination. He took a moment to order his thoughts.

"Of course, truthfully, I'd rather you were older and well settled, but I haven't a doubt in the world but that you'll be a very, very good mother," he said, and then added, "and that the baby is best off with you."

Michael was ashamed that for a few seconds he had been tempted to respond differently. Adriana's greed for Jane's baby infected him. He was relieved that he'd managed to say the right thing to Jane, and Jane's obvious relief at his words told him that the real point of her question was to be assured that he, too, did not have designs on her child. How cruel Adriana had been. Every day, it seemed to Michael, she became a little more wicked, a little more willing to betray, lie, and hurt. And although as a man of science he was supposed to understand that what he reacted to as wickedness was in fact sickness, a broken mind rather than a bad one, he felt otherwise. Sometimes, he could see Adriana as ill and feel compassion for her, but more often it seemed as though she suffered from a corruption of conscience. It took all his strength to resist complicity with it.

When Jane had gone, relieved and comforted, he considered how he might protect her from the hungry-wombed demi-demon his wife seemed to have become. On second thought, he was not nearly as confident that he could as he had led Jane to believe. He doubted Adriana would actually follow through on the threat to give the prosecution information against Andrés. But she might dream up some other grotesque, mad plan. Worst of all, she might approach Charles and Anne, a possibility that tormented Michael from the moment Jane left until he returned home. Adriana was out—with Barbara, he remembered now. For an hour, he sat in the living room waiting for her, too preoccupied for reading or music, and then he heard the familiar noises of her arrival—key, door, shufflings at the hall table and closet.

"You here, Michael?" she called from the foyer.

How pleasantly ordinary her voice was, and comfortable, like a wife's voice. That was what he had married her for. How was it that the baby business had so overthrown Adriana? He knew many women who had struggled with infertility, and though some seemed to be made permanently sad, not one had disintegrated the way Adriana had. Most had adopted children and seemed happy. One or two got close to nieces or nephews or children's friends. Others devoted themselves to work, a cause, hobbies, or various pleasures. Michael sometimes wondered whether any other significant deprivation—of money, security, health, status—would have had the same effect on Adriana. A baby was the only great good that hadn't been handed to her. Would she have come apart if he had been ill, say, and had never become a successful, influential man? He knew only that there was something crooked in Adriana's desperate need for pregnancy and that he himself had done something crooked in marrying her, having known from the beginning that she lacked some core of self and sanity. How mercilessly life punished sins like hers and his—sins that seem so harmless compared to, say, murder or torture.

"What's the matter?" Adriana asked, seeing his face.

He looked at her curiously. "Did you think I wouldn't find out?"

Although she had come in with an air of cheerful, urbane self-possession, she now looked suddenly depleted and frightened. She sat in the chair across from him, her bag between her legs.

"I don't know what I thought," she said. "I suppose I thought she'd agree, and that would fix things between us. I thought you'd love it."

"And when she didn't agree, you thought you'd try to threaten and frighten her?"

"That's an exaggeration."

"No, it isn't. Adriana, I won't raise a baby with you—adopted or otherwise. It's all over. We won't injure any child with our deficiencies."

"With mine you mean."

She began to weep, but he was unmoved. He sat and stared at her, not sure what he meant to do next.

"But don't leave me," she said, through sobs. "I can't give you a reason to stay. But, please, don't go. What would I do if you did? What would I do?" She got up and went to him, curled up against his chest, her face pressed into his coat, and sobbed. And, being a man who could not endure the sight of suffering, he put his arm around her and spoke soothing words. After a while, he carried her to bed and left her sleeping there. The thought circled in his mind that Adriana was the only child he'd ever have, and he would have to carry her all his life. That was his punishment for trying to bring the dead back to life.

CHAPTER 31

"That was your best—last night was," Anne said at breakfast Monday morning, speaking of Charles's recital at Trinity Church. " 'Ich habe genug' had me in tears." Anne had wiped the tears away, grabbed Jane's hand, and rushed home to the other children as soon as the last notes were sung, leaving Charles to take bows, and she had fallen asleep before he returned. This was their first chance to discuss the performance.

"You know what I think it was?" she went on. "I think it's all this business with Andrés. It's changing your timbre so that . . . Charles, Michael was there—with Wyatt Younger! Jane and I were talking with them at intermission. Michael was dazzled. He could hardly talk straight, he was so moved. Even Wyatt got it. He actually smiled when he saw us."

"Did Professor Selvnick approve?"

"He wasn't there as far as I could see."

"Oh, God. Surely Michael's not replacing him."

"Michael's a better father for Wyatt than Selvnick," Anne said. "Isn't that an interesting theory? I can see the article in *Psychoanalytical Quarterly:* 'Effects of Father-Hunger in a Twenty-eight-Year-Old Billionaire.' In some ways, Michael is even a more fatherly man than you, Charles."

"That's because he's childless," said Charles. "He has unexpended capital in that account. Morning, Janie."

Jane came to the table in the plaid, pleated skirt that she wore to all interviews and official occasions. "I'm not going to school. I'm going to court," she announced. "It's no use arguing with me. Daddy, last night you were a miracle."

Over the past week, the Braithwaites had gotten regular reports about jury selection and pretrial motions. Opening statements would begin the first thing this morning. Charles and Anne's pretense of ignorance about Jane and Andrés was hard to maintain, for they understood that she would have to go to the trial.

"We'll all go," said Charles, to the surprise of both his wife and daughter, and he put an arm around Jane's shoulders for a moment. "Anne, could your mother pick up the boys after school? When Ellen gets home, she can babysit if we're not back by then."

At nine-thirty, Jane, Charles, and Anne arrived at 100 Centre Street just as Peter Frankl did, and the four of them entered the courtroom together. Andrés was there already, sitting at the defendant's table with Mark Berman, and Greg was behind them in the spectators' section, leaning forward and talking to Andrés. Michael Garrard, to their surprise, sat next to Greg, and Carla Winter was alone in a back row. Everyone looked strained and tense except for two dark-suited men at the prosecutor's table. The young prosecutor, Charles thought, behaved like an athlete before a big game—nervous but eager to play.

Andrés was so thin that his face was all dark eyes, but he had a new short haircut, and he wore a sports coat and pressed khakis. He was startled when the Braithwaites appeared at his side but managed to stand and shake hands with Charles and avoid looking at Jane. A smile, they saw, was beyond him.

"Sit here, close to Andrés," Greg whispered to the Braithwaites, motioning to the empty space beside him. "Make it clear you're with him."

Charles and Anne, once seated, could not take their eyes off the prosecutor, a Mr. Spiker, and his assistant. How dangerous he is, Anne thought, observing Spiker, who was all energetic anticipation as he arranged papers and files on the table before him. It was terrifying to

watch this man, a perfect stranger intent on doing dreadful harm to Andrés. If only she could talk to him for a minute and explain the whole situation. Wouldn't he understand that Andrés was not the villain that they
took him for? That he deserved help and understanding, not attack? Peter
said he wouldn't. Peter said the prosecutor did not think that was part of
his job. The judge and the defense attorneys were there to worry about
such things. The prosecutor attacked, the defense counsel defended, and
the judge moderated. Justice resulted when each did his job. But how
could a rational human being believe that such a silly, medieval contest
would result in justice? The whole room, with its license to break lives—
its armed bailiff, its ravenous demands for money to buy defense, its insistence on humility and obedience, its stiff distortions of the supple
realities of human motive—it was terrifying and loathsome to a mind like
Anne's. How was it that such primitivism survived in the legal system, and
why didn't people complain about it? In fact, the only human being Anne
had ever personally heard raise a complaint against such ills was her own
mother. Helen's rants against the criminal justice system provided Anne
with the vocabulary of her present musings. Anne wondered whether she
would still think the system so appalling if it acquitted Andrés.

Justice Knight strode in, wearing a long black robe that announced his
authority. He was somewhere between sixty and seventy, and a suspicious,
sour anger already showed on his face as he took his seat. Andrés didn't
have a chance. Anne inhaled as though in pain. It was already over. Justice
Knight was angry because he knew he was about to sentence a young boy
to many cruel years in prison. His was the disgruntled face of a man who
knew he had to do something he didn't want to do. Anne looked at Jane
and saw that she, too, understood. She put her arm around her and felt her
body shaking.

"Do you want to go out?" she whispered.

Jane shook her head.

When the jurors were brought in, both mother and daughter searched
their faces hungrily, but there was no sign of independence or mercy in
any of them. They looked mostly shy and uncertain, desirous of being led
and let off the hook. You could see that in the affection that quickly
sprang up between them and Justice Knight. He had no sympathy for the

lawyers or the defendant. He felt for the jury, who were in the same boat he was. He was all consideration for these seven women and five men, settling them in with kindly instructions and little jokes about their lunch and the jury room. He'd done the dance many times, Anne thought; he could have led the balkiest partners through it to the conclusion he wanted.

By the time the jury was settled and opening statements were over, it was lunchtime. Andrés, who had been distressingly still and pale through it all, was too sick to eat. Michael and Greg walked him to a drugstore, where Michael wrote out a prescription for his nausea and had it filled.

Andrés's other friends gathered in a diner and took stock.

"That was a bad start," said Peter. "The prosecutors believe in what they're doing, and Berman is too neutral. The prosecutors' story is simple and easy, and Berman's saying nothing except that there's room to doubt. That's not going to work."

"Well, big surprise," said Carla. "Berman told you himself it wouldn't work."

"I'm starting to think Andrés would have been better off with me in there. At least I believe in him. But what really gets me," Peter went on, "is that it looks like no one's going to call Juan. Juan could be a believable witness for Andrés. I myself might even have put Andrés on the stand in this case."

"Come on, Peter. They'd rip Andrés up. All they'd have to do is describe this druggy mess he grew up in and everyone would say, 'Oh, yeah. Too bad, but with that kind of background of course he's guilty.' And they'd ignore anything Juan said because it would be obvious he was just trying to protect him for Gabriela's sake. It would get Andrés nothing, and it would just make Berman's story more complicated. He's trying to make it a no-brainer."

"I'll tell you what, Carla. I don't know why you think you have to defend Berman. You suggested his name, but I thought he was a good idea too. Still, speaking as someone with a few courtroom instincts, there were better strategies for this case than Berman's. I mean, if you remember, we hired him because he's good at plea-bargaining. He doesn't like trying cases. I'd say he decided on this strategy because he thought he'd lose no

matter what he did, and he's not a man who'd put a lot of effort into a case
he thinks he'll lose. Don't forget, what we're paying him is not a lot compared to what he gets from major-league drug dealers."

"You're wrong, Peter. The man has a reputation to maintain. And Andrés never had a chance at trial."

"I think you're terribly right, Peter," Charles put in, his voice anguished. "The judge knows it too. Let's fire Berman. You can take over
right now."

"The judge would never allow it. He's already mad that Berman insisted on going to trial. I mean, jaws must have dropped when he announced that. See, we put the judge in a hell of a bad spot," Carla said.

"That's probably true," said Peter. "We'd have to weigh whether the
risk is worth it. Right now, I think Andrés doesn't have a chance, so maybe
it is."

"You're crazy, Peter. How the hell can you tell the judge you want to
fire Berman? What if he says no?" Carla asked. "Then you're stuck with a
lawyer who's furious with you. Or what if Knight says okay, fire him, but
no continuance. Are you prepared to step up there this afternoon or tomorrow morning and call witnesses and do cross? What you really should
do is try to convince Andrés to take the plea bargain. They might still go
for it. The judge might even make them. Charles, help me make everyone
see reason."

Peter was not prepared to step up and call witnesses or do cross. The
idea was terrifying.

"He won't take a plea bargain," said Jane, looking at Carla with contempt. "He won't lie about Juan, and he won't lie and say he did what he
didn't do."

"Jane is right," said Charles. "Everyone has been trying to convince
Andrés to do it. He's just not going to."

That afternoon, two of the three police officers who made the bust testified. They said that Juan had mentioned a partner several times. They said
that they had heard Juan talking to Andrés before he opened the door, and
that he had said, "Who says you get half? I told you four thousand, and

that's it." They also said that Andrés shouted at Juan, while they were being arrested, "You said you knew the guys! You said you knew them."

The fury on Andrés's face as he listened to the officers testify did not prevent them from staring brazenly at him as they passed by, going to and from the witness stand.

Peter sat forward expectantly when Berman began cross-examination, but afterward he passed a note to Carla: "Lamest cross you ever heard. Admit it."

Carla read the note, crumpled it in her hand, and shoved it into Peter's pocket.

When the jury had been dismissed for the day, the judge spoke to the lawyers. "This might be over by tomorrow night," Justice Knight told them coolly. "Mr. Berman, you're still just going to rest, hmm? No witnesses? In that case, I expect to send the jury out right after lunch." He glared at Berman, as though to ask, once more, why he had put them all through this absurd exercise. A good lawyer controls his client. Justice Knight knew who Berman was, and he disliked him. Berman represented big drug dealers—kingpins, real bad guys who paid him generously out of their illegal profits. Justice Knight wondered what lay behind Berman's tactics in this case. Maybe it really was what Berman said: the boy just wouldn't plead. But maybe Berman was afraid that something even worse than what they had would come out if he called witnesses. Maybe he was just minimizing the damage. There was no way to know. The case stinks, thought Justice Knight, back in chambers.

The Morningside Heights people, except for Jane, stood in the back of the courtroom while Andrés talked to Berman at the defendant's table. Andrés, with a sideways glance, suddenly became aware of Jane at his side.

"I'll be here tomorrow," she whispered. "Nothing is changed. Everyone knows they're lying."

He would not look at her, but he gave a slight nod in acknowledgment. Satisfied, she went back to the others and glided in among them. Only Anne seemed to have noticed what she had done.

CHAPTER 32

Andrés went home again with Greg after the first day in court, and Greg cooked dinner for him—tacos.

"I'm not such a great cook," Greg said, setting a plate before him.

"No, it's good," said Andrés politely. But he ate almost nothing. "I can't. It just doesn't go down—stops here," he said, pointing to his throat.

After weeks at the shelter, Greg's apartment seemed a fairy tale of luxury to Andrés. But he tossed and turned on the pullout sofa, despite the real sheets and pillows and a blanket, and when dawn came he had hardly slept.

Greg had a bad night too, and when he heard Andrés stirring, he got up and made coffee. Coffee, it seemed, Andrés could get down—even a piece of toast, which he dunked.

They were in court early, in the same seats, with the same friends on the spectators' benches behind them. Greg and Michael sat directly behind Andrés. The Braithwaites and Peter grouped on either side of them, and Carla sat in the back. This time, when Jane came in with her parents, Andrés knew it immediately, and looked out of the corner of his eye. He felt a series of hands grip his and heard encouraging mutters he could not make out. His expression throughout was, as it had been the day before, indignant, serious, and most poignant of all, Anne thought, hurt.

When the judge came in and the clerk announced "All rise," Andrés held his middle and took a deep breath as he stood.

"All right?" Michael Garrard whispered, his hand on Andrés's shoulder.

The three morning witnesses testified about the quantity of cocaine the police had seized, Andrés's relationship with Juan, and the layout of Juan's room. Then both lawyers gave closing statements. Berman's was short, clear, and low-key. Peter's hope rose as he heard it. If the jury could think straight for just a yard or two, they'd see that there really was a reasonable doubt. A reasonable person *could* easily doubt that Andrés had done what they said. By law, they *had* to let him off. Spiker's statement was longer and impassioned, winding up with a diatribe about what the plague of drugs had done to so many of the city's neighborhoods. Everything he said was true. Peter agreed with all of it. He hated the drug lords as much as Spiker did. The question was what any of that had to do with this poor skinny, scared kid. Berman objected where he should have and pointed out, sarcastically, when and how it was all irrelevant, but the judge didn't stop Spiker and didn't strike anything he said from the record—not that it would have helped if he had. Peter knew they had to get a jury verdict because, though the judge and Berman made plenty of errors, none were bad enough to get an appeals court to order a new trial. No, they just had to hope that the jury could make their way through the maze. That would be hard work, though, and a jury worked hard only if defense counsel gave them a motive to, which Berman hadn't. The jury would find it hard to motivate themselves; they knew nothing about Andrés, who he was or what he was like.

During all these proceedings and during his instructions to the jury, the judge continued to be good-natured and fatherly to the jury and surly with the lawyers—especially, the Morningside Heights observers thought, with the defendant's lawyer.

"Don't ask me," Peter said, in response to the look on Michael's face as everyone went to lunch. "Coming?"

"I think I'll stick with Andrés again—make sure he's all right," said

Michael, looking to where Andrés still sat, sullenly listening to Berman. "He's too upset for lunch."

"Remember, if it goes badly, there are appeals," Charles and Anne told Jane. They did not tell her what they themselves had been told: that Andrés would all but certainly be imprisoned while the appeals were pending. Greg and Michael, with Andrés between them, walked out together.

"I never got to tell what happened," Andrés told them. "I never got to say they were lying. This is all stupid."

They did not want to discourage him by agreeing, but he was right. Greg looked crushed, and Michael was agitated and angry. The three of them wandered for the entire lunch hour. It was a tender spring day, and the downtown crowd seemed cheerful. Meanwhile, thought Greg, people are being ground to bits in all the courtrooms around here. No one ever knows. Everyone believes it's all so wonderful.

At one o'clock, they circled back to court; the judge briefly instructed the jury, and the wait for the verdict began. They paced, stole looks at Andrés, went for coffee, and had meaningless conversations. Jane once again approached Andrés and said a few words, and, this time, Charles saw the way Andrés looked at his daughter. Anne had not gotten this one wrong. The sight of them together gave Charles painfully conflicting feelings. He was actually able to be glad for Andrés's sake even as he was angry and frightened for his daughter's.

After two hours, the ennui of waiting had soothed them. Even Andrés was calming down. Waiting, obviously, would go on forever, and life under these circumstances, sitting with friends, eating candy bars, and remembering trivia, was quite bearable—even, you could say, worth living.

Thus the bailiff's announcement that the jury had returned a verdict was a violent shock, completely unexpected.

"It's too soon," Charles said, "for a guilty verdict. They'd think harder if they were going to impose this brutal sentence on a kid."

"But they have no idea what sentence they're imposing," Peter reminded him as they all reentered the courtroom. "They don't know what the sentence is, and they don't know who they're imposing it on. In this country, blind justice means making sure our juries have no idea what they're doing."

Everything happened next, Michael thought, just as things happen in the movies; only the tempos seemed wrong. There was no dramatic pause before the verdict, and there was a strange drag in time afterward. The judge asked the foreman if they had reached a verdict, and was told they had. He ordered Andrés to rise to hear it, and the foreman read it out: Andrés was guilty. The spectators murmured, and Jane cried out softly. But before reciting his own next lines, the judge paused to be tender toward the jury, all of whose faces were somber. It wasn't easy, what they had done, he said. Everyone was grateful for the serious way they had approached their task. He turned to address Andrés next, but before things could proceed further according to the ordinary script—in which the judge would formally announce Andrés's guilt and the need for a sentencing hearing and Andrés would be cuffed and taken off to Rikers Island—Andrés's knees began to buckle, and he vomited.

Michael started up from his seat and grabbed him under the elbows.

"Hang on," he whispered to Andrés, "just hang on."

"Sir, let go of the defendant," said the judge. "Bailiff!" The judge was agitated and tense.

The bailiff, who had stood bored at the rear of the room throughout these proceedings, moved up the center aisle in no particular hurry. He had seen it all before.

"Your Honor, I'm his doctor," said Michael, his hand still under Andrés's elbow. "He's been sick since yesterday, and I've prescribed something for him. Why don't I just take him to the men's room—right around the corner? I can help him wash up and give him some medication, and you can proceed in just a minute. I'm Dr. Michael Garrard—on the faculty at Columbia Presbyterian. Several people here know me. I'll clean him up and give him something, and he'll be back right away."

The judge sighed and looked at the jury. Two women were crying. They'd be damned unhappy if they had any idea what they'd just done to this kid. The judge was not very happy about it himself, but his hands were tied. He'd leaned on the prosecutor; he'd leaned on the defense attorney. They had both refused to change course, and he had no powers that could make them.

Andrés should have thrown up earlier, thought Peter. Then they would have known that he was human. As it is, they only just found it out.

"All right, Dr. . . ."

"Michael Garrard, Your Honor." Michael said his name slowly and distinctly, to inspire trust.

"Just make it quick." That Dr. Garrard was the real thing, with his English accent, enormous dignity, and exceptionally fine suit, was obvious, and Andrés's distress deepened the judge's dismay about the verdict.

"Yes, Your Honor. Certainly."

"Bailiff, stick with them."

The bailiff, still bored, followed Michael and Andrés out of the room. And not a minute afterward, Jane, too, jumped up and ran out, tears streaming down her face. Charles half stood and called after her, but Anne pulled him back down.

"Let's all be seated and maintain quiet, jurors and spectators," said Justice Knight. "We're not finished here. The doctor assures us this won't take long. We can afford to show some compassion. We're so close to the end, I'm not going to recess."

Judge, jury, lawyers, and spectators sat for more than ten minutes in churchly silence, during which a great pall came over everyone, as though they had woken to the enormity of what had just happened in the noise-less room. If this was justice, justice was perhaps a ghastly, frightening thing, the jurors thought. And others thought, if this was the law, the law was perhaps a force for evil.

After ten minutes, Justice Knight became impatient and spoke to the prosecutor. "If they don't show in another minute, Mr. Spiker, you go and get them. He'll just have to be sick while we wind things up. But make sure he gets medical attention as soon as he gets to Rikers, you hear me? I'll fol-low up on that, so you better be sure. Ah, there's your transportation com-ing in, I see. Finally."

Two stony-faced police offers, with handcuffs on their belts, had just entered at the rear of the courtroom. But immediately behind them, no longer looking blasé, came the bailiff, at a run.

"Your Honor, I think they're gone," the bailiff called from the back of the courtroom. "Somehow, I don't know, they got out of there and I didn't—"

"Officers, the bailiff thinks the prisoner may have escaped," said the judge. "Go see . . ."

But the officers were already out the door, the bailiff behind them. In the courtroom and outside in the corridor, people stood and milled about, asking other confused questions.

"They can't be gone," said Anne. "Jane must be with them. They're talking somewhere or something. Charles, one of us should go look."

"You wait. I'll go," he said, grim-faced, as unhappy possibilities rose up in his mind. Greg, too, made for the door.

"No one leaves the room," the judge called out, banging his gavel. "Return to your seats. No one leaves."

After more confusion and the buzzing arrival of hordes of blue-suited, irate police who seemed to have erupted from some angry hive of cops somewhere, Spiker approached the judge, talking rapidly and pointing emphatically toward Charles and Anne.

"Bring them up here," said the judge.

There was some question in Spiker's mind, it seemed, as to whether the whole thing had not been planned ahead. The bailiff, who was by now distraught, said that he had been talking to the unhappy young lady, who told him that the defendant was her boyfriend, while the doctor and the defendant were in the men's room. He waited for them to come out, but finally, when he went in to get them, they were gone, so he ran back into the courtroom, leaving the weeping girl in the corridor. She had called after him, "What's the matter? Is he all right? What's going on? Can I go in now?" But when they went back, she was gone too. All three were gone.

Charles and Anne explained their connection with Andrés to the judge and the prosecutor and assured them that nothing had been planned and that there had to be some innocent explanation for all this, but no one seemed to believe them. Justice Knight wondered aloud whether the boy had given Dr. Garrard the slip. Maybe Dr. Garrard had pursued him, hoping to get him back before anyone realized what had happened. If they walked into the courtroom this minute, Justice Knight was prepared to be understanding. But Spiker suggested again, to their faces, that Jane had been in on a plot to help Andrés escape.

"What are you talking about?" Anne said, with highly convincing outrage. "How could anyone have planned what just happened? Mr. Spiker, in my mind, if they're really gone and if there's a guilty party here, it's *you*—for driving three innocent people to something desperate."

"Wait, Anne," said Charles. "We don't know yet. Jane may have just gone home."

"That's true," said the judge hopefully. As angry as he was, he didn't want to issue a warrant for the arrest of another eighteen-year-old or for that doctor. And now that he had had a moment to think, he could see that it was most unlikely that anyone had planned this sequence of events. For one thing, the boy had been genuinely sick. Anyone could see that.

"And Andrés and Michael could be—"

"Michael? You know this man?" asked Spiker.

"Michael Garrard is his name," Charles said, "just as he told you. He is our friend, and he's a well-known, upstanding, longtime member of the community. There is going to be some perfectly reasonable explanation—"

"Maybe it was a medical emergency," Anne said. "We should check the hospitals."

"Okay, you two just sit down and stay out of this," said Spiker. "No more conversation."

"No, they won't do that," said Peter, who had approached the bench uninvited. "And if you speak to either of them again in that tone of voice, I'll file a complaint against you with the ethics committee. I might do it anyway, after seeing the nonsense that went on in this room today. It's their daughter. They're upset, and they've committed no crime. You have no right to detain them or tell them what to do. If you two want to go, just go," he said, turning to Charles and Anne. "No one has a right to keep you here. Don't worry about Jane. She's probably so upset that she just went home."

"Who are you?" asked the judge, who looked indecisive for the first time that day.

Too bad he couldn't have been less sure of himself a little earlier, Peter thought. "I'm their lawyer, Peter Frankl," he said. Peter searched in his pockets for his card. In fact, Peter had just appointed himself to that office, for until that moment the Braithwaites' lawyer had been a mild, plump fellow down on Park Avenue South who handled mostly wills, trusts, and taxes.

"Then you ought to know that their daughter is in big trouble, and they could be too," said the prosecutor.

"Jane is probably on her way home. And with you on the loose, we're all in trouble, Spiker. Are you familiar with the penalties for causing false testimony to be presented in a court of law?" Andrés's trial had succeeded in entirely convincing Peter of his innocence—he'd never been confident that he was guilty. The testimony of the police was just too neat, and Andrés's injured response too authentic.

Surprisingly, Spiker was two seconds late with his outraged denials, which Justice Knight noticed with considerable alarm. Although the judge hadn't doubted the boy was guilty, he had certainly seen that his defense was poor. Should have had some witnesses. Terribly ineffective cross. Justice Knight thought, belatedly, that he should probably have thrown in a few of his own questions. In fact, he had thought about it, then decided that he wouldn't because Berman was not exactly a novice—or a nice guy, either. The hell if he was going to help out Mark Berman. An hour later, when the entire mess had been handed over to the police and the judge was in chambers, he said to his clerk, "Case should never have been tried. I told them that."

Berman said the same to himself, but he also admitted that if he had it to do over, maybe he would have done a couple of things differently. He'd take the appeal pro bono. They'd catch the kid by morning, and there'd be another trial on the escape charges. He'd do that trial pro bono too. What a mess. Spiker was just an ambitious jerk trying to make points off this stinker of a case.

Even Spiker, walking the deserted street back to his office in the melancholy twilight of the court district, clutching a black court bag in each hand, for a moment or two wished that he'd offered Andrés something better than four years. He even admitted to himself that his confidence that Andrés was guilty had a crack in it—now that he'd watched him during the trial. He had a few qualms about his witnesses too.

I let Carla talk me into things against my better judgment, Peter thought, walking toward the subway station. *I* could have gotten an acquittal. I should have known that. I could've hired someone to assist on criminal procedure. I could have . . . In the end, with his energies roused by Andrés's flight, he discovered that there were many things he could have done. A lot of this whole mess was due to people doing what was easiest and excusing themselves from responsibility. But the law offered no fix for the confluence of lethargy, minor misjudgment, and cruel laws that produced this tragedy. In fact, the judge and the lawyers knew that this was how most cases went. Once the verdict came in, no one was free to say, "Wait a minute, let's try again. This feels all wrong. What's going on here?" There was no common sense, no chance to be taught by chastened second thoughts, no course of action that would save an innocent boy from years of torment. The law offered no remedy at all.

CHAPTER 33

That evening, Charles and Anne had to tell the police that they had no idea where Jane was, and Michael and Andrés had still not been found. The nightly news added Jane to the list of fugitives. Helen and Anne switched on the television as soon as the children were asleep, and simultaneously burst into tears on hearing her name.

The Braithwaites pieced together a rough outline of what they guessed had happened in the back corridors of justice late that afternoon. Michael and Andrés, according to the bailiff, had gone into the men's room, which was small and windowless and was located down a short, dead-end hallway with two other doors, a janitor's closet and a conference room, both locked. There was a stairwell about ten feet from the hallway, and an elevator beside the stairwell. After determining that no one else was inside the restroom and trying the other two doors, the bailiff had left Michael and Andrés alone there and stepped to the entrance of the narrow hallway to wait for them, certain that there was no way out except past him. As soon as he stationed himself there, Jane had appeared, weeping.

Charles and Anne could only speculate on much of what had happened next, but knowing their daughter, they found some parts of it not terribly hard to imagine. By the bailiff's own admission, she had distracted him, no doubt innocently at first. She had repeatedly, desperately, begged to be allowed to go into the restroom with Andrés, the bailiff said, and he had refused. They argued; she got him all upset with her tears and pleas. It was a scene Charles and Anne had played out with Jane a hundred times. No one could beg and plead like Janie when she thought she was entitled. The bailiff had stepped forward a few paces. Oh yes, the Braithwaites understood perfectly. Meanwhile, Anne guessed, at some point Jane had seen Andrés and Michael appear behind the bailiff's back. Suppose one of them had just put his finger to his lips; Jane would have taken it from there. She would have been off and running, improvising cover for them. With some ploy or other—and they knew just how good she was at that sort of thing—she succeeded in inducing the bailiff to move just a few more paces away from the doorway so that Michael and Andrés could slip out behind him silently. Obviously, she had managed to keep the bailiff distracted long enough to give them a good start. And why did the bailiff let himself be fooled this way? Because, they concluded, regardless of the courtroom nonsense and the depiction of Andrés as an antisocial villain, his take on Andrés and his friends, based on all the unconscious cues he had been absorbing during the trial, made him trustful. On a level out of his control, much deeper than that of the courtroom accusations, he believed that Andrés and his friends were trustworthy and therefore did not fear that they would try to do what they did.

Some parts of the story were harder to figure. For one, how had Jane met up with Michael and Andrés afterward? Did they signal something to her? That seemed unlikely. Did she call them on a cell phone? It was not believable that Michael would have permitted her to come to them. Was it accidental?

"I think the three of them were together from the beginning," said Charles, with no qualifying doubt in his voice, "but it all happened more or less accidentally. I'm guessing that what happened was, Andrés and Michael ran down the steps while she kept the bailiff busy, and then she just happened to catch an elevator the minute the bailiff ran off. She could have arrived at the ground floor just after they did or even before them. They could have been delayed getting down—whatever. Pure accident."

"And no one saw three people leaving together because they all pretended to be moving separately," Anne said. "But they watched each other."

"Then once they got outside, I think they probably hopped a cab," Charles said. "That's what I would have done. And a couple of them hunkered down in the backseat. They knew they had only a minute or two to get out of the area. The cops would cover the subways as soon as they were missed, and it would be too easy to get trapped in the subway. The cab was probably across the Brooklyn Bridge before the cops got it together to follow them. And, anyhow, there were three of them, but until just now the police bulletin said two males."

"But they're all in such trouble. What happens to them now? How can Janie come home?" Helen said, her voice broken with sobs. Anne leaned against Charles and wept again.

The next day, Morris and Merrit came and took Ellen and the boys for dinner, to give Charles and Anne a chance to go to pieces and consult their lawyer friends, Peter, Carla, and Greg. The boys seemed frightened and had been crying for their sister, and Ellen was behaving strangely. Ellen was a favorite of Merrit's—my honorary daughter, she called her— and Merrit was so astonished by Ellen that she phoned Anne about her.

"What's with her?" she asked. "She's like a crazy little thing. She was crying when she walked in the door, and now she's giggling totally out of control. She knows something, Anne."

"She told me she didn't know anything about it or about where they are," said Anne, "and I believe her."

"But she's not saying something."

"She probably thinks we don't know Jane had something going with Andrés. But we did know."

"That could be it," Merrit said. She doubted it, but this was no time to argue with Anne.

"Jane must have been amazing," Carla was saying when Anne rejoined the others. "What guts. What quick thinking. I'm sorry, Anne, but my main reaction is just that she really must have put on a show."

"Carla," Greg said, worried—signaling her to drop it. Charles and Anne couldn't be seeing things that way. He was astonished when Anne looked lovingly at her, and Charles nodded, gravely surprised and rather moved by what Carla had said.

"She's always been like that. It's been hard for her, living the life we gave her," Charles said.

Peter, himself the devoted father of two grown children, had his doubts about whether living in the bosom of her loving, understanding family had really been all that hard on Jane, but he kept them to himself. By and large, he recognized parental instincts like his own in the Braithwaites. Your daughter springs a convicted drug dealer out of jail? Well, but he was innocent, and she is a brave, right-thinking darling—and creative too!

"Where do you think they are, Charles?" Anne asked.

Pictures of the missing three had appeared on last night's late news and were shown again this evening, along with new, sordid, and sensationalist descriptions of Andrés, his alleged crimes, and even the two friends who had apparently engineered his escape. Jane was a "troubled teen," the "convicted man's secret girlfriend," and the daughter of Met baritone Charles Braithwaite. Dr. Garrard was mysterious and standoffish, a brilliant physician to the international elite, with a pronounced English accent. They would be recognized everywhere they went. It was only a matter of time until the call came. They would soon be in custody upstate somewhere, perhaps in some Catskills town. They would be arrested trying to rent a car in Poughkeepsie or getting off the train in Boston or Washington. None of them could have said whether they more dreaded or hoped for this inevitable outcome.

As the cab sped away from 100 Centre Street, Michael gave calm instructions to the driver, while keeping a steadying arm around Andrés's shoulder. Jane sat on the other side of Andrés, gripping his hand with the fierce strength of terror. Michael noticed himself relying on the same tense control in this situation that he used for medical emergencies. Truly, he thought, what is the difference?

"Brooklyn," he called up to the driver. "Uh . . . the boardwalk at Coney Island. Andrés, ever been there?"

"No, why are we going there?"

"We need to go someplace with lots of people where we never go. Jane?" Michael spoke softly and motioned with his hand to Jane and Andrés, too, to keep their voices low.

"Not since I was ten."

"Just thinking now, scoot down, Andrés—you too, Jane. Stay low." Michael whispered these words, looking nervously at the driver, but the man was speaking some African language into his cell phone and seemed oblivious. "And I'll make a call as soon as we're well into Brooklyn. I'll find a phone booth."

"Here, I have a cell," Jane offered, holding it out to him.

"No, no, dear," he said. "You mustn't use that. Don't call anyone. Don't call your mother. Just turn it off and leave it off. Andrés? Yes, that's right. Just leave them off. Oh God. Oh God, oh God." Michael rubbed his face with his hands until it was scarlet.

"So we're going to hide?" Andrés said. "But we have to get Janie home."

"I won't go," said Jane.

"You have to," Andrés said. "Don't be stupid. Just tell them you were wandering around because you were upset or something."

Michael looked at Jane sorrowfully. "It would be best if you did," he said. "Andrés is right. If you go home, I doubt they can prove you did anything."

"How can you say that after you watched Andrés's trial? I'm coming with Andrés. I'm already in this. It's too late for me. *You* know I have to stay with Andrés." Jane looked meaningfully into the doctor's eyes as she said the last words. "Andrés, I'm much happier this way. We'll go someplace and change our names and— But Dr. Garrard, what about you? This is not your problem. You'd better just drop us somewhere."

"Well. Let me think now. Oh God. Children, I think we're all in this together. Let's just stop all this trying to send each other off, and . . . and pull together."

Andrés knew he wasn't worth the sacrifice they were making for him, but it still made him happy, extraordinarily so. Despite his terror, he began to feel like laughing. Jane was going to run away with him. Dr. Garrard was going to help. It was the first time in his life that anyone had left safety to share his trouble. It made him brave. Whatever came next, he could take it. But if Jane went to prison? The thought checked him for only a moment. Jane could take it too. He would let her risk loving him; he was brave enough even for that. Andrés smiled at Jane and gripped her hand tightly, and she laughed, a girlish giggling peal of a laugh, like she got it—and she did, too. He loved the way she got everything so fast. He loved everything about her. He just loved her.

"All right then," Dr. Garrard was saying. "Where are we? This looks good. Driver, could you stop for just a moment at that pay phone, right there. Whatever you do, don't move. Wait here. I'm coming right back." He spoke in loud, slow English and made exaggerated gestures, pointing to the ground, to be certain the driver understood.

He made his call, anxiously watching the car. Despite the coolness of the early-evening breeze, sweat poured down his face while he waited for an answer, the receiver to his ear. Then a look of deep relief came over his face.

"Wyatt," he said into the receiver. "I need your help badly."

CHAPTER 34

Three days after her sister's disappearance, Ellen told her parents that Jane was pregnant, that Dr. Garrard had known it, but that Andrés, who was the father of her baby, had not. Charles and Anne considered themselves beyond shock, but Ellen's disclosures taught them otherwise. As they sat trying to decide how much to blame Ellen for the entire tragedy, Willie rang their bell and told Anne that he needed to talk with her for a minute. He sounded cagy. They knew that the police were watching the building. The plainclothesman had been spotted by the doormen and the super within an hour after he parked a blue Toyota just across the street, slightly east of the building.

How was it the building employees were so expert on things like that? Charles wondered. Certainly, the entire staff seemed to have known about Jane and Andrés, but none of them had ever told him or Anne. Not only was Willie amazingly well informed about every particular of Andrés's life, but suddenly all these men adored Jane. Jane was a goddess. They would have done anything for Jane and her parents. They asked after her with grave affection and concern. "Any news?" they'd say, and Charles and Anne would shake their heads. They couldn't really be angry with them. It wasn't their job to tell tales. It was the parents' job to keep track of their children.

Willie brought Anne an envelope addressed only to "Braithwaite." "I waited an hour," he said, "because I didn't want the guy out there to know you got anything."

Anne was impressed by his cleverness. The envelope contained a handwritten note that said, "Jane is well. Andrés is well. Forgive me. mg." Milligram? Anne thought. Her overwrought mind often miscued itself these days. "Oh my God—Charles!" she cried.

"Who gave you this?" Charles asked Willie.

"I didn't know the guy."

"What did he look like?"

"He had on, like, cycler's gloves, with a fanny pack. He took off on a bicycle. Just a regular-looking guy. I had a feeling it was about, you know . . ."

The second note came several weeks after that—on the day Gabriela died. Anne had visited her at the hospice only once. It was so hard to get there, and she couldn't help feeling angry with Gabriela, though she knew Gabriela wasn't really to blame for Jane's flight. They had just contributed two hundred dollars to the fund Greg was raising to send the body to the Dominican Republic and pay for a modest funeral when Willie rang again. The second note, too, was hand delivered—by a jogger this time—and said exactly what the first note had. When Willie left, Anne wept for hours, for Gabriela and Jane both. There were brief third and fourth notes, which came midsummer in anonymous e-mails addressed to Ellen.

Anne and Charles leaned over Ellen's shoulder to read the message: "All are well. mg."

"Why don't they tell us more?" Ellen complained.

"I'm guessing this is sent from some cybercafé just before they take off for someplace else because they're afraid of being traced to whatever city they're in. And also, I think Michael wants to keep us ignorant of information that might make us guilty of obstructing justice or aiding and abetting something or other. Right now, if the police ask us questions, we can answer with complete truthfulness that we don't know anything," said Charles.

"I guess we know they're together," said Anne.

CHAPTER 35

Morris Malcolm called one Saturday morning, an unseasonably warm day in November. "Let's take the kids down to the playground at 112th," he said.

Charles and Anne agreed. And since Ellen was off running errands with her grandmother, they would both come, with Stuart and Gilbert. After all these months, Anne still had trouble letting any of her children out of her sight. When Merrit heard that Anne was coming, she decided to tag along, although she had planned to use the time to work. She was worried about Anne.

Merrit and Morris's boys, five-year-old Gabriel and three-year-old Clement, showed up with plastic bats, and soon Morris and Charles had all four boys playing in a diamond whose bases were marked with the coats they defiantly flung off. Despite being short, Stuart had considerable athletic talent. But it was hard to talk him into letting the younger ones have extra strikes and softer pitches; he was too worried about giving up his advantage, being beaten by a baby, to be generous. He sulked and hit one ball after another far over the moral fence they had marked between two trees.

"Did you ever think about gymnastics for Stuart?" Merrit asked Anne. Again she was struck by how gray Anne had gotten in just a few months, how lined her face looked and how her shoulders slumped. They were the same age, but Merrit looked far younger. Charles, on the other hand, was sad, and he wasn't as ready to roughhouse with the boys. But, oddly, he was better tempered these days, and he looked no older—and handsomer than ever. He no longer seemed aggrieved, the way he had as long as they had known him.

"His violin teacher threw a fit at the idea. I would have let him anyway, but he convinced Stuart that it wasn't worth the time or the risks. So I butted out."

"He's just so unbelievably coordinated."

"I guess." Anne could no longer enjoy her children's talents. She had become suspicious of her own maternal confidence. Maybe her flawed mothering was the reason they had lost Jane.

"Mom, did you see?" Stuart called, one muddy foot on third base, which was Gilbert's blue parka.

"Nice hit, sweetie," she called back.

"I got it low, right between Daddy and Morris—on purpose."

"Really good, Stuey," Anne said in a dutiful singsong.

But Merrit saw that Anne withheld what he wanted. That glint was missing from her eye. No *nachas.* "Oh boy," said Merrit, sighing.

"What?" asked Anne.

"I don't know," said Merrit. She had leaned on Anne, and Anne's mother, her whole life. They had always been full of confidence and hope. If Anne's new outlook gave Merrit such a sense of loss and abandonment, she could imagine how Anne's children felt. They sat and watched in silence.

"You know what, Anne?" Merrit said, when the players paused for a water break. "I think you're messing up here. You're fixing a lot of things that weren't broken because you blame yourself for what happened with Jane. It's not good for the kids, what you're doing."

"I don't know what's good for kids," Anne said.

"Garbage." Merrit thought she knew what Anne was secretly accusing herself of, but she couldn't tell her. It might sound as though she, too, accused her. Morris always said that Anne and Charles spoiled Jane because they were overinvested in her music. He wasn't crazy about Jane. In fact, when she was younger, he couldn't stand her. Merrit, on the other hand, while she had often longed to see Jane's parents win in one of their many showdowns, had also seen attractive sides of Jane's character, and now that Merrit was dealing with the willfulness of her own sons, she was much less inclined to be critical of the way the Braithwaites had coped with Jane. Charles and Anne, after all, had managed to run an orderly ship. Jane had not refused to obey the rules of the household. She came home on time, did her homework, and practiced and all that. Although Jane and Ellen quarreled, Jane was really good with her little brothers—kind, affectionate, always ready to babysit. In fact, she was Clem's and Gabriel's favorite sitter. Jane tormented Charles and Anne, of course, with her nasty tongue, her peculiar boyfriends, her hatred of school, and social-pariah tendencies. Considering how difficult she was, just how badly had they done with her? Maybe not at all.

While Merrit was getting up her courage to speak, trying to condense haphazard impressions into sentences that would be both clear and kind, Anne's cell phone rang in her hand, making her start. This had happened over and over in Merrit's presence. Anne couldn't help expecting a call from Jane every minute.

"Ellen and Mother are back. They're going to walk down and join us," Anne told her, folding up the phone. But she didn't pocket it; she kept it in her hand. The day before, Helen had taken Ellen on a shopping expedition as a present for her fourteenth birthday. Anne knew that Ellen's bed would be laden with clothes, earring boxes, CDs, books, and more.

"What, she wants some little thing and I can pay for it, I'm not going to give it to her?" Helen would say, pained, if anyone objected to her largesse.

She was always generous to all the children, but maybe lately she overdid it a bit with Ellen. Everyone knew why. In a few minutes, Helen and Ellen came down the promenade, hand in hand. Anne's mother had also changed remarkably in six months. She had been lively and youthful for a woman in her late sixties, but now her step dragged a little and she had lost her fresh color. Although even Ellen was a little less perky these days, she was doing better than the rest of the family. Merrit thought, fondly, that Ellen was probably the one who best understood the whole thing. She suddenly adored the girl, looking so much like a younger, happier Anne with her dark curls.

"Oh, Ellen, you're such a teenager," she cried, and she wrapped her arms around her, over Anne's, so that she was hugging mother and daughter together. Ellen giggled and struggled to escape. Then Merrit stood and embraced Helen.

"Hello, darling," Helen said, patting her back. "How pretty you look. Anne, didn't you sleep? Where are . . . oh, there they are. My goodness. Gillie can really hit!"

"Look there," Merrit said over Helen's shoulder. "Anne, there's Lily and Jonathan—walking a dog." The dog was tiny and wayward, a black Labrador puppy on a long leash. It suddenly sat on the sidewalk, ignoring their tugs and commands—"Come on, Sam. Here boy! Let's go, Sam!"— while it looked around. Then, panting affably, it trotted to the grass and tentatively chewed a few stems.

"What an adorable puppy!" Ellen called, running toward Lily and Jonathan. "Is it yours?" She knelt on the pavement, and it climbed into her lap, licked her face, and chewed manically on any part of her it could reach. Ellen and the dog were in raptures with each other. "I love baby things," Ellen said to Anne, who had walked over to greet Lily and Jonathan.

Anne's face fell a little. "Me too," she said, stooping to pat the little creature, which was now writhing and rolling its eyes, frenzied with the excitement of so much attention. "Lily, this is one frantic little dog."

"It's only nine weeks old," Lily said defensively. "I don't buy this disciplinarian stuff they've got in all the dog books. You don't want a dog with no spirit."

Morris and Charles, smelling of sweat, also came to greet Jonathan and Lily. Charles laughed at Lily's remark. "No worry," he told her.

"We've got spiritedness down," Jonathan said with acid stoicism.

Morris snorted but said nothing. Before he married Merrit, he had been engaged to marry Lily and had broken the engagement against her wishes. Seeing how ineffectual—incompetent really—Lily was with the puppy, he congratulated himself anew on his narrow escape.

"*No!*" Lily told the puppy firmly, holding up her forefinger instructively. It had grabbed Clement's shoelace and pulled it untied. Now it put its tiny face down between its paws and pulled harder, growling a treble growl. Ellen laughed, but Clem burst into tears. "*No, Sam, no,*" Lily repeated. Jonathan bent down and tried to part the fierce little jaws but succeeded only in pulling off the shoe. Clem howled tragically, Lily dropped the leash to comfort him, and Sam took off with the shoe, pursued by Jonathan and the other three boys, who whooped with joy.

Morris picked Clem up. "He just wanted to play," he said to the weeping child. "He's only a baby dog. He doesn't know."

"He's *bad!*" Clem shouted, between sobs.

Lily joined Charles, Anne, and Helen at the park bench where they had retired to observe the spreading chaos.

"I've been thinking about Jane a lot," she said, "and I wanted to tell you what I thought."

Anne looked up at her hopefully. Lily had a psychoanalyst's frankness, and Anne trusted her insights. Their other friends were more reticent on the subject of Jane. They waited for Anne and Charles to bring it up.

"I thought that if I were you, I'd trust her," Lily continued. "No matter how everything might look to strangers, I'm sure there's nothing self-destructive about Jane. She's protective, she's loving, and she has a sense of justice. So I'd just trust her and wait." Lily then gave a hesitant, wincing smile. "And also, I'd keep in mind the pitfalls of guilt here. You know— like if you'd ever wished she was gone or something like that. That could affect your reactions to everything very painfully. Just a word to the wise. Oh, excuse me, I'd better rescue Jonathan."

"Thanks, Lily," said Charles. While he listened to her little speech, his brows had risen in an ambiguous expression that could have signified either respectful attention or amused skepticism.

"Thank you very much, Lily," said Anne with complete sincerity.

Lily ran off to Jonathan, who had finally captured the fugitive puppy. It panted joyfully in his arms. "It knows no remorse," Jonathan told Lily. "It's sociopathic."

"I would have taken what she said a lot more seriously," said Charles, "if I hadn't just been watching her with that puppy." Anne snickered, and he put his arm around her.

"They say you should never judge psychoanalysts by their kids," said Helen. "I'm sure that applies to their dogs too."

"Sweetie, let's ask everyone up to our place for lunch. It's so late," said Anne. "The boys are starting to go to pieces."

That afternoon the Braithwaite household sounded and felt more the way it used to before Jane went away.

CHAPTER 36

Not until the day before Thanksgiving, many months after her flight, did Charles and Anne learn what had become of their daughter. On that day, they received a long letter from Jane herself through the regular mail.

Jane, Andrés, and Michael had set up house together in Buenos Aires, and their legal situation was now stable. They could correspond safely. They had passports, and there was no danger of extradition, but, as they would all face arrest if they returned to New York, they would stay in Argentina. They had received generous help, but she could not disclose who was giving it.

She and Andrés had married months ago, and they had a beautiful little boy named Miguel. The baby and Andrés made her happier than she had ever known she could be. She wanted everyone at home to love Miguel and Andrés. Miguel was the most astonishing baby who had ever lived— an assertion proved with a full page of detailed evidence, which Anne took in avidly. A woman helped with the baby and the house.

Andrés was a student at the Universidad de Buenos Aires, already near the end of his first term and doing extremely well, delighted with everything: marriage, fatherhood, and his studies. (They'd had no problem at all getting his SAT scores sent down. Did they know he had 800 in math?) Dr. Garrard had a wealthy backer who was funding his efforts to open a clinic for poor people there. He was excited about it and had made many new friends. His wife was divorcing him. He felt terrible about her, but Jane couldn't stand the woman and thought he'd be much better off. They had ordered a piano—a Baldwin, not a Steinway. She hoped Charles and Anne wouldn't think that was a mistake.

Jane had found a good vocal coach and had one promising audition. They wouldn't believe how wonderful and popular opera was there. There seemed to be all sorts of singing opportunities for younger and less-known singers, lots of new groups staging very good opera, and some had already shown interest in Jane. The major opera there was, of course, out-standing, and the opera house, the Teatro Colón, gorgeous. She was hope-ful, but for now she wanted to take things slow because Miguel was not even a month old yet. They worried about their family and friends in New York. Andrés had managed to get in touch with Gabriela before she died. He grieved for her still, but otherwise they were as happy as people could be, given his losses and hers, and Dr. Garrard was happier than she had ever seen him back in New York. The four of them were a family. But she missed her parents and siblings all the time and longed to see them. She couldn't bear the fact that they had never even set eyes on Miguel. Couldn't they come for a long visit? There was plenty of room. Dr. Garrard wanted them to come very much, even though he worried about their being angry with him. P.S. Could they possibly send some of her clothes, as they would probably fit again now. Could they also send her CDs, iPod, music, et cetera?

Charles and Anne sat and stared at each other when they had taken turns reading the letter through.

"She's not going to City Opera, I guess," said Charles, his face grow-ing red with repressed weeping. "Or even to Juilliard. Not to college at all. She doesn't even have a high school diploma."

"She didn't really want to go," said Anne. Her own tears squeezed out, one by one. "You know she would have hated it."

"But think of her raising this baby. She just turned nineteen. And they'll end up divorced and pulling the kid back and forth between two continents and two worlds."

"Why do you think so? You and I started going together when I was nineteen. You were not much older than that, and here we are."

"But we didn't start out with a baby and no degrees. We finished school, and did European tours, had fun, all that."

"Janie had a hard time doing things that way," Anne said, her voice breaking.

Sadness silenced them again.

"Anne, do you ever think about whether what they did was wrong?"

"You mean running away instead of letting Andrés go to prison and then appealing and all that? If it had been one of our children, you would never ask that question. You'd know the answer."

"That's probably true. But this isn't civil disobedience, and it can't be justified that way. Not that I mind, I guess. In fact, that's what bothers me. I feel only relief that Andrés got away. I never once felt anything but contempt for the law and the people administering it, beginning on the day we found out he'd been arrested. I might have felt pretty much the same way even if he had actually committed a crime. That's new for me."

"The world has changed," said Anne. "Things are more cruel than they used to be. People decided they'd be safer if the world was meaner."

Anne read Jane's letter again and this time smiled a little over how Jane it was. "In a way, it's a happy ending," she said.

"It's a comedy," said Charles. "If everyone gets married, it's a comedy. If everyone dies, it's a tragedy. So it can't be a tragedy, can it?"

"It really isn't, Charles. First of all, I like Andrés a lot—really a lot. I can't think of Jane with anyone besides Andrés anymore, and I'm so relieved that Michael is looking after them. That's why they're not destitute, and Andrés is in school. You know, it might not really be Michael's fault about Janie. I can easily believe that she insisted on going with Andrés, and he just couldn't control her—any more than we could."

"I decided long ago that's how it probably happened."

"And keeping the pregnancy secret—well, I can see how he thought a few weeks more wouldn't matter. He didn't know what was going to happen. It all sort of works out though. Now Andrés gets a father, just when he really needs one, Miguel gets a nifty paternal grandfather, and Michael finally gets some children and gets free of his miserable marriage. He seems to be making a good new life for himself. He always should have had children. I just kind of wish he didn't take one of ours. Charles, do you ever think that you might like to leave Morningside Heights and try out someplace else?"

"No," Charles said. He was not as ready as Anne to regard Jane's exile in a hopeful light and certainly not ready to consider joining her in it. But that seedling thought was apparently already sprouting in Anne's mind. "Would you like to go visit them on Christmas break?" he asked.

"Christmas break?" Anne said. "Yes—we could take as much as three weeks if we keep the kids out of school for a few extra days. You'll have to cancel a couple of performances. Charles, I can't wait."

The job of spreading the news about the fugitive three turned out to be less difficult than it might have been because nearly everyone who had to be told was invited to Thanksgiving dinner the next day: Helen; Peter and his wife, daughter, and son-in-law; Merrit and Morris and their kids; Greg (who assured them that he had no problem with Carla being there); Carla (who said it wouldn't bother her at all if Greg was there); Anne's brother, Paul, and his family; and others. More friends, like Lily and Jonathan, were going to drop by after dinner for dessert and music.

Anne read parts of Jane's letter aloud to the stunned friends and relatives. The first reaction was subdued. Although everyone already knew that Jane had been pregnant, they still found the news of her nineteen-year-old motherhood a little sad. But their second reaction was that things were turning out far better than anyone could have hoped. Carla was elated.

"But they can never come home," Greg told her and Peter in the living room after dinner, "and for a family as tight as this one, that's real misfortune."

"Well, we'll see," said Carla. "Maybe it isn't all over yet."

"Don't be so mysterious," Greg said. "What do you know?"

"She's been busy," said Peter. "Carla decided to appoint herself their lawyer in absentia. She's working to get the judge to overturn the verdict. She's also submitted new evidence in support of Andrés's innocence."

"And I've got something else," said Carla. "Something unbelievable— in writing as of just yesterday."

"We were troubled," said Peter, "by the fact that the prosecutor never called the third cop. It might have meant nothing. But maybe there was a reason. So . . . you tell, Carla."

"So I called the third cop—over and over. He wouldn't say anything for a long time, but I got him to listen and I told him about all my new evidence. Finally, he agreed to meet with me to look at the stuff. I was able to show him by Juan's and Andrés's phone records that they had never called each other, not once, during the relevant period. Also I was easily able to prove that Andrés was at the Braithwaites' on every one of the cru- cial days when Juan was out putting the deal together because he was al- ways on Anne's computer—for hours and hours, writing poems and making journal entries that basically recorded every thought he had and every move he made, with not a word about drugs or Juan on those days. The computer never left the house, and when Andrés wasn't in the house, he was at work or school, which I also documented. I mean, none of this was hard proof he was innocent, but it certainly made it look very unlikely that he was in on Juan's deal. And then I told this cop all about the situa- tion—with Gabriela being sick and homeless, and how before Juan got mixed up with the undercover cops he had tried welfare and charities— anything to get a place for her. There are records on all that. The poor guy must have visited a hundred different offices and filed requests every- where. So this cop got the picture, and he confessed." Carla interrupted her recital to sip wine and gauge Greg's reaction. She had eagerly antici- pated telling him this story, but the look on his face as he listened was odd—certainly not what she had hoped to see.

"Confessed to what?" he asked.

"To knowing that the other two cops lied. He said Juan and Andrés never said those things they testified about in the trial. He didn't come forward because he thought Juan and Andrés really were both guilty and also he didn't want to rat on his pals. But once he started to doubt that Andrés was guilty, he just couldn't stand it. He thought it was probably

entrapment with Juan, too. He hated the whole case. He signed an affi-
davit, and I'm submitting it to the D.A. and the judge. We're going to get
those guys. A lot of convictions are going to be in question after this—
including Juan's."

"Perjuring cops," said Peter. "As a former colleague said, they're the
demon in the criminal process. It's terrifyingly common."

"Nice work, Carla," said Greg. He made his voice kind, but Carla still
looked disappointed. "What got you started on it?"

"A lot of what happened was my fault. I was the one who kept insisting on keeping Berman on the case. Berman should have done everything
I've been doing, and he did nothing. I kept saying he was handling it right,
but he wasn't—I *knew* he wasn't. I even kind of knew that he was the wrong
sort of lawyer for this case, but I pushed for him anyway—I don't know
why, to tell the truth. I just tried to stop Andrés from going to trial, and
then when he insisted on it, it was like I was kind of pushing for it to go
wrong."

"Sounds like you were sacrificing Andrés so as to convict the system."

"That's very sweet and understanding of you, Greg, pointing out how
I'm even worse than I thought. I thought your theology says you're supposed to forgive."

"You can't really forgive anyone, including yourself, unless you face up
to what you're forgiving."

"Yeah, and unless you really make the sinner suffer and squirm, right?
That always makes forgiving a lot easier. Your friend Greg is such a nice
guy," Carla said, suddenly addressing Peter, who was wincing on her behalf. "And to think he's telling me these things out of pure generosity—
with the best interests of my immortal soul in mind."

"Just your happiness," Greg said hesitantly, "because the reason you
got yourself into this jam is you tried to insulate yourself from the kind
of pain that would have alerted you to what you were doing. You do that
all the time, Carla. That's all your cynicism is. You're a modern Antisthenes. You got yourself into a position where you get very irritated and
self-righteous about other people's fur coats and perfume while you're
completely numb to your own life." Greg's manner in this speech, which
evidently seared Carla, was tentative and circumspect, as though he were

thinking it out as he went, and, when he had finished, he looked at Carla with eyes full of appeal and apology.

"Sure. For my happiness, you'd sacrifice your whole theology."

"Actually, what I just said about happiness *is* my theology," Greg said.

"I'll bet."

"Cut it out, Carla," said Peter. "He's not condemning you. He's understanding you. And if you didn't think he was right, you wouldn't be doing what you're doing."

"What a pair of know-it-alls," she said, but astonishingly, her face reddened, and she stalked out of the room.

She looked as though she was going to cry. No one had ever seen Carla cry.

"So go," Peter told Greg impatiently, pointing after Carla, when Greg just stood there, looking tragic. Otherwise he would have to go himself, he thought, and clearly it was Greg's job.

"Who's Antisthenes?" asked Anne, who had joined them, bearing cups of coffee on a tray, near the end of Greg's speech.

"He was the founder of the ancient Cynic sect," Peter replied. "The Cynics believed that the only way to be happy was to stop caring, and be indifferent to everything, even pleasure. They also didn't believe in the niceties—manners, ordinary social decencies. They were considered churls and ruffians."

"Imagine your knowing that," Anne said. She was always impressed by Peter's store of information.

"An amazing analysis coming from our mild-mannered priest," said Peter, modestly ignoring her admiration. "He understands Carla. I wouldn't have thought so."

Greg found Carla in Jane's bedroom, and the two of them sat on the bed and talked for half an hour. Ellen, sent by Anne to fetch them to hear the music, came back and announced confidently that they'd made up.

The next morning, while Carla slept on in his bed, Greg sent Michael a warm note. This was the beginning of an energetic correspondence in which they renewed their friendship and traded reflections on everything from the foundations of success in marriage to the psychology of social reform. In time, Michael was delighted to hear of Greg's engagement to Carla, and confessed that he himself had met someone "interesting"— a doctor who was helping him learn his way around the medical world there. He invited the penniless new couple to honeymoon in Buenos Aires—if it would not be too unromantic to stay in a house that was filled with university students, a miscellany of other houseguests, and the competing vocalizations of a young soprano and her infant. Greg assured him it would not and hoped to accept the invitation before too many more months had passed. The rector was demanding that they marry; Carla had all but moved into the parish house. She said that she could not bear her old apartment, even after three visits by the exterminator.

The Braithwaite family reunited in Buenos Aires at Christmas. Charles and Anne, with Ellen, Stuart, and Gilbert, made their way from Ezeiza to a once-fine, now slightly shabby house in a marginal district.

"Neighborhood's not so great," Charles said, looking around dubiously.

"Probably no worse than Morningside Heights back in the eighties, when we moved in on 117th Street," Anne pointed out.

The children grew shy as they waited for someone to answer the door, and when Jane herself opened it, holding a tiny dark-eyed infant who stared alertly at his relations, they could only grin and hang back. But Charles and Anne had their arms around the pair of them in a moment. And soon Ellen was curled up on a sofa with her little nephew in her arms. She looked worshipfully into his inky eyes, leaning against Jane, who was rapidly exchanging with her parents all the minutiae of their lives that had not been passed on in the last month's barrage of letters, calls, and e-mails. Charles and Anne, though, were so mesmerized by the tiny perfections of their grandchild that they could hardly follow.

The little boys sat and stared curiously at the baby, then looking up, shouted with joy as they saw Andrés enter the room, looking so different that Charles and Anne hardly knew him. The hollows in his face had filled in, his color was fresh, his eyes were no longer circled in rings of black despair. Dressed like an ordinary student, he was definitely an appealing-looking kid now, and the shy smile he gave them was not to be resisted.

They had always liked him. They had liked him enough to have to make excuses for failing to adopt him. They were going to hate him now that he was their son-in-law and the father of their grandson?

Andrés had apparently hung back so as to give the others a chance to meet without him. But he was an old friend to Gilbert and Stuart. Soon the two boys were all over him, and he took them outside to play.

Charles joined the three of them by the fountain in the backyard, casting around awkwardly for some acceptable topic of conversation. "Do you expect Michael?" he asked.

"In about an hour," said Andrés.

Another planned delay, Charles thought, so that there could be an uninhibited reunion before Michael got there. "Your studies going well, I hear."

"Very well—it seemed strange at first, all in Spanish. My Spanish isn't as good as my English, but I'm doing fine. I don't know. When I start doing more math and science—that might be harder."

"Science? Is that what you're interested in?"

"I think, maybe . . . medicine," Andrés said. For some reason, this made his face turn crimson.

Charles maneuvered around his sense of injury to find a way to offer some paternal support. "That's good," he said. There was too much relief in the word, however, as though he had been entertaining fears on the subject of Andrés's future. He had, of course, but he didn't want Andrés to know it. "You'd be a great doctor. And you and Michael could practice together," he added, more convincingly. Michael, obviously would be Andrés's hero.

"That's what I hope," Andrés said with enthusiasm, and Charles was relieved that he had said something right. "But he gives everything to us, you know. He does everything. I don't know why. I said I'd work, but he insisted I go to school."

"Absolutely right," Charles said, with extra energy in his voice. "Whatever it takes, you stay in school. I want to help out a little too, by the way, if you need anything. It doesn't have to be all on Michael's shoulders."

"It's embarrassing that I don't even know if we need help," said Andrés. "But when I'm finished, someday, I'll take care of everything myself."

"Of course you will," Charles said. He sounded a little gruff, as he was trying not to overdo it. He wanted to give Andrés the same matter-of-fact confidence he gave his own children—all except Janie, anyway. It struck Charles that he didn't really need to talk himself into that confidence. In many ways, Andrés impressed him as being steadier, more reliable and cautious, than Jane herself. It was among the most satisfying thoughts he had had in months, a happy revelation.

Andrés felt the change instantly and relaxed.

"It must be hard, though, attending classes and getting up at night with Miguel," Charles said. "Does it interfere with studying?"

"Really bad," Andrés said, with a smile.

Charles had to smile too. Of course, Andrés would study hard whatever the obstacles, and soon Miguel would be sleeping through.

They gradually wandered back into the house, and Anne and Charles had the unnerving experience of seeing that Jane was more intimate with Andrés than with them. She seemed quite like his wife when he leaned down with a serious face to ask her something in a low voice, and she responded in the same low, businesslike tone—in Spanish! Then she handed Miguel to Andrés, whose adoring pride was evident behind a display of fatherly insouciance.

"Be right back," she said. "I have to check something in the kitchen."

Charles and Anne fell into grief again. It wasn't fair that they had traveled to the bottom of the world to find their daughter only to learn that she had disappeared forever. They'd had no chance to prepare themselves for this—this in-charge young matron who was not Jane at all. Jane was too young to have all this on her shoulders.

At just this anguished moment, Michael entered the room. More tan and lively than they remembered him, his cowlick bouncing energetically, he walked briskly toward Charles, his hand outstretched, with an expression half apologetic and half delighted. He liked Charles tremendously and was very glad to see him. He was equally fond of Anne, who greeted him with less ambivalence than Charles did. Charles and Anne were slightly brittle around Michael for at least a day, and then their resentments were charmed away by the realities of their daughter's life.

Throughout their visit, Jane was contented, competent, and impossibly sweet. Jane hadn't been sweet since she was five, Charles said to Anne the next night as they lay in bed. More like four, Anne said. The home the three fugitives had made was a perfect blend of Michael's middle-aged dignity and care, the teenagers' passion and sense of discovery, and Miguel's infant anarchy. Anne feared that Michael would find having so many Braithwaites in his home for so many weeks beyond his endurance. But he seemed not only to delight in their presence, even the fights and noise of the little boys; he actually invited more visitors to increase the chaos. In the third week of their stay, two women, both doctors, joined them. Michael appeared to be excellent friends with one of them, a rather attractive obstetrician who, it seemed, had delivered Jane's baby and was talking about joining Michael's clinic when it opened. She was so warm, motherly, and familiar with both Jane and Miguel that Anne had to fight off a little jealousy. Nearly every day, she and her friend brought various acquaintances to join them for dinner or outings. Michael presided over it all with low-key benevolence. It was as though the house could not be full enough for him. They all visited the future site of the new clinic—another rambling old house not far away from their own, which was to be renovated in what was evidently a beloved joint project. Andrés was as knowledgeable about it all as Michael, and the two of them conferred expertly on the architect's drawings.

Andrés and Jane were surprised to hear about Carla's work on Andrés's behalf, and Jane instantly forgave all Carla's crimes and gave her credit for every virtue. But both she and Andrés seemed more depressed than happy at the news about the third cop's testimony, as though they could not bear to remember the terror of those last months in New York.

"But Andrés, Jane," said Anne. "If we could get assurances that you wouldn't be prosecuted, wouldn't you prefer to come home?"

"I don't really know," Andrés said, looking troubled. "If Jane was homesick, I guess . . ."

"No," said Jane. "I won't be. This feels like home to me. You know, I didn't really have a lot of friends in New York. But I'd like to be able to come back to visit."

"You're sure?" Charles asked sadly. "You know, some scary things have happened in this place, and not that long ago."

"For me, the United States is a scary place," Andrés put in. "I know about the terrible things that happened here, and I see how poor it is. There are so many desperate people here, and lots of bad, greedy people. They say sometimes there's *no* law here, but to me that's no worse than *crazy* law like in New York. Anyway, for poor people there's no law anywhere. And—I don't know how to explain this—people here are not as rigid. They listen more, and they change their minds easier," he said. "And we can help people here. They want us, and they're glad we're here. In New York, we were always getting pushed out. No place to live, no job, you can't do anything, not even help people."

This was the longest speech any of them had ever heard Andrés make. Michael's influence was obvious in the more fluent way he expressed himself. Michael would help him learn to be a father too.

"I think you all should come here," Jane said. "Daddy, I bet you could get an offer to spend a year at the Colón. It would be so wonderful. Ellen, you could go to the American school."

Ellen found the idea attractive. She adored her little nephew, her sister, her new brother-in-law, their new city. She was in love with all of them, including Dr. Garrard. She begged her parents to stay an extra week. She told Jane that Nana had agreed to come down in the summer, and Ellen would come with her and they'd both stay until school vacations ended.

"A year here is not a bad idea," Charles said. "I'll look into it. I've wanted to do something like that for a long time. I had thought about La Scala or—"

"No, no!" said Jane. "Look into opera at the Colón. You'll love it, Daddy."

"They'll never come home," Anne said on the flight back. "I don't really blame Andrés. I know I shouldn't, but I blame Gabriela, even though I feel so sorry for her. She had a sad, short life, and she deserved better, but I can't help feeling that she took all her problems and unloaded them on us—through deceit too. She lied to us from the beginning. She wrecked our family."

"I don't blame Gabriela. She took by deceit what she had a right to be given because she knew no one would give it. What she did was not so different from the three of them running away together, which you said was not wrong."

"Maybe."

"I blame us, not Gabriela. Gabriela was just trying to survive. The simplest explanation for everything that went wrong is that we didn't hand Gabriela a check for a few thousand and say, 'Here. Get yourself a place to live, and let us know if that's not enough.' We should have taken her to a good doctor right away. We didn't want the responsibility. We had this idea that society had been unfair to Gabriela, but we'd be foolish to give her more than our share of what society owed her. I wonder whether you wouldn't have done all the right things, no matter how overgenerous it felt, if you hadn't been worried about making me mad. Maybe *I'm* the real problem here. But you know, Anne, it's your job to fight with me when I'm wrong. Anyway, our family isn't wrecked. We've had a misfortune. Jane is fine. She's just not going to have the life we planned for her."

Anne did not believe that she would have done the right thing but for Charles. She had indeed been tempted to give Gabriela money behind his back and to take her to her own doctor, but she hadn't done so because she had thought Charles was right. She, too, had thought it would be giving too much. The idea that she and Charles were not innocent in Gabriela's death undermined Anne's resentment. She was silent for a few moments, and when she spoke again, her mood had shifted.

"By the way, Lily was saying that sometimes she thinks women should have kids very early instead of very late if they want to join the professions. In fact, now that I see Jane's life," Anne said, "I wonder what would have happened to her if we had succeeded in shoehorning her into another one. You realize, Charles, that the same social mentality that made Andrés into a criminal in Manhattan also made Jane into an outcast there."

"Of course. The two of them were natural allies. We have to do better when the other ones get to the age of choice. They may not have a Michael Garrard hanging around looking for an opportunity to escape his life and become a saint."

"Or a grateful billionaire with a jet in the process of adjusting his ideas of right and wrong."

They looked across the aisle of the plane to where Ellen sat reading beside her sleeping brothers.

"You know," Anne said, some hours into the flight, "Jane is such a super kid. You have to be proud of her. What an interesting life she's making. What strengths she has. You have to admit it, Charles, we know how to raise 'em."

"Oh, we're the envy of the neighborhood," he said. "They all want to bring up high school dropouts who get pregnant out of wedlock, marry convicted felons, and flee to South America."

Anne wouldn't have thought this at all funny a month ago, but now she did. "It's true, though," she said. "All our friends *are* impressed. No one thought Andrés should have let himself get locked up for years because he'd had his minimal due process. Even Rebecca's mother told me just before we left that she thought what Jane and Andrés had done was awesome."

"Don't kid yourself," said Charles. "She'd jump off the George Washington Bridge if Rebecca ended up like Jane. She can afford to be high-minded because we've been through such hell. It subdues her envy."

"No doubt," Anne said, "but that doesn't mean she wasn't also sincere. That's partly why Rebecca is such a wonderful girl: her mother really, truly does think that way, under all her out-of-control competitiveness—and she didn't ten years ago, when they moved in. She absorbed that kind of thinking in the neighborhood. Yes, we're all too envious, competitive, selfish, cowardly, and worse. But in the end, we really want our kids to be good, not just successful, and Jane got the message. You watch. All these kids are going to be something. Really, I think Morningside Heights is still the best place in the world to raise children."

CLIPPINGS

Missing Doctor Divorced

New York Family Court, Pizutto, J., today issued a final divorce decree in *Simmons-Garrard v. Garrard.* Adriana Simmons-Garrard was married for eleven years to Dr. Michael Garrard, the Columbia Presbyterian professor of medicine who mysteriously disappeared two years ago after allegedly aiding in a prisoner escape from a Manhattan courthouse. Simmons-Garrard attempted suicide twice in the months following her husband's disappearance.
—*New York Law Journal,* September 12, 2006

Officers Plead to Perjury

New York City police officers Vincent Smiley and Jason McGrew pleaded guilty to charges of perjury relating to their testimony last year in the trial of fugitive Andrés Valiente. Prosecutors said that Valiente's conviction on drug charges would be vacated. Valiente, who maintained his innocence, made a dramatic escape from a Manhattan courthouse immediately following his conviction, apparently in the company of Dr. Michael Garrard, a prominent Manhattan physician, and Jane Braithwaite, the teenage daughter of the Metropolitan Opera baritone Charles Braithwaite. The prosecutors refused to comment on what the perjury pleas in today's proceedings would mean for Juan Santiago, who is appealing his conviction in a related case, claiming entrapment. Valiente, Garrard, and Braithwaite are still wanted on various charges related to Valiente's flight. —*The New York Times,* October 17, 2006

Father Gregory Merriweather Married

Our own Father Gregory Merriweather and Carla Winter took their vows here at Saint Ursula's on Saturday, December 9. Charles Braithwaite sang "Grosser Herr, O Starker Koenig," from J. S. Bach's *Christmas Oratorio,* and flowers and a wonderful reception at the parish house were provided by the Thursday Night Club. The newlyweds are honeymooning in romantic Buenos Aires. Way to go, Father Merriweather! —*Saint Ursula's Biweekly Newsletter,* December 15, 2006

Former Misanthrope Turns Philanthrope?

Your keen-eyed, on-the-scene Morningside Heights reporter has learned that Wyatt Jesse Younger, the neighborhood's resident billionaire, has begun leasing apartments to low-income locals for far-below-market rents. He's also severed relations with libertarian philosopher Richard Selvnick, who is now a full-time media spokesperson for a libertarian think tank. —Mallory Holmes, www.E-Tablet.com, December 24, 2006

ABOUT THE AUTHOR

CHERYL MENDELSON received her Ph.D. in philosophy from the University of Rochester and her J.D. from Harvard Law School. She has practiced law in New York City and taught philosophy at Purdue and Columbia universities. She is the author of *Home Comforts: The Art and Science of Keeping House* and the novels *Morningside Heights* and *Love, Work, Children. Anything for Jane* is the final novel in her Morningside Heights trilogy. She lives in New York City.

ABOUT THE TYPE

This book was set in Centaur, a typeface designed by the American typographer Bruce Rogers in 1929. Rogers adapted Centaur from the fifteenth-century type of Nicholas Jenson and modified it in 1948 for a cutting by the Monotype Corporation.